**THE ONLY PERSON** in the waiting room today is a teenage girl, sitting cross-legged in one of the armless wooden chairs, her eyes closed.

I shouldn't stare. Emily Post may not have written about therapy, but some things are unspoken. You ignore the other people in the waiting room. You do not make small talk. You keep walking when a maladjusted third grader hurls a toy at you, though it is permissible to step on his bag of Goldfish in revenge.

I shouldn't stare at this girl and her loose, long, wavy hair, the color of an old penny. And scraggly at the tips, like it hasn't been cut in a while. She's in faded jeans and a navy hoodie that's way too big for her. It engulfs her torso and hides her hands. Her feet are tucked under her legs. I wonder if she's even wearing shoes.

And as I'm standing there, staring, the girl in blue opens her eyes.

Also by Katie Henry

*Heretics Anonymous*

*This Will Be Funny Someday*

LET'S CALL IT A

DOOMSDAY

# KATIE HENRY

KATHERINE TEGEN BOOKS
*An Imprint of HarperCollins Publishers*

Names: Henry, Katie, author.

Title: Let's call it a doomsday / Katie Henry.

Other titles: Let us call it a doomsday

Description: First edition. | New York, NY : Katherine Tegen Books, an imprint
of HarperCollins Publishers, [2019] | Summary: Ellis Kimball, sixteen, whose
anxiety disorder causes her to prepare for the imminent end of the world, meets
Hannah, who claims to know when it will happen.

Identifiers: LCCN 2018034313 | ISBN 978-0-06-269891-9

Subjects: | CYAC: Anxiety disorders—Fiction. | Mental illness—Fiction. | End of
the world—Fiction. | Emergency management—Fiction. | Family problems—
Fiction. | Mormons—Fiction.

Classification: LCC PZ7.1.H4646 Let 2019 | DDC [Fic]—dc23 LC record available
at https://lccn.loc.gov/2018034313

Typography by David Curtis
20 21 22 23 24   PC/LSCH   10 9 8 7 6 5 4 3 2 1
❖
First paperback edition, 2020

For Leah, who always reminds me it's not the end of the world

LET'S CALL IT A <u>DOOMSDAY</u>

# ONE

**HERE IS ONE** way the world could end:

In a peaceful corner of northwest Wyoming, under the feet of park rangers, herds of deer, and thousands of tourists to Yellowstone National Park, lies a giant reservoir of burning, deadly magma called the Yellowstone Caldera. First, there would be earthquakes, the kind you can't sleep through. Then would come the supereruption, a rare seismic event. Rare, but possible. Rare, but overdue. The park would be a lake of lava, but the real problem would be the ash, which would blanket the entire United States, coast to coast. In the Rockies, the ash would crush buildings, devastate crops, suffocate animals and people. Even a few inches would make national highways impassable, ruin farms, shut down air travel. Life as we know it would be over. The entire planet would grow colder.

Here is another way the world could end: I could fail my driving test for a third time.

"Twice isn't even that many times to fail. Two times, that's all, and my parents look at me like I've murdered something. Something cute. And fuzzy." I take a breath. "There are bigger problems in the world than me not being able to drive my sister to ballet. Millions of people don't have clean drinking water. Two-thirds of the animals on Earth might be dead in five years, did you know that? And at any time—*any time*—a gamma-ray burst could destroy the ozone layer and kill us all."

"Could we bring this conversation back to you?" Martha asks.

We're not actually having a conversation. She's a therapist and I'm a client, and even though her office is made to look like someone's living room, we're not doing this for fun.

"Sure," I say. "Forget the world, *I* could have bigger problems than not being able to drive. I could be an alcoholic. I could be a shoplifter. I could be selling my dad's muscle relaxants in the park across from school, did they think about that?"

"Do you think there are some fears wrapped up in this experience?"

"It's not irrational to be scared of driving. It's the most dangerous everyday activity."

"It's good to take safety seriously," Martha concedes. "And I know I've said this before, but fear can be a very useful tool. Everyone experiences fear, and there's a good reason for that. It helps us identify danger. It helps us survive."

"Yeah, exactly, we should all be *more* scared."

"But sometimes, people experience fear that's constant, or very intense, or out of proportion to the situation," Martha adds gently. "And when fear keeps you from living your life freely, that's when it has to be addressed. Not eliminated completely. Just managed."

"My mom says I can't go to college if I don't know how to drive," I say. "Like it's the equivalent of a high school diploma. And I'm not getting that for almost two more years, so what's her rush?"

"It sounds like you're feeling a lot of pressure."

"For no good reason! I can take the bus to school, I can walk to church and your office and the library, I can get on BART if I want to go to San Francisco. I'm fine." I pause. "People are too dependent on cars. Like, sure, if a geomagnetic storm destroyed the electricity grid and society collapsed, you could use a car to get somewhere safer—"

Martha clears her throat. I keep going.

"—but we live in a city; the freeways would pile up. And gas expires, it oxidizes, so all the cars would be rusted from the inside out, anyway. You can't count on cars."

"Do you think this is a worthwhile thought pattern, Ellis?"

*Is anything you do worthwhile, Ellis?*

I shake my head.

"Let's talk about what happened during the driving test."

"Nothing happened."

"What do you mean?"

"I sat in the DMV parking lot with the . . . driving evaluator, or whatever—and *nothing happened*." I pause. "Because I couldn't turn the car on."

Martha tilts her head. "Couldn't?"

I've only been seeing her for a few weeks, but I know what it means when she repeats a word I've said. It's like when you insert your card at the train station and the turnstile spits it back out. Try again. She's looking for me to say *wouldn't* or *didn't want to* in place of *couldn't*. But I really couldn't. I had my finger on the button and my foot on the brake but my brain was already out of the parking lot and on Claremont Avenue, calculating exactly what would go wrong.

> *You could hit a pedestrian.*
>
> *You could hit an elderly pedestrian.*
>
> *You could hit a child pedestrian.*
>
> *You could hit an elderly pedestrian carrying a child pedestrian and get arrested for manslaughter and your parents will have to pay restitution to the elderly/child victims and you'll never go to college because of your horrible guilt and will instead live in the basement for the rest of your life and befriend the rats.*

Alternatively, I could humiliate myself in front of a DMV employee. At least I've got a road map for that.

"What feelings are coming up, right now?"

I shrug. "I'm fine."

"'Fine' is not a feeling."

"Is 'annoyed' a feeling?"

She smiles. "Yes. Is that what you're feeling about your driving test?"

"It's not a big deal to me. So I guess I'm annoyed it's such a big deal to other people."

"That's understandable." Martha pushes a dark, springy ringlet back from her face. "Is this something you've experienced before? Or is this a new feeling?"

For someone so serene and unflappable, she talks about feelings a lot. Never hers, though. Only mine.

"It's not new." I hesitate. "It's actually kind of constant."

"Tell me about that."

I slump back on the couch. The more information you dredge up and vomit out to someone, the more they seem to want.

> *Is it really that horrible to have someone listen to you? Your parents are paying for this. You're wasting their money.*

"Everything my mom and dad think is important, I don't want anything to do with. They want me to get my license. They want me to be in AP classes. They want me to hang out with girls from church more. I don't care about the things they care about. I just don't."

> *Not only are you wasting your parents' money, you're using it to talk crap about them.*

"It goes the other way, too," I say, trying to seem like less of a

5

jerk. "They don't care about what I care about, either." I pause. "They don't *want* me to care about the things I care about."

"Can you give me an example?"

I give her a look like, *Come on*. She smiles. She waits.

"Like disaster preparedness," I say. "Like the end of the world as we know it."

"Where do you think your interest in survivalism comes from?" she asks.

I shake my head. "I'm not a survivalist."

"Oh?"

"Survivalists have skill sets. Hunting and fishing and living off the land, and I can't do any of that. I'm a prepper. I have supplies, not skills. Or, I would have supplies, except my mom told all my relatives they can't give me gift cards anymore because I'll spend them on 'bizarre internet stuff,' as if she won't appreciate properly filtered water you don't even have to boil first."

"Okay," Martha says. "Prepping. Where do you think your interest in prepping comes from?"

My palms itch. I try to put my hands in the pockets of my cardigan, but they don't fit. I take them out.

"Do you know," I ask Martha, "where the word *interest* comes from?"

"Where it comes from?"

"The history of the word. Its etymology." She shakes her head. "It's Latin, if you go back far enough. The noun form of *interesse*, which means, literally, 'to be between.' It was more a legal term, though, not like we think of it now."

"It's impressive you remember all that."

"Well, I wrote it down," I say. "I can remember anything if I write it down."

Absentmindedly, I touch the front pocket of my backpack. That's where my notebook is. Kenny #14. The first Kenny was an eggshell-blue diary from Deseret Books, a gift from my aunt on my ninth birthday. My mom suggested I name it. I chose Kenny. She hated that so much I stuck with it for thirteen more notebooks.

Martha shifts in her chair. "How much progress have you made in your workbook?"

I've made exactly no progress in *Stress Free and Happy to Be Me* because I buried it in my sock drawer the first day I got it.

"The workbook is one tool," she says. "It's designed to give you strategies for situations like your driving test. When you feel overwhelmed, or anxious."

Hearing that word always makes my throat tight. I'm not in denial, I know it's what I am. Martha was the first person to say it like a diagnosis, not just as an adjective. All the diplomas on Martha's office walls—Howard University, Smith College, UC Berkeley—only make it feel more official. Generalized anxiety disorder. It's not the word itself, it's what people mean when they use it.

"But maybe it's not the right tool for you," she admits. "I'd like to give you an assignment for this week."

7

"Okay."

"You've probably written down some facts about how the world could end. Or change drastically. Yes?"

I nod again.

"Have you looked up any of the times people thought the world would end, and then it didn't?"

No. Those people were wrong, whoever they were, whenever they were. Why would I care about things that didn't happen? I shake my head.

"This week, I'd like you to look up some end-of-the-world predictions that didn't come true. They can be from last year, they can be from a thousand years ago."

I can do research in my sleep. "So you want a list, or—?"

"Go deeper than that. Look at what happened to those people afterward. When the world kept going, what did they do? What changed in their lives, and what didn't? How did they move on?" She looks at her watch. "And then next session, we can talk about it. Sound good?"

If it means the workbook can stay buried in my sock drawer, it sounds great. I nod.

"Wonderful." She glances at her watch. "Our time's about up for today."

I grab my backpack. Martha opens the door for me.

"Have a good week," she says. "And try not to focus too much on the driving test, okay?"

But as I walk past the other offices and the eternally wilted potted plant at the end of the hallway, that's all I can think about. Me at the wheel of a car, and all the things that could go wrong. Martha calls this "catastrophizing."

> *You could hit the gas instead of the brake. You could run over a kindergarten teacher or a volunteer firefighter or the Dalai Lama.*

Never mind that the Dalai Lama doesn't even live here.

> *What if he was giving a lecture at UC Berkeley and you murdered him, what then? It's possible. Anything terrible is possible.*

When I walk into the waiting room, I expect to see the little redheaded boy who sees Martha right after me. He's usually here when I get out, destroying a *Highlights* magazine and demanding more Goldfish from his exhausted mom. I've taken to calling him the Red Demon.

> *You're a horrible person. He's a child.*

He did whip a Tonka truck at my face once.

> *And everyone still likes him better than they like you.*

But the only person in the waiting room today is a teenage girl, sitting cross-legged in one of the armless wooden chairs, her eyes closed.

I shouldn't stare. Emily Post may not have written about therapy, but some things are unspoken. You ignore the other people in the waiting room. You do not make small talk. You keep walking when a maladjusted third grader hurls a toy at you, though it is permissible to step on his bag of Goldfish in revenge.

I shouldn't stare at this girl and her loose, long, wavy hair, the color of an old penny. And scraggly at the tips, like it hasn't been cut in a while. She's in faded jeans and a navy hoodie that's way too big for her. It engulfs her torso and hides her hands. Her feet are tucked under her legs. I wonder if she's even wearing shoes.

And as I'm standing there, staring, the girl in blue opens her eyes.

I squeak and stumble back.

She smiles, big and broad, like we're best friends reunited. "Hi," she says, and the way she says it, it's clear she remembers me, even if I can't remember her.

"I'm sorry," I say, and don't even know for what. For staring at her? For forgetting her name? "Do we—how do I know you?"

She tilts her head. "You don't know me," she says. "Not yet."

This is how serial-killer shows start. In five network-TV minutes, a grizzled detective is going to find my corpse by a drainage pipe, strangled with a navy blue sweatshirt.

The girl's still smiling. It's like she doesn't even know I'm internally debating whether she's a criminal mastermind. I have to say something. Anything. Anything not about murder.

I clear my throat. "Um. What?"

She opens her mouth, but closes it fast as we hear high heels clipping down the hallway. Martha appears in the waiting door almost inhumanly fast. She looks at the girl in blue, then at me. Her serene mask, the nonjudgmental face she wears in our sessions, vanishes. Only for a second.

Martha looks back at the girl in blue. "You're very early." She pauses, awkwardly, like she swallowed a word.

The girl gets to her feet. She is, in fact, wearing shoes. "I walked, and it didn't take as long as I thought it would."

"We'll start now," she says to the girl. She flicks her eyes to me. "See you next week."

Martha starts to usher the girl through the door. The girl glances back at me as she goes. "See you sooner than that."

She grins. Martha shuts the door behind them. I stand in the empty waiting room alone.

If we were in a session, Martha would ask me to name what I'm feeling right now. It's easier to do inside my head than out loud.

Confused. Intrigued. Nervous, as always.

I can name Martha's feelings, too, the ones on her face when the mask dropped. Surprised. Wary. Maybe even scared.

I can't do that for the girl in blue, because I don't know her.

I don't know her, but I think I will.

## TWO

**I TAKE THE** bus straight home. I'd rather have walked, but it's Monday, and Monday means family home evening. So I squeeze myself onto a packed 51A bus. Wedged between a pack of middle school kids drawing boobs on the wall and an elderly man who clearly regrets having chosen the back row, I think about the girl in blue.

*You don't know me.*

*Not yet.*

And though I rack my brain for what that could mean, even after I'm off the bus, down my block, and opening my front door, I'm no closer to figuring it out. I shake my head. I need to forget about this, for now.

Family home evening—everyone shortens it to FHE—is the one night a week reserved for family time. No extracurriculars, no late nights at the office, no holing up in your room alone. We're Mormon, and that means we're big on family. It makes sense. If you're going to spend all eternity together, you might as well become close while you're still on Earth.

I know a lot of people do this kind of thing, not just us, but we're the only church I know of to give it a name and make it a weekly expectation. Not that I mind. As far as expectations go, this is an easy one. Hang out with your family, eat something sugary, play a game or watch a movie? It's nice. I like my family.

"Ellis?" Mom calls from the kitchen. "Can you come in here?"

I mostly like my family.

When I walk into the kitchen, Mom is still in her work clothes, though she's probably been home for a while.

"Hey, sweetie," she says, closing the oven door and then straightening up to look at me. She frowns. "I wish you wouldn't do that."

I'd ask what I possibly could have *done*, since I'm standing here motionless and silent, but I know she'll tell me.

"What's in the oven?" I ask as she walks over to me and gently untucks the hair behind my ears.

"There," she says, pushing the hair back away from my forehead and fluffing the ends like I'm some kind of prized Pomeranian. "It looks so much better that way. Don't you think?"

When it's behind my ears, it's out of my eyes. I don't care what it looks like. "It's fine."

13

"Or up," she says, starting to gather it into a high ponytail. "You never wear it up."

I shrug her off. "Mom, *stop*."

She lets my hair down. Steps back. She nods at a bowl on the counter next to the sink.

"Can you wash your hands and mix that coleslaw for me, please? I'm bringing it to the Jensens tomorrow. You can put it in the fridge when you're done."

She knows I don't like the feeling of cold food on my hands, but the last time I reminded her, she said, "Well, there's not much you *do* like, is there?" And the Jensens just had a baby, which makes this an act of service. So I roll up my sleeves and start.

It's quiet, but the wrong kind. Maybe she's counting down the seconds, just like I'm counting down the seconds until my dad or little sister comes home and rescues me.

"So." I hear Mom turn toward me. "How was it?"

"How was what?"

She tries to sound casual. "Therapy."

Now I know why she gave me this job. My hands are covered in mayo and I can't walk out. I mix the slaw with shredded carrots and shredded trust.

"It was fine," I say, and can almost hear Martha: *"Fine" is not a feeling.* Mom doesn't know that, though.

"Just fine?"

Or maybe she does.

"I talked. She talked. I didn't cry," I say. "So, yeah. Just fine."

"It's a lot of money for 'just fine,' Ellis."

"It's therapy, not Disneyland, Mom."

Mom closes the oven door and checks the slaw over my shoulder. "It's not mixed enough."

"I'm not *done*, I—"

"What did you talk about?"

I close my eyes. "I don't know."

"You don't know?"

"No."

"You don't know what you talked about for an hour?"

"I mean, a lot of stuff," I say. "I didn't take notes."

She waits a beat. "Did you talk about me?"

"Mom!"

She has the absolute audacity to look shocked. "You don't have to yell."

"Why do you always ask that?" I've stopped mixing.

"I have a right to know what's being said about me."

I shake my head and start mixing again.

"No, Ellis, not like that—here." She digs her hands into the bowl, taking over.

"Do you have to criticize every little thing I do?" I snap, but step back.

"You're being dramatic."

"You're kind of proving my point."

Her nostrils flare, but at that moment, Dad steps into the

15

kitchen, two reusable grocery bags over his shoulders. He was smiling, but that dies when he sees the way Mom and I are looking at each other.

"Hey," he says, cautiously, hands out like a zookeeper faced with two snarling wolverines.

Mom flicks one last look at me before kissing him hello and rinsing her hands off at the sink. "I told my sister I'd call her back before dinner. Can you check the lasagna in five?"

"Sure," he says. I unload the groceries. Once we hear the click of her heels on the second floor, Dad turns to me. "What happened?"

I don't say anything for a moment.

"Come on, Elk," he says, knowing I can't resist my childhood nickname. Elk, for my initials—Ellis Leah Kimball.

"She wanted to know what I talked about in therapy."

He sighs.

"She wanted to know if I talked about *her*."

"She likes to be in the loop," he says. "Just like you."

I roll my eyes. Mom and I could not be more different. Like I'd ever host parties or stand up in front of a crowd to teach Sunday school. Like I'd ever have as many friends as she does, or know how to comfort someone who's grieving, or argue with a salesperson over a gift card balance and win.

Mom is afraid of nothing and no one. And I'm—well, there's a reason she asked Dad to check the oven, not me.

"I'll talk to her," Dad assures me, running a hand through

16

hair that's the same deep brown as mine, the same thickness and inability to curl. My sister inherited my mom's dark yellow hair—she won't let anyone call it "dirty blond"—her slight build and light coloring. Dad was adopted as a baby, so I'm the only one in our entire extended family that looks like him. Tall and broad-shouldered, capable of tanning when the rest of them just burn. Oddballs in a family of pocket-size blonds.

There's a lot I don't like about myself, but I do like the way I look. I can stand in the back row and still see, unlike my mom. I can go outside in summer without putting on sunscreen every ten seconds, unlike Em.

I didn't always like it. Like when I was nine and at a family reunion, running around with my cousins, and one of my dad's sisters said I was like a "moose in a deer herd." I was old enough to know it wasn't a compliment. When I told Dad, he said, "You like eating venison, right, Ellis?"

"Yeah."

"And that's deer."

"Yeah."

"Have you ever eaten a moose?"

"No."

"That's because it's a lot harder to take down a moose." He winked. "Or an elk."

He talked to Aunt Karissa, and she never said anything like that again. So maybe he can get through to Mom. Eventually.

Mom's phone call and the lasagna are both done before Em

bursts through the door—late, as always. Ballet slippers falling out of her dance bag, bun half unraveled, talking about eighteen things at once, as always.

"Sorry, sorry, sorry I'm late." She dumps her bag and kicks off her shoes in the middle of the kitchen doorway. I start counting the seconds until she trips over them. "Lizzy's mom drove me home but first she—oh wait, I have a permission slip for—" She turns back for her bag. "Whoops." There's the trip, seven seconds in. She retrieves a crumpled blue form. "But so anyway, Lizzy's mom wanted to ask about the date for the winter recital—are we going to Utah for Christmas this year? Because we can't fly until it's over—okay, but then so after Lizzy's mom asked, I remembered *I* wanted to talk to Miss Orstrevsky about—ugh, these tights are killing me."

She plops down in a kitchen chair and rolls her dance tights farther up her legs. "*I* was thinking it would be cool if we did a piece from Tchaikovsky's *The Snow Maiden* because it's not like I *don't* like *The Nutcracker* but it's kind of played out."

"I hope you didn't hold up Lizzy's mom too long," Mom says. "She's very nice to drive you home."

"Don't worry," Em says to Mom, as if they aren't both biologically incapable of worrying about anything. "She loves me."

Of course she does. Everyone loves Em.

"If we could start eating before midnight, please," Mom says, and ushers us all into the dining room.

We fold our arms as Dad says the blessing over the food,

then dig in. Conversation is, as usual, heavily dominated by Em. Today at school, she had to complete a ten-year plan. She thought this was exciting, which only shows how different we are. Not only do I not know what I'd do in a decade, I'm increasingly unsure the world will even last that long. But my sister's got plans.

"First I'm going to graduate high school," she reports. "Then I'll go to college on the East Coast, then I'll go on a mission, then I'll get married in the temple and become a wildlife biologist."

Mom raises her eyebrows. "I thought you wanted to be a nurse."

"Yeah, but I don't know, you have to be inside all day."

"Didn't you want to be a garbage truck driver?" Dad says, and Em groans.

"*Ugh*, Dad, when I was, like, *six*."

"Why a wildlife biologist?" I ask her. "I mean, it's cool, but why?"

"I watched this thing on YouTube about this lady wildlife biologist who lived out in the Canadian wilderness for years tracking this wolf pack," Em says, "and she eventually made friends with them and became, like, a member of the pack and—it was so cool. She wasn't studying them, she was *part* of them, you know?"

"I bet she didn't have any children," Mom says. Dad clears his throat.

"Maybe," Em says. "She didn't say. What's it matter?"

"I think it would be very hard to do something like that and raise children, too."

Emmy's knife squeaks against her plate. "Maybe I won't have kids."

Dad looks at Mom. Mom looks at Em. "Don't be silly, you love babies."

"Well, you just said I can't do both."

"That's not what I said. You weren't listening closely."

"Lisa," Dad says.

"I said it would be very hard," Mom says. "You'd have to think carefully about what was important to you. Or most important to you. And I don't really think that's following wolves around, but I could be wrong."

Em's mouth twists. "It was just an idea."

"It's a great idea," I jump in. Mom's always on me to hold people's tiny, extremely breakable babies, but that's because she knows I don't want to. Em's always wanted to cuddle newborns and wipe snot off toddlers' faces. Why does Mom push like this when she doesn't even *have* to?

"Emmy," Dad says. "It's okay. You're thirteen. Don't worry about this right now."

Em stabs at her lasagna with a fork. Mom touches her shoulder.

"I didn't mean anything by it," Mom says, and Em smiles. But she smiles like she thinks she's supposed to. Not because what Mom said didn't hurt.

"You know what we should really be worrying about," I say. "Emergency food storage."

Em frowns. Mom closes her eyes.

"You don't need to worry about that, either," Dad assures Em, who's closely watching Mom's reaction.

"No one's going to get to live with wolves *or* have babies if we can't get through an earthquake," I say.

"Okay," Dad says. "Let's not do this tonight."

"We only have three months' worth of food."

"That's enough," Mom says, and I don't know whether she means that's enough out of me, or that we have enough food.

"Bad things can happen," I say. "They do. And when people aren't prepared, they suffer. I don't want to us to *suffer*, what's so terrible about that?"

Em looks to Dad. He sighs. "No one is saying it's bad to be prepared, but we are, and the more you obsess over this, the worse it gets for you—"

"The worse it gets for all of us," Mom cuts in. "It's not only about her."

You'd think I was holding them at gunpoint or forcing them to eat dirt. All I want is to make sure we survive. All of us, together.

"What do you think's going to happen?" Em says with a tilt of her head.

Biological weapons released into the air. Superviruses that

21

can't be cured. Terror attacks at the university, at my school, on the Golden Gate Bridge. I open my mouth to answer.

> *She's a kid. She's your little sister. You want her to have nightmares? You want her to start checking for fire exits whenever she walks in a room? You want her to be like you?*

I shrug. "Earthquakes."

Mom and Dad share a look. They know it's more than that, but I doubt they want Em to know about it, either.

"We're perfectly prepared for an earthquake," Mom says. "A power outage, a fire—this is California. We don't have hurricanes, we don't have tornadoes or snowstorms. We. Are. Prepared."

"Three months of food storage is the bare minimum," I argue. "Aunt Karissa has three *years*."

"She also doesn't vaccinate her kids," Dad mumbles. "She should not be your role model."

"Your aunt lives in the middle of nowhere," Mom points out. "If something happened—and *nothing is going to happen*—it might be a while before help could get to her."

"We have Safeway right down the street," Em says, taking a bite of lasagna.

"We have five grocery stores in walking distance. And food banks. And—" Mom holds up her hands. "No, you know what? I'm not doing this." She turns to Em. "Emmy, why don't you go pick out a board game for after dinner? Anything you want."

She quickly adds, "Anything but Trivial Pursuit."

"Why not Trivial Pursuit?" I ask.

"Uh, you know why not," Em says, getting up from the table.

"Sometimes the answers on the cards really *are* wrong, Em," I call after her as she pads into the living room.

The second Em's out of sight, Mom grabs my wrist, not lightly. I try to pull away.

"Mom—"

"No," she says. "No more of this. I know you worry about these things. But it's irrational."

"Lisa," Dad says. "She can't control what she worries about."

"She can control what she says," Mom counters. "I know it's hard. And I'm glad you're working on it with Martha." She tightens her grip. "But you are not allowed to hold this whole family hostage because you're *anxious*, Ellis."

There's the word. The word that always tightens my chest, but only slices my skin when she says it. She drops my wrist.

I don't always like my family, but I love them. And I'm going to keep all of us safe, whether they like it or not.

# THREE

**HERE ARE THREE** things my school doesn't have:

A dress code

Detention

Any real rules besides "no murder, no arson, no water guns"

Here are three things my school does have:

A campus the length and width of several city blocks

Nearly four thousand students

A halfway decent library

So though we also have an open campus during lunch, there's only one place I'll eat, and that's the library.

No one's actually supposed to eat in the library, which I understand, but it does present practical difficulties. Late in the spring semester of my freshman year, I went looking in the library stacks for a book on extreme weather patterns. It took me all of lunch to find it—the shelf it was on was in the back corner, with a wide, perpendicular set of bookshelves blocking outside sightlines. My first thought was, *This would be a perfect place for a mass shooter to hide.* My second thought was, *This would be a perfect place for me to eat lunch.*

It's a perfect place within another perfect place. And maybe a public school library wouldn't be everyone's perfect place, but it's mine. Everything about the library is routine. Every time I walk inside, the steps I take are as replicable as a lab experiment, and much safer.

I walk in the A-building and up the stairs to the second floor. I push open the glass door. I smile and say hi to Rhonda the Lunch Librarian, who does not smile back. Ours is a clandestine friendship. I head straight to the reference section and scoop up the heavy maroon book on the top shelf, five books from the left: *Barnhart Concise Dictionary of Etymology.* I make a beeline for the corner by the Meteorology/Climatology section. I sit with my back against the corner stack, the most tactically advantageous position. I spread the etymology dictionary out on the mauve synthetic carpet. I take out Kenny #14. I breathe in the solitude, the books on every side of me like a cocoon, the smell of old paper and ink and a little mildew.

And for the first time all day, I can breathe out.

I unwrap my PB&J sandwich as I flip through the etymology dictionary. Sometimes I'll go in order, word by word, page by page, but today, I skip around. *Parabola. Galore. Kestrel.*

I feel someone standing close by. Ugh. Rhonda the Lunch Librarian, here to demand I throw away my sandwich even though I never leave crumbs.

"Okay, okay, I'll put it away," I mumble without looking up, though it doesn't seem fair. Food is a human need. Books are a human need. It's cruel to make a person choose.

"Put what away?" asks someone who is not Rhonda.

My head snaps up. Standing a foot away from me is the girl from Martha's waiting room, the girl in blue. She's still in blue, actually—same shoes, same Cal Berkeley hoodie. It might even be the same outfit, which is weird, but not as weird as the fact that she's standing *here*, in my corner where nobody else goes.

Half her body is still behind one of the other bookshelves. She's leaning in like she knows she's invading something private. But she doesn't look nearly as surprised as I feel—she doesn't look surprised at all.

I think she knew I'd be here.

"Can I sit?" she asks, indicating a vague portion of the carpet next to me.

I peek my head around the stacks. There are many available chairs in the center of the library.

"Um. Sure." She plops down but keeps her backpack on. She says nothing as her eyes move up from the tips of my sneakers to the tips of my hair. I untuck the strands behind my ear.

"Yeah," she says softly, on a breath out. "It's you."

I still have no clue how we know each other. But we must; she wouldn't say it like that otherwise. But where? Church girls' camp? Freshman-year PE? The two weeks I played soccer before discovering that I lack both hand-eye *and* foot-eye coordination?

"I'm really sorry," I say. "I don't remember your name."

"It's Hannah," she says. "Hannah Marks. And you don't have be sorry. We only met on Monday. And I didn't tell you my name then."

*What?* "We met on Monday?" I bleat.

"Yeah," she says, then looks concerned. "In Martha's office? I mean, in her waiting room. You came out of your appointment and—"

"No, I remember," I say. "I thought maybe we were on the same sports team, or in the same grade."

"We are. You're a junior, right?" I nod. "Me too."

I wait for her to elaborate, as if all I could possibly want to know is that she's Hannah, a junior. After a long silence, it's clear I'll have to speak first.

I clear my throat. "I'm Ellis."

"I know."

"Okay," I say. "That's kind of creepy."

I didn't really mean to say that last part aloud, but she brushes it off with a wave of her hand.

"I only know because I snuck a look at Martha's appointment book."

"That's . . . actually creepier."

She shrugs apologetically. "Martha wouldn't tell me, so."

"You asked her about me?"

"Only what your name was."

"Why?"

She blinks. "Because I didn't know."

"Why did you want to know?"

"I've seen you before," she says, though I'm not sure that answers my question.

"Where? Did we have class together?" I ask. "Like last year or something?"

"No," she says. She nods at the dictionary, still flipped open to *kestrel*. "What are you reading?"

"A dictionary."

"You're reading the dictionary?"

"An etymology dictionary," I clarify. Like that makes it better.

"Whose class is that for?" she asks.

"Oh, no, it's for . . . fun."

"Oh. Okay. Cool," she says, so now I know she is Hannah, a junior *and* a liar. Her eyes move to my half-eaten sandwich. "Do you eat lunch in here?"

I nod.

"Every day?"

I nod, slower.

She sits back on her hands. "You should eat lunch with us."

"Who's 'us'?"

She ignores the question. "We hang out in the park. During lunch and usually after school, too. We meet under the tree across from the Little Theatre. Look for knitting needles."

I'm overwhelmed by the number of things that don't make sense here. I'll start with the most basic.

"We haven't had class together, I didn't even know your name, but you want me to eat lunch with your friends?"

"We should be friends," she says. "We're supposed to be friends."

"Supposed to—I don't—*why*?"

She considers this. "I have a couple working theories."

I should leave. I should get up and walk away from this weird girl with her cryptic riddles who invaded my secret spot. But I don't get up. It's *my* secret spot, after all. Why should I leave?

"That's really nice of you," I say, and focus back at my book, "but I like eating lunch here."

She stirs beside me. "It doesn't have to be lunch. You could come after school."

I stare so hard at the words on the page they blur. "I have chemistry lab."

"We could get coffee."

"I can't drink coffee—look." I close the book. I've never had someone work this hard to hang out with me. "You don't want to be friends with me."

She wrinkles her nose. "Yeah, I do."

"No, you don't. I'm not fun, okay? To hang out with. I'm . . . the opposite of fun."

"Boring?"

"Boring is the opposite of interesting, not fun, the word 'fun' implies—" I shut my eyes. "Do you see what I mean? Please save yourself. Save us both."

I keep my eyes closed for a long moment. When I open them, I expect to see that Hannah's left, like any normal person would. But Hannah hasn't moved from her spot on the carpet.

"Why do you see Martha?" she asks.

My mouth drops. "You're not supposed to ask that."

"Why not?"

"It's . . . private."

"What if I guessed?" she suggests.

"Um," I say, which she somehow interprets as "Sure, go ahead."

She rests her chin on one hand. "Are you secretly convinced your entire body is made of glass?"

"No, I'm not—how is that your first guess?"

"Do you suffer from dancing mania?"

"I don't know that means."

"Clinical lycanthropy?"

"Oh my gosh, *no*, I have *anxiety*. I see Martha for *anxiety*."

"Oh." She looks disappointed. "That's not so bad. Everyone has anxiety, right?"

I think that's supposed to make me feel better, but it only makes my temper flare. "No," I snap. "Everyone feels anxious. Sometimes. About normal things, about tests, or getting into college, or—" I swallow. "I'm anxious about *everything*."

"Not everything," she says. "I'm sure not every single thing."

"I worry that people are talking about me, I worry that people hate me, I worry that the guy sitting next to me on the bus is a kidnapper or a murderer or a Scientologist. I worry that I talk to my lab partner in chemistry too much, I worry I talk to him too little. I'm worried that I'll fail chemistry and every other class because I'm bad at school, and of course I am, I'm bad at everything, so yeah, I *do* worry about everything—every single little thing."

I suck in a deep breath. Hannah folds her hands in her lap. "That," she says, "must really suck."

A laugh bursts out from somewhere near my rapidly beating heart. "It's not great." I sigh. "I don't mean to make it seem . . . it's not just silly stuff like that. I worry about big stuff, too. Terrorist attacks, the apocalypse, MRSA—"

"What?"

"Methicillin-resistant *Staphylococcus aureus*, it's this bacterium that doesn't respond to most antibiotics."

"No, I know what—" She shakes her head. "The apocalypse? You're scared of the apocalypse?"

"Yeah." She closes her mouth, looking at me intently, purposefully. She looks like someone trying to do multivariable calculus in their head. Or me trying to do math at all.

"Not the Four Horsemen, specifically." She only looks more confused. "I mean, not necessarily a *biblical* apocalypse, though

31

it could be, but it could also be a flood, or an asteroid, or a human-created black hole. I worry about all the ways it could happen."

"The end of the world?"

"Yeah. That's my biggest one, probably. Doomsday, the apocalypse, the end of the world. That's what I worry about most."

She nods once, then again. "The end of the world. That's awesome."

It's not awesome. It is not awesome to dream about tsunamis and wake up in a panic. It is not awesome to sweat through your shirt at airport security because there might be a bomb by the baggage carousel. It is not awesome to imagine your skin peeling off in the wake of a nuclear attack.

I try to say all these things, but I'm so flustered that it comes out more like, "Bflugh."

Hannah moves closer to me. "Ellis. You and I were—" She hesitates. When she speaks again, each word is deliberate, like she's choosing them carefully. "We were meant to meet."

I shake my head. "I don't understand."

She doesn't hesitate this time. "We were meant to meet. It's fate."

*Fate*, from the Latin *fata*, the neuter-plural of *fatum*. *Fate*, which broken down literally means *a thing spoken by the gods*. *Fate*, a word that people use in both wedding announcements and obituaries.

"Fate?" I whisper. She nods, but I can't tell which kind of fate she means.

The bell rings, sudden and jarring. Hannah jumps up. She tightens her backpack straps, ready to go. The spell's been broken.

"I meant what I said. You should hang out with us," Hannah says, hand on the edge of the Human Anthropology bookshelf, two steps away from turning the corner and out of my view. "You remember where?"

"The park, a tree," I say. "But—wait—"

"Look for knitting needles," she says, interrupting smoothly. "And dead writer ladies. That's how you'll know which tree."

"That doesn't make any sense!" I say, as if one single part of this interaction *has* made sense. "A dead writer—?"

"Dead writer ladies," she clarifies.

"Let's go, everyone." I hear shoes scuffing the floor and Rhonda the Lunch Librarian shooing kids out, from what seems like a million miles away.

Hannah looks over her shoulder. "I'll see you soon, Ellis." She moves to slip around the corner.

"You didn't answer my question!" I yell after her, scrambling to gather my things.

"Which one?" she says.

Not a bad point, since she barely answered any. "You said we were meant to meet, that it was—fate?"

She takes her time answering. "You're afraid of the end of the world."

33

Is that all she can do, repeat what I already know? I throw down my bag in frustration. "Yes. I am. So what?"

Hannah takes a step toward me. She leans down, and for the first time since she came into the library, she speaks in a whisper.

"So I know how it's going to happen."

# FOUR

**MARTHA SWITCHES MY** appointment day. She tells Mom it's because she's had to rearrange her Monday schedule for personal reasons, but I know it's really because she doesn't want me running into Hannah again. Not that it would make a difference at this point. Not that I'll tell her that.

I was raised to be honest. Since I was a toddler in the church nursery, someone's always been telling me to "Choose the Right," which makes it seem so obvious. What's right should be clear. Martha might not know Hannah thinks the end of the world is coming. *Knows*. Hannah is Martha's client, and Martha deserves to know that kind of thing about someone she's trying to help. It would be right to tell her.

But when I sit down on Martha's couch on Tuesday, and she asks me how my week's been, I enter a morally ambiguous fugue state. I hear myself say, "Fine."

"The first couple weeks of school can be stressful."

"It's been okay," I say.

*She knows, she knows you're a lying liar who lies.*
*Bail. Bail on this lie. Bail on this therapy session.*
*Set the couch on fire as a distraction.*

"I think you can give me more than okay," she says gently.

*She knows you've been stalked by a doomsday*
*prophet. She knows you want to talk to Hannah*
*again. Immolate this polyester blend sofa and run.*

But I'm scared of fire, so I decide on something less destructive but still evasive. "I did the assignment you gave me. On eschatology."

"On—what?"

"Eschatology. The study of things at the . . . end. End of life, end of eras, end of the world. It's a good word, right? I'd never heard it before."

"It's a great word," she says. "So what did you discover?"

"It's weird," I admit, "reading all these accounts of people who are so sure the end of the world is coming—and knowing it won't. Because it hasn't."

"But they believed it, very strongly," she says. "How does that make you feel, when you read about these . . . true believers, you might call them?"

*She wants you to call them stupid, she wants you*
*to call them gullible. Hannah knows you're stu-*
*pid and gullible, that's why she found you in the*
*library. It's a joke, a big practical joke. If you even*
*went to find Hannah in the park, she wouldn't be*

36

*there. It's been a week. She's probably forgotten about you.*

I look away. "The hoaxes are actually more interesting."

Martha tilts her head. "The hoaxes?"

"People who knew the world wasn't ending but wanted other people to believe it was."

"Can you give me an example?"

"Okay." I pull out Kenny #14 and flip through, looking for the page. "So in 1806, there was this woman named Mary Bateman. She lived near Leeds, in England, and everyone in the area knew her as a—well, as a witch, but a good one. Someone who could cure curses. No one wanted to burn her or anything. But then she started telling people that the end of the world was coming. Because of her chicken."

"Her chicken?"

"Its eggs. Her hen started laying these eggs and they all said 'Christ is coming' on them."

Martha laughs, and then I do, too. Because it is ridiculous, hearing it out loud.

"How did her neighbors react, when she told them?" Martha says.

"Oh, they freaked out. People started coming from miles around and paid money for a glimpse of the prophet hen laying its miracle eggs. Everyone started getting *real* religious. But then, one day, two visitors dropped by the farmhouse. Early in the morning. And they saw Mary Bateman writing on a fresh egg and stuffing it *back inside* the hen."

Martha leans forward. "Really?"

"Really. It was all an elaborate hoax." I pause. "And also animal abuse."

"So what happened to all those people? The ones who had believed Mary?"

"I don't know. No one wrote about them. Just Mary."

"But what do you think?" she presses. "Do you think they were relieved?"

I shrug.

"Well," Martha says, "they were scared the world was ending. And now they knew it wouldn't. I'd be relieved."

I shake my head. "They only knew this wasn't *how* the world was ending. I think . . ." I pick at the couch threads. "I think maybe they were more relieved before. When they thought they knew for sure. Maybe they wanted to know, even if it was bad."

"That's important to you, having as much information as you can," Martha says.

"You can't do anything unless you have all the facts. You can't make choices." No, that's not exactly right. "You can't make the *best* choice."

"What about the choices the townspeople made?" Martha asks. "Do you think they made the best choices?"

Not the people who paid money to see fake prophetic eggs. Why would a woman who believed the apocalypse was imminent want money? What would she do with money, during Armageddon? They should have seen they were being played. But—

"The two men," I say. "They made the best choice, those two men who caught her in the lie. They didn't go along with everyone else, they didn't believe or disbelieve anything based on what other people told them to. They went and looked for themselves."

"So when you're looking for answers," Martha asks, "what do you think your next step will be?"

Hannah believes the world is ending. Maybe she's Mary Bateman in twenty-first-century clothes, a hoaxer waiting to shake me down for money. Or maybe she's a true believer, like the Leeds townspeople who desperately cleansed their souls. And maybe she's wrong.

But maybe she isn't.

"Ellis?" Martha prompts. "What will you do?"

I look at Martha straight on. "I'll do exactly what they did," I say. "I'll investigate."


My mom has this saying: "Avoid the appearance of evil."

She didn't make it up, it's a church thing. Basically, it means you should be careful about where you find yourself. It's not enough just to technically avoid breaking the rules; you shouldn't even *look* like you might be breaking them. Like my cousin Sarah, who won't buy hot chocolate from Starbucks because people might think she was drinking coffee. My mom rolled her eyes when Sarah told her that, but I think she'd feel differently about Civic Center Park.

Everyone at school just calls it "the Park." During lunch and after school, it transforms from a public park into a bacchanalian fun-fest of drugs, cigarettes, and the occasional bottle of something clear and very alcoholic on special occasions like St. Patrick's Day. Or so I've heard.

At the edge of the park, the corner closest to my bus stop, I scan the groups of kids on the grass, looking for Hannah.

> *Everyone's looking at you. Everyone sees you're alone. Everyone's looking at you and if they aren't looking at you it's because they're embarrassed for you and how alone you are.*

She's nowhere to be seen, and neither are knitting needles or dead literary figures. For a second, I lock eyes with Paloma from English class, lounging with the rest of the field hockey girls, their sticks tossed in a pile behind them. She smiles at me, and I make myself smile back, closemouthed, before looking down at the ground.

> *Don't stare at her. Why were you staring at her?*

I squeeze my eyes shut. I have to make a choice, either way. The longer I stand here at the edge, the more people are going to stare at me, and the worse I'll feel. Hannah mentioned being close to the Little Theatre, I think, which is almost one block south, along the park. I'm not going to happen upon her by chance. I'll have to look for her. I'll have to want to find her. With the tips of my shoes on the grass and the rest of me still on the concrete sidewalk, I wonder if I'm the person who walks forward or walks away.

I walk forward, shoes squishing into damp grass, past kids I know and kids I've never seen before, until I'm standing with the Little Theatre behind me and a particularly sturdy tree in front of me. There are three boys under it, none of whom, obviously, are Hannah.

"I'm not saying you're wrong, Theo, but—no, you know what, you are wrong," says a boy with sandy hair who I half recognize. Sam. He sat in front of me in Latin freshman year and spent the whole time drawing party hats and astronaut costumes on the portraits of Roman emperors in our textbook.

"You are wrong like people who recline their airplane seats," Sam says to the lanky kid next to him. "You are wrong like pineapple on pizza."

The boy—Theo, I guess—looks unmoved. "I don't know why you think ad hominem tactics will convince me."

"I don't know why you think I know what that means," Sam says.

"It means you're attacking Theo, not his argument," says the third boy, tan and curly haired and oddly familiar, though I don't think we've had a class together. "You might know if you hadn't skipped AP Language and Composition today."

Sam throws up his hands. "You skipped with me!"

"Yeah, but I did the reading."

From behind him, Theo pulls out a periwinkle ball of yarn and two shiny knitting needles.

Wait. Knitting needles?

Just like Hannah said. Maybe she's around here after all. I take a couple of steps closer to the tree and pull out my phone, pretending to text someone.

"Ms. Heaney's having after-school tutoring today. You should go," Theo says. "Maybe she could help you construct a better argument than 'If you don't jizz yourself over Jane Austen, you might as well be an actual monster.'"

"She's a genius," Sam says. "The way she writes dialogue. Revolutionary."

"It's just people being dicks to one another. But they're British, which makes it culture, I guess."

"You don't give her enough credit," Sam says. "So she's not all *serious* and *dark* and *borderline sanctimonious* like the Victorian princess of your heart, George Eliot."

"Now, she was a genius," Theo says.

Jane Austen. George Eliot. Both writers, both dead, both ladies. Just like Hannah said. This has to be the place; she must just not be here yet. I'll wait for her. I continue to fake-text on my phone. But then I hear someone say, "Hey, are you waiting for someone?"

I look up, and they're all staring at me. I guess I was more conspicuous than I thought. And much closer to the tree.

"Um," I say.

"Because no one's walked by or anything," Sam says.

"Hannah," I blurt out. "I'm looking for Hannah, she told me to go across from the Little Theatre, to a tree, and she said to look for dead lady writers which I took more literally than I probably should have." I gulp in air.

"Okay," Sam says.

"She used us as, like, treasure map directions?" Theo says. "That's weird, Hannah, even for you."

I look behind me, but she's not there.

"She'll come back soon," Sam says, scooting over so there's space between him and Theo. "You can sit down."

"Thanks." I sit. The curly-haired boy stares at me like I'm a particularly unattractive fish at the aquarium.

"Your name's Ellis, right?" Sam asks.

I nod. "Ellis Kimball. And you're Sam . . ."

"Segel-Katz, yeah. You still doing Latin?"

I nod again.

"Of your own free will?"

"It's a lot more fun once you start translating."

He shrugs. "I'll take your word for it."

Theo shifts his knitting supplies to one hand and holds out the other. "Theo Singh."

I shake his hand and turn to the last boy, expectantly, but he's only frowning harder. Sam clears his throat. "And this ray of absolute sunshine is Tal."

"Hi," Tal says, digging his hands deep into his hoodie pockets.

"Do I know you from somewhere?" I ask him.

"No," he says definitively. So definitively I don't think it's true.

Sam turns back to Theo. "What I was going to say was, you can't say you hate Jane Austen if you've only read *Pride and Prejudice*. So you don't like that one book. She did write others."

"I don't hate the book," Theo says. "I hate Mr. Darcy."

"Yeah, because you wish girls liked you as much as they like Mr. Darcy."

"Oh hell no," Theo says. "He is literature's biggest asshole."

Tal sticks his hand up. "Bigger than Voldemort?"

"Fine, he's literature biggest non-genocidal asshole," Theo says. "Happy, Tal?"

"Almost never."

"He loves Lizzie Bennett," Sam protests. "They're perfect for each other."

"He's not even *nice* to her for most of it—he spends the entire first half brooding in a corner and refusing to dance. And then he tries to wave it away with, 'Oh, I'm so *weird* and *fucked up* and how could anyone *ever love me*.'"

"You refused to dance at my bar mitzvah," Sam points out.

"Only the Electric Slide," Theo says. "Because it sucks."

"Wow, are all your opinions this wrong?"

"Screw you." Theo leans back into the grass and stares up at the sky. "You're with me, right, Hannah?"

Hannah—where? I swivel my head around. Sam sees me looking and taps my arm. He points up. From somewhere in the tree branches, a voice says, "I haven't read it. Sorry."

No way. I've only heard Hannah's voice once, and that did sound like her, but . . .

"Is she—?" I ask. "She's not in the—?"

Sam and Theo crack up. Tal tilts his face up at the tree. "Would you come down now? This girl's not here to see us."

> *He hates you. They all hate you, but he really hates you. He hates you so much he called you "this girl." He hates you so much he won't even say your name.*

Mom would say "kill with kindness"—which really means shut up and smile—but I don't like how he said *this girl*. I open my mouth to remind him of my name, but then a pair of blue Converse hits the grass with a thump. Hannah stands at the base of the tree, the legs of her jeans dusty and a couple of reddish leaves mixed into her hair. We lock eyes, and she brightens.

"Hey," she says, taking a seat next to me. "Awesome, I wasn't sure you'd show."

> *She didn't really want you to come. She hangs out in trees and probably makes friends with the squirrels and birds, but you are a bridge too far.*

"Have you met everybody?" Hannah says. "Theo, and Sam, and—"

"She's been here awhile," Tal cuts in.

Hannah looks surprised. "How long was I gone?"

Gone? She was in the tree. Wasn't she in the tree?

Theo shrugs. "Same as usual."

"I wish you'd start doing it on the ground," Tal says.

"Doing what?" I ask. "Where do you go?"

"She teleports," Sam says.

"To another plane of existence," Theo says.

Hannah shakes her head. "I'm only meditating," she says. "*I don't really go anywhere, my brain does.*"

I'm not a meditation person, despite a semester-long, mandatory "elective" on mindfulness in middle school. I can't make my mind go quiet like that. My brain stays right where it wants to, thumping inside my skull like a migraine that never stops.

"But why in a tree?" I ask.

"Because she has a death wish," Tal answers.

"People used to meditate in all kinds of places. In caves. In forests. On top of poles in the desert." She carefully pulls a leaf from her hair. "It helps. To go somewhere no one can see you, and you can't see them. It helps me see . . . things. More clearly."

*Things* is such a vague word. It didn't used to be. It used to mean a meeting, a council, a matter of great importance. Maybe she means it blandly, metaphorically. *See things the way they are.* But that pause, that little hesitation, makes me think it might be something more.

"Do you see it?" I blurt out before the smarter half of my brain can pump the brakes. "Is that how you know— Is that how you see it?"

Hannah freezes, her fingers around another leaf in her hair. She stares at me, wide-eyed and quiet.

"What did you say?" Tal asks.

"See it?" Sam repeats.

"Oh, do you mean, is that how I see things?" Hannah smiles back at me, with the barest hint of strain.

"Uh," I say. "Yes."

Hannah crumples the leaf. "Then yes."

"It's colloquial, Sam," Theo says. "Go to class for once."

"I know what a colloquialism is!"

Tal's eyes bore into me. "Where did you two meet, again?" he asks Hannah.

"Library," I say.

"Therapy," Hannah says at the same time. I close my eyes.

"That's great," Tal says, in a tone that strongly implies otherwise. "So how—"

"Hey," Hannah interrupts, reaching across me to nudge Sam, still arguing with Theo about colloquial language. "Can you smoke me out?"

Sam puts his hand to his heart. "I'm offended. To just *assume* I have the necessary supplies for such a thing. I am a scholar, an artist—"

She rolls her eyes. "Yeah, you're some kind of artist."

"You shouldn't insult your personal charity service." Sam pulls a film canister out of his backpack. "What would Emily Post say?"

Hopefully nothing, considering she's dead. Next to me, Sam tips a small rolled joint from the film canister into his hand.

You can't grow up in Berkeley and not know what weed looks and smells like, even if you're part of a religion that strictly forbids it. But I've never seen a joint this close. It almost feels like a setup.

"Who's got a light?" Sam says. "Mine's out."

"Hey, um," I say, trying to sound casual, "you guys know City Hall is sort of . . . right there?" I point across the street at the domed white building.

"Not like it's new," Tal mumbles, digging a lighter out of his pocket.

"But there are, I mean, there are police officers there," I say. "Who might see what you have?"

Hannah smiles at me like I'm a cute toddler. Sam laughs. "They've way got bigger problems. They're not going to bother us."

"Sam," Theo says, leaning back on his hands. "That might be the whitest thing you've ever said."

Sam grins. "I can do better—'Megan, turn off NPR and get in the Kia, we're late for Hunter's lacrosse game.'" He holds out his hand for Tal's red lighter. "Or, or—'I lost my North Face jacket at Whole Foods, so I have to replace it at REI before we go camping in Yosemite.'"

"'This casserole needs more mayo,'" Theo offers up.

"Weak," Sam says.

"Yeah, well, I'm Indian, give me a break."

I watch as flame sears the end of the joint, smoking and blackening the tip. My parents would lose it if they knew about this. I should leave. I should tell them to stop. I should avoid the appearance of evil.

But they were nice to me. Most of them. They didn't have to be, and they were. And even though the smell wrinkles my nose and I'm still half certain a Berkeley cop is going to pull up in his department-issued Prius, I don't get up. It feels good to be sitting here. It feels good to have someone to sit with.

After taking a hit, Sam extends the joint toward me like a Christmas present.

"I don't do that," I say, and cringe at how sharp it sounds.

He shrugs and passes it across my body into Theo's hand.

I feel like I need to explain myself. "It's against my health code."

"It's cool, doesn't matter why," Sam says.

"What do you mean, health code?" Hannah asks. "Like a diet, or are you asthmatic?"

I steel myself for an inevitable turn as Mormon Ambassador. It's a really fun game in which I explain that yes, I'm a Mormon, so yes, I have a health code that involves no drugs, no tobacco, no alcohol or coffee or tea. Then I have to cheerfully field whatever questions come next, no matter how insensitive or condescending. Half the people in Berkeley are gluten-free or vegan or freegans—actual, literal dumpster divers—but sure, *my* diet's the weird one.

Before I can open my mouth, Tal says, "She means the Word of Wisdom. She's a Mormon."

I spin around to stare at him. Not because he's wrong; that *is* what we call our health code. But it's what *we* call it. How does he even know what church I belong to? I never said.

Then it clicks, in a tumble of disjointed, hazy, little-kid memories. Shorter hair, a collared shirt and tie in place of a hoodie, and instead of a Zippo lighter in his hand—actually, no. There was a lighter then, too.

"I do know you," I say to Tal, more accusingly than I intended. He avoids my eyes. "You're a member, you're LDS."

"What?" Theo says.

"LDS," I repeat.

"No, this is weed," Sam says.

"Latter-day Saint," I clarify, gesturing at Tal. "I'm one, and he's one, too."

"No, I'm not," Tal says.

"Yes, you are. You're the one who accidentally lit the auditorium curtains on fire at the Oakland Stake musical when we were nine."

"Shit," he mutters, and takes a drag on the joint.

"You're Mormon?" Hannah says. "I thought you were Jewish."

"No way. He gets his bagels toasted," Sam mock-whispers. "I've seen it."

"His name is *Tal*," Hannah says to Sam. "I have a cousin in Israel named Tal."

"It's not really Tal," I say, bits of old memories piecing together. Playing in the basement of the Oakland Ward building one Sunday when I was five. Red Kool-Aid and cookies at someone's baptism. "Your name is Talmage. Isn't it?"

Theo and Sam look at each other. They collapse into giggles.

Tal gives me the blackest of glares. "It's a nickname."

"Where did your parents get *Talmage*?" Hannah asks.

"Family name. My mom's idea."

"James E. Talmage was an apostle in our church," I add.

"It's not *our* church," Tal says.

Hannah checks the watch around her wrist. "Oh, shit." She reaches behind the tree trunk and drags out her backpack. "I've got to go, you guys." She stands, and I experience a moment of pure panic. She's not leaving me here with these boys, is she?

"Which way are you going?" I ask, scrambling to my feet so fast I almost slip on the wet grass.

"Um—" For the first time, she doesn't look serene and all-knowing. She almost looks panicked. "You can walk me as far as Yogurt Park, if you want."

I nod.

"I have to get something out of my locker," Hannah says. "I'll meet you at the gate."

She's gone in a whirl of hair and leaves. I roll up my jacket and stuff it in my backpack. "It was nice to meet you," I say to the boys as I leave. I only make it a few feet away before Tal catches up and steps in front of me.

"Hold up," he says.

"I'm sorry I embarrassed you," I say, and then for some reason start saying *everything.* "I didn't know you didn't like your name; I mean, *I* like your name, and I'm sorry I told them you were a Mormon, though, you know, you can *tell* people, *I* tell people—"

"I'm not a Mormon," he says, cutting me off.

"But I know you. I've seen you at—"

"I used to be. I'm not anymore."

*Used to be* is different from *never was.* I stand still for a moment, trying to wrap my head around the idea of leaving the church. I know people do. I know they don't do it without a reason. But I can't quite imagine it. It's like leaving your whole family. Not just on Earth. After, too.

"I'm sorry," I say, like I've forgotten how to say anything else.

He shakes his head. "I didn't want to— This isn't about that. This is about Hannah."

"Hannah?"

"Why did Hannah invite you to hang out?"

What, because my very presence ruined his afternoon? My cheeks burn. "I don't know. Ask her."

"I don't know what your deal is or why she's suddenly decided you've got to be besties, but Hannah's dealing with a lot, okay?" he says. "More than just that thing with Paloma. A lot more."

Paloma from my English class? "Paloma Flores? What about her?"

Tal raises his eyebrows. "They broke up, right before school ended last year. In the cafeteria. Very publicly, very loudly?"

I shake my head.

"Are you sure you *go* to this school?" Tal asks.

"I don't know why you're telling me this," I say.

"Hannah's having a hard time. And she's coping with it in . . . her own way. But it's a problem." He pauses, then leans closer to me. "Don't be part of the problem."

I hate the word *problem*. My dad uses it a lot, when he doesn't want to say what he means. He used it when we were late to Em's kindergarten ballet recital because I had to check all the doors in the house and make sure they were locked. And when it took us forever to get home from Sea Ranch because the mountain roads were too narrow and I couldn't stop hyperventilating and asking him to drive slower. "Everything's fine. We just had a small problem," he told people when they asked why we were late.

The problem was me, and everyone knew it.

I wonder if Tal understands what that feels like, knowing things would be easier for everyone if you weren't around. If you were different from how you are.

"I won't be," I say, and I leave Tal in the grass. And I mean it.

Hannah and I aren't problems. But we might be each other's solution.

# FIVE

**WHATEVER HANNAH HAD** to get from her locker, it must be small. Because when she meets me at the main gate, all she has is her backpack.

"Ready?" I say. She nods and touches the front zipper compartment of her bag. That must be where it is, whatever she needed to retrieve. And it must be secret, because that touch—light, quick, confirming—that's what people do when they're hiding something.

I won't ask about it. I wouldn't want anyone asking about the mini survival bag I keep in *my* locker. Not because I'm selfish and wouldn't share the bandages or antiseptic wipes or even the particulate-filtering respirator mask, if it came down to it. But I've also got a multi-use knife in there, and I really don't want to get expelled.

We walk up Allston Way and turn right onto Shattuck, with the beautiful art deco central branch of the Berkeley public library up ahead. That's where I would normally be right now, ensconced on the top floor where it's quiet and empty. That's where I *should* be. I pause when we reach the library, but Hannah glides right past, as if she knows I'll follow. And I do.

"Is this on your way home?" she asks as we walk. "Or do you live up in the hills somewhere?"

"No, by the Oakland border. Off College Ave. You?"

"North side of campus."

We're taking a circuitous route for that. I guess she isn't going straight home.

> *Some people have lives, some people have hobbies and friends and places to go after school. Not you, obviously, but other people have those things.*

"Do your parents work at Cal?" I ask.

"Yeah, they're professors. Yours?"

"My dad's a dentist, and my mom does admin stuff for him. What do they teach?"

She laughs. "My mom barely teaches at all. She does research and has, like, one five-hundred-person lecture. My dad mostly teaches Freshman Comp but he's super popular; my brother couldn't even get into his class last year—" She shakes her head and pushes up the sleeves of her hoodie. "God, why does it always get hot *right* when we go back to school?"

"You have a brother?"

She blows air out her cheeks. "Yeah. Do you have siblings?"

"A sister, she's thirteen." I pause. "It's nice your brother goes to Cal, you must still get to hang out a lot."

"Not really," she says, and it's almost a snap.

> They're probably having a fight and you brought it
> up, why would you bring that up? Shut up, Ellis.
> JUST SHUT UP.

We keep walking. When we hit the steep part of Durant Avenue where the ground begins to climb, Hannah turns and asks: "Why are you always looking around like that?"

I startle. "What?"

"You're never looking straight ahead," Hannah says. "You're always, like . . ." She searches for the word. "Scanning."

Oh. "Sorry," I say. "It's weird. Sorry."

"You don't have to be sorry about it," Hannah says gently. "But why do you do it?"

"It doesn't matter."

She shrugs. "I bet it matters to you."

We're at the corner of Shattuck and Durant. The traffic light is on our side, and she steps into the crosswalk, but I grab the loose sleeve of her hoodie and stop her. She wants to know? Okay. I'll tell her.

"I'm thinking about where we are," I say. "I'm thinking about what we'd do if, ten seconds from now, a nuclear bomb was dropped on San Francisco."

She steps back in surprise, then recovers. "An earthquake's more likely."

"An earthquake is easy. We're outside, far enough from a

building, not under a utility wire." I point up. "We'd move away from the streetlight, then duck, cover, and wait. Like they taught us in kindergarten. This city was built for an earthquake. Half of this city was built *because* of the 1906 earthquake."

Hannah shifts her gaze from the streetlight above us, back to me. "But a nuclear bomb?"

"Totally unprepared. Fallout shelters went out of style with poodle skirts and—"

"Jell-O?" Hannah suggests.

Maybe in her family. "So I'm thinking about what we'd do if we saw the white flash. I'm thinking about how we'd drop to the ground, right here, and wait for the shock wave to pass. I'm thinking about how Pegasus Bookstore might have a basement for storage, and whether it's concrete, because that's where we'd want to go next, to wait out the radiation. Or maybe we'd want to go back to school, because there are showers there and I don't think any conditioner, which is good."

"What? Wouldn't you want shampoo?"

"But not conditioner. It binds radioactive material to your hair." I sigh. "I'm thinking about the science test I have tomorrow. I'm thinking about how my hair looks right now and whether my mom's going to leave me alone or make some comment she doesn't think is mean but is. I'm thinking about whether this paper cut I got is going to turn into MRSA and whether the turkey sandwich I ate at lunch is going to give me listeria."

"And the possibility of a nuclear attack," Hannah says.

"And that."

"All at once?"

"All at once."

> *She feels sorry for you, which she shouldn't. She probably doesn't. She probably thinks you're deranged. Either way, she's ten seconds from fleeing the scene of the disaster that is you.*

Hannah doesn't run. Hannah doesn't even look fazed. She grins. "But what about zombies?"

I've never understood the fascination with zombies. With so many real things to be terrified of, things that could and do happen every day, why spend a moment's thought on something fake?

"Aren't zombies scared of fire?" I reason. "I have fire steel in my Altoids box."

"I think it's Frankenstein who's scared of—" She stops, cocks her head. "Wait, your what?"

I swing my backpack around. I unzip a side compartment and pull out an Altoids mints box, still remarkably shiny and new-looking despite being tossed around in my bag every day. I hesitate for a moment, my fingers on the lid. If I show Hannah, she'll only have more questions. But if I show Hannah, maybe she'll answer some of my questions. I open the box.

"Fire steel," I say, pointing to a two-pronged compact tool on a string. "One part's a rod, one part's the striker. When you scrape them together, the friction creates and ignites metal shavings, and that creates sparks. You can make a fire in any weather, no matter how cold, no matter if it's raining."

She pokes her finger in the tin, moving the contents around. "Band-Aids. Alcohol pads. Superglue. Is that—dental floss?"

"It's stronger than you think. You can use it as thread. Replace a shoelace. Make a clothesline or a pulley system or a trip line."

"You carry this around with you all the time?"

"We call it 'everyday carry.'"

Her eyebrows go up. "'We'?"

"Prepared people," I say. I try not to say "prepper" unless I have to. It instantly creates this image of some Unabomber type with dead eyes stockpiling peanut butter and AK-47s in his bunker. "All the emergency gear in the world won't help if you aren't close enough to it during a disaster. You never know where you'll be when shit hits the fan."

"I didn't think Mormons were supposed to swear."

"We're not," I say, returning the tiny survival kit to its pocket. "But 'when stuff hits the fan' just doesn't have the same emotional resonance. You know?"

She laughs, and we cross the street together. We're nearly to Yogurt Park now, so if I'm going to ask the question I really want to know, I'd better ask it now.

"How do you know the world is ending?"

She takes a sharp breath in but doesn't say anything.

"Is that what happens when you meditate?" I press her. "Do you see it happen?"

"It's more complicated than that."

After all I told her about the things I worry about, the things I carry around, that's all she's going to give me? I fold my arms. "That's it? It's complicated?"

"Up in the tree, I'm—I'm trying to see something. I'm supposed to be seeing something. But I can't force it."

"Literally see it. In front of you."

She nods.

"You mean a vision."

"Yes."

"Of the end of the world."

"Yes."

"Does it work?"

"Only when I'm asleep."

Not visions, then. Not quite. "So they're dreams."

She shakes her head. "I mean, I'm asleep, I'm always asleep, but these aren't dreams."

"How do you know?" I can't count the number of dreams I've been certain weren't dreams. I've woken up panicked, ready to grab my go-bag under the bed, reaching for the flashlight on my nightstand because I'm certain the world has plunged into the Three Days of Darkness from the Book of Revelation.

"Dreams are fuzzy," Hannah says. "Dreams are unclear. But you can control your dreams, you know? You can switch locations. You can make things appear by imagining them. You can change your fate." She closes her eyes. "When I go to sleep, I'm not dreaming. I'm remembering."

"But it hasn't happened. You can't remember what hasn't happened."

"I know I can't. But I am." She twists her sweatshirt sleeve. "It feels exactly like a memory. Something that has already been and can't be changed. Something . . . fixed. I don't have each second of it, I'm not reliving it, I'm seeing the parts that mattered most. Will matter most."

"What do you see?"

"The night where everything changes, forever," she says. "The night the world ends."

My heart is pounding in my chest, my pulse is in my throat and my guts at the same time, my body is defying medical science just like Hannah is defying logic and reason and I want to know more. *Why* do I want to know more?

"What does it look like?" I ask, again, certain I don't want to know how life will fall to pieces but asking all the same. "When will it happen?"

She looks away. "I can't."

I stop walking. Why tell me this, if this couldn't give me any real information? Why tell me the world is ending if she's going to leave me powerless to stop it? My heartbeat picks up, my lungs constrict. "You *can't*?"

Hannah grabs my arm and pulls me to the edge of the sidewalk, out of the way of other pedestrians.

"I wish I could," she says in a whisper. "I wish I could, but I can't, because I don't know, either."

"But you've seen it!"

"It's so vague. It's so confusing. I need . . ." She trails off. Swallows. Focuses back on me. "I need someone to help me figure it out. Interpret it."

I shake my head. "I don't know how to do that."

Then it's her turn to shake her head. "Not you, Ellis. There's this—guy, who lives in Berkeley. Prophet Dan. He knows a ton about religion, and prophecies and things. He studied it. He helps people figure out this kind of stuff."

"Like a psychic?"

"Like it's a language, and he speaks it. But he's really, really hard to track down."

"You don't know where his house is?"

"Well," she admits, "he doesn't exactly have one."

"He's homeless."

She nods. It's not shocking. This city has a huge homeless population. It's warm year-round, we've got tons of public transport, and we've got history, too—people have been sleeping in Berkeley parks and panhandling on Berkeley streets since the hippies showed up in the sixties.

"I need you to help me find him," Hannah says. "I—I know that if we find him, he can tell us what we need to know."

"Why me?" I ask. "I don't know anyone named Prophet Dan, I don't know where he is, I don't even know—"

I cut myself off before I can tell the truth. I stop talking before I can say *I don't even know if I believe you.*

Hannah grabs my hand, and her fingers are cool and firm. "You can help me find him. I know you can, because when the end of the world comes, you're going to be right next to me."

"How do you know that?" I whisper, but I don't pull away.

"Because I've seen it."

The way she says it, so casually but so definitively, turns blood to ice in my ventricles. I freeze. She notices.

"Sorry," she says. She drops my hand. "I didn't mean to . . . Do you still want some frozen yogurt?"

I nod. Sugar is always the answer.

We walk the rest of the way to Yogurt Park in silence. I pile my cone with chocolate and mint yogurt, and enough toppings to decorate a large gingerbread house. It's not until I'm accepting my precarious, lopsided order from the cashier that I notice. Not only is Hannah not behind me in line, she's not in the store at all.

I take a giant bite and race out of Yogurt Park, but she's gone. I know she said she would only walk me this far, but I didn't think she meant it quite like this.

My brain feels frozen, and not from the yogurt. How could she dump something like that on me and then leave?

I'm about to turn the corner onto Dwight Way when I see her. Across the street, in the shade of the trees and under an unlit street lamp, Hannah is standing in the middle of People's Park.

It's not a typical park, because nothing in this city is typical.

People's Park was never intended to be a park at all. It was an empty lot until the Free Speech Movement, when students and hippies and runaways used it as a meeting ground and sort of communal property—a park for the people. When the National Guard tried to clear the park, the protesters fought back. Decades later, it's still a park of the people—homeless people. Mostly men, mostly during the day. A sanctuary for people with nowhere else to go.

And Hannah is standing in the middle of men and grocery carts and bundles and used needles. All by herself. Or—no, not all by herself. She's with a tall, spindly man in a long coat, and they're talking like they know each other. She asks a question. He nods. She pulls a small, white paper bag out of her backpack. She hands it to him, and they wave to each other as she walks through the uncut grass, back the way we came.

## SIX

**I LIKE CHURCH,** but I don't like the minutes before church starts. I feel all this pressure to stand around and chat, like everyone else in the ward seems so comfortable doing. I'm sure it's nice if you're a new convert or a visitor or an ultra-mega extrovert like every single one of my family members. It's a warm place. A welcoming place. But I want a quiet one.

That's why I'm standing in the corner just outside our ward meetinghouse trying to avoid the eye of the newest straight-out-of-Zion sister missionary. Sometimes I wonder if the missionaries from little towns in Utah and Idaho think we're all a bunch of heathens, with our oddball congregation and our liberal-as-Mormons-get vibe. They'd never tell us that, of course. They're sweet and sunny and positive no matter what, because that's just how we do things. We fake it until we make it. We're supposed to, anyway. So I spot the girls my age, shove my discomfort down somewhere near my pancreas, and walk over.

Lia is the first to notice me. "Hi, Ellis," she says, brushing some of her waist-length hair off her shoulder. It's perfectly black and perfectly straight.

Everything about Lia Lemalu is perfect, actually. She's the president of our Young Women's class. The top of her grade at her all-girls private school. And everyone knows not to perform after her at a talent show, because her expertly executed Samoan dance routine will put any boring piano solo to shame. She's also easily the prettiest girl in our ward, and seems not to have to work for it at all, which is profoundly unfair. Or it would be, if she wasn't so nice.

"How was your week?" she asks me. "We missed you on Tuesday."

I was supposed to go to Mutual, a combined Young Women's and Young Men's church activity, but after my walk with Hannah, I couldn't do it. Not only did I feel emotionally drained, but I hate ice-skating. So I faked a headache and watched myself into a reality-TV stupor.

"I wasn't feeling great," I say. "Was it fun?"

"Cameron Wright kept trying to help Lia on the ice, even though she's a way better skater than him," McKenna Cooper says conspiratorially, wrinkling her freckled nose. "He is so obvious."

"You should go out with him," April Lee says to Lia. "You guys can come out with me and Tanner, it'll be fun."

"Cameron's okay, I guess," McKenna says. "I'm not trying to

be mean or anything, but Lia can do better."

"I like Cameron," Lia says, and of course she does. She doesn't understand meanness. It may as well be ancient Sumerian to her. "Not like *that*, though." She touches my shoulder with a warm, delicate hand. "I'd rather have skated with you."

I take a feeling I won't name and shove it down, all the way down, past my pancreas and into the quietest, safest corner of myself.

The girls keep chattering about Tuesday and boys, and what we'll do in class today. I stand there and smile, and feel like I'm drowning on land. I've known these girls since we were babies, eating Goldfish and fighting over stuffed animals. But sometimes, it feels like they've moved on without me, like everyone got a handbook in the mail explaining how to be a teenage girl, and I'm still a glue-stick-eating toddler. Not because they're mean. They aren't. But even though I'm standing right in the semicircle, sometimes it seems like they've stopped seeing me.

> *You're not allowed to feel sorry for yourself. As if you'd really want them to know you. As if you'd want them to know what kind of a person you really are. They're better than you, you're—*

I shudder. Lia frowns. "Are you okay?"

"Yeah," I say too quickly. "Hey—where's Bethany? I saw her mom outside."

"She got her tonsils out on Thursday and I guess she still feels pretty bad," Lia says.

"She *must* be feeling really bad," McKenna says. "When *I* got my wisdom teeth out *I* still made it the next Sunday."

Lia rolls her eyes. "McKenna."

"I'm not judging! I'm saying she must be feeling awful, or she'd come."

"Come on, she was so out of it when we saw her on Friday," April says, then looks at me, suddenly panicked. McKenna grimaces. Lia stares at the floor.

They went without me. It's okay they went without me. I get why they went without me, but there's no way to explain that without embarrassing everyone involved.

Lia glances up at me, mouth open, but I beat her to the punch. "That's good, that's good she got her tonsils out."

"Yeah," April says, looking relieved. "They made her sick all the time."

"Also," I say, "think of how much less bacteria she has in her mouth now."

"What?" McKenna asks.

"The tonsils are a huge breeding ground for bacteria," I say, and then the words start to tumble, because if I stop, they might be embarrassed again, they might feel sorry for me again. "The whole mouth is, not just the tonsils. There are actually more individual bacterium in your mouth than there are *people on Earth*."

"That's . . ." Lia clears her throat. "That's really interesting, Ellis."

Lia might be a perfect Disney princess in the flesh, but it doesn't mean she can't lie.

"But you know," I say, trying to save myself, "there are also more chickens on Earth than people. So."

"Cool," April says. She nudges McKenna, who is struggling valiantly not to look weirded out. She is failing.

"Wow," McKenna says.

"Yeah," I say, letting the pit of awkwardness I've built envelop me.

My mom, in an act of true and unintended motherly love, calls to me from the front doors.

"See you in class," I say to the girls, and head over to where Mom is standing with her back to me, next to Sister Jensen.

"Hi, Sister Jensen," I say. "How are you feeling?"

"Tired," she laughs, looking down at the tightly swaddled, impossibly tiny infant in Mom's arms. "But he's worth every three a.m. wake-up, aren't you, buddy?"

Mom cradles Sister Jensen's new baby like her arms were designed for it. "What a sweet face. Look at those eyelashes."

I peer down at the baby, who looks shriveled and angry, to be honest. And you can't even *see* his eyelashes. I don't get it. I wish I did.

Sister Jensen puts her hand on my shoulder. "Would you like to hold him?"

Panic floods my bloodstream. "Oh," I say, looking at Mom with wide eyes, silently begging her to help me. "That's so nice of you, but—"

Mom all but shoves the baby into my arms.

"Support his head, there you go."

This is how I die.

"Oh, I do miss this age," Mom says. "So precious."

"I think you'll have a newborn in your life soon enough," Sister Jensen says, and I don't have to look at her to know she's talking about me.

Maybe the baby can sense my sheer terror, or maybe he needs to be changed, because he opens his tiny mouth and wails to shake the rafters. Sister Jensen scoops him from my arms as the clock hits nine a.m. and everyone moves toward the pews.

Mom and I find Dad and Em in our usual pew. They aren't assigned, it's more of a habit than anything else. As always, they let me have the aisle, closest to the emergency exit. Right before I sit, I catch a split-second glimpse of a boy on the opposite side of the chapel, obviously out of place in a colored button-down shirt—not white—and a half-undone tie.

"Tal?" I whisper, but he's too far away to hear, and disappears in the crowd. Em looks up and frowns.

"Who?" she says.

I sit down. "Never mind."

Bishop Keller welcomes us from the pulpit and calls for the opening hymn. I hear the rustling of hymnbooks around me, but I don't bother taking one from the pews. I know this one by heart. I know most of them by heart. I close my eyes, breathe in, and sing.

It's not that it all disappears. It's not that church is some magical forcefield that banishes the nagging, gnawing voice inside

70

my head. It's only that it's quieter, or maybe I just can't hear it as well over the organ and the voices around me. Maybe it's only that I can ignore it better at church, but even so, that's why I come here. Not for the awkward conversations in the vestibule, for all the rules, or even out of duty to my ancestors who crossed the prairie with handcarts. I come here to stand with my family and people who might as well be. I come here to feel whatever's always squeezing my lungs release, to feel my shoulders loosen and my mind calm.

I come here because when we sing *all is well, all is well*, I believe it. If only for a moment.

As part of ward business, Bishop Keller calls one of the little girls, Caroline Collins, to the front. She's eight years old and shy, but gamely allows herself to be introduced as a newly baptized member of our congregation. Some churches baptize kids much younger than this, I know, but we wait until eight. Old enough to make a choice, old enough to read from the Book of Mormon and feel a confirmation that what's been written is true. Old enough to feel that warm feeling of peace inside, what we call feeling the Spirit.

Sacrament—our kind of Last Supper reenactment and the whole point of this all-ward meeting—comes next. Some of the boys twelve and older—but only the boys—pass through the pews first with the bread, torn into bite-size pieces, then the water, poured into individual cups. When I eat the bread and drink the mini Dixie cup of water, I can feel myself letting go of the week. I can forgive myself for not being a better daughter. I can forgive myself for being an awkward mess around Lia and the other girls. It won't last forever, but for now, I can let it go.

Bishop Keller turns the pulpit over to the first speaker of the day. The ward is a family, a collaboration, and we all speak at one time or another, on some assigned topic. Even little kids will give their testimony. I'm a much happier listener than lecturer, especially when one of the speakers is my dad.

Dad takes the pulpit. He clears his throat. He's not much of a speaker, either, but he accepts every call without hesitation or complaint.

"When I was ten, I went camping with my Boy Scout troop in Zion National Park."

Oh, it's this story. I've always liked this story.

"We were hiking, and I fell behind. By the time I'd looked up again, my troop was gone, and I couldn't tell which way they'd went. Soon, I was completely lost, and the sun was getting lower. I was standing at a crossroads, terrified and helpless. I dropped to my knees and prayed, begging Heavenly Father not to let me die in the wilderness, when I heard a still, small voice, from somewhere deep inside. It told me to get up. To walk forward. And when I did, I felt the strongest prompting to take the left fork. So I turned left, and discovered a little stream. Every Boy Scout knows that water flows to civilization. I followed the river downstream and found my way back to the world.

"Brothers and Sisters, I tell this story because it shows how important it is to listen to Heavenly Father's prompting. Jesus Christ appeared to Joseph Smith, a fourteen-year-old farm boy, when he could have chosen a king to restore His church on Earth. No one is too young or too average to receive revelation. When the Spirit speaks to us, we must listen."

He goes on, but I can't hear him above the thrumming in my heart and the buzzing in my brain, because of course. Of course. Why didn't I see it before? It's in the word itself. *Apocalypse*. It comes from the Greek word *apokalyptein*, meaning to uncover, to unveil what has been concealed. The word *apocalypse* means a revelation. I know how to decide if Hannah's telling the truth. I know how to know. All I have to do is ask.

After a couple more speakers and the closing hymn, we break for the next part of services. We'll gather in smaller groups according to age and gender. Mom's in Relief Society, the women's group, Dad meets with the other Elders. Em and I are both in the Young Women's program, but she's a Beehive and I'm a Laurel, so after a short prayer and hymn, we'll split up. On the way, I stop by the water fountain in the hallway.

"Well, good morning, Sister Kimball."

I shoot up, water dribbling from the corner of my mouth. Leaning on the wall next to me is Tal, his hands shoved in his pockets, his tie threatening to unravel completely.

I swallow the water in my mouth. "I thought I saw you."

"In the flesh," he says.

I open my mouth to ask who he's here with, but my eyes

snag on his tie. It looked normal from far away, but up close, it's awful—paisley patterned out of mustard yellow and a nauseating shade of maroon.

"Ugh," I say, out of instinct more than cattiness.

He raises an eyebrow. "What, you don't like my tie?"

My cheeks go hot. "Oh, no, it's—"

"The ugliest tie you've ever seen, right?" He grins. "They said I had to wear one, they didn't say it had to be tasteful."

"What are you even doing here?"

"I'm here under duress," he says. "I had to stay at my mom's this weekend. So, not optional."

"Your mom?"

"You'd know her as Sister Collins."

Sister and Brother Collins are recent transfers from an Oakland ward, with two little kids. She's older than most of the moms with kids that young, but I didn't know she'd been married before.

"I didn't know she was your mom," I say.

"I live with my dad. He's gone this weekend for some conference, and I thought I made it pretty clear I could take care of myself, but . . ." He shrugs. "Here I am."

"Oh."

"Of all the fucking weekends," he says, and I wince. I try not to be too precious about other people swearing, but a portrait of Jesus himself is staring at us from across the room. "Caroline's baptism yesterday, two hours of church today. Jesus Christ, it's never-ending."

I know it's a painting, but I swear, the Jesus-portrait frowns.

"It must have been nice to see your sister baptized."

He picks at his shirt collar. "Well, the cake at the reception was good."

Maybe he thinks this prickly-hedgehog routine is endearing, but I don't. "Yeah, sorry you were forced to hang out with your sister on one of the most important days of her life. My condolences."

He drops his eyes. "No one forced me. I was always going to go. And you're right. It was nice—it was nice to see her so happy."

That's the thing about hedgehogs. They're all spikes on the outside, but soft when you get underneath.

He looks back at me. "There. Is that better, Sister Kimball?"

Kids don't call each Brother and Sister. He's doing it to tease me. "It's perfect, Brother—" But then I stop, because I have no idea what his last name is.

"It's Santos, but—call me Tal, call me Talmage, call me goddamn Ishmael, but please don't call me Brother Santos."

"Deal, if you stop swearing in front of my Savior." I indicate my head at the Jesus portrait.

"He is entirely too white to be Jesus," Tal says, "but deal." He pushes himself off the wall. "You skipping Young Women's? Going to play with the babies in Nursery? Caroline loves doing that."

Yeah, Em, too. "I'm not a fan of babies," I say before I can think better of it. He looks surprised, but doesn't rush to offer me reasons I should be, which is a nice change. Still, I feel like I need a reason. "The crying. I have sensitive ears."

"Not to mention all the germs," he says.

"Did you know there are more germs in the human mouth than there are people on Earth?" I blurt, because I'm apparently incapable of learning from my mistakes.

"Really?" he says. "That's fascinating."

Is it? I think it is.

"Yeah," I say, "a little terrifying, but fascinating, right?"

He considers. "It's not terrifying."

"It's not?"

"We need those bacteria, right? The bacteria, mites, all of that. It's this hugely complicated ecosystem, right inside of us, everything working together. Even the tiniest part matters. Even the bacteria."

Huh. I've never looked at it that way. I grin. "Fair point, Tal." He smiles.

Sister Olsen, the resident ward busybody, appears in the chapel doors. "Don't you have somewhere to be?" she says to me. I start toward my classroom.

"Young man," I hear her say to Tal, "would you like some help finding *your* destination?"

"Nah, I'm good," he says. "You know what they say, everything in moderation. Even Jesus."

I stifle a laugh and turn around to see him halfway out the front door, to Sister Olsen's disapproval. He catches my eye. "See you around," he says. Then after a pause, "Ellis."

As usual, it takes forever to leave church. From the way Mom clings to her friends, just needing *one more minute* eighteen minutes ago, you'd never guess they see each other weekly, at the absolute least.

And as usual, during the ride home, the car transforms into a Broadway stage for Em to perform her one-woman show: *Everything I Saw, Did, and Thought During the Two Hours You Were Not in My Direct Presence.*

After a particularly meandering story about another girl in her age group who wants to get a second (forbidden) ear piercing, Em takes a breath, and my mother seizes the opportunity.

"Sister Olsen said she saw you talking to a boy outside the chapel," she says, glancing back over the seat. Em nudges me, grinning, and I push her elbow away. "But she didn't know who he was."

"His name is Talmage," I say, using his full name in a deliberate act of misdirection.

"Who was he there with?" Dad asks.

"Sister Collins. He's her son."

Mom and Dad look at each other. Dad focuses back on the road. "Oh," Mom says. Weird.

"Did you know she had an older son?"

"She's mentioned him," Mom says. "I think their relationship is . . . complicated."

"So he's Caroline's brother?" Em says.

"Yeah, half brother, I guess," I say.

"How do you know each other?" Dad asks.

"School." This is technically true. The park is part of school. Hannah is part of school. But my parents don't need to know about either.

"Is he cute?" Em asks.

"I— He's—" Is he cute? In a completely objective sense, yes, he is. If you like boys with holes in their jeans and dark curls and green-brown eyes, *not that I've noticed at all.* "We're friends," I force out, though we might not even be that.

"Uh-huh," Em says, and I'd strangle her if it didn't mean I'd be all alone with my parents.

"Good," Dad says. "You don't need to get involved in anything else." I roll my eyes.

"She's sixteen," Mom says. "She's old enough to date."

"Ellis can't date Caroline's brother," Em says.

I glare at her. "Really, you too?"

She looks at me with a bit of pity. "Because he's *gay*, Ellis."

Oh.

"Emmy," Mom scolds. "Don't gossip."

"His sister told me. It's not gossip if his *sister* told me."

I feel so stupid. Not because he's gay, it's fine that he's gay, but I thought when were inside—I thought maybe he was flirting with me. Maybe.

> *Obviously not. Why would he flirt with you, why would anyone flirt with you? You're weird and awkward and no one will ever, ever like you that way. Not Tal, not—*

78

I shake my head to bury the thought. "What did Caroline tell you?" I ask Em.

"She said he got caught doing stuff with another boy at some sleepaway camp. And his mom—well, I think more his stepdad—wanted him to see a therapist about it, but his real dad said he didn't have to. And it was a big thing."

Mom sighs. "Oh, poor Jessica."

Jessica is Sister Collins. "Poor *Sister Collins*?" I say, with an edge. "Not poor *Tal*?"

Mom looks back at me. "You don't think it was hard for her?"

"There's nothing wrong with being gay," I say.

"Of course not," Dad says.

We believe that, my family. Not everyone in the church does. Some of my cousins say things that make me cringe, and the leadership isn't exactly progressive. But my family believes that.

"I don't mean it's wrong," Mom says, choosing her words with care. "I mean it's a hard row to hoe."

And she's not wrong. Because no matter what my family believes, even what our local community believes, it doesn't change the reality of being gay and Mormon. It doesn't change the reality that same-sex relationships are considered contrary to God's plan. That Tal could never marry a man in the temple. That until recently any children he and his husband had couldn't be baptized until they were adults. And even then, they couldn't be baptized unless they disavowed their fathers' relationship. That's the reality. And it sucks.

There are so many terrible things that the end of the world would bring. Famine, war, displacement. All those people who get to hurt Tal and people like him, all those people who think anything under the rainbow flag is immoral or shocking, well. At the end of the world, maybe they'll have a chance to see what immorality really looks like, what shock really feels like. There's not much of a bright side to the apocalypse, but maybe this is one: when the world as we know it ends, no one will care whether two people love each other.

As soon as we get home, I rush up to my bedroom. There's no road map for determining the truthfulness of a teenage dooms-day prophet, so all I can do is follow the routine I learned as a child.

I shut the door. I drop one knee to the carpet, then the other. I rest my weight on the back of my legs. I fold my arms across my chest, bow my head, close my eyes.

I'm not sure how to start. I've never asked for a revelation before. My previous pleas to the universe have been, I real-ize, remarkably self-centered. *Please let me find my missing library book. Please let me pass this math test. Please let me be different, better, someone other than myself.* Asking for divine inspiration isn't any less selfish, but it's on another scale entirely.

I replay each second with Hannah in my mind, from the moment I saw her in the waiting room to the moment I saw her sweep through People's Park.

*I know when it's going to happen.*

*It's going to happen.*

*I know.*

Maybe it's wrong to be doing this. Maybe it's wrong to be asking for an answer when I know my parents, my bishop, my sister would all say Hannah's wrong. That she's delusional at best and dangerous at worst. But all Hannah wants is for someone to believe her; there's nothing sinister about that. She wants someone to hear her dreams and repeat them back without fear or doubt. She wants to speak and have someone pull her words close, not scatter them into the wind. She wants someone to believe she's seen what she's seen, and what's so strange about that?

I want to be believed when I beg my family to be prepared. I want to be believed when I say I'm afraid, when I say I don't want to be in AP classes, behind the wheel of a car, with a baby in my arms. Even Mary Bateman, hoaxer and liar that she was, only wanted to be believed when she said she'd been granted something special, that she was more than a poor woman in a small town.

Everyone just wants to be believed.

And as that thought rides the synapses of my brain like lightning, I feel it. The Spirit, exactly like I felt it when I was eight years old and preparing for my baptism. When I asked if the only life I'd ever known was true, was right, was real. My parents told me I'd feel a burning in my chest, a still, small voice, a sense of utter peace. That isn't what I felt. What I felt was so much more.

Trying to capture it is like describing salt without mentioning sugar. Like painting a wall with a color you can't see. Like holding the sun in a jar or pinning down the wind. I love words. I love finding out what they mean, where they come from, cataloging and categorizing and *knowing*. But this is beyond words.

Everyone just wants to be believed. Hannah wants to be believed and I want to believe Hannah, because I'm kneeling on the carpet on my childhood bedroom gasping for air, flooded with adrenaline and endorphins and that indescribable feeling. I know. I know. I know Hannah is telling the truth.

But feeling that something is true, even *knowing* that something is true, is one thing. Belief is another. Belief is a choice.

And I've chosen.

## SEVEN

I LOOK FOR Hannah at lunch on Monday, but no one's seen her. I sit through my afternoon classes and seventh-period chemistry lab in a state of profound agony. Who cares about sines and cosines when the world is going to end? Who cares that my lab experiment bubbled over and oozed brown sludge onto the lab table? In a postapocalyptic society, no one's going to ask about my junior-year grades.

I escape the classroom as soon as my chemistry teacher dismisses us, all but trampling a tiny freshman on my way out the G-building door. *Please*, I pray, *please let Hannah still be here, please don't make me wait another day to tell her.*

I'm panting by the time I reach the Park, but my breath stops in my throat when I see Hannah's tree with no one under it. She's not there. No one's there.

> *You missed her. You waited too long. She'll never tell you what you need to know and the end of the world will come and you'll die—*

"Ellis!" someone shouts behind me. I spin back around, and there's Hannah, standing by the front gates. I must have run right past her and not even noticed. I try to say "hi" back, but I can't seem to say anything at all. And maybe Hannah has seen this moment, or maybe she can read the look on my face, because she grabs her backpack and walks over to me without another word.

And though I want to shout it the whole time she's walking over, I wait until she closes the distance.

"I believe you," I whisper.

"What?" she says. I don't know if she can't believe it, or simply couldn't hear me.

"I believe you," I say again, more firmly. As Dad would say, with *conviction*, a word that means determination but also prison sentences.

"You do?" she says, not sounding surprised, but somehow still relieved. "You do."

"Yes."

"Okay," she says on a breath out. "Okay."

"So you'll tell me now?" I ask. "You'll tell me how it happens?"

Hannah opens her mouth, but then hesitates. She sticks her hands in her pockets, then takes them out. Suddenly, she's speaking rapid-fire. "I don't really know, I wish I could tell you, but I don't really know, that's why we need someone to interpret—they're so confusing, the dreams are so vague and

84

weird and I have them every night but it never gets any clearer."

I put out my hands to stop her. "Okay," I say. "Please breathe." She takes a deep, audible breath in. "We'll figure it out, we'll . . ."

But I don't know how to finish that sentence. I've done so much research into surviving disasters, surviving attacks, surviving all the ways the world could end. I have no idea how to untangle a prophecy. It didn't seem like a useful skill.

She still looks like she's having trouble catching her breath. "Let's sit down," I suggest, ushering her to the Little Theatre steps, a few feet away. No one's going to bother us here. More important, no one's going to overhear us here.

"Is there anything you do know? For certain?" I ask her as she twists her hands in her hoodie sleeves. "A date, a place?"

"Just . . . feelings," she says.

"Feelings," I repeat.

"I know how I *feel*, when it happens. I can remember that."

"So, what do you feel?"

"Cold," she says.

"Cold?"

"Because it's snowing," she explains.

"Where are we? When it happens."

"Here," she says.

I gape at her. "Here?"

"Not in the Park," she clarifies. "But in Berkeley."

It doesn't snow in Berkeley, except maybe a couple flakes

way up in the hills. It's never enough to stick. I'm not prepared for a blizzard, or an Ice Age, or anything like that. I never thought I needed to be.

"What about inside?" I press on. "Like, what do you feel internally?" I pull one of Martha's favorite lines from the back of my brain. "Can you name the feeling?"

She closes her eyes. "Confusion. Panic. Like someone's ripping my heart out and I can't stop them."

I really hope that's a simile. Murderous bands of cannibals shouldn't show up until *years* into a post-doomsday society. Months, at least.

"What about your senses?" I say. She opens her eyes and frowns. "No, keep them closed." She obeys. "You've only said what you feel. But there's more to memory than that."

Smell is the sense most closely connected to memory—I remember writing that in Kenny #11 or #12. We'll start there. "Smell. What do you smell? Breathe it in."

She breathes. "It's like . . ." She hesitates. "It's like my mom's perfume."

"Is she there?" I ask. "Is she with us?" Maybe our families come with us.

"I don't think so," Hannah says. "It's like her old perfume, when I was little. She has a new one now, but it's not that."

"Do you remember what it was called?"

Hannah shakes her head. "It was in a green bottle. That's all I remember."

Okay, well, that was a bust. "What do you hear?"

"Wind."

"What do you taste?"

"Salt."

Somewhere near the ocean, somewhere that smells like per-fume. I've got nothing. One last sense, one last shot. "What do you feel?" I ask. "Not inside, but . . . touch. What do you *feel*?"

She is still for a long moment. "Your hand, in mine. I feel you grabbing my hand, and holding on tight."

That's as comforting as it is terrifying. On the one hand, I won't be alone when the world ends, and neither will Hannah. On the other hand, that means that I'll be there, unprotected, on some sea cliff. It's fated. Fate takes the uncertainty out of things, but it doesn't take the fear.

"You're sure?" I ask Hannah. "You're sure I'm there?"

"It's about the only thing I am sure of."

That shouldn't make me happy. It should worry me, that she's not sure when the world is ending, or how it's ending. It should completely freak me out that all she knows is I'll be there. It shouldn't make my heart swell. But it does.

"That's why we need to find someone who can help us interpret," she says. "Like I said before."

I nod. "I remember."

"I know you like our school library," she says, "but what about the public one?"

"Which branch?" I ask, as though I haven't made it to half the branches at some point.

She seems confused by the question. "Up the block."

The Central branch. "All the time, I go there all the time." I'm talking too fast, too eagerly. I don't even know why she's asking, but I'm desperate to be helpful all the same.

"Great," she says, nodding to match my eagerness. "That's great. I've got a lead that the guy we're looking for—"

"Prophet Dan?"

"Yeah, Prophet Dan. I've got a lead that he hangs out there, sometimes. And since you know the place . . ." She trails off.

"Okay," I say. "When do you want to check it out?"

She gets to her feet. "How about now?"


As we walk to the library, Hannah gives me the lowdown on Prophet Dan.

"Brown hair, brown beard, brown eyes," she says. "Tan-ish skin. Five foot ten. He might be wearing a red buffalo plaid coat."

"Buffalo plaid?"

"Red and black, checked."

"It's too hot for a coat, though," I say. But then again, Hannah's wearing a hoodie. I've never seen her without it on, now that I think about it.

"He'll be wearing the coat," she says. "It's kind of a protection . . . thing."

"Protection from what?" I ask, slowing down.

"Nothing real." She looks at me out of the corner of her eye. "So does it matter?"

It suddenly occurs to me that this might not be the safest plan in the world. "Are you . . ." I hesitate. "Are you sure he'll be okay talking to us, if we find him? Because if he's paranoid or something, maybe we should leave him alone."

Hannah spins and grabs my arm. I stop. "We need him," she insists. "He knows about this stuff, okay? He studied it at Cal, mysticism and religion and prophecies and everything. He's good. He's, like . . ." She pauses. "A legend."

"I've never heard of him."

She tilts her head. "Yeah, I don't think he exactly runs in your circles."

Fair point.

"Look," Hannah says, hands in front of her, like she's worried I'll bolt. "He won't judge us. He won't call our parents. And he's not dangerous, if that's what you're worried about."

"How do you *know* that, though?" I ask.

She chews on the inside of her cheek. "We have friends in common."

It's not as much reassurance as I'd like, but it's better than nothing. I start walking again. "Well, okay, I guess."

Hannah heaves a sigh of relief. "Great. Good. How many floors is the library?"

"Six."

"I guess you'll have to check them all."

"Not necessarily," I say. "If he's really big into mysticism and that kind of stuff, all those books are on the first floor."

Hannah raises an eyebrow. "Did you memorize all the rooms in this library?"

"No," I say, feeling heat rise on my cheeks, "just the Dewey Decimal System."

"See," she says with a smile, "this is how I knew I needed you."

Well. That, and the apocalyptic nightmares.

"Wait," I say, my mind jumping back to an earlier comment. "Did you say *I'd* have to check them all?"

"No, not if you know which floor."

I slow down, because we're just about to reach the library. "Are you not coming in with me?"

She stops in her tracks. "Oh, shit," she whispers, looking past me. I follow her gaze to the benches in front of the library. Right by the flower planters are Sam, Theo, and Tal.

"Are you okay?" I ask her.

"Don't tell them who we're looking for," she says, her eyes still on the boys.

"Maybe they could help," I suggest.

She shakes her head. "Nope."

"But—"

Just then, Sam turns his head and spots us. He waves.

"We'll just hang out for a minute," Hannah says to me as she waves back. "I'll keep watch on the door. Just in case."

I open my mouth to ask fourteen different questions—Why don't you want your friends to help? Don't you want your friends to know what you do? Don't you want to protect them, don't you—but Hannah's already walking over. So I just sigh and follow.

"I think I bombed our pop quiz in chemistry," Theo's telling Sam as Hannah and I reach them.

"The last time you said that, you got a B," Sam reminds him.

"There was a dead spider in the corner this time. It was distracting." Theo shudders.

"If it makes you feel better," Sam says, "it might not have been dead. It might just have been a shed exoskeleton, which means it's still alive, only now it's bigger."

"*Why*," Theo says, with a full-body recoil, "would that make me feel *better*?"

"Why do you only know the grossest things about animals?" Tal asks Sam, making room for Hannah and me on the flower planter. I sit next to Hannah, careful not to block her view of the library doors.

"Spiders aren't animals."

Tal chooses to ignore this. He turns to Hannah. "Where were you two going?"

"We were looking for you," Hannah says with such cool nonchalance I almost forget it's fake.

Tal looks skeptical. He nods over at me. "Then why does she look so uncomfortable?"

"You can have that effect on people, Tal," Sam says. Tal throws a leaf at him. Hannah laughs.

And then I think—maybe Hannah hasn't told them because the second she did, moments like this would disappear. Maybe Hannah wants more time, just a little bit more time, to pretend like everything is normal. I can understand that.

"You guys want to play Five-Word Books?" Sam asks. "It's more fun with more people, anyway."

"Sure, I'm game," Theo says.

"What's Five-Word Books?" I ask.

"Just what it sounds like," Sam says. "Without using the title, the author, or any character names, describe a book in five words and the rest of us see if we can get it."

"We play it at Quiz Bowl practice," Theo says. "But Ms. Jacobs never lets us swear or make sex jokes, which takes all the fun out of it. I'll start. Two horny teens ruin everything."

"*Romeo and Juliet*," Tal says. "One horny teen hates phonies."

"*The Catcher in the Rye*. Mass-murdering teen in love triangle."

"That was six words," Theo says to Sam.

"'Mass-murdering' is hyphenated."

"Fine. *The Hunger Games*."

"Orphan boy, obvious Jesus allegory?" Theo says.

"*Oliver Twist*?" Sam guesses.

"I was thinking *Harry Potter*," Theo says. "But yeah, Dickens did love angelic orphans."

"And corpses," I add.

"What?" Theo asks.

"Did you say corpses?" Hannah asks.

"Yes," I say. "He liked to visit the Paris morgue and stare at them. The corpses. He also went to Italy and asked—*asked*—to see an execution by guillotine and study the headless body. He liked looking at corpses so much that one time, he went to the morgue on Christmas."

"Well, damn," Sam says.

"If *A Christmas Carol* had ended like that, I might've liked it better," Tal says.

"What, with Tiny Tim getting embalmed?" Theo says.

"'What's today, Mr. Scrooge?'" Tal says in an awful British accent. "'Why, it's Christmas Day, sir, and the morgue is open for tours!'"

"Too dark, you guys, too dark," Hannah says. And this coming from a girl who regularly dreams about the apocalypse.

Thinking about the apocalypse makes me remember why we're actually here. Hannah said she'd keep an eye on the door, but it can't hurt if I do too. I twist around to see the entrance. Nothing. Ten seconds later, I do it again, even though I know it's excessive.

"You looking for something?" Tal asks me, flicking his eyes to the library doors and back.

"Um," I say.

"Ellis wanted to look for a book," Hannah cuts in smoothly.

She nudges me with her foot. "It's cool. Go ahead. We won't leave or anything."

"I don't want to go alone," I say through gritted teeth. "You didn't tell me I'd have to . . ." I trail off at the look on Hannah's face. Just for a second, it's gone from cool and composed to something panicked and pleading. It says, *help*. Just a flicker of real need. But I see it.

No one's ever needed my help before. It's always been the other way around. I get up.

Inside, I pass by the low-cost bookstore by the front entrance—they sell books for dimes and dollars, but still, I'm guessing Prophet Dan uses the library as a place to rest, not just a place to read. I scan the checkout line briefly, but no luck.

"What's it called?" says a voice behind me.

When I turn around, Tal's standing there. I don't understand why he's here. He looks like he might not understand, either.

"Uh," I say.

"Your book," he clarifies. "The one you're looking for."

"That's okay, I don't need help."

"I'm sure you don't." He sticks his hands in his pockets. "But you said you didn't want to go alone."

"Oh." It seems wrong to default to suspicion. I try not to. "Okay."

He nods at the reference computers. "You need to look it up?"

"No, I'll . . . figure it out."

I lead Tal on a quick sweep of the first floor, and we end

up in the stacks at the back, housing "Nonfiction 000–899," Computer Science all the way through Austronesian & Other Literatures.

I run one hand along the shelves as we walk through the aisles, stealing as many glances as I can at the reading tables. I don't see anyone matching Prophet Dan's description. Next to me, Tal paws through the Astronomy section. He holds up a book called *The Seven Planets*.

"I wonder if they cut the pages about Pluto out of this. Since it got demoted from planet status."

"Do you know where that word comes from? 'Planet'?" It's got such a good etymology I can't help myself. "Earlier astronomers noticed that some stars in the sky weren't fixed. They moved around. So they called them *asteres planetai*. 'Wandering stars.'"

"All stars are wandering." I must look confused, because he adds, "They only look fixed, to us. When we think we're seeing a star, we're really seeing where it was thousands of years ago. That's how fast they're traveling, and how much light they leave behind." And then I must look surprised, because he ducks his head and mumbles, "Whatever, I like stars."

Stars. Who would have guessed. It's so . . . wholesome.

"Huh," I say. "Theo's into nineteenth-century literature. Sam knows some terrible things about spiders. And you like stars."

"I do."

"You're just full of surprises." And then, in case it wasn't clear: "Not bad ones. Good ones."

"Thanks," Tal says, returning the book. "Next time you see my stepdad at church, you should tell him that. He'll be horrified."

My shoulders drop, remembering what Em told me. I can't imagine how hard that must be. My parents might not be thrilled with my general personality, but they'd never, ever treat me like that. No matter who I kissed at summer camp.

"I'm sorry," I say.

He shrugs it off. "I try not to take it personally. *I'm* a bad influence on Caroline and Matt? He drinks, like, eight Red Bulls a day and wears tube socks with shorts. But sure, the things *I* do are godless and unnatural."

"Is that why you left the church?" I ask. I drop my voice. "Because you're gay?"

Tal stares at me. "Who told you *that*?"

"Your sister told my sister. About summer camp."

Tal sighs. "Caroline," he says, "has an un-nuanced view of human sexuality."

"What does that mean?"

"I'm not gay," Tal says. "I'm bisexual." When I wait too long to respond, he continues. "It was a boy, at camp. But it could have been a girl."

"Oh," I say. "Okay." I drop my voice again. "Bisexual."

"You don't have to whisper," he says.

"We're in a library."

"That's not why you're whispering."

"Can I help you two find anything?" says a crisp voice behind me. I turn around to see one of the librarians, a young-ish woman who always wears vintage dresses, looking at me from behind her cat-eye glasses.

"Yeah," Tal says, "we're looking for a—"

"Person," I blurt out before he can say "book." I feel him swivel to stare at me. "We're looking for a man we heard might be here."

"Jesus Christ," Tal mutters under his breath.

"Nope, not him." I wave Tal off without looking over. "A different itinerant preacher."

The librarian shifts the stack of books in her arms. "All right."

"He's a homeless man, five ten, kind of tan," I say, trying to remember every bit of Hannah's description. "Brown beard, brown eyes, red-and-black jacket—"

"I'm sorry," she says, "there's lots of guys like that. But if he's a regular, you might ask Lydia."

"Lydia?"

"Yeah, she's been coming here for decades, she's sort of like an ambassador," the librarian says. "Very friendly. She usually reads on this floor. You'll know her by the hat. Big and straw."

"Thank you," I say as she goes, then look around. There are college students juggling textbooks, older Berkeley hippies in hemp perusing the Metaphysics section, and a group of middle school boys pelting each other with paperbacks, but no women

97

in straw hats. I choose the most central reading table and sit down. Tal sits next to me. It's not a great tactical move—if he sat across from me, we'd be able to see the whole room, between us.

"Quick question," he says, faux-casual. "Do you have any idea what the hell you're doing?"

I fold my hands. "I'm in the library, waiting for Lydia—"

"You're in way over your head."

"—*waiting for Lydia*," I push through, "to see if she knows how to find—"

"Yeah, I know who," he interrupts. "I've been friends with Hannah a lot longer than you have."

She said I couldn't tell the boys who we were looking for. Do they already know?

"This isn't helping her," Tal says, shaking his head. "I know it seems like it would, but it doesn't. We figured that out a long time ago."

"I believe her," I tell him. "Maybe you don't think it's real, but I do."

His eyebrows knit together. "Of course it's real. No one thinks it isn't."

Huh. Maybe he only *thinks* he knows what Hannah's doing, because there are many, many people who don't think the apocalypse is real. And maybe I've already said too much.

"Anyway," I say, quickly steering back to our earlier conversation, "it's probably easier, being bisexual, right? For you. Than if you were gay."

"What," Tal says, long-suffering, "could you *possibly* mean by that?"

I cringe. "I don't know. Sorry. Never mind."

"Oh, no, no," he says. "Come on, lay it all out."

"You kissed a boy, at camp, right?"

He nods.

"And your—some people were upset about that, right?"

He nods.

"And you just said it was a boy, but it could have been a girl. Right?"

"All correct," he says.

"If it *had* been a girl, no one would have been upset. So isn't that—easier?"

He runs his hand over the table. "I think it's all hard. Being not-straight. But the ways it's hard can be different. When you're bi—if you're a dude, at least—people assume it's just a stop on the road to gay. They think you're pretending to like girls. Like their walnut brains can't process it's not an either/or situation, for you."

"Well—have you ever kissed a girl?" I ask. He shakes his head. "Then how do you know you like them?"

"Have you kissed anyone?" he asks. I shake my head. "But you know who *you're* attracted to, right?"

Yes. No. "That's a weird question," I say, too fast, too defensive.

He holds up his hands. "All I meant was, you don't have to kiss someone to know you like them. I've had crushes on boys

99

and girls, both, since . . . forever, I guess."

A crush doesn't mean anything. A crush doesn't *have* to mean anything. "Crushes are different. It's not the same thing as being . . ." I falter for a second. "It's not the same as *being something.*"

> *You're saying all the wrong things. You wouldn't know the right thing to say if it punched your vocal cords out. Which would be a net gain for the world.*

Tal frowns, but not like he's offended or mad. Like I'm something written in code, something cryptic. *Cryptic*, from the Greek *kryptos*, meaning hidden.

Maybe I want to stay hidden.

Before he can ask me anything else, I steer the conversation back to him.

"So is that why you left?" I ask again. "Because you're bisexual?" He didn't have to, necessarily. Gay Mormons exist; I know some. And sometimes I wonder, *How do you stay? How do you stay when the whole system was designed without you in mind? When there are so many things you have to give up? When it's cruel and unfair and wrong that you should even have to?* But I know how; I know why. They stay because they believe this church is true. I wonder if sometimes they wish they didn't.

"That was part of why I left," Tal says. "Not all of it."

"You could marry a girl," I point out. "If you married a girl, you could get sealed in the temple like everybody else."

He shakes his head. "I could marry a girl. But never in the temple."

"Why?"

"I don't want to get married in a place that tells me some of my feelings are part of a beautiful Celestial plan and some of my feelings are—sinful, at worst. Something to chastely *suffer through*, at best. All of me matters. Not just the part that could marry a girl, someday."

After a moment of silence, I ask, "So then why else did you leave?"

"Why do you want to know so badly?"

"I'm just making conversation."

"That's kind of a hard-core conversation for someone you barely know."

> *You're making him uncomfortable. You make everyone uncomfortable.*

"Okay, whatever, sorry."

"You don't have to be sorry. But if you're only asking because you think I made a mistake, that you can *convince* me I made a mistake, please don't. I'm good. I'm happy."

*Wickedness never was happiness*, that's in the scriptures themselves. I believe Tal, though, when he says he's happy. Maybe the passage is backward. Can real happiness, the kind that doesn't hurt a soul, ever be wickedness? I don't know. I don't *think* so.

"Was it because of something you read? On the internet?" I ask, because I still want to know. He rolls his eyes. "I'm not trying to be mean, but that stuff can be biased. That stuff can be really wrong."

"What should I have read?"

"There's the church website."

"Because that's sure not biased."

"They wouldn't lie."

"Just because something makes you uncomfortable doesn't mean it's a lie."

That's a pretty good line. I don't love how it's being used against me, but it's still good. I'll have to remember that, for when Hannah and I tell the world about its imminent destruction.

"Look," he says. "I didn't leave because I wanted to sin. And it wasn't because someone offended me. It wasn't because of what I read online, though I did read a lot of weird stuff. I just didn't believe. I wanted to, I tried to, I doubted my doubts and shut myself down. But you can't force belief. And when I realized I liked other boys, when I realized I'd rather peel off my skin than go on a mission, I decided I had a choice. I could live my life for the church, or I could live my life for myself." He shrugs. "I chose myself."

I wonder what's that like. I wonder what it's like to be that proud of who you are. To choose yourself, rather than change yourself.

"Are you guys—" There's suddenly an itch in my throat, and I cough. "Are you still together?"

Tal looks confused. "Who?"

"The boy you met at camp."

"No, it was just for the summer. He lives in Connecticut. And plays polo. The kind with horses."

"What does that matter?"

"He and I were not meant for eternity." He grins at me, lop-sided. "I prefer my partners a little more salt-of-the-earth. And a little more local."

Before I can say anything, or do anything, or even breathe, I spot a giant straw sun hat, and a tiny woman underneath. She's carrying an improbably large stack of books, which she gently sets down on a table a few feet from us, then eases herself into a chair.

Before Tal can see her, I push myself back from the table. And before he can say anything to stop me, I walk in her direction, trying to ignore the lump in my throat.

*You're going to mess it up.*

From behind me, I think I hear Tal get up too.

*Hannah's counting on you and you're going to mess everything up.*

I approach her slowly, with light steps, like I'm stalking a skittish woodland creature.

*You're going to ruin it, you're going to say the wrong things to her just like you said the wrong things to Tal—*

The woman looks up. From somewhere outside my stupid body, I hear myself say, "Excuse me, I'm so sorry to bother you, but—are you Lydia?"

She blinks at me, and takes off her hat. She's not quite as old as I thought—maybe midseventies. Her face is round and wrinkled, and her mouth crescents into a warm smile. "Yes, dear. I'm Lydia."

"One of the librarians said you might be able to help me?" It's not a question, but my voice goes up at the end anyway. I cringe. Mom's always telling me not to do that. It makes you sound unsure.

Lydia doesn't appear to care. "Please, sit down."

I take the seat across the table from her. Without being invited, Tal sits to my left.

"My name's Ellis," I say. "This is my— This is Tal." He waves. Awkwardly.

"What can I do for you, Ellis?"

"We're looking for a man, and the librarian said you might know him. Prophet Dan." Tal takes a sharp breath in, so I keep going before he can interrupt. "He's got a brown beard, a red-and-black coat, likes books about mystics—?"

"Yes," she says, and sighs. "Danny. He's so young. It's so sad, when they're so young."

I always assumed he was older, one of those neighborhood fixtures. How else would Hannah have known about him?

"You wouldn't know it, though, from the way he talks," she says. "So smart. Mind like a steel trap. Now, I'm not much for all that religion stuff, but he could talk to me about botany, about birds. He never forgot a thing."

"Has he been by today?" I ask. "When do you usually see him here?"

"I haven't seen him in weeks," Lydia says, and my heart drops. "He didn't think the library was safe anymore."

The library is the safest place I can think of. I think it even qualifies as a fallout shelter. "Why wouldn't it be safe?" I ask.

"It didn't *seem* safe. To him." She leans across the table and pats my hand. "You can't make a person believe in what they don't."

Tal shifts, and I bet he's looking at me. *You can't force belief.* That's what he said, too. But I don't know—this seems different.

"Do you have any idea where else he might hang out?" I ask. "I'd just really love to talk to him."

"I'd suggest People's Park, maybe Willard, maybe the encampment by City Hall, but I'm figuring you've looked there."

Is that why Hannah was in People's Park? Was she looking for him then, too? Lydia misinterprets my silence as agreement.

"Well," she says. "When you find him, tell him I miss our talks. And those muffins he used to bring me—carrot zucchini, who knew you could make muffins out of that? But mostly our talks." Lydia looks up at the ceiling for a moment, and blinks hard. "He's a special kid. He deserves better."

I thank her for her help, and she gives me the number of the senior center where she's living. Tal looks like he'd like to ask several more questions—of me, not Lydia—but I take a page from Hannah's book and set a brisk pace for the front doors. By the time he's caught up, I'm already outside, where Hannah is waiting, her hands twisted in her sweatshirt sleeves again.

"Did you . . . find the book?" she asks.

I shake my head, deciding to tell her about Lydia tomorrow, or whenever Tal isn't just a couple of inches to my left.

"I thought we all agreed to stop looking for *that book*," Tal says to Hannah under his breath.

Hannah folds arms. "*We* definitely didn't."

"Anyone want to go to La Burrita?" Sam asks, hopping up from the bench. "I'm starving."

"When are you not starving?" Theo asks.

"Whenever I've just finished eating at La Burrita."

"I'm in," Tal says, with one final long look at Hannah.

"I have to get to therapy," Hannah says, pointing her thumb in the direction of the Martha's office.

I check my watch. "Yeah, I should go too."

Everyone's going the same direction but me, so I say good-bye to them there. But at the last second, I turn around and catch Tal by the arm. He looks surprised, but stops. The rest of them keep walking.

"I'm sorry," I tell him, "if I was weird, back there. If I said the wrong things. You didn't have to tell me those things, and you did, and I'm sorry if I made you uncomfortable."

"No worries. We're cool."

"Are you sure?" I ask.

"Yeah. Look, I'm not thrilled about what you're helping Hannah do, but your heart's clearly in the right place. So I'm

106

figuring your heart's in the right place just . . . in general."

Something warm and unnameable surges in my chest and floods the veins in my arms and legs. I take a sharp breath.

"I know," he says. "I'm as shocked as you are."

He salutes me with two fingers as he walks away.

## EIGHT

**LATER THAT WEEK,** Hannah corners me in the hall after English class.

"I've been thinking," she says, "we should hang out this weekend."

I can't remember the last time someone asked me to hang out during the weekend. Or more accurately, I can't remember the last time someone asked and it wasn't out of obligation or pity.

"Yes let's do that yes please," I say, too fast, too eager.

Hannah pretends not to notice. "Awesome. Saturday?"

Then I remember. "Oh. I have to go to a wedding on Saturday."

"So, Sunday."

"Well, I have church. . . ."

"After, then," she says with a shrug. "It's only, like, an hour, right?"

"It's two hours. It used to be three."

Her eyes widen. "Jesus. Do you read the whole Bible from start to finish?"

I laugh. "Do you want to come with me and see? You don't have to," I add quickly. "But if you wanted to . . ."

"Okay."

"Are you sure?"

"Yeah." She grins. "It'll totally freak my parents out. With any luck."

"I don't get your family dynamic," I admit.

"Me neither," she says, turning to go. "I hope the wedding's fun."

The wedding's a disaster, and we aren't even there yet.

"I told you we were going to be late," I say to Mom from the backseat of the Volvo. "I *told* you."

"Ellis, it's going to be fine," Dad says, hands on the wheel.

"It's starting in fifteen minutes and we're still on the bridge," I point out. "We're going to be late, just like I told Mom we would be."

"Weddings don't start right on time," Mom says without turning around. "And I don't appreciate you blaming me."

I slump in my seat. Who else is there to blame? Was it me who only started to get ready a half hour before we were supposed to leave? Did *I* do that? No, what I did was check the traffic report. What I did was give Mom a fifteen-minute warning. But it was like she hadn't heard me.

"Which shoes, do you think?" she had asked, showing me two identical pairs of black pumps.

"They look the same."

She held one pair up higher. "These are suede."

"Mom, whatever, who cares, we have to go."

She shrugged so quickly it almost looked like a wince. "I'll ask Emmy."

"Seriously, if we're not in the car by—"

"I only have to do my makeup," she said, padding to her attached bath. "And my hair."

"That's going to take forever, you don't have time!"

Mom looked away from the mirror, three different lipsticks in hand. "This is one of Dad's partners getting married."

"It's not his partner, it's a junior dentist we barely know."

"It doesn't matter who," she said. "They invited us to celebrate their marriage. It's one of the most important days of their life. The least I can do is look presentable."

"The least you can do is be on time."

She glared at me, then sighed. "Why don't you put on a little makeup while you wait for me? This color would look so pretty on you." She selected one of the lipsticks and held it out. "Here."

"I don't wear lipstick."

"First time for everything," she said, pushing it closer. "Come on, I'll show you how to do it."

*Is that all I'm for?* I thought. *To make the world look prettier? Is that all I get? Is that all she wants for herself?*

I folded my arms and turned away. "No, thanks."

I heard the lipstick clatter on the sink counter. "Fine."

And now here we are, crawling through traffic on the Bay Bridge. I check my watch.

> *Thirteen minutes until the wedding starts. You're going to be late.*

I didn't even want to go. I know some girls daydream about their future wedding, making mock-ups of their modest-but-still-hot bridal gowns, debating over color palettes and whether tiaras are tacky. But every time the topic comes up, my brain shuts itself off like a panic-sensor light switch.

> *Twelve minutes until the wedding starts. You're going to be late and everyone will see and stare at you.*

I don't daydream about my wedding. I *actually* dream. I dream that I'm in a white dress that's slowly constricting. The light is so bright I can't see around me. I can't see my family, or the other wedding guests, or even where I'm going. All I can see is my new husband, who has a suit, a crew cut, and a blurred-out face. I asked Martha about it once, if it meant anything.

"We don't use dreams as diagnostic criteria," she said. "They don't say anything either way about your mental health. But . . ." She paused. "Sometimes they do reveal things we don't like thinking about in the daytime."

> *Eleven and a half minutes until the wedding starts,*
> *eleven and a quarter minutes until—*

I try to breathe deeper. It's just a wedding. A wedding like in the movies, with the bride walking down the aisle, to have and to hold, till death do you part. My mom has already told me my temple wedding won't be like that. Not even the *till death* part, because we marry for time and all eternity. My wedding won't *just* be a wedding, it'll be an eternal bond to the man I'll live with forever. Having a baby won't *just* be giving birth, either, it'll be giving a waiting spirit the chance to have a body. Everything is something more, and I know that's a good thing, I know I should be happy my life has such a clear, straight path forward.

My chest is caving, I'm breathing in air but it's not reaching my lungs. I put my head between my knees.

"If we're going to talk about mistakes," I hear Mom say from the front seat, "if you're so comfortable talking about other people's mistakes, maybe we should all talk about your grades."

Why now? Why would she bring this up now, when we're already late and I'm already upset and it's all her fault? I breathe in heavier, but only drown faster.

"Pull over," I croak.

"What?" I hear Dad say.

"Pull over, you have to pull over!" I repeat, even though

I haven't done this for years, beg for him to stop the car like this. But the walls are caving in on me, I can smell Mom's perfume, feel her elbow on the back of her seat as she twists around to look at me. I'm trapped, I'm so trapped, and I need to get out.

"Dad . . ." I hear Em say, soft and hesitant.

"She's fine," Mom interrupts. "Emmy, don't worry, she's fine."

I'd protest this, but feel I should concentrate my energy on not passing out.

"She doesn't look fine," Em says.

"She's only doing it because she doesn't want to talk about failing her chemistry test."

I find some air in the atmosphere, push myself up, and look my mother in the eye.

"A C-plus," I tell her, "is not *technically* a failing grade."

After what feels like eons, we're off the bridge and in San Francisco. And in a stroke of luck or divine intervention on my behalf, we find a parking spot right outside Grace Cathedral. I practically throw myself out the car door when I heard Pachelbel's Canon from inside the church. Em is right behind me, smiling tightly, smoothing down a nonexistent stray hair.

"This is all her fault," I whisper to Em. "We're going to be walking in with the bride herself all because Mom couldn't be bothered to—"

"Oh my *gosh*, shut *up*," Em snaps. And I do, if only out of surprise. Em doesn't tell anyone to shut up. Not even when she should. She keeps her smiles sweet and her words sweeter, even when she'd rather storm or cry.

"Don't blame me," I say. "This isn't my fault, she—"

Em stops dead in her tracks, and I only put one stumbling foot forward before stopping too.

"You made it worse, Ellis," she says, and every word is a precision dart. "Why do you always have to make it worse?"

She turns and stomps up the church steps, leaving me to quietly bleed out on the sidewalk.


When we get home late that afternoon, everyone seems to split apart. Em goes upstairs to change. Dad decides to return a work call in his room. Mom announces she's going to Safeway for groceries. And suddenly, I'm in the living room, all alone.

*They don't want to be around you.*

I turn on the TV, but I can't hear it, no matter how much I turn up the volume.

*Your own family doesn't want to be around you. You make their lives worse. You make everything worse.*

My eye catches on the family computer. There are some things I know that they don't. There are some things I won't make worse. I walk up the stairs to my room, open the top

114

drawer of my desk, and pull out the thin plastic card I've taped to the top.

It turns out that if you keep a bag of change under your bed for half a decade, you end up with quite a bit of money. Turns out, those coin-counting machines at the supermarket actually work, though they will steal one quarter out of every fifty or so. Turns out, you don't have to get your payout in cash. You can get it in the form of an Amazon card.

*I shouldn't be doing this on the family computer*, I think as I turn it on and open a browser. I should do it at school, or the library, but no one is here, I have a window, and time is of the essence.

*You make everything worse.*

But I can make things better. When the end of the world comes, Em will see, I'll make everything better.

I scan the order list, second-guessing and reconsidering, as always.

A solar charger.

A survival weather radio.

Several extra-large packs of dehydrated food essentials, including ramen, vegetables, fruit. Also jerky, which I find disgusting but could be bartered for matches or protection in the New Ice Age.

Various winter clothing items, the warmer the better. Snow-shoes, collapsible ones.

Dozens of single-use hand-warmers. Not just to keep your

palms toasty, but to melt snow, keep liquids from freezing, and heat up an IV line, if it came to that.

Enough wool socks to free every house elf in the Harry Potter extended universe.

Good enough. For now.

I click order.

# NINE

HANNAH'S ALREADY STANDING outside the ward building when we pull up on Sunday morning. As I get out of the car, I realize I forgot to mention certain things to her. Namely, the dress code. After introducing her to Mom, Dad, and Em, I pull Hannah off to the side. "I just want you to be prepared," I say. "The other girls probably won't be wearing pants."

She startles. "Girls can't wear pants?"

"No, we *can*." There's no rule against it. Just like there's no rule against men wearing non-white dress shirts or forgoing a tie. I never thought about how many expectations are unspoken. "We can, just most girls don't." She frowns. "It's not a big deal at all, I swear."

Hannah shrugs. "These are the nicest pants I own. I don't even own them. They're my mom's."

They do look a bit big on her. But really, she doesn't own a pair of dress pants? I mean, I guess I don't, either. I've only got skirts.

Mom, Dad, and Em are already ahead of us, so I lead Hannah into the building. Before we reach our pew, Lia appears in front of us, a vision in seafoam green. Her sundress has cap sleeves and a sweetheart neckline, the kind where you could almost see the top of her cleavage. If you were looking.

> *Are you looking? Why would you even be looking?*

"Ellis!" Lia says, reaching her hand out to me. I twitch my arm back, without meaning to.

> *You're being so weird. This isn't weird, friends can touch each other and it's not weird. You're just friends. It's not weird. STOP BEING WEIRD.*

Lia must not notice, because she follows through and grabs me by the elbow. My muscles turn to Silly String. She smells like citrus and clean laundry.

> *It's not weird for her to touch you, but it is definitely weird for you to be SMELLING HER, ELLIS.*

I breathe in deeper.

"Hi, I'm Lia." She extends her left hand to shake Hannah's, but keeps her right hand on my elbow, and warmth spreads from her hand through my arm, through my veins, into my chest.

"I'm Hannah."

Lia nudges me. "You didn't say you were bringing a friend!"

I try to think of something funny to say. I try to think of

something to say, period. But I feel like my mouth is stuffed with cotton balls. "Surprise?"

"You're always full of surprises," Lia says. When she shifts her weight, her long hair brushes against the bare skin on my arm. I almost shiver.

Hannah's looking at me out of the corner of her eye. "Yeah, Ellis has a few of those."

And I stand there like I'm waiting for something just out of reach.

Lia smiles at me, then turns back to Hannah. "Lucky for you, I basically planned our whole class today, so it'll be fun. See you later!"

She waves and glides into the chapel. Sunlight streaming in from the open door catches her hair, and for a moment, it gleams. When I turn back to Hannah, she's looking at me strangely. But she's always looking at something strangely, isn't she?

"What was her name?" Hannah asks. She couldn't possibly have forgotten already.

"Lia." I'm glad I'm not as pale as McKenna or even Hannah. Otherwise, I might be blushing.

"Right. Lia."

"Are you ready?"

Hannah looks like she's got more to say, but she nods. I lead her through the doors and to our regular pew.

"Today's not like regular church," I whisper to her during

the opening hymn. That's another thing I forgot to mention. "It's fast and testimony."

"What's that?"

"People are going to stand." I point to the podium up front. "And they're going to talk about why they're LDS and what it means to them." That's the idea, anyway. Sometimes it's a free-for-all.

"And the fast part?"

"It means the audience might get hangry."

Here are the first three people who get up to the mic:

McKenna Cooper's dad, bearing his bragimony—

I mean, testimony—about his three perfect children and the joys of six a.m. family scripture study until the entire ward feels inadequate.

Sister Keller, who weeps through the entire thing. The only part I catch is about the Spirit helping her find lost car keys.

Sister Olsen, who takes this opportunity to reflect on what a blessing the Gospel is to our souls, and similarly, what a blessing essential oils are to our bodies, and did she mention she has some free samples in her car, if we're interested?

Here are my thoughts on these testimonies, respectively:

Why

Lord

WHY

Hannah must think this is completely ridiculous. If I didn't know us, if I wasn't *part* of us, I'd think that. Why aren't the people with beautiful testimonies standing up? Why isn't Brother Chang talking about how converting helped him recover from alcoholism? Why isn't Sister Christiansen telling the story about how knowing she'd see her dead daughter in the Celestial Kingdom helped her survive the grief? There are so many stories about our church family seeing each other through tragedy and loss. There are so many stories that explain why we're here, week after week. Hannah isn't hearing any of them. I wish she could.

Instead, she's watching six-year-old Hunter Cannon clench the mic with sticky hands and repeat the testimony his mom wrote for him.

"I know . . ." Sister Cannon whispers in his ear, as a prompt. Lots of testimonies start with these words: *I know.*

"I know the church is true," Hunter lisps. "I know Joseph Smith was a pocket."

"Prophet."

"Prophet."

"I love my family. . . ."

"I love my family," Hunter continues. "I love my mama and my dad and my sister. I love Heavenly Father and Jesus and my dog, Buster." Sister Cannon smiles and starts to pull the mic away, but Hunter latches on with both sticky hands. "And please forgive my dad because yesterday he said *dammit* and he's not supposed to. *InthenameofJesusChristAmen.*"

Sister Cannon goes red and hustles Hunter away from the altar. Hannah snorts. Well, at least I gave her some free entertainment. To my right, my mom puts three delicate fingers on my back. At first, I think it's a signal to stop Hannah from laughing, which would be weird, since everyone's laughing. But then, I realize Mom's pressing on my spine. If we weren't in the middle of church, she'd probably demand a full-on posture check. This involves touching your hands to your head, first, then laying them on your own shoulders. You put them to your waist, then all the way down. Heads, shoulders, perfect posture.

Tal would probably try to make this about religion, but none of the other moms in my ward do things like this. He'd say my mom acts this way because the church conditioned her to think her purpose was to be a perfect mother to perfect children. But I know she doesn't believe that. I know she'd be this way no matter what religion she followed, or if she followed nothing at all. This is who she is. I should be annoyed at her. I *am* annoyed at her, but I also feel . . . sorry for her.

I clench my teeth, but straighten my back.

Hannah is a real trooper. She sits through the entire testimony meeting, then through my Laurels class, without complaint. Hannah is such a trooper that she even lets Sister Olsen drag her to the parking lot and give her essential oils sales pitch. And maybe Sister Olsen has some latent hypnotism powers, because Hannah appears to have a religious experience with one of the bottles. She takes a deep inhale and then visibly freezes. Her eyes go glassy, and she stares straight through me, unfocused.

"Hannah?" I say cautiously. She snaps out of it and covers the awkward moment with a smile and a question.

"What's in this one?" she asks Sister Olsen.

"Eucalyptus. Very good for relaxation and clear breathing."

Hannah doesn't look relaxed. She looks wired. And her breathing might be clear, but it's way faster than normal.

"I don't have any money on me," she says to Sister Olsen with an apologetic shrug. "Or I would."

"I'd never ask anyone to spend money on the Sabbath, dear." Sister Olsen presses something into Hannah's palm. "You just take my card."

Mom invites Hannah to stay for dinner, and Hannah accepts. It's the right choice. The dinners Mom makes after we've fasted all day are comfort-food heavy, and they're always delicious. When we get home, I take Hannah up to my room.

"Wow," she says, turning in a circle to get the whole view. "This is . . . not what I expected."

"What did you expect?"

"For it to look like you, I guess."

She's not wrong. The pastoral blue print on the curtains matches my bed skirt. The bookcase is a pink floral, the rug is a pink floral, too, and there are enough pink pillows to make up a whole other bed.

"I didn't decorate it," I explain. Hannah looks at the bulletin board over my desk, with pictures and ticket stubs and a single blue ribbon from my fourth-grade spelling bee. She touches a photo of my Young Women's group at girls' camp, all of us with knee-length shorts over one-piece bathing suits.

"Lia's pretty," Hannah says, looking at me out of the corner of her eye. "Really pretty."

"She's Mormon."

"Does that mean she can't be pretty?"

"She's not gay."

"Does *that* mean she can't be pretty?"

"It means don't ask her out, or anything."

Hannah squints like she's trying to read something very far away. "I wasn't going to. I just thought maybe—"

"It doesn't matter anymore, right?" I interrupt, out of breath for no reason. "Those kinds of things."

"Pretty girls?"

"There's no dating in the apocalypse," I say, and mentally file it in my Top Ten Most Ridiculous Statements. "When the snow comes it doesn't matter who you want to snuggle up with. Except for body heat purposes. Which reminds me, we should talk about heat sources, because—"

"I'd want to know," Hannah blurts out. I stop talking, but then she hesitates. "I'd want to know who I was. If I didn't already, I'd want to figure it out. Before the world changed."

"But you do know," I reason.

"Yeah."

"So, you're fine."

"Yeah." She nods. "I'm fine."

"Good, that's good," I say briskly. Like if I rush through the words, I can rush away from this entire topic. I sit down on the bed, and she settles in next to me. "Hey, what happened in the parking lot? With Sister Olsen?"

"It was the right smell."

"The right—for what?"

"For the last day in the world."

It takes me a second to grasp it. "It smelled like your mom's old perfume."

She nods.

"Eucalyptus," I say. "You smell eucalyptus."

She nods again.

That's all at once so specific and not nearly specific enough. Eucalyptus grows all around Berkeley. It's not a plant that was even meant to grow in our dry, fire-prone hills. It's native to Australia and was brought over in the 1900s by people who needed lumber, but were unaware eucalyptus makes for crappy houses. The lumber companies folded. The trees were abandoned. Then they spread, multiplying and surviving against the odds. Now they're in every grove, foothill, and nature preserve, filling up the air with the deep, strong smell of mint and honey.

"It's not a person," I say, slowly getting to where Hannah already is. "It's a place. We need to go somewhere that smells like eucalyptus."

"I think so."

"Do you know where?"

She bites her lip. "There's so many eucalyptus trees."

I scoot closer to her. "Will you . . . tell me about it, now? The end of the world."

She looks away. "When we find Prophet Dan, he can help us—"

"But we might never find him," I point out. "He might have left town. He might be in jail, who knows?"

Hannah bites her lip, and her eyes are suddenly glassy. *Oh, I shouldn't have said that. She thinks we can't do it without him. I'm freaking her out.*

"Sorry," I say, touching her shoulder. "It's okay, though. We can do it, we can interpret it. At the very least, we can try. Right?"

She waits a moment in silence before swallowing hard and nodding. "Okay. Okay."

"So first off . . ." I clasp my hands together and focus all my attention on her. "What kind is it?"

Hannah blinks. "Kind?"

"What kind of apocalypse?" Her expression doesn't change, so I elaborate. "A meteor. A nuclear attack. The Rapture, biblical or otherwise."

"Is there a *non*-biblical kind of Rapture?" she asks.

"I don't know, my church doesn't do the Rapture—I'm asking what we're looking at here."

Hannah thinks for a moment. "There's snow."

"I remember, but—what does that mean? A blizzard?"

"I've never seen a blizzard," she admits. "But it's a lot of snow. Falling fast."

"How much snow?" I ask. It must be a lot, and over days, weeks, months, or it wouldn't destroy the world. A freak storm in an unprepared place would do damage, for sure. Roads would close, new shipments of food and medicine would be delayed. People on the road could get stuck. They could freeze. Everything could freeze, things that were never meant to. Pipes could break and flood houses and buildings. It would be a mess. But it wouldn't be the end of the world. "Exactly how much snow?"

She wipes her hands on her jeans. "I don't know."

"You don't *know*?"

"They're dreams," she says, with an edge. "Not the Weather Channel."

I deflate like a factory reject balloon. "Sorry."

She rubs at her arms, as if she's suddenly got hives. "It's not like I can just answer any question you ask. I see what I see, and I know what I know, but I don't have every answer."

"It's okay," I say. "Just close your eyes, and tell me what you've seen."

Hannah shuts her eyes. Her shoulders rise with an inhale, then descend with an exhale. "It's snowing. In my dreams, it's always snowing."

"Okay. It's snowing."

"It's winter."

"Are you saying that because it's snowing?" It could be a nuclear winter. It isn't necessarily winter*time*. This is the apocalypse, and anything is possible.

She shakes her head. "It's winter. I remember. You . . . say something about Christmas tree lights."

"So we must be in someone's house."

"No, we're outside. I know we're outside because snowflakes are falling on me. They're melting in my hair. It's cold. It's really, really cold, so cold my hands hurt, even though they're in my pockets."

We shouldn't be outside during a storm. It's not tactically advantageous. We should be taking shelter.

"We're somewhere unpaved," Hannah continues, "because it's grass and dirt under my feet, not sidewalk."

"What do you see?" I ask her. "From where you're standing, what do you see?"

"Nothing," she says, and it's almost a gasp. "I don't see anything."

"Because it's too dark?"

She shakes her head. "I should see something. From where we're standing, I should see San Francisco."

"But you don't?"

She shakes her head again. "There's nothing there. It's gone."

Something cold grips my chest. Then it spreads, like ice

water, out from my lungs, to my shoulder, down my arms and legs into my fingers and toes until I'm one shivering mass of fear. It's *gone*? An entire city is just *gone*?

"You're sure?" I ask.

She nods. "There's only snow."

I don't even know what would cause that, an entire city disappearing. A nuclear bomb? Possible, but then we *definitely* shouldn't be outside, not even on higher ground. A superstorm so large it alters global temperatures? Glaciers moving in from the ocean and destroying the city? San Francisco has low-lying areas, for sure, but it also has hills. Lots of hills. How could they all disappear?

"And you're there," she says, opening her eyes to look at me. "That's the clearest thing. The only clear thing. Every night, in every dream, you are there with me."

She pauses, running her hand over my bedspread. "When you came out of Martha's office, you were like . . . God." She shakes her head.

"I was like God?" I joke. "I made a believer out of you?"

She cracks a smile. "Not the way you mean, but yeah. I'd been having these dreams for months, and nothing was clear and nothing made sense, except I saw this girl. I didn't know her, but I did. I'd been waiting so long for things to make sense, so long to figure out who you were. And when I finally did . . ." She lets out a breath. "That's when I knew it was real. You were real. So it was real."

A sign from the universe. A revelation in a human body. I'm a lot of things, but I never thought I'd be someone's revelation.

"And then that's when I started . . ." Then she trails off, looking away from me.

"What?"

"It's going to sound ridiculous."

"At this point, nothing does," I assure her.

She reaches into her hoodie pocket and pulls out a folded piece of notebook paper. "I started writing stuff down. Things I—well, not heard, exactly, in the dreams. Things I know."

"I don't understand."

"When I wake up each morning," she explains slowly, "I've got, like, phrases in my head. Facts. Things I know."

"But how do you know them?" I ask.

"When you wake up in the morning, you know the sky is blue and your name is Ellis. You don't have to open the curtains or check your ID. You already *know*."

"I get it," I say, then reach my hand out hesitantly. "Can I . . . see it?"

She gives it over with both hands, like it's something fragile. I can't read most of it. Her handwriting's awful. Even what I can read is confusing and strange.

*The city disappears*. San Francisco, I guess.

*A star falls from the sky and breaks to pieces*. A meteor is a star, but they don't break when they hit land, so I don't know.

*A red sky before midnight*. I've got nothing.

*One becomes two, then two becomes one.* Ditto.

"I can see why you wanted Prophet Dan," I admit.

"I might understand the first one," she says. I gesture for her to continue. "First, there was just me. One person, having dreams, one person who believed they were real. And then I told you, and—" Her voice wavers slightly. "You believed me. So there were two. And I think, when we're up on the higher ground, when we're watching the world end and you grab my hand, we'll be . . . bound. You know? Tied together. One."

"Hannah," I say. "There's nothing here about when it's going to happen." She stares at me. "Like, the date. We can't warn people if we don't know the date."

"It's before the end of the year," she says. "I wrote that." She points to another line. "And that."

I read the line. It's only three words. *The longest night.*

"That's the day?" I ask.

"No. It's night. It happens at night."

"I mean, that's the *date*? That's not actually a date."

"They're connected," she insists, taking the paper back. "It happens on the longest night."

The longest night. Maybe it's a worldwide power grid failure. A solar flare could cause that, and so could the skilled detonation of an electromagnetic pulse—maybe it's the longest night because the artificial lights never come back on. I can work with that. EMPs are the bread and shelf-stable butter of the prepping community.

131

"Do you see house lights?" I ask Hannah, anticipating a no, already making a mental list of next steps. Wind-up flash-lights, citronella oil for outside lamps, storing cell phones in the microwave as a makeshift Faraday cage.

"Yeah. And car lights."

My list erases. "You do?"

"Yes."

So much for that. "I should be writing this down." I grab Kenny #14 and a pen off my desk, flip to a fresh page, and scrib-ble everything she's told me so far. *The longest night. Eucalyptus. One becomes two, then—*

"Of course!" I shout. "*Of course.*"

Hannah looks over my shoulder. "What?"

My dad once told me something he learned in dental school: when you hear hoofbeats, look for horses, not zebras. Basically, that means when presented with a problem, look first for the most obvious solution, not the most interesting or exciting. I was so fixated on a (literally) flashy EMP, I almost didn't see what was right in front of me. I put my finger on what I've just written:

*One becomes two, then two becomes one.*

"That's it." She looks up at me, confused. I write next to the line:

$1 \rightarrow 2 \ 2 \rightarrow 1$

Then, on a new line:

*12 21*

"Oh!" Hannah says, and takes the pen to add the slash herself.

*12/21*

"One becomes two," she says. "Then two becomes one. December 21st."

"Do you know what that date is?" I ask.

She looks shocked, the blood drained from her face. "Do *you*?"

"Yeah. The winter solstice. It's the longest night of the year."

"Oh," she says, recovering. "Right. Yeah."

We sit for a moment with this. A date. A real date, less than two months from now. The last day of the world we know.

"What's it like?" I blurt out. "After. Can you see after?"

"I can't see it," she admits. "I can feel it, though."

"What's it like?" I sound like a child. It's frustrating, having to ask for every scrap of information, but I can't pretend I'm not grateful to have it.

"It's . . . complicated. Good and bad. Joyful. Crushing. Like every feeling at once."

"The end of the world," I say slowly, "as we know it."

Hannah nods, solemn and sure. I grab her arm, harder than I mean to. Her eyes go wide, but she doesn't pull away.

"We have to tell people," I say.

Her eyes get wider. "We don't need anyone else. As long as you're there, things will happen the way they're supposed to."

"We might not need them, but they need us." Hannah only frowns. "If the world is ending . . ." I swallow. "The world *is* ending. People have a right to know that. They have a right to decide what they're going to do with their last normal days."

She still looks confused, and unsure. And you can't have a prophet that's unsure. "People have a right to know," I say again. "So that means we have a duty to tell them."

We sit there, staring at each other, until a knock on my door breaks the silence.

Hannah gets to her feet and opens the door for Em.

"Mom says to help me set the table," Em says. "Ellis, are you okay?"

I must have been staring straight through her, my mind in overdrive with everything I've learned, everything I now need to do. Knowledge is power, but it's also responsibility, didn't Dad always say that? We need to make a website. We need to make flyers and pass them out, we need to get our message to the world. We need to stockpile the supplies we have and buy new ones. We need to get prepared.

But first, dinner.


After dinner, my dad asks Hannah if she needs a ride home, but she declines.

"It's not far."

Mom looks worried. "It's dark, though. I'm sure your parents wouldn't want you walking in the dark."

"You'd think, wouldn't you?" Hannah asks.

"So Andy will drive you," Mom says.

"That's very nice of you," Hannah says. "But cars and I don't mix. Thank you, though."

Then, Mom does something truly miraculous: she defers to a teenage girl.

As I walk Hannah out our front door, I can't help but ask, "Are you afraid of cars?"

"No," she says.

"It's okay if you are. I'm afraid of cars. Driving, not being a passenger, but—"

"I just don't like them, it's not the same . . ." She trails off, staring at something ahead. She walks to the end of our driveway, where the mailbox is. Then I see it. A package, wrapped in newspaper and tied with a bedraggled ribbon.

Hannah immediately grabs it, which is so odd. It was tied to our mailbox, it's probably for us. I'm about to ask if there's a label, but she's already undoing it. Inside the newspaper is one long, thin piece of scarlet string.

"What is it?"

"A gift," Hannah mutters, letting the newspaper fall to the ground. She winds the string around her left wrist.

"What for?"

"To keep away the evil eye."

"The evil eye?" I have so many questions. What evil are you afraid of? How do you know this gift is for you? What's string going to do against evil, anyway? "Who is it from?"

Hannah ties the string around her wrist, like a bracelet. "I'll see you at school. Good night, Ellis."

And then she walks into the dark, leaving me, as always, with more questions than answers.

## TEN

I DON'T SEE Hannah the next day at school. Or the next. Or the next. I ask the boys, but they haven't seen her either. It's Thursday before I happen to spot her on my way to the bus stop. She's standing outside a restaurant across the street, talking to a man with a knit hat, a shopping cart, and very long hair. He says something to her, and it must be weird or gross, because she immediately goes to leave. She only gets two steps away before she turns back, makes an apologetic gesture, and they trade goodbyes. Then she really does leave, with a wave.

So it wasn't something weird or gross, and why did I even assume that? He told her something important.

I break my long-held rule on jaywalking, not wanting to lose Hannah in the crowd. She's practically speedwalking, and not in the direction of the Park.

"Hannah!" I call out, when I'm close enough to be heard. She whips her head around.

"Hey," she says, stopping before the crosswalk, shifting her weight from one foot to the other.

"I feel like I haven't seen you in forever," I say.

"Yeah, I've been . . ." She shrugs, apparently declining to finish the sentence.

"Where are you going?" I ask.

"Home."

"Oh. Okay." I try to hide my hurt. She's not the first person to blow me off. "See you tomorrow, I guess." I turn to go.

"Wait," she says, and I stop. "I'm coming back, I just have to pick something up."

"Oh. What?"

"A package, I think—look, if you want to come with me, you can, but I've got to keep walking."

I'm not going to pass up an opportunity to see anything that helps me understand Hannah better. Especially not something like her house. So we walk on.

Hannah's house is one of those modern Berkeley homes built on an upward-sloping street. Square windows, clean lines, so unlike the older, more ornate ones you find farther up in the hills. Hannah's house is minimalist, just like her. On the outside.

Inside, it's warm and cluttered and a bit dusty. Shoes under the dining room table, coats and jackets on the backs of chairs rather than hung up, and books on every available surface. Hannah's fluffy dog jumps to greet us, leaving white fur all over my black sweater. My mom would never tolerate a house like this. I never want to leave.

Hannah drops her backpack by the door, but I keep mine on. She leads me through the kitchen and out a set of glass doors to the back porch. I walk forward to take in her backyard, which is beautifully overgrown. The kind of place where you could curl up with a book and a sandwich and not worry about getting crumbs anywhere or accidentally squashing freshly planted tulip beds.

"This must have been the best place to be a kid," I say, turning back to Hannah. But she doesn't hear me. She moves to the porch wall, where, nearly hidden by recycling bins and a compost pail, something beige and thin is stuck in the wooden lattice.

"When were you even *here*?" she whispers, plucking the letter from the slat.

It's a basic envelope, and it's addressed to Hannah. But there's no return address. And no stamp. How did it get here? Who left it?

Before I can ask, a balding middle-aged man in a blue suit appears in the open doorway.

"Hey," he says to Hannah. "You're home early."

Hannah slides the letter into the waistband of her jeans. "You too, Dad."

"We had to get changed—Mom was just about to leave you a note." He leans over to shake my hand. "I'm Jacob."

"It's very nice to meet you. I'm Ellis."

"Like the island?" he says.

Like Ellis Shipp, one of the first female doctors west of the Mississippi, but sure. "Like the island."

"You and Mom are going out?" Hannah says, eyes flicking from his suit jacket down to his dress shoes.

"Some thing with her department. We're meeting up with Matt Mackenzie at his place first."

Hannah's impassive shrug doesn't quite hide her disappointment. "Fine."

Just then, Hannah's mom breezes into the room. Everything she's wearing is flowy but still expensive looking. That's a big thing around here. Hippie chic. Less Birkenstocks and hemp, more Eileen Fisher and locally sourced statement earrings. She smiles, and introduces herself as Isabel.

"What are you doing out here?" she asks Hannah.

"Just showing Ellis the backyard," Hannah says. "Are you going to be home for dinner?"

Her mom adjusts an earring. "I doubt it."

"You shouldn't wait on us," Hannah's dad says.

"Get whatever you two want for dinner," Hannah's mom tells her. "You've got the card number."

"Okay."

"Lock the back door before you go to bed."

"Okay."

"The dog's been fed, no matter how she acts."

"Okay," Hannah says, as the aforementioned dog paws at her. "Laska, get *down*."

Huh. Hannah's mom is nice to her—no comments about her outfit, no poking or prodding or passive aggression. But it's weird. She doesn't ask Hannah about her day. She doesn't even ask about me. Hannah's mom doesn't talk to her like a daughter. She talks to her like a roommate.

They're out the door before I can even thank them for offering to feed me, an almost complete stranger. When I look over at Hannah, she's staring at the door—past the door—eyes narrowed, shoulders slumped.

"Hey," I say. "Are you—"

"Sorry they were so awkward," Hannah interrupts, pulling the letter out of her jeans. "It's not that they didn't want to meet you, or whatever."

"Oh."

"They don't like being in the house," she says. "Which is fucked up, but I get it."

That's concerning. "What's wrong with your house? I love your house."

But she doesn't hear me. She's torn open the letter with no stamps, revealing crumpled, smudged notebook paper inside. I resist reading over her shoulder. For all of five seconds. I can only make out the first few words of each line.

*Don't keep asking around you don't understand what you're doing*
*Join me if you believe me but this isn't helping you're the one who needs*
*Making sure you're safe but you'll never be until*

The first letter of each line is darker, bolder, like someone was making a point. As I try to read over her shoulder, that's what I see, those first letters repeated down the page. *D, J, M. D, J, M.* I could read more, if Hannah's hand weren't shaking.

*Just let go Hannah you need to let*

Hannah folds the letter up just as it came, on each original crease.

"Are you—" I ask, but then I don't know how to finish the sentence. *Okay? In danger?*

"I'm fine."

"Hannah, what was that letter? Who *sent* that to you?" I ask.

"Sometimes I'm not even sure, anymore," she says, which makes zero sense, especially as she tucks it gently, carefully, into her backpack.

I could ask her again. I should ask her, I should demand she tell me what's going on, refuse to help her with one more thing until I'm certain I know everything. But she wouldn't tell me, and then where would I be? Certain the world was ending, uncertain about everything else. If I have to choose, I'll let the letter go.

Hannah zips her backpack. "Let's go to the Park."

When Hannah and I get to the Park, Theo and Sam are in the throes of a contentious game of Five-Word Books.

"Mice, cats, pigs, and fascism," Sam says.

"*Animal Farm?*" Theo guesses.

"Um, no. *Maus.*"

"*Animal Farm* works too."

"No, it doesn't. There aren't any mice. There are horses, human, and allegorical Marxist pigs, but no mice."

"You're the worst."

"I'm a treasure," Sam says.

"That must be why I want to bury you on a desert island and not come back for twenty years."

"Can you two go one day without a death threat?" Hannah asks them as we approach.

"Never tried," Sam says.

"Where have you guys been?" Tal asks.

"I'm going up in the tree," Hannah says, one foot already on the trunk. I didn't see her take it out of her bag, but the letter's in her back pocket again. Tal frowns, then looks at me.

I shrug. He frowns harder.

"Five-Word Books, I'm in," I say, settling down in an empty spot between Tal and Sam. "Here's one: British children create murder society."

"*Lord of the Flies,*" Theo correctly guesses, then passes a joint across me, to Tal. "Hey, can you relight it?"

Tal flicks on his Zippo, and I try not to shrink away. I fail.

"You okay?" Sam asks.

"I don't like fire," I explain.

"That's a little weird," Tal mumbles, but sticks the lighter back in his pocket. "What did fire ever do to you?"

"It burned down the Library of Alexandria," I say.

"I don't think that was personal, Ellis," Tal says.

"That's a rough thing to be afraid of," Sam agrees. "Fire is life."

He has no idea. Surviving practically any doomsday scenario requires the controlled, skilled use of fire. The world hasn't even ended yet and I've got lighters, accelerants, and fire steel. What's going to happen when the snow comes and I'm too scared to light a match?

"Tell me something I don't know," I say to Sam.

"Sea cucumbers hurl their own internal organs at predators when they feel threatened."

Theo coughs. "What?"

Sam gestures to me. "Well, did you know that?"

"No," I admit.

He turns to Theo. "See?"

Theo ignores him, focusing on me. "Fire's not as destructive as you think. Sometimes it's not even as destructive as you *want* it to be."

I shake my head. "What do you mean?"

"Okay," Theo says. "So one time, when I was, like, thirteen, my mom came into my room to ask me something. But then she stopped, and paused, and was like, 'I can tell you have drugs, your room smells like drugs.'"

"What did it smell like before?" Sam asks. "Masturbation and Doritos?"

Theo shoves him. "I have no idea how she did it. It was this one tiny baby joint in my sock drawer. How could she possibly have smelled that?"

"Dude, she didn't." Tal laughs. "She probably saw it when she was putting your laundry away. She already knew it was there, she wanted to see if you'd tell her."

"Yeah, well, I did," Theo says. "She can be very scary."

"So then what happened?" I ask. I can't imagine what my mom would do if she found drugs in my room. We'd probably abandon the house entirely and start over in Antarctica.

"She took the joint into the kitchen and—" Theo grins. "I'm not sure what she was thinking. I guess she meant it, as like, some big dramatic gesture, but . . . she lit a stove burner and set it on fire."

Tal bursts out laughing. It takes me a second to realize. "Oh no," I say.

"The whole house," Theo says, "smelled like the Grateful Dead tour bus."

"And what, now your parents are okay with it?" I ask, eyes flicking down to the joint in Theo's hand.

"Hell no," he says. "But I don't bring it home anymore, my grades are excellent, somehow, and they're never had to bail me out of jail." He leans back on one hand. "A little bit of denial goes a long way."

Sam sticks his hand up. "I was in denial the first time I found my dad's weed."

I choke. "*You* found your *dad's*?"

"Sixth grade. I needed a stapler, went looking for one in his office out back, and found, like, four film canisters in the top drawer of the desk. And at first, I just shoved them aside, but then I was like, wait, he doesn't even own a film camera, so what the hell's in here?" Sam looks up at the sky pensively. "A lot of things suddenly made sense. No adult is that happy at Disneyland."

I think my mom had a borderline religious experience at Cinderella's castle one time, but I'll keep that to myself.

"It's almost like a Gettier problem," I say. "Drugs in a film canister."

"A what now?" Tal asks.

"A Gettier problem, it's a philosophy thing," I say. I can just about see the pages in Kenny #12 where I copied the information down. In red ink. "It's supposed to show that you can have a justified true belief of something, but that doesn't mean you have knowledge. You know?"

"Nope," Theo says.

"That 'nope,' but squared," Sam says.

"Okay, okay." I spread my hands out. "Sam. Let's say you're standing on the edge of a really big field in farm country. There are lots of hills."

"Does it matter that it's hilly?" Tal asks.

I point at him. "It actually does. Don't interrupt." I turn back to Sam. "You're standing by this field. In the distance, you see something that looks exactly like a sheep. So your first thought is, 'There's a sheep in the field.' Just like your first thought when you saw a film canister was, 'There's film in this film canister.' You have a justified belief in that, but that doesn't mean it's true. Because your dad was hiding drugs, and that sheep is actually a dog dressed up to *look* like a sheep."

"Oh, this is why philosophy sucks," Tal says.

"Whatever, I'd rather go pet a dog than a sheep," Sam says.

"No, but then wait," I cut in. "Let's say there *is* a sheep in the field. It's behind one of the hills. So your original thought was a justified *and* true belief, even though you couldn't *see* the sheep. But does that count as knowledge? If not, what is it?"

Two feet thump to the ground, just inches away from my hand. I pull it back and stare up at Hannah. She doesn't look like she's dropped gently from the branches this time. She looks like she's been hurtled down to Earth.

"That's not Sam's fault," she says, sinking down next to me and resting her back against the tree. "That's not fair."

I draw back, surprised by the fierceness in her voice and the tightness in her face. "It's not real, Hannah."

"It's a metaphor," Tal explains.

"What's a metaphor?" Sam asks.

"A place to keep your cow," Theo says.

I throw up my hands. "It's a sheep, not a cow, and it's a thought experiment, not a metaphor."

"It's not fair," Hannah repeats. "Someone set him up to see a sheep and then got mad when he did?"

"No one's mad," Sam says quietly.

"People don't see things out of nothing," Hannah says, even quieter. "It comes from somewhere. It always come from somewhere."

Theo touches Hannah on the shoulder. "Hey. Let's get snacks from E-Z Stop." She shakes her head, but he doesn't let up. "I was there yesterday, they got the weird Israeli peanut things you like back in stock."

She cracks a smile. "Bamba. They're delicious. Don't knock it."

Theo stands. "Come on, my treat."

Hannah gets to her feet. Sam scrambles up, too.

"You guys want anything?" Theo asks me and Tal. We shake our heads. After the three of them walk away, Tal pulls out his lighter again and starts to singe the tip of a grass blade, holding the grass close until it blackens and shrivels.

> *He's going to start a fire, and you're going to get burned, or blamed, or both.*

"Should you really be doing that?" I ask. I'm starting to get less freaked out about people doing drugs around me, but arson is a bridge too far.

> *He's going to start a fire big enough to have its*

*own weather system, which is a real thing that can happen. And it's windy, so then it'll become a fire tornado, which is another real thing that can happen.*

"Relax, you're perfectly safe," he says, but does stamp on the burnt grass blade. "I'm very careful."

"I've seen you light curtains on fire."

"I was nine!" he protests. "Which makes it a little more forgivable than the time I was fourteen, bored at my mom's house, and wanted to test out—for science—the difference between flammable and *in*flammable."

"They both mean you can light it on fire."

"Yeah, I know that now," Tal says. "One gigantic steel wool fireball later."

I've only used steel wool to clean our kitchen sink but I laugh at the image. "I don't get it. Weren't you scared? Aren't you scared?"

He frowns. "Of what?"

"Getting burned. Getting . . . hurt."

"But that's the whole point of life," he says. "Isn't it?"

I stare at him. "Lighting yourself on fire?"

"Yes!" he says. "I mean, not on purpose, but everything's got danger. Everything's got risk. If it's good, anyway."

"Things can be good and safe," I say. "It's possible."

He leans forward. "Humans need water, right? Water's good. But water can drown you. I bet you like funeral potatoes right out of the oven, but that pan could burn you."

"You're supposed to let them sit for fifteen minutes before serving."

"Ellis, oh my *God*," he says. "My point is, everything good in the whole world could hurt you. Doesn't mean it will."

> *But it could, it always could. Anything could hurt you, everything could hurt you, he could hurt you. Don't get comfortable. Don't forget all the terrible things that could happen.*

*Could* is a horrible word.

"You only want the safe parts," he goes on. "It doesn't work that way."

"It can," I say, thinking of the stockpiled supplies in my closet at home. All the facts, the knowledge scribbled down in my notebooks. I've worked for years to make myself safe, and now he's saying it's not even possible?

"It can't!" he says. "It's part of the deal. Sometimes you just get burned. Just, like, as a hypothetical," he says, "What if one day, you want to tell someone you like them. They could shoot you down. That burns. It hurts."

"But they could . . ." I clear my throat. "They could also say they like you back."

"Yeah," he says, looking down at the grass. "They could."

I look over his shoulder at Sam, Theo, and Hannah returning with armfuls of snacks, and think maybe, occasionally, *could* isn't such a horrible word, after all.

★ ★ ★

The second I shut the front door, Mom is already yelling down to me from the second floor.

"Ellis!"

She's never upstairs when I come home. The computer is down here, the TV is down here, the only thing upstairs is our bedrooms.

"What?" I call back up.

"Come up here."

I sigh and dump my backpack by the couch. When I get to the top of the stairs, I turn left, toward the master bedroom.

"No." I whip around to see Mom standing in the doorway of my room. "In here."

For a moment, I just stare at her. Then, feeling eerily like I'm walking toward a newly constructed gallows, I follow her into my room.

It isn't the way I left it. The drawers on my dresser are open. Books have been moved, restacked. My closet door is ajar, and I always close it before leaving.

"Is there something you'd like to tell me?" she asks.

*How about get out of my room?* I think. What she means is: "You're in trouble, and I'd like you to figure out why."

"Don't bother lying," Mom adds. "I know all about it."

In another life, my mother would have made a great lawyer. Or cop. Or CIA black-site interrogator. But this is not my first cross-examination, and I know the only way to minimize the damage is to minimize my words. So I swallow hard and wait her out.

"You were seen," Mom says, "at the drug park."

My body goes cold all over. She stares me down.

"Do you mean the dog park?" I ask, trying to sound casual, trying to keep my bubbling panic from leaking out of my pores.

"Why would you be at a dog park? We don't have a dog."

"Why would I be at a drug park? That's not a thing."

"Helen Olsen *saw you*. She was leaving the YMCA and she saw you."

Ratted on by a woman who sells essential oils out of the trunk of her Subaru. My life is a joke.

I spread my hands. "I don't know what Sister Olsen thinks she saw, but—"

"She saw you at the park next to your school, a known hangout for children to drink and do drugs."

"The park, or the high school?"

She glares at me. "She saw you with boys. Several boys. She thought they were passing something around."

I get a sudden image of Sister Olsen crouching behind a bush with binoculars and a tape recorder, like a private eye. I fight back a giggle. The giggle wins.

"Is this funny to you?" Mom says. "Are you high? Are you high right now? Let me look at your eyes." She reaches for my face, and I bat her away.

"This is ridiculous, you're tearing my room apart because

Sister Olsen spied on me in a public park?"

"Oh, so you *were* there?"

I walked into that. "Yes, but—"

"And what were you doing with those boys?"

"Just hanging out. They're my friends."

"Do these friends share your standards?"

I resist rolling my eyes. What she means is: *Your friends are not like you, and this is worse than having no friends at all.* What she means is: *Avoid the appearance of evil, even if that means you never do anything at all.*

"They were nice to me. They like me. I like them."

"People will judge you by the company you keep, Ellis."

"Do what is right and let the consequence follow," I say, just to piss her off. That hymn has been quoted for a lot of purposes, but I doubt it's ever been used to justify befriending a group of stoners.

"Well, here it is." She yanks open another desk drawer and starts pawing through it. "Here's the consequence."

"Mom—"

"Go downstairs."

"But you can't—"

"Don't tell me what I can't do," she snaps. All my bubbling panic is suddenly replaced by anger, red-hot and unstable. She's blocking me from my room, the place that's safe, the place that's mine. We stare at each other, but she has to tilt her head up. That's not new. I've been taller than her since I was fourteen.

But for the first time, I realize that if I wanted to, I could push her out of the way. For the first time, I seriously consider it.

"Downstairs," she says. "Now."

I swallow my pride. I swallow all my terrible thoughts. I leave her in the doorway.

# ELEVEN

**OUR COUCH ISN'T** as nice as Martha's. I'm sure it was more expensive. I'm sure it ties the room together. But I can't sink into it. And sitting here alone, while Mom is upstairs systematically destroying my room, it's never felt more uncomfortable.

When Dad comes in the door, it's obvious Mom texted him, because he heads straight for the stairs.

"Dad," I call out to him, half rising from the couch. If he'd stop, I can explain before Mom sets the stage for Our Daughter's Downward Spiral, a three-act tragedy ending with me selling my teeth for black-tar heroin. If he'd stop, I could make him understand. But he only throws me one sidelong look before continuing up the stairs. The disappointment in his eyes socks me in the stomach. I slump back down on the couch.

After ten minutes of hushed conversation and a couple of disconcerting thumps, Dad comes back down. He sits in his favorite chair. I avoid his eyes, focusing on the dark wood of the table between us.

Upstairs, something solid and heavy lands on the floor.

"What's she doing?" I look up at the ceiling.

"She's looking at the things you bought."

Oh no. "Do you mean my new books?"

"I mean your new subzero sleeping bag."

There's another bang upstairs. My temper crackles again.

I meet Dad's eyes. This time, I don't look away. "Why aren't you stopping her?"

He does an honest-to-goodness double take. "Excuse me?"

"She's trashing my room, she's going through stuff I bought with my own money. It's not fair."

"Fair," he repeats, like he's never heard the word before.

"They're *my* things."

"They're in *our* house and you're *our* sixteen-year-old daughter."

That only adds heat to the brush fire inside my chest. "So you and Mom own me like you own the house?"

"We have a mortgage, Ellis."

That's fine. The bank can raise me. I'd prefer it.

"Is this okay to you?" I ask. He shuts his eyes. Sighs. "Do you think what she's doing is okay?" I ask again, willing my voice not to crack.

"I wish she wouldn't handle it like this."

"Then do something about it."

He shakes his head, like, *Not going to happen.* I wonder if it's hard sitting upright, with absolutely no backbone.

"You're my dad." And this time, my voice does crack. "She's awful to me, all the time, and you know she shouldn't be, so why don't you ever do anything about it?"

Dad opens his mouth, but stops when we both hear the stomp of Mom's shoes on the stairs. With flinty eyes and perfect posture, she lowers herself next to me. I shrink away.

"Explain," Mom says.

I explain. Or, I explain as much as I need to. I tell them about Hannah, a girl who has dreams about the end of the world. I tell them about the way she seems to know things before I say them. I tell them that the last days are coming soon, with snow and ice.

I don't tell them what day it's coming. I don't tell them Hannah is a client of Martha's. I don't tell them Hannah has secrets she hasn't yet shared. I'm exactly as honest as I need to be, and nothing more.

When I'm done, Mom and Dad just look at me. *Bewildered*, a word that implies being lost in the wild. That's exactly how they look. Totally lost.

Mom sighs, long and heavy. "You bought these things because your friend told you the world was ending."

"Yes."

"And you believed her."

"Yes."

Mom blinks at me. "Why?"

What an odd question, coming from her. I've heard Mom asked the same question, by family friends who are secular: Why do you believe what you do? And I've seen her smile serenely and say: *Because first I felt its truth, and then I lived its truth.*

There's no other answer to give.

"I had a personal revelation."

Mom and Dad look at each other. Then back at me.

"I prayed to know if it was true. And it is. Because when I prayed, when I asked if it was true, I felt the Spirit."

More silence. More staring.

"I felt the Spirit," I say again, because clearly they didn't hear me. "I asked for a revelation, I got a revelation, I felt the—"

Mom waves her hand, pushing the words away. "No, honey, you didn't."

My throat constricts. I force it open. "Yes, I did."

"I'm sure it seemed like the same thing," Dad says, "but it wasn't, not if it you made you afraid like this. 'Faith is the opposite of fear,' didn't we teach you that?"

I have faith. And I have fear. I believe in my religion. And I believe in Hannah.

"I prayed to know the truth," I say. "You taught me that, too. And I received an answer."

"Because you *wanted to*, Ellis," Mom insists. "Because this is something that worries you and you want to feel like you're in control of it." She throws up her hands. "And apparently, you'd believe any crackpot on a street corner who said you *could* be in control of it."

My eyes sting. Who is she to talk about *control*? If I want control, at least it's for something bigger, something that matters, not policing how my daughter looks and talks and feels. When I look back up at Mom, her face has softened, just a bit.

"What you felt was not the Spirit," Mom says. "What you felt was your anxiety."

I don't believe that. If she were right, how could you ever know what you were feeling was real? How could anyone trust a revelation or prompting? How could anyone trust someone *else's* revelation? The church is built on new revelations. If I can't trust my own promptings, how can I trust any at all?

"How do you know this isn't the Spirit?" I say, my eyes flicking from Dad to Mom, then back to Dad. "How am *I* supposed to know it isn't real, when it feels so real?"

"The next time you have a 'revelation,'" Mom says, and I can *hear* air quotes around the word, "you should tell Bishop Keller."

"Or I can pray with you," Dad offers, "and tell you whether this is a real prompting."

Oh, of course. Men. Men with power and Y chromosomes and righteous dominion over me. The only people who could possibly tell me which of my own feelings to trust and which to dismiss as hysteria are *men*.

I stare at Mom. "Why would Bishop Keller automatically

know better than me? Because he's a priesthood holder and I'm just a girl?"

"Of course not, that isn't—" Mom flounders. "This is his job. He was called to be our spiritual leader."

"Yeah, well, a year ago he was just your accountant."

"Ellis!" Dad gasps.

Mom shakes her head. "What's the matter with you?"

I have no idea what's the matter with me.

But I also know what I felt was real. And true. And mine.

"I don't care what you say," I tell my mom. Her jaw sets. "I don't care what Dad says. I don't care what Bishop Keller or the stake president or every priesthood-holding seventh-grade boy says. The end of the world is coming, and it's coming soon."

I push myself off the couch and storm toward the stairs. Mom springs up and grabs my upper arm in a death grip.

"I am not letting you do this to yourself," she says. "You are not going to hurt yourself like this. It ends now, Ellis, do you understand me? Right now."

"December, actually," I tell her. "It'll all end in December."

I feel a cold kind of triumph at the flicker of real fear that passes over her face. She steps back a half inch but doesn't let go of my arm.

"From now on," she says, and I can tell she's working to keep her voice even, "you will come straight home after school. Therapy, church, or home. That's it. No internet, no hanging out in parks, and no seeing Hannah ever again."

"Fine!" I yell, when what I really mean is *try to stop me*. Her grip tightens.

"I mean it," she says, soft and deadly. "Don't push me on this."

"Or what? You'll take away all the *freedom* I have? You'll trash my room again? You'll yell at me, you'll make me feel horrible and worthless?" I lean in. "Or will you come up with something new?"

Then Dad is there, prying Mom's hand off me finger by finger. "Go to your room," he orders me.

"Fine!" I yell again. This time I do mean it.

Dad knocks on my door an hour later, and opens it without pausing for me to invite him. I guess I've given up any kind of privacy. He sits down on the bed next to me. I wait for him to say something. I guess he's waiting too, because we sit like that, in silence, until finally I can't take it anymore.

"Why does she hate me?" I blurt out.

Dad looks stricken. But he doesn't have to ask who I mean. "She doesn't hate you."

"She does."

"Don't say that."

"Why not?" I demand.

"Because it's not nice."

"What does it matter if it's nice, it's true!"

"It's not." I look away. He touches me on the shoulder, but I don't look back. "Elk. You don't believe that."

161

He doesn't know what I believe. I rub at my eye.

"Your mom doesn't hate you. She loves you, she loves you like you can't even imagine. She just . . ." He sighs. "She just wants what's best for you."

But how is she so sure what that is? How does everyone seem so sure of what's best for me? And don't I get a say in that?

"She doesn't always handle it the right way," Dad acknowledges, "but it's never because she *hates* you. Just before she got pregnant with you, she had this dream—"

I screw my eyes shut, because I know this, of course I know this, they've only told me a thousand times.

"We'd only talked about having a baby—hadn't made a decision or anything—but she dreamed of being in a green, beautiful garden, with sky all around her, and a graceful, beautiful young woman sitting beside her. Your mom could feel how special this girl was, how pure and precious. The girl said her name was Ellis, and that they'd see each other again soon."

When I was little, I loved this story. I loved the idea that my mom had met me when I was still a spirit just waiting for a body. I loved the idea that I was fated to be born into my family, that my very existence was ordered and planned. But the older I got, the more distant I felt from the girl in the garden. Beautiful? Not especially. Graceful? Almost never.

The older I got, the more I thought my mom was given the wrong daughter.

"She doesn't like me as much as Em," I tell Dad. "You can't

argue with that, even if she doesn't hate me, Em's her favorite."

"Your mom doesn't have a favorite," he says.

"Just an unfavorite."

"That's not true."

"But that's okay," I say, blinking my eyes until they stop stinging. "That's okay, I don't need her to like me as much as Em, it's okay that I'm her unfavorite. Because—" I take a gulp of air. "I'm *your* favorite. Aren't I?"

His shoulders sag as if I've thrown him something heavy. "I don't have a favorite, either."

I used to be. He can say that all he wants, but I remember. Me on his shoulders at Disneyland, even though Em was smaller. Me helping him fix the kitchen sink, even though I only made the mess worse. Me telling the whole story of the First Crusade at the dinner table and him not once stopping me, even though everyone else was bored. "I used to be your favorite."

Dad clears his throat. He clasps his hands. "Before you were born—"

"Don't tell the dream story again, please, I know."

"This isn't that one," he says, suddenly gruff. "Just listen."

I listen.

"Before you were born," Dad says, "I didn't know a single person on Earth with my eyes."

His eyes? They're brown. Like mine. Nearly the whole world has brown eyes, and I tell him that.

"Not my exact eyes," he says. "Same shape, same color, same

163

dark lashes. Everyone in my family has blue eyes, every single one. I never knew anyone with my eyes."

Dad is my grandparents' only adopted child, their longed-for son, a hand-picked boy chosen after the birth of their fourth daughter and my grandma's hysterectomy. His parents love him. His sisters adore him. Aunt Karissa used to dress him up like a doll; I've seen the pictures. But they don't have his eyes.

"But with you . . ." He trails off. Looks up. Tries again. "That first moment I held you, Ellis, it was—you were early, you know, and so, so small. But your nose was my nose. Your ears were my ears. And when you opened your eyes . . ." He breathes out. "It was something holy."

In my family, we don't call something holy unless we mean it. Unless we really mean it.

"You don't know what that's like," he tells me. "To see yourself in another person, for the very first time."

I grab his hand, and hold on tight, the way I used to do when he'd read to me at bedtime. Like if I gripped his thumb hard enough, he'd never turn the light off. Like if I never let go, he wouldn't, either. "Dad," I whisper.

"I don't have favorites," he says. "I mean that. I don't love you the most, I couldn't love either of you kids more than the other. But maybe—" He squeezes my hand. "Maybe it's true that I needed you the most."

# TWELVE

"SO, I KNOW this isn't our usual day and time," Martha says. "Do you have any feelings about that?"

I feel like it wasn't necessary. After sleeping the night in my still-trashed room, I came down for breakfast the next morning and told my parents that I'd thought about what we'd discussed. I'd prayed about it. And I'd decided they were right, after all. If they were skeptical of the sudden change of heart, they didn't say anything. Maybe because Em was at the table too. But Dad texted me at lunch and told me to go to Martha's after school, all the same.

"Your parents and I had a conversation this morning," Martha says.

I bite my lip.

"Do you have an idea of what we talked about?"

"Snowshoes?" I say. "Global cooling patterns?"

"We did talk about your recent purchases."

"I don't know how my mom made it seem," I say, "but I didn't steal, and I didn't even lie, because no one asked me about it."

"Do you think that's what made them concerned enough to call me?" Martha asks. "The money?"

"They think it's stupid. They think caring about it makes *me* stupid."

"It sounds like the way they reacted to it really hurt you," she says. "I'm sorry that happened."

It only makes me feel worse, when someone tells me they're sorry. I know it hurt. But if I'm the only one who knows that, I can shove that hurt deep inside my chest cavity. I can nestle it right next to my parents' disappointment, and Tal touching my arm, and the way the light hit Lia Lemalu's hair—

I dig a fingernail into my palm. I picture sewing my insides shut with my mom's embroidery thread, pulling each stitch tight.

"Would you like to talk about what happened yesterday?" Martha asks. "Your mom didn't go into a ton of detail, but I'm thinking it was probably a tough night for you."

> *If you talk, you might tell her about Hannah. You might ruin your only chance at survival, just like you ruin everything.*

I shake my head.

"Are you sure?"

> *If you tell her, she won't understand. Your own*

*parents don't understand. You can't trust them and
you can't trust her.*

"I did more research," I say, and ignore the disappointment
on her face. "I think we should talk about my eschatology
research."

"Okay," Martha says, but doesn't look thrilled. "Maybe you
can tell me about a time when it didn't happen."

"But that's every time," I say. "Because it hasn't happened
yet."

"That's true," Martha says. "Just tell me about one."

I don't even have to take out Kenny #14. I know the one I
want to talk about.

"There was a woman named Thiota. And she lived in—
we'd call it Germany now, but it was the Carolingian Empire.
It was before the first millennium. And Thiota lived in a
world where the Catholic Church ruled, totally. The Church
was the Empire and the Empire was the Church and you
didn't get to pick your beliefs. You didn't get to pick anything, really, if you were a commoner, like Thiota. Or a girl,
like Thiota. You did what your priest told you. And he did
what the bishop told him. And the bishop did—well, you get
it, right?"

"Yes," Martha says. "A rigid society with lots of rules but not
a lot of freedom."

"But then—and we don't know how old she was, or why she
started, or even what she said, but Thiota started prophesying

about the end of the world." I pause. "People listened to her. Even though she was a girl. And a nobody. Even though they could have listened to wealthy men with power and the whole church behind them, people listened to her. They brought her gifts. They asked for her blessing. Not just other women, but men, even some priests. She had a following."

"Do you think they were scared, her followers? Maybe they needed someone to tell them it would be all right?"

"Maybe." But I also wonder—is that all she was preaching about? Was it just the end of the world, or was it Judgment Day, too? About the meek inheriting the Earth and the rich being turned away? About justice, and fairness, and rightness?

Maybe they were angry too.

"It didn't matter that she had a following. Probably made things worse. She got hauled up in front of this big council of bishops and they told her it was heresy, what she was saying. That she didn't have the right to say it, or anything else about God, because she was just some peasant girl. They made her say some priest told her to do it. They didn't even believe her words could *be* her words."

"And then?"

"And then she was publicly beaten and thrown out of town. And that's it."

"No one knows what happened to her after?"

"Someone did. She did. But the priest who wrote down her story didn't, because he didn't *care*."

"Why do you think this is so upsetting for you?" Martha asks. "Thiota's story?"

"They erased her. They erased her even more than if she'd never been in history books at all. They made her an example of someone who shouldn't have dared to think she was anything more than what they told her she was. They made her a joke. They made her a footnote."

"History is long. Lots of people don't make that cut."

"But it's not fair. Why are some people allowed to have a vision and other people aren't?" I ask. "Why do some people get religions and churches and songs praising and hailing them as a prophet, and some people get dragged through the mud and treated like a joke?"

"Why do you think that is?"

"I don't know," I say, even though I do. Some people have power, or magnetic personalities, or unbelievable luck. Some people are the right *kind* of people to change the world. Some people aren't weird teenage girls with the charisma of a chainsaw.

"If it's okay, I'd like to circle back to you, here," Martha says. I'd rather not, but I can't really say so. After all, we're here because of me.

"Okay," I say, picking at the couch threads again because I have a feeling I know what we're going to circle back *to*.

"Your mom said you'd agreed to stop talking to your . . . new friends," Martha says. "She says you came to accept that the world was not ending in December."

I nod.

"Is that what you told her?"

I nod.

Martha hesitates. She purses her lips. "And is it true?"

There's heat on the back of my neck, pressure in my shoulder blades. "What," I say, "you don't believe me?"

"I'd like to," she says, "but you answering a question with another question lowers my confidence."

I look down at my lap.

"Tell me if I'm off base here," Martha says, "but I think maybe you felt like you had to tell your parents what they wanted to hear. That there wasn't another option. So you did what you had to."

When I meet her eyes again, she's watching me carefully, waiting for my answer. I have to be careful too. She can't tell my parents what we talk about in sessions, except if I'm a danger to myself or others. I'm not going to hurt people—if anything, Hannah and I will be *helping* people—but Martha might not see it that way. So I stare back at her, lips pressed shut.

"Ellis. I'm not here to judge you."

"No. Just to tell me I'm delusional."

"You're not delusional. That's a real condition, and it's not one you have."

"Then what do you think is wrong with me? Because you do. Everyone does."

"I think you're feeling scared. And overwhelmed. And mis-understood."

*Don't you dare cry. Don't you dare tell her she's right. Don't you dare let her see inside you, don't you dare let her get any closer.*

"I think you've been feeling that way for a very long time, and I think you're so sick of feeling like that, you've latched on to something, anything that doesn't make you feel that way."

*Don't you dare believe her. You're fine, and if you aren't, you brought it on yourself. Stitch yourself up tighter and cut the thread.*

I chew on the inside of my mouth. "It's not that simple."

"I'm sure it's not."

"You haven't heard her—" I stop. No Hannah talk. "I really believe this. I know what I believe."

Martha sighs. "Will you do one thing for me?"

"Okay."

"For the next week, here's what I want you to do: instead of research, instead of looking at what happened before, I want you to make a plan."

"A plan?" I have plenty of plans, plenty of ideas about how to survive the winter, plenty of lists and facts and worst-case scenarios in my head.

"I want you to consider the fact that the world may not end." I open my mouth, but she holds up her hand. "You don't have to believe it, just consider it. And I want you to think about this: What will you do if it doesn't? If you're given the gift of more days, or years, or decades, what will you do with them?"

I don't know what I'd do with a future wide-open like that. It fills me with an inexplicable, inescapable feeling of pure dread.

"Can you do that for me?" Martha asks again.

I smooth my hand over the couch cushion. "I'll try."

Mom is twenty minutes late to pick me up. I could have taken the bus. But Mom texted me after school informing me that I was to wait right outside Martha's office. So that's what I'm doing.

She finally pulls up on the wrong side of the four-lane street, just across from the office. Then she waits. And I wait. Does she really expect me to dash between the cars? Sure, maybe it's not super busy right now, but that's dangerous.

> *You could get hit and die.*
>
> *You could cause a three-car collision and be named in a civil suit after one of the passengers is paralyzed.*
>
> *You could get yelled at by an angry cyclist.*

It's just not worth it.

So I keep waiting. And when it's clear Mom has outright refused to circle the block and re-park on the right side, I walk the half block to the crosswalk, cross with the green light, and walk the half block back to her car.

"Hi," I say, sliding into the front seat.

"What is wrong with you?" she snaps back as I pull my seat belt tight.

"What did I do?" I ask, though I guess it would be more accurate to ask, "What did I do *now*?"

"I've been sitting in this car for five minutes waiting for you to cross."

"I would have been quicker if you'd parked on the right side of the street."

She glares at me. "You could have crossed three times while I was waiting."

"Mom! There is no crosswalk! I could have been hit by a car!"

"That's the problem with you, Ellis," Mom says, jerking the car into drive. "You want everything covered in Bubble Wrap. And if you can't have that, you shut down. Well, that's not the world. I'm not letting that slide anymore."

She has never let a single thing slide.

"It's not just about you," she says, a death grip on the steering wheel. "It's not just about your comfort. Do you have any idea how much I have on my plate? I have laundry and a meat loaf dinner just waiting to be done at home."

Oh good, meat loaf. My absolute least favorite.

"Not to mention I'm bringing meals to three people in the ward this week, Emmy needs to be fitted for new ballet shoes, and I have to train the new receptionist who is, bless her heart, completely incompetent."

I'm starting to think this isn't about me at all. I'm just a safer target.

"How was your day?" I ask, hoping she'll land on another person to be mad at.

She shakes her head. "Oh, don't even try that with me."

I wonder what her friends would think, if they saw her like this. My mom is such a smiler at church, at dinner parties, at parent-teacher conferences. She's almost aggressive in her cheerfulness. I'm the only one she gets this angry at. I'm the only person she *can* get this angry at.

"I was just asking." I slump back in my seat.

"You couldn't care less. You couldn't care less about my day."

"Could you give me a break? For once?"

"Sometimes I feel like that's all I do."

My mother has many talents. She can bake a perfect root beer Bundt cake, embroider the most delicate flowers on a baby gown, and slice me off at the knees in six words or less. There's a lump in my throat and salt in the corner of my eyes, but I swallow it down, brush it away. She keeps going.

"I can't talk to you the way I can with— You can't handle things. Anything could make you melt down. So we walk on eggshells, the whole family, you know that? We do. We handle you with kid gloves. And now you start with this— I don't even know what to call it. A cult?"

"It's not a cult."

"No, it's not, it's a cry for attention. As if you don't get enough. As if Dad and I don't spend half our lives worrying about you, trying to figure out what on Earth to do with you."

She talks about me like I'm a rug that clashes with every room in the house. Like a cat that won't stop clawing at the curtains. She talks about me like she has buyer's remorse.

"You can blame him for this, by the way. He was the one who insisted I drop everything and pick you up."

"Maybe he thought it would be nice," I say. *Maybe he thought you would be nice*, I don't say.

"He didn't rearrange his schedule for it, did he?" Mom asks.

"If he could have, he would have," I mumble.

"He could have." Mom steals a glance at me. "He's not perfect. I know you need me to be the villain in your life, but he's not perfect, either."

Martha would call that "deflection."

I roll my eyes. I would call that "a fair response."

"I bet that's what you tell your therapist," Mom says. "I bet you tell her your father is perfect and your mother is a monster. Well, let me tell you, my mother didn't do half of what I do for you."

Grammy Kit isn't in a position to contradict this superconvenient story. She's in a nursing home in Salt Lake City.

"She didn't chauffeur me around, not when I was your age. And why do I have to do this, Ellis? Why do I have to cart you around like this?"

"Because I can't drive," I mumble.

"Because you *won't* drive. It scares you. So you just *won't*." She huffs, gathering steam. "It's my fault. I can only blame you so much, because I allowed you to get this way. I got my license on my sixteenth birthday. I was independent. My mother didn't *care* how my day went; she didn't pick me up, talk to me."

I watch the houses pass by, trying to imagine who lives in them. I picture myself on the second-story porch of a classic Berkeley brown shingle, in the overgrown front garden of a light blue cottage, reading on the window seat of a gorgeous modern house my mom would hate.

"So with all I do . . ." Mom says, starting in on me again, but quieter this time. "I don't think it's wrong of me to want some appreciation. Is that so terrible? Does that make me so terrible to you?"

I don't know what to say. How did we even get here? How did she take it from me not crossing the street to me not appreciating her? And I almost ask that, but then I think—is that how *my* logic seems to other people? Is that how my catastrophizing makes me sound? Maybe this is Mom catastrophizing. Maybe—the thought catches me by surprise—maybe my mom feels like I do. Like her life is spinning out of control too. I plan and prepare and worry, and she arranges and prods and perfects.

My mom and I could not be more different.

Or maybe we could.

"Thank you," I say, breaking the silence, "for picking me up from therapy."

"All the way across town," she adds.

She's not making this easy. "Thank you for picking me up from therapy all the way across town."

Her shoulders drop a half centimeter. She looks at me. I try for a smile. She frowns. Shakes her head.

"I'm sorry you have to," I say, because maybe what she really wants is an apology. "I'm sorry I have a mental illness."

She stops at a red light and twists to look at me. "You don't have a mental illness," she says. "You have an attitude problem."

"You sent me to a therapist all the way across town for an attitude problem?"

Mom shakes her head. "Schizophrenia. Psychosis. Dementia, like Gammy Kit has. Those are mental illnesses. You do not have a mental illness."

She's wrong. I know she's wrong. If she'd take a half second to research it, or just listen to me for once, she'd know she was wrong, too.

"This doesn't have to be your life," she says, stealing a look at me. "You aren't helpless. You can change, if you want to, and I hope Martha can help you do it. That's what makes this different. You can get over this, you can have a normal, happy life. You just have to try."

I see it, all of a sudden, with the clarity of a key in a lock. My mom is *scared*. Her fears don't look like mine, but that doesn't mean she doesn't have them. And she's wrong, she's still so wrong about everything, but it's not because she's unfeeling. I thought she couldn't see the way I struggled and hurt and clawed against my brain, but she can. And it might scare her more than it scares me. She's scared I won't get to have the life she imagined I would. She's scared I'll let myself suffer forever. She's scared to see me suffer.

*I do try*, I want to protest.

*I'm not going to get over this*, I want to tell her.

*I can get better at living with it*, I want to assure her.

But I just stare out the window.

The rest of the car ride passes in silence. When we reach home, I half expect Mom to beat me to the door and lock me out of the house, but she waits patiently for me to gather my things and get out of the car.

"Wash your hands when you get inside," Mom says. "I need you to grate cheese for the tuna casserole."

Tuna casserole? Mom hates tuna casserole. She can't stand the texture, and Em isn't a fan either, but it's my favorite. I ask for it on every birthday, and that's about the only time she'll make it.

"I thought we were having meat loaf."

She locks the car. "I changed my mind."

I hold up my hands and walk away from the car. I won't argue with tuna casserole.

At the top of the stairs, with the key already in the lock,

Mom stops and looks at me. Her mouth is still in a hard line, but her eyes are softer. "Ellis," she says, and sighs, and I hold my breath. "I'm—" She swallows. "Your hair looks very nice today."

It doesn't. It's frizzy and messy and tucked behind my ears. But I know what she means. I know that sometimes you say one thing when you mean another.

"Thanks, Mom."

## THIRTEEN

**MOM'S ULTIMATUM CHANGES** very little about my life. It means I have to lie more—or maybe just better.

The next Monday, as soon as I leave sixth period, I text my parents saying I'm going to math tutoring after school. It's barely a lie. I should be going, and I would be going, if the world weren't ending. But I highly doubt knowing my sines from my cosines is going to help, and sticking close to Hannah might. So I choose that.

Well, as close as I can get, when she's up in her tree. Staying on solid ground and playing Five-Word Books appeals to my need for self-preservation, anyway.

"Rodents who were monks, weirdly," Sam says, counting five words on his fingers.

"*Redwall*," Tal says. "God, you're right, why *were* they monks? What were they worshiping? Was there a mouse Jesus?"

"Maybe they pray to Cheesus," I suggest. Tal laughs, and

my stomach leaps for no reason at all.

"Okay, okay, I've got one," Theo says. "Exiled prince defeats demon king."

We all look at Theo blankly.

"It's *Ramayana*," Theo says. "The ancient Indian poem? Epic? Super important to the, like, six million Hindus of the world?"

The three of us shrug guiltily in unison.

"You are all," Theo declares, "a bunch of colonialist monsters."

"The Brazilian half of me is offended," Tal says.

"If you just say 'colonialist' I think the 'monster' part is implied," Sam adds.

Suddenly, Hannah jumps down from her tree. The boys keep playing, but she peers out across the Park, then drops down next to me.

"Hey," she says to me, low. "Do you have a dollar?"

"Yeah. What for?"

She points out a man walking through the park with his arms full of newspapers. I think it's the same one I saw her talking to before. "I want to buy a *Street Spirit*."

*Street Spirit* is a paper run by homeless people in Berkeley. The reporters get paid for their work, and it's sort of an alternative to panhandling. A product people living on the street can sell. It doesn't cost much, and I know it helps, so I dig four quarters out of my backpack and hand them to her.

"Thanks," she says, and walks off. The boys are still deep in Five-Word Books.

"Okay, okay, how about this," Tal says. "Sociopath child slowly dismembers friend."

"*The Giving Tree*," Theo answers, with a touch of horror. "Jesus, Tal."

"Am I wrong, though?"

Sam nods his head over at Hannah. "What's she doing?"

I shrug. "Buying a *Street Spirit*."

"From the guy who hangs out by Ashby BART and tells you he knows when you're going to die?" Tal asks.

"That's a different guy," Sam says. "They look kind of the same, but the dude at Ashby BART's way shorter and has that green Army jacket."

"Oh yeah, you're right."

"Why is that?" I wonder out loud. "Why are all the homeless people you see men, usually middle-aged, living alone? Or maybe with a dog."

Theo scoffs. "Those are the only homeless people you *think* you see."

"What?"

"Not everyone who's homeless sleeps in a park," Theo says. "They live in their cars, or on friend's couches because they lost their house or apartment because shit happens. Most homeless people are families. With kids. You've definitely been on a bus or in a class with one, and just didn't know it."

I'm surprised he knows this much about it, and my face must show that, because he shrugs. "My mom's a social worker. And I'm a good listener."

"Are you?" Sam asks.

"Yeah, and I'm also good at nonverbal communication," Theo says, holding up both middle fingers.

Hannah wanders back over, her nose buried in the newspaper. For a moment, I think she'll take it up in the tree with her, but she walks a few feet past me and plops down on the grass, her back to us. The boys either don't notice or have decided it's best not to bother her. I go over and sit down next to her. She doesn't look up, but meticulously combs through each page. "Hey."

"What are you doing?" I ask as she reaches the last page, then shakes the newspaper like she expects something to fall out.

"I thought maybe he'd left a note."

"Prophet Dan?" I ask, and she nods. Why would she think that, though? He doesn't even know we're looking for him.

Does he?

"I'm sorry we haven't been able to find him," I say to Hannah. "But we've done so much already, to figure out your dreams, maybe we don't . . . need him."

"We do," Hannah says. "Trust me, we do."

"Hannah," I say tentatively, "I don't think he wants be found."

Hannah's face tightens. She buries her head in her hands. That's not the reaction I was expecting, and I have no idea what to do. I touch her shoulder as gently as I can.

"It's okay," I assure her. She doesn't move, and I hear myself start to babble. "It's okay, okay? We'll keep looking, I'm sure someone's seen him. He's got friends, right? We'll find his friends, and we'll find him. He's a nice guy, of course he has friends, I mean, he brought that lady at the library muffins every week—"

Hannah perks up instantly. "Muffins? What muffins?"

"Yeah." I dig back in my brain. "Carrot zucchini muffins. That doesn't even sound like a pastry, right? It sounds like a salad. . . ." I trail off. Hannah's jumped to her feet. She zips up her backpack.

"Are you okay?"

She spins around to me. "Why didn't you tell me that before?"

"I didn't think it mattered."

"I know where we need to look," she says. "Come on."

I scramble to my feet without hesitation, then feel immediately annoyed with myself. How can she do that, get me to change my plans with two words? It's like those magnets we used in middle school science. How some were strong enough that you could feel them pulling in the smaller ones. You could actually feel the draw.

It's obvious, but I never really thought about it before: that's what "magnetic personality" means.

"Me and Ellis are hungry," Hannah says to the boys. "We're going to get something to eat."

"I'm in," Sam says, even though she didn't invite him. Theo follows suit.

"Yeah, why not." Tal shrugs. I glance over at Hannah, my eyebrows raised. She looks less than thrilled.

"We're going kind of far . . ." she says, rubbing at the back of her neck, but they're on their feet and have started a new round of Five-Word Books. She sighs. "Fine. Whatever."

"Where are we going?" I whisper to Hannah as she sets a brisk place up the block, the three of them behind us.

"The only place that would sell carrot zucchini muffins," Hannah whispers. "Berkeley Bowl."

Berkeley Bowl is not, as the name suggests, a bowling alley. It's a grocery store. It's the kind of place that lets you grind your own peanuts into butter. It's the kind of place that has kombucha on tap. It's the kind of place where just to get in you must brave three separate ponytailed men wielding petitions.

"Do you really think Prophet Dan shops here?" I whisper to Hannah. "It's kind of pricey."

She looks at me like I'm six years old. "They throw out food. Or give it out. At the end of the day."

"Why are we here?" Sam complains, and Hannah looks away from me. "This is the worst place to get free samples.

One time, my mom bought nutritional yeast here. Nutritional. Yeast."

"Was it good?" Tal asks.

"Does it *sound* good?"

Suddenly, Theo stops. "Hold up a second. Yo, Ravi," Theo calls out. A young man down the aisle wearing a red T-shirt turns, and grins broadly. He walks over to us, and he and Theo fist-bump.

"Hey, Theo."

Theo turns to the rest of us. "Our parents go to temple together." Then, back to Ravi: "What's up, man, when did you get back?"

"August," Ravi says. "I'm doing post-bac stuff at Cal. I have to get my science GPA up or the MCAT's not even going to matter."

"That blows. So you picking up study snacks or something?"

"Oh, no, I'm working here," Ravi says. "Just a few shifts, in the bakery."

Next to me, Hannah goes very still.

"Sweet," Theo says. "Any free samples?"

"I think there are some chocolate éclairs over by the customer service counter," Ravi says. "Tell them I sent you."

Theo and Ravi say goodbye, and all three boys walk off in search of the éclairs. I'm about to follow them, but Hannah's hanging behind. As Ravi passes her, she turns and taps on his arm.

"Excuse me?"

Ravi stops and turns around.

"Sorry to bother you, but . . . at the bakery, do you ever . . ." Hannah pauses. "You guys ever give out food? Maybe to the homeless?"

Ravi shrugs. "I've never closed up, but I mean, what doesn't get sold . . ." He narrows his eyes. "Why?"

"Could you maybe take me back there?" Hannah blurts out. "Maybe I could ask your coworkers?"

Ravi takes a long pause, then a longer look at Hannah's tense, desperate face. "Okay. Come on."

He leads her away, and I head in the direction of free dessert. I stop when I find Tal wandering the canned food aisle.

"You didn't want an éclair?" I ask, meeting him in the middle.

He wrinkles his nose. "I don't actually like chocolate."

That's practically blasphemy for someone raised Mormon. Sugar is our only vice.

"Oh my gosh, I'm so sorry," I say. "I had no idea you were secretly an inhuman cyborg."

"If I were a robot, I wouldn't be this cold. God, it's like an icebox in here," Tal mutters, rubbing at his arms.

It is, but I appreciate that. It tells me they're committed to food safety standards. I'd rather be cold than get staphylococcal food poisoning from overheated chicken.

"That's why I love layers," I say, hugging my cardigan closer.

"You never know when you're going to need something extra, especially if the fog rolls in."

"You're like an onion."

"Uh," I say. "Because I smell, or because I make people cry?"

"Oh my God," he says, horrified. "No, because you like layers, onions have—oh my God." He looks up. "Why would I say that?" he appears to ask the giant ceiling fan.

I bite the inside of my mouth to keep from laughing. "It's okay."

"For the record, I *like* onions," he says. "I make a kickass salada de cebola, that's all onions."

"You cook!" I say. "That's a surprise. Who knew you had so many . . . layers."

He looks back down at me. He narrows his eyes. "You're enjoying this."

I shrug, with a smile. "Just a little."

He smiles back, and then we're smiling at each other, and if the silence goes on, I might say something inappropriate in the middle of a supermarket aisle. So I clear my throat and turn back to the shelf.

"Don't ever try canned onions, though," I say, rummaging through the cans with suddenly clammy hands. "They're the worst."

"Does anything canned taste good?"

"Some things are better than others." I pick a can off the shelf. "Pretty much any fruit is good. But you've got to be careful with meat."

Tal looks revolted. "No one buys canned meat."

"I've got a bunch of ham in my personal storage." And then, because canned ham probably deserves an explanation: "It's important to have lots of different kinds of foods so you don't get appetite fatigue. If you eat the same things every day, you'll get sick of them and that's just as bad for you as whatever disaster you're trying to survive."

"A disaster," he repeats, slowly. "Your *personal* storage?" I pick at my cardigan collar. He's going to find out eventually.

"Yeah. I'm sort of a . . . prepper."

"Like for doomsday?" he asks, even more slowly this time.

I hesitate. This is a lot all at once. Doomsday can wait another day. "Like for any kind of natural disaster. Floods, earthquakes."

Tal stares at me for a moment, like he's trying to solve a riddle. "Is it your parents?"

"My parents?"

"Did they get you into it? Is your whole family a bunch of weird preppers?"

"No," I say, resenting the implication that *I'm* a weird prepper. I'm a normal prepper, as far as that goes. When you spend practically years of your life browsing the forums, you see what weird really looks like. You meet the really hard-core survivalists, the ones with bunkers in the woods and bullet magazines to last decades. In comparison, I'm the picture of normalcy. June Cleaver with freeze-dried casseroles. Betty Crocker in a gas mask.

"My parents aren't into this at all," I say. "They hate it. They blame it all on my anxiety. As if my anxiety caused the tides to rise, and erratic weather patterns all over the world, and potential economic collapse. Like my personal anxiety did all those things."

"They don't even have food storage?" Tal asks.

Every family in our church is supposed to be prepared for a minor disaster—bottled water, nonperishable food, space blankets and lamps with extra batteries, that kind of thing. But it's not enough to make it through something big, not nearly enough to stretch through an endless winter. It's about self-sufficiency, not surviving a destroyed world.

"That doesn't count."

He shrugs. "Maybe it does."

"You sound just like them," I say. "'Oh, Ellis, we're prepared. Oh, Ellis, you don't need another pocket water filter. Oh, Ellis, don't tell us a turkey wishbone could be whittled into a fish hook, you're *ruining Thanksgiving.*'"

"That's not what I mean."

"Then, what?"

"It's the mind-set, you know? Be on alert. Be ready. Be afraid."

Maybe LDS people care more about emergency preparation than most people. But not everyone's ancestors spent years on their feet, getting kicked out of Missouri and Illinois, watching their prophet murdered by a mob. They were on alert because they had to be, I remind Tal.

"Yeah, okay," he says. "Don't oversell it. There were a lot of people way worse off than our pioneer ancestors."

"I know that."

"Like, for instance, all the Native people they trampled along the way."

"Oh my gosh, Tal, obviously," I say. "It doesn't come close. But it did happen. There really *was* an extermination order against Mormons in Missouri. They really *did* get massacred at Haun's Mill."

"Yeah, and then they turned around and slaughtered a bunch of random people at Mountain Meadows and stole their kids."

I throw up my hands. "It's not a competition!"

"I'm just saying, if it were, you would lose."

"And *I'm* just saying they had good reasons for staying prepared," I say. "But I don't do this because I'm Mormon. I do this because I'm me."

He shakes his head. "You of all people shouldn't be afraid."

"Of the *apocalypse?*"

"Not if you believe it'll end with Jesus coming back to rule over Earth for a thousand years of sunshine and joy," he says.

And he's right. That's what the scriptures say. After years of pain and suffering on Earth, after natural disaster, war, and plague has ripped the world to shreds, Jesus Christ will return in glory and usher in the Millennium, a thousand years of perfect peace throughout the universe.

*But not for everyone. Not for you.*

"We all still have to live through it," I counter. "There's no Rapture, you know Mormons don't believe in that. There's no avoiding what the world could become. We could all still *die*."

"But what's it matter if you die in a nuclear bombing or a flood or a zombie attack?" Tal presses. "What's it matter if you'll just be resurrected, perfect and whole, with your perfect forever family in the Celestial Kingdom?"

"Because maybe I won't!" I burst out. "Because maybe I'm not worthy. Not worthy enough. Maybe I won't make it there."

> *Too much. Way, way too much, even for a friend, and he isn't your friend.*

"You don't think you're worthy?" Tal asks quietly.

I knew it was too much. "I don't know. Never mind."

"Why wouldn't you be worthy?" I look away, but Tal moves so he's in my line of vision again. "Why not?"

I don't know. I should be. I follow the rules, I pray every night, and I almost never fall asleep during early-morning seminary class.

> *Your family is worthy. Your family is good and kind and holy, true believers, effortless believers.*

I believe. If I doubt, I doubt my doubts. I turn cartwheels to fit myself into my faith. I stay in the boat even though the water is rough and the shore looks so peaceful. I work to believe, and that alone should make me worthy. So why don't I ever feel like I am?

> *One day your doubt might be stronger than your belief. One day you might not fit into your faith.*

> *One day you might not be able to live the life your*
> *family wants for you.*

There's a nagging, clawing feeling in the pit of my stomach, and sometimes it feels like it could slice me open entirely. And it can't, I can't let it, because who knows what would spill out?

> *A faceless man with a crew cut, you in a white*
> *wedding dress.*
> *A baby, or two, or three, who look like angels to*
> *everyone but you.*
> *Lia Lemalu's hair in the sunlight.*

"I don't know," I say. "I'm just not. I need—"

"What?" Tal prods.

"Time. I need more time."

"To do what?"

"Become someone different."

"You don't need to be different, you're perfect," Tal says. My eyes widen, and so do his.

"Um," I say.

"I didn't mean that," he says quickly. "That's not—"

"I know," I say.

> *Of course he didn't mean that, you're the opposite*
> *of perfect, the anti-perfect, everyone knows it, and*
> *if you thought Tal would be different you're wrong.*

"You're not perfect. I'm not perfect, no one is, no one has to be. You don't have to be."

"But that's the whole point!" I say. "The entire point of being on Earth is get to a body, make good choices with it, and be as close to perfect as possible."

"God," Tal says. "Someone has done such a mind-fuck on you."

"Tal!"

"Is that really worse? Is me saying 'fuck' worse than someone beating you down with 'perfect'? Is it worse than you thinking that if you aren't perfect, you're worthless?" He shakes his head. "No one expects you to be perfect in this life, not even those old dudes in Salt Lake City. I'm not a fan of the church. You know I'm not. But that's not even *doctrine*."

"I can be closer, though, I need to be closer, because that's what a person gets judged on. How close they came. That's what determines if you go to the Celestial Kingdom with your family or—"

Then I stop, because I don't want to say it. Mormons don't believe in a binary heaven-or-hell situation. There are levels to the afterlife, different kingdoms that spirits are sorted into, and good people don't suffer eternally in a lake of fire. The highest level is the Celestial Kingdom, where families get to be together. When you're sealed together on Earth, you're sealed for all eternity. Families can be together forever—people say it all the time.

That's the key word, though—*can*. Not *will*. It won't happen if someone's unworthy, and certainly not if someone leaves the church and never comes back. Like Tal.

But as I'm standing across from him, I realize I don't believe that. I don't believe the God I love would separate a person like Tal—someone funny, and kind, and only sometimes prickly—from his mother or his half siblings, I don't believe He'd ever do that to one of His children. I know it like I know that the sky is blue and my name is Ellis. There's doctrine, and then there's belief.

Maybe my belief is stronger than I thought. Maybe it's different than I thought.

"You are worthy," Tal says. "If there were a Celestial Kingdom, you'd get there. I believe that."

Tal, who doesn't believe in so many things. Tal, who questions and doubts everything. Tal believes that.

"Thank you," I say, and it's almost a whisper.

"No big deal," he says, sticking his hands in his pockets.

"You're worthy too," I tell him. "You should get to be there too. With your family, I believe you'll get to be there—"

He smiles thinly. "It's a relief, really. I don't want to become a god and create worlds. I didn't even like building dioramas in elementary school."

That's a pretty flippant way to describe deep doctrine, and I almost say that. But then—maybe there's a reason he talks about it that way. Maybe it makes the whole thing hurt less. Everyone deserves to hurt less.

"Well," I say, and find myself stepping closer. "If I were creating a perfect world"—I swallow—"I'd want you in it."

"You don't have to wait, you know," Tal says. "You shouldn't have to wait for that."

I close the gap with another step. "For what?"

"For the afterlife. Whatever comes next. You deserve to be happy on Earth, too."

Does happiness just come to a person? Does it arrive in a package labeled and addressed? Or is it something you have to want, something you have to take rather than ask for?

An inch away from Tal's body, eye to eye, I think about how I could take it.

That's how we're standing—almost touching, barely breathing—when Sam rounds the corner and crashes straight into Tal.

"They were out of éclairs." He holds out something that looks like beef jerky, only flatter. "You guys want some dehydrated fruit leather?"

When I get home, all the living room furniture is pushed up against the walls. Em is standing in the middle of the rug in leggings, a T-shirt, and socks. She stares, unblinking, at the far wall, then throws herself into a spin. I'd call it a pirouette, but the last time I did, she patted my arm and said it was a *fouette, actually.* Her left foot doesn't even touch the ground as she spins once, twice, three times. Em is even more spectacular in practice than in recitals. In recitals, they have to make it look effortless. In practice, you can see Em's clenched teeth and razor-sharp focus, the ache in her legs she's pushing past. You can see how hard it really is. You can see how *good* she really is.

She drops out of the spin with a sigh.

"That was amazing," I say, leaning against the doorframe. She startles and turns to me.

"I wish you'd tell Miss Ostrevsky," Em says. "She says my spotting needs work."

"Your spotting?" I doubt you can spot anything under those blinding stage lights.

"Spotting the wall. It's something you have to do when you turn." She points. "You pick a spot. You focus on the spot. And you keep your eyes on that spot as you spin."

That makes zero sense. "But you're turning. At some point, your head's the other way. How can you keep your eye on something you can't see?"

Her face lights up. "I'll show you. That's the best way to get better, right, teach someone else?"

Em takes my arm and guides me to the center of the room. She puts her hands on my shoulders, which requires standing on her tiptoes. She points at the wall. "Choose a spot, right at your eye level. Focus on it, really hard, and *don't* take your eyes off it."

I struggle to find a spot. The wall is just one vast, perfect ocean of light blue. Eventually I find an almost minuscule dent. Em takes my hands in hers and lays them gently on my shoulders. "Keep your hands here."

I do, even though it reminds me of Mom correcting my posture.

"Start turning to the right," Em commands. "Slowly. Slower. Keep your head still and your eyes on the spot. Your body moves, your head doesn't."

This is unnatural. My head wants to turn with my body; they're attached. Ideally. I'm starting to feel for those Barbie dolls I decapitated as a kid.

"When you absolutely have to, whip your head around and find the spot." I attempt that, but stumble and lose the spot. I look over at Em and shrug.

She tilts her head. "That's supposed to prevent you from losing your balance."

"Well, you tried."

She wrinkles her nose. "You're doing it again."

"That's okay."

"Ellis, you're doing it again." She folds her arms. "Did you expect to be good at it instantly?"

It's not that. I'm good at so few things, and terrible at so many. That's fine when I'm on my own, in my room, but not with someone else's eyes on me. I don't like people seeing me fail. But Em looks serious, and I don't have anything better to do, so I fix my feet, find the spot, and try again.

I fail again. I fail a third time. But I fail with more grace.

"Miss Ostrevsky says that usually, we know exactly where our bodies are in space," Em tells me as I whip my head around again. "That's how we keep our balance without trying. But when you're spinning, your body gets confused. It thinks it's free-falling. It can't figure out where it is."

"Proprioception."

"What?"

"That's what it's called. A body's unconscious spatial orientation."

"Proprioception!" Em says with triumph, like I've given her a treasure hunt clue. "So if you don't have that, you need something else to help you stay upright. You need your eyes, and your eyes need to stay where you put them."

When she puts it like that, it feels scientific. It feels like a fact. I stare at my spot on the wall. I imagine myself as a horse with blinders. I imagine myself looking through an old-fashioned telescope. When I twist my head around, my eyes zero back in on the spot, and I remain upright.

"Hey!" Em says. "There you go."

It wasn't beautiful like hers, and I doubt I'd be able to do it in a real spin, but I stayed upright, and that's a victory. I failed, until I didn't. I kept my eyes ahead and my feet solidly planted. I kept my balance as the world around me tilted.

Em's grinning like that creepy cat clock Grammy Kit had. "I knew you could do it," she says. I should be annoyed by such self-satisfaction from my baby sister, but I'm not.

"I'll let you practice," I say. "Thanks for the lesson."

"Wait, can you braid my hair first?"

I nod, and she places herself in front of me, shaking out her long hair, blond with the occasional ribbon of chestnut. I

199

separate the top layer. For all of Em's absurd flexibility, she's never been able to French braid her own hair. Mom can do it, but I'm better, with both Em's hair and mine. It's never seemed like a skill, something to brag about. But as I plait and fold, I reconsider. If not a skill, maybe it's a gift. Not a gift of mine, but a gift for Em. She can gift me with dance lessons and grit, and I can gift her with new words for her thoughts and beautiful hair.

I've nearly finished when I notice an odd twist in the braid, halfway up. And a strand I missed, near Em's ear. The left side is slightly uneven, now that I look closer. I almost let the braid go, almost run my hands through her hair, almost start over. But then I don't. Em can't see that it's imperfect. She probably wouldn't care that it was. It's imperfect, but that doesn't mean it's worthless.

I slip my own hair tie off my wrist and finish the braid.

# FOURTEEN

**TEEN MOVIES HAD** led me to believe homecoming was about football and maybe a dance, but two years of real high school have clued me in: it's Mardi Gras for teenagers. At least at this school. We don't even call it homecoming.

"Why do you think they named it Rally Day?" Sam wonders aloud during lunch as he rolls a joint. The Park is packed with kids in face paint, school colors, and varying levels of intoxication.

"I think we're supposed to be rallying the football team to murder our rivals," Theo says.

"Wait, who's our rival?" Tal asks.

Theo shrugs. "Sobriety?"

"No kidding. This place is lawless," I mutter as two boys I half recognize from AP US History drink out of a water bottle I'm certain is not filled with water. "It's like a Roman bacchanalia."

"Fewer goat sacrifices," Sam points out.

Behind Sam, on the other side of the Park, Hannah sits on a bench, something small and gray in her hands.

"Be back in a second," I tell them. Tal frowns, but doesn't stop me.

I slide down next to Hannah on the bench. She looks up and smiles, but it's thin and tight.

"What's that?" I peer over her shoulder at the small package in her lap. It's badly wrapped, in what looks like a thicker kind of newspaper print.

"I think it's a present," she says.

"From who?"

She clears her throat. "Prophet Dan."

I feel a stab of betrayal. She finally found him, after all this time, and she didn't come looking for me?

"When did he give it to you?" I ask. "What did he say? About your visions, will he help us?"

Hannah shakes her head. "It was in my tree, this morning. Tied to a branch."

She's been carrying it around all day, unopened. Maybe she's scared to see what's inside. I touch the package.

"Do you want me to?" I offer.

Hannah shakes her head and unwraps. She's going painfully slow, pulling at each piece of tape instead of tearing, until finally, we can both see what's inside.

"Oh," she whispers, like she's just gotten a paper cut. Surprise and a little bit of pain.

All I have is surprise. "It's . . . a fish."

Not a real one. A stuffed toy, the kind you'd give to a little kid. When Hannah picks it up, its fins and tail flop.

"I liked fish," Hannah says softly, rubbing her thumb against its plush blue scales. "When I was little. I knew all the kinds."

How would Prophet Dan know that? Did he see it, just like Hannah sees the end of the world? I almost ask, but Hannah's curled into herself, her eyes welled up, holding the fish in her hands like it's breakable. Maybe this isn't the best time.

So instead, I pick up the wrapping paper. It's crumpled, torn, and taped back together out of order, but the print's still visible. Not that it makes much sense. Half of it seems like a menu, with words like *lentils* and *eggplant* and *cashew ricotta*. The other half is random adjectives.

"Giving. Evolved. Humble," I read. "What *is* this?"

Hannah, who has been focused on the fish, looks over my shoulder. With a gasp of recognition, she plucks the wrapping out of my hands.

"Thanks Café," she breathes out.

"Huh?"

"Thanks Café, it's this vegan restaurant. All the food is called something positive." She points. "See, the tempeh Caesar salad is called Glorious, so you have to tell the waiter, 'I am Glorious' and then when he brings it to you, he says, 'You are Glorious' and it's supposed to be affirming, or whatever."

Sometimes, this city is a parody of itself.

"We have to go," Hannah says. "It's on Shattuck, it's not far."

I don't understand. It's not a clue, it's just wrapping paper. Weird wrapping paper. "Why?"

"He's been to the restaurant. Where else would he have gotten it?"

"I don't know, from their trash?"

"Pretty sure they recycle."

"But so what if he has been to the restaurant?" I ask. "I doubt he's still there."

"He might be a regular. They might know where he hangs out." She scrambles to her feet.

"Wait," I say, because I still have so many questions. *Why did Prophet Dan send you this? Why does it seem like he's hiding from you? How many things aren't you telling me?*

"Come on," Hannah says, holding out her hand to help me up.

Now? She wants to go right now? "I have class."

"Like anyone's really teaching today."

"I have a test in English." Not that my grades matter at this point—I just don't want my teacher to think I skipped it because I was drinking in the Park. It might be the end of days, but I still have standards.

"You can make it up," Hannah says. So casually, so definitively, like she's already seen the future and the future is me following her around like a puppy on a leash. Like I always have.

*No.* I don't want to trot along at her heels anymore, I don't want her to assume that I will. I don't say *No.* I only think it. But I don't move, either.

"Come on," Hannah repeats, but it isn't commanding, like before. It's more of a beg. "Come with me."

"After school," I say. I want to help her. I do. But this isn't a beehive, and I'm not a drone. "We'll go after school."

"It'll be fast. You'll barely miss fourth period."

Not every language has a singular word for *no.* Even in English, I wonder how often people actually use it as a full sentence. A straight refusal. I wonder if I can do that, say *no* without caveats or explanation. Not just to Hannah, to anyone.

My feet stay on the grass. I literally dig in my heels.

Hannah reaches closer. "Ellis. Please."

"Hey," Tal says, appearing out of nowhere at Hannah's side. I didn't even see him walk up. I wonder how much he heard. "Can I talk to you real quick?"

Hannah frowns. "We were just about to—"

"Real quick," Tal says again, then steers Hannah a few feet away. Purposefully out my earshot. I don't try to eavesdrop, exactly, but I do watch them. Hannah's got her arms folded across her chest. Defensive. Tal's talking with his hands, and he's talking a lot. Word by word, they're getting louder, and I don't think either of them realize it. Finally, it looks like Hannah's had enough.

"You know, Tal, you don't know everything!" she shouts.

"I know you have her completely snowed," Tal says, matching her volume.

"She's helping me."

"I know you think this is helping, but—"

"Which is more than I can say for you."

I'm far away, but I think Tal flinches. He runs a hand through his hair. "Hannah."

Their voices drop, or maybe I can't hear over the pounding in my chest. Are they talking about me? I am helping Hannah, and I think I'm the only one. But the way Tal's saying it, it's like he thinks I'm not smart enough to have chosen that for myself. Like I'm helpless. It prickles my skin like hives.

"You don't know what's best for me," Hannah says, her voice rising again. "And I know you think you're her . . . *knight in stoner armor*, but you don't know what's best for her, either."

"She doesn't even know who she's looking for!" Tal shouts. It's loud enough that for the first time, Hannah looks away. And straight at me. My heart flops into my stomach, because now I'm certain. The *she* is *me*.

"Well?" Tal throws his hands up. "Does she?"

Hannah is silent for a long moment, eyes still on me. She spins away from Tal and stalks back in my direction. I open my mouth, ready to tell her I'm not going. To actually refuse when she asks. But she doesn't ask. She doesn't say anything. All she does is scoop up her backpack and walk away from school as the end-of-lunch bell rings, without a word.

Without me.

★ ★ ★

My afternoon classes pass by in a blur. I can't stay focused on anything, and not just because of the Rally Day chaos.

*She doesn't even know who she's looking for.*

I know Hannah hasn't told me everything. But I know who we're looking for—we're looking for the only person she believes can help us survive the end of the world.

But then again—what has Hannah done, to prepare people, to warn them? Not enough. Maybe she doesn't know how. And maybe I haven't pushed her hard enough. I'm not nearly as helpless as Tal thinks I am. Maybe it's time for me to stop following Hannah around and make some decisions of my own.

I'm the last one out of the locker room after PE, and by the time I'm dressed, the field hockey girls are starting to change for their away game. I go to my locker to retrieve my backpack, and find Paloma Flores in the same bay. I've had at least four classes with her over the past two years, but I know almost nothing about her. She plays field hockey. She wrote the best opinion piece our school paper ever printed, in which she called the all-male Barbecue Club "a school-sanctioned cult of toxic masculinity." And she dated Hannah.

"Hey," she says.

I smile back. "Hi."

We watch as a senior girl walks by, glassy-eyed and cradling a half-empty water bottle like it's her infant child.

Paloma shakes her head. "This day is always such a shitshow."

"Yeah," I agree.

"All my classes were basically free periods," she says. "We watched *The Godfather* in chemistry. That's not even about science."

"My Spanish teacher at least tried. But have you ever seen someone try to play Scrabble Español drunk?" I ask. "It's painful."

"Yeah, my tito Carlo, every Christmas. Just replace Scrabble Español with Pusoy dos." Then, off my confused look: "Card game. Filipino thing. A little bit like poker."

As she stuffs her bag in her locker, I realize this is an opportunity to learn more about who Hannah was, before I knew her. Another piece of the puzzle. Another part of the truth, since I clearly don't have it all.

"You and Hannah Marks," I blurt out, but then don't know what else to say without sounding creepy.

"What about her?"

I steer into the skid. "You two were together, right?"

She closes her locker. "We dated for almost a year."

"But not anymore."

"That is what *dated* means."

I decide to power through the skid and over a cliff. "What happened?"

Paloma leans against the locker bank. She folds her arms. "Are you interested in her, or me?"

My cheeks burn. "Neither."

She laughs. "Well, I'm taken, sorry, and if it's Hannah, save yourself the trouble. Or maybe just save yourself. In every sense."

I take a step back. "Hannah's not . . . dangerous."

"Of course not," Paloma says. "She's funny, and sweet, or at least she was, before she got so—" Paloma puffs up her cheeks with air.

"Weird?"

She blows out. "Beyond."

"Because of her dreams?"

"The one about all her teeth falling out? Lots of people have that dream."

Hannah never told Paloma about her dreams. Hannah never told her own girlfriend about her visions. Why?

"I'm only telling you so you don't get too invested," Paloma says. "Friendship or otherwise. Hannah got really into—what's it called, when you go and live in the desert because the world is evil?"

It takes me a second to locate the word. "Asceticism?"

Paloma shrugs. "Probably. Hermit bullshit. Beyond weird."

It's more than that. An ascetic isn't necessarily a hermit, though they could be. An ascetic is anyone who practices self-denial or purposefully detaches themselves from earthly pleasures. Some of it is simple stuff, like living frugally, but it can be hard-core and scary, too, like fasting for days or sleeping on a bed of nails.

"Hannah's not a hermit," I tell Paloma. "She lives in a house. She's sixteen, it wouldn't even be legal."

Paloma puts her hand on her hip. "It started with gifts."

Even more evidence to the contrary. Hermits don't give gifts, unless you count spiritual advice, which I guess I should, as a religious person.

"There was this one coat of hers I always loved," Paloma continues. "One day, she gave it to me. And I thought, okay, maybe a late birthday gift. Then came sweaters. And jeans. And books and DVDs and there probably would have been shoes, too, but we're not the same size."

Okay, that is a little weird.

"She must have given almost all of it away, her clothing, because eventually it was a rotation. Three pairs of pants. Five or six shirts. That one stupid Cal sweatshirt that doesn't even fit her. She said it was simpler. And *I* said, is it really simpler if you have to do laundry every week?"

Now that I think about it, Paloma's right. The clothes I've seen Hannah wear could fill a single drawer. Even when she came to church with me, it was a shirt I'd already seen and her mom's pants. And that sweatshirt. Every single day.

"And fine, do a capsule wardrobe if the spirit moves you, I guess," Paloma says. "But then she stopped cutting her hair. She wouldn't go to movies, she wouldn't go shopping, even if it was just for me. Then I see Laura Jacobs wearing the earrings I got Hannah for our six-month anniversary, and she says Hannah gave them to her. I storm over to her house after school and go into her room, and it's all gone. Her clothes, except for a few outfits. Her books, except for, like, this stack of weird text-books about mystics and hermits and whatever. Her room was basically empty. Like she'd just moved in."

No wonder Hannah wouldn't let me go upstairs.

"I *get* big dramatic gestures," Paloma says. "But this was something else."

"What did she say?" I ask. "Did she say why?"

"She said . . ." Paloma hesitates, though I can't tell if it's hard to remember, or just hard to say. "Hannah said she didn't have a choice. It was the only way to make things right again."

"Make what right?" I wonder aloud.

"If you're looking for logic," she says, "look somewhere else."

"Is that why you two broke up? Because she gave away the earrings?"

Paloma stares at me incredulously. "We broke up because she wouldn't talk to me. We broke up because she didn't trust me enough to tell me what was wrong."

Hannah hasn't told me her secrets, either. Maybe she doesn't trust me, either. Maybe she doesn't trust anyone, even the people she cares about the most.

"Hannah's not exactly attached to the world," Paloma says, turning to go, "and that means you shouldn't get too attached to her."

## FIFTEEN

**WHEN IT'S COLD** or raining Telegraph Avenue looks like any block in a college town. There's a drug store, a bagel shop. Stores that sell branded sweatshirts and blue books. But on a day like today—bright, sunny, and unseasonably warm for early November—Telegraph comes to life. A college kid devours two slices of pizza in one gulp, like a reticulated python consuming a goat. Vendors' carts and stands crowd the already narrow street. There's a girl doing henna body art. A lady selling tie-dyed T-shirts to tourists. A man in rainbow suspenders and no shirt hawking bumper stickers that say THE PEOPLE'S REPUB-LIC OF BERKELEY and feature a Cal Golden Bear hugging a Communist Party sickle.

It smells like weed. It smells like the incense used to cover up that weed. It smells like home.

"I still don't know about this," Hannah says, her hands dug deep in her pockets.

It's been nearly a week since she walked off without me in the Park. She found me later, to apologize for pressuring me. I didn't mention what I'd overheard, and neither did she. And when she asked if I wanted to keep looking for Prophet Dan this weekend, I agreed, on one nonnegotiable condition: that she take the plunge and tell the world about her visions.

"This is a good spot," I assure Hannah. "It's a T. We'll get the people going up Bancroft *and* everyone going down Telegraph."

She looks skeptical. But she's been skeptical of just about everything I've suggested, evangelism-wise. No, we couldn't go door-to-door, it was creepy and we'd get the cops called on us. I told her practically every eighteen-year-old boy in my church does exactly that for two straight years and no one gets arrested, but this didn't sway her.

No, she wouldn't get up and make speeches downtown, or at school, or even in the middle of the Cal campus where these things are practically expected. She isn't good in front of crowds.

No, we couldn't make flyers—*not even flyers*—because all she knows is the date, and what good would that really do?

And then I suggested Telegraph, where she wouldn't be put on the spot and we'd still get to talk to lots of people. "Who knows," I said. "We might even see Prophet Dan."

So here we are.

"Are you ready?" I ask her.

"Not really."

"Come on, Hannah." I scan the crowds, trying to pick out someone approachable. "Shoulder to the wheel."

"What the hell does that mean?"

I put on my brightest, sunniest smile. "It means buck up, buttercup."

Here are three of the people we talk to:

A couple waiting for their friends outside a restaurant

An older man shopping at the jewelry stand

A college girl who is very and obviously hungover

Here are the people we convert:

No one. I still think flyers would have helped.

I get better, as we go along. My explanation of our message is smoother, clearer. The last time, my voice doesn't shake at all, and neither do my legs. Hannah only gets worse. Every single time, she mutters something vague about snow, and then turns her head away. Outwardly, I smile and thank them for their time. Inwardly, I'm seething at Hannah, who has to be the worst street preacher I've ever seen. And I've seen a few.

"Are you okay?" I ask finally. "You seem kind of . . . off."

"I'm fine," Hannah says. "A little light-headed."

"Do you want me to get you some water? Or maybe a bagel, Noah's is just down the—"

She's already sidling away. "I've actually got this errand, so."

"We barely started!"

"I've just got to drop something off. With a guy. It's close by."

"What do you need to drop off?"

She waves the question off. "Don't worry about it."

I hate it when people say that. I hate that they assume it's an option for me, *I hate that*.

"Of course I'm going to worry!" I shout at her, throwing my hands up. "I'm not capable of not worrying about it. It's built into my faulty toaster of a brain, *of course I'm going to worry*."

"Ellis," she hisses, eyes darting around, as if anyone's paying attention to us. This is Berkeley, we could be jousting on unicycles and we wouldn't be the weirdest thing to stare at. "Would you please chill?"

"No." I fold my arms. "No. I won't. Because there's something you're not telling me."

She chews on the inside of her mouth. "I don't know what you're talking—"

"Yes, you do," I say. "There's something big you're not telling me, there's something weird going on and I'm sick of pretending there isn't, and we only have less than two months until . . ." I take a giant breath. "If you can't trust me enough to tell me what's going on, why should I trust you?"

Hannah stands very still, her arms wrapped around herself. She sighs. She nods.

"Okay," she says. "I'll tell you."

## SIXTEEN

"I CAN'T BELIEVE you hang out here alone," I say to Hannah as we sit on a chipped-paint picnic table in People's Park. "I'd be freaked out."

To tell the truth, I *am* freaked out, even with Hannah by my side. We're two teen girls in clean clothes. We obviously don't belong here.

She looks at me with a bit of pity. "Why would I be freaked out?"

"Well." I look around the park, at the scattered mini liquor bottles. I can't see any needles, but I bet there are some. "They drink, don't they? And do drugs?"

"Some do. And wouldn't you want something to make you forget you were living on the street? If you were cold and tired and dealing with some serious shit, wouldn't you want a drink?"

"I'm Mormon."

She shrugs. "I'm not a drinker, either. But I might be, if this were my life."

I've never thought about it like that. It's always been about choices. We've all been given a body and the agency to make choices with that body. All choice takes is willpower, I thought. But maybe it's not that simple. Maybe some choices aren't all our doing. Maybe sometimes, genetics or bad luck or fate pushes our hand.

"But what about, like . . . that guy." I nod my head at an older man walking in circles around a bench, carrying on an animated conversation with no one.

"His name's Jerry."

"He's talking to himself."

"He has schizophrenia."

"And that doesn't make you nervous?"

"Why would that make me nervous?"

"Come on." She stares at me. I wait. She says nothing. "He's obviously really sick. He could attack you. He could be dangerous."

"You know, Ellis," she says evenly, "if you don't know what you're talking about, it's okay not to say anything at all."

My face burns. My spine coils.

> You offended her. You offended her and don't even
> know why, which only makes it worse. You are the
> RMS Titanic in human form.

"I'm sorry," I say. "I didn't mean to—whatever I did, I'm sorry."

"Jerry," Hannah says, pushing dirt off the bench seat with her shoe, "is a lot more likely to hurt himself than me. Or be attacked by someone else. People with mental illnesses are targets way more often than they're perpetrators." She sighs. "Mental illness is—"

"You don't need to explain mental illness to me." I have one. Hannah doesn't.

"No offense," Hannah says, "but no one thinks a person with anxiety is a public menace. They save that for psychosis. Or delusions." She points at herself.

"You're not delusional."

She shakes her head. "Just because you don't think so doesn't mean other people feel the same way."

She must mean her parents. And maybe Martha, since that's got to be why Hannah's in therapy. But didn't Martha tell me that dreams don't count? Hannah's not having dreams, though, not the normal kind. She's having visions in her sleep. Is the only difference between a vision and a delusion whether someone else believes it? Does it take ten people believing it, or a million? Was every belief on Earth once a single person's delusion, until enough people with enough power believed it?

Or does it take only one person, no matter how powerless?

Hannah shifts on the bench, looking across the park at a tall, lean man in a long brown coat. He's older, with tightly coiled hair and a military-green rucksack. Hannah cups her hands around her mouth. "Chris!"

The tall man turns his head. He raises a hand in greeting as he walks over to us. "How are you doing today?" he asks Hannah.

"I'm alive. You?"

"It's like you read my mind," he says, then flicks his eyes over to me. "Hello."

"Chris, Ellis. Ellis, Chris," Hannah says.

Chris nods. "Nice to meet you."

I start to say it back, but stop short, because the rucksack slung over his shoulder is *moving*.

"Your bag," I say, as if he doesn't know it's moving. "It's—?"

The world's most adorable shepherd puppy pops his head out of the rucksack.

"Oh!" I squeal, and then feel completely ridiculous. "Um. Your puppy is very cute, sir."

Hannah hides a laugh behind her hand. Chris sets the rucksack on the ground, and the puppy wriggles out. "You want to hold him?"

I have never wanted anything more. "Yes, please."

He scoops the puppy up and places him in my arms.

This is how I die. Of joy.

"What's his name?" I ask as the puppy licks my arm.

"Frank Zappa," Chris and Hannah say at the same time.

"Like the musician?"

"Like the legend," Chris says. He turns to Hannah. "So what's up?"

Hannah jerks her head toward the basketball court. "Let's talk over there."

While Chris and Hannah talk, I play with Frank Zappa, letting him gnaw on my hair and failing to eavesdrop on their conversation. It's taking all my willpower and fear of divine retribution not to kidnap this puppy. I've never had a dog. My mom grew up rural, where dogs were meant to be useful, not pampered. My dad is allergic.

I'd never *really* steal Frank Zappa, of course, but Chris doesn't know that. Chris doesn't know me at all, but he trusted me to take care of his most precious possession. I couldn't do that. I couldn't choose trust over fear.

Or maybe I just haven't. Yet.

Hannah and Chris head back over. Frank Zappa wriggles off my lap and bounds over to his owner. Chris pulls a leash out of his pocket and clips it to the puppy's collar. His bag looks full.

"Good to meet you," Chris says to me.

"You too," I say, then lean forward to scratch Frank Zappa behind his soft ears. "Bye, buddy."

He looks to Hannah. "No promises. I'll do my best, but . . ."

She chews her lips. Nods. "Thanks, Chris."

"Call if you hear something. You've got my number."

"I couldn't forget it," she says, and they both laugh. They wave to each other, then Hannah starts walking to the park exit near the Christian Science church and I scramble to follow.

"What did you mean?" I ask as we cross the street. "That you know his number?"

"Oh," she says, "it was my phone, first. I gave it to him."

I always assumed she didn't have a phone because her parents wouldn't let her have one, or she was taking a strong stand

220

against modern tech. "You gave him your phone?"

"Yeah."

"Why?"

"He needed one."

*And you didn't?* I think, but don't say.

"Hey," she says, shifting her backpack, "Do you have to go home right away?"

I told my parents I was doing a service day with girls from church. This is the perfect excuse, because Mom doesn't like the woman in charge of my Laurels group and will therefore never ask about it. Not that she'd admit it. What Mom says is, "Sister Miller is always *so* well put-together." What Mom means is, Sister Miller is a snotty jerk who never shows up for her church-cleaning assignment.

"I've got time," I tell Hannah. "Do you want to go back to campus and try street-contacting again?"

"No. I want to show you something."

"Just for ten minutes," I suggest, trying not to let my impatience creep into my voice. What's wrong with her? Doesn't she understand how important this is? She has information no one else has access to. People have a right to know their lives are going to change.

"You said you wanted me to tell you everything," she says. "You said you wanted to know."

"Yeah, but—"

"Then we've got to get up there before the sun sets," she says, and picks up the pace.

Hannah leads me up Haste Street, toward Cal stadium, toward the Greek Theatre where we'll graduate. Would graduate. If the world weren't collapsing before our senior year even started. The streets incline steeply as we walk, until Hannah stops at a small, paved path tucked in between a university building and a Mediterranean-style house.

"Is this private property?" I ask, looking up the path.

"It's the fire trail. You're never been on it?"

"No." We haven't had a big fire here since before I was born. You can see it, though, in the Oakland hills. Large overgrown lots in prime locations, where a house once was. Even though the ash and char were cleared away decades ago, there's still a hole that hasn't been filled.

Hannah and I arrive at the top of the path, where concrete gives way to dusty dirt and patchy yellow grass. I catch my breath and look to my left. A huge hill is in front of us, the path winding up past where I can see. I take a breath, preparing to remind Hannah that I'm scared of heights, scared of falling, scared of breaking bones, and pretty much everything else associated with hiking, but she's already several feet in front of me. "Are you coming?" she calls over her shoulder. She doesn't wait for the answer before continuing up.

It's clear that either I'm going to walk forward or I'm going to be left behind.

I walk forward.

★ ★ ★

Hannah sets the pace, so we're up the hill to the first lookout point in what's probably fifteen minutes, but feels like hours to me. My legs are sore, my lungs burn, and my shoulders ache from tensing them. But I didn't fall.

"Isn't it amazing?" she says when we reach the lookout spot.

It is. From the bench off the trail, you can see downtown Berkeley, the port of Oakland with its towering cranes, all the way to San Francisco. It's hazy today, but if it weren't, you could probably see the Farallon Islands, too. In the gradually dimming afternoon light, the bay shimmers and the city gleams.

I slump down on the bench, focusing out onto the water. I don't look past the cliff, just a few feet in front of us. I keep one hand on the bench seat and one ankle twisted around the bench leg. It's bolted into the earth, and I will myself to feel that steady too. After a moment, Hannah sits down next to me. Her gaze is straight ahead, but her eyes look unfocused. Like she's seeing what I'm seeing, but her mind is somewhere else entirely.

"Hannah." She doesn't look over. "Hey. Hannah."

She blinks, then rubs at her eye with one fist. "Yeah?"

"Why are we here?"

"On Earth? You'd have a better answer for that than me."

"Why are we on this hill?"

"This is the place."

"What place?"

"The place where it's going to happen. The place where we'll be when it does."

223

"The end of the world?" I ask, and Hannah nods. This isn't good. It's uncovered. There's no shelter at all. This might be the worst place to ride out an apocalyptic blizzard. "How do you know?"

"Breathe in," she orders, and I do. "What's it smell like?"

Clean, sharp air. Dirt. Urban wilderness. "Lots of things."

"Eucalyptus."

You can't really smell it up here, but she's right, we passed through a eucalyptus grove as we climbed.

"There's eucalyptus all over," I remind her. "In Tilden. At Lake Anza. Down by campus. How do you know it's *here*?"

"I just do."

"You've been here before," I say, and it isn't a question.

"We used to come every Saturday," she says, brushing her hair out of her eyes. "Early in the morning, all four of us."

*Four?* I think, but then remember. Hannah has a brother. She told me on our first walk together, but never mentioned him again. I guess they aren't close.

"It was Dad's idea," she continues. "I think he missed going to synagogue. Or, not that exactly, he was pretty done with religion, and my mom is, like, a third-generation atheist, but I think he missed that weekly *thing*, you know? One day of real rest."

There are so many religions, so many denominations to choose from. I'd never really considered you could have one no one else shared. A church without walls. A religion without authorities. A faith for you alone.

"He made his own church?" I ask.

"It wasn't church," she says, "and it wasn't just his. It was all of ours." She stares out onto the water. "My brother called it 'the place where the light comes in.'" She smiles. Then hesitates. Then speaks. "Danny called it that because he loved watching the sun get higher and higher in the sky. My mom told him he'd fry his retinas."

"Danny," I repeat, and that's not a question, either. I know what I heard. "You said—Danny."

She looks down at her lap. "That's my brother's name. Daniel Jacob Marks."

Daniel like Dan, the street preacher we've never been able to find. Danny, like Lydia called him. D, J, M, like the bolded first letters of the note stuffed into Hannah's backpack. A name, a name she's been so careful never to mention.

"Hannah," I ask, "where's your brother?"

She's quiet, until the sound of an engine breaks the silence. I look out to my right, where a car is climbing a paved road down below. Hannah looks too.

"It would be cool to live up here, don't you think?" she says lightly. Too lightly. "There's even a house right up the path. They rent it out for weddings and things." She points up the steep dirt path, but I don't see any house.

"Where is Danny?" I repeat.

She swallows. "Around."

"That's not much of an answer."

"It's the only one I have!" she snaps, and I shrink back at the sudden fierceness.

"I'm sorry, I—"

"I'm not avoiding the question," she says. "I'm not in denial. He's not dead, he's not away, he's not even missing, really. He's somewhere close by. I just don't know where."

Oh. Oh no.

"It started in his freshman year at Cal," she says, and then her voice hitches.

"You don't have to tell me," I say.

"I want to," she says. "More than anyone else, I think you'll understand."

I know she's about to tell me something terrible, something painful, but still, my heart swells.

"It happened in his freshman year at Cal," she begins again. "Or maybe it started earlier than that, because he was always—" She hesitates. "I don't know. Sensitive. Secretive. Maybe there were always things that hurt him. Things he couldn't tell us.

"The fall started off okay. I don't remember, it's not like I was paying attention to that, but my parents say it started off okay. Even when he was weirdly quiet or getting irritated about the smallest stuff, they thought he was just nervous about college. And his first semester, he actually seemed to like it. He was taking this History of Mysticism course he was in love with, he thought he might major in comparative religion." She smiles, just a little, at the memory. "He bought, like, twelve books that weren't even required, which pissed my parents off because that academic stuff's expensive and he didn't even use his student discount."

Those must be the textbooks Paloma saw, after Hannah purged her room. They must have belonged to Danny—Prophet Dan, who knows so much about religion and mysticism and visions. Hannah lied, but not all the way. She only lied as much as she had to.

"He'd come over for dinner every week," she continues. "At first. And it was like—every dinner, something new was . . . off."

"Off?"

"Like he'd be so nervous, even though it was only us. The next week, he'd refuse to eat what my dad made and wouldn't say why. Then he left this cryptic, scary voicemail on the home phone, saying he 'knew the truth about our family,' and my parents got really worried. They told him something was wrong, he needed help. They asked him to see a doctor, a therapist, someone. Then they begged him. He wouldn't go. He started talking to me. Only me. He told me our parents weren't really our parents. Or, no, I guess they were, but they were evil and going to hurt us both."

"Oh my gosh, Hannah."

"It was awful. Because he really believed it. He wasn't telling me to be *mean*, he was telling me because he was *terrified*."

"But how could he even think that?"

She bites her lip. "Because the human brain is complicated."

I do know that.

"So he's . . . schizophrenic? Or something else?"

She shakes her head. "He's never been diagnosed with anything."

"I mean, that *sounds* like—"

She shakes her head harder. "Bad idea."

"What is?"

"Diagnosing someone you don't know."

"Why didn't he get diagnosed by a doctor?"

"I told you, he wouldn't go."

"They can force people. Commit them."

"Would you like that?" she says, on a razor's edge. "If someone did that to you?"

"No," I admit. "But I'm not . . . sick. Not *that* sick."

"You could be," she says. "Five years from now. Ten. Tomorrow."

The words stick in me like needles. Like knives. I turn away from her.

"Sorry," Hannah says, and touches my hand. "I only meant, anyone could be."

Is that true? Are we all just one illness, one crisis away from losing control over our own lives?

"It was his whole life, this fear. It consumed him." Hannah pauses with the weight of that word. *Consumed*. It means—or meant, in the original Latin—something destroyed. Something broken down into parts that can't ever be rejoined.

"My parents threatened to withhold tuition if he didn't see someone. Not that it mattered. He stopped going to class. Around spring break, he left his dorm room in tatters and his roommate threatening to sue for pain and suffering. He smashed his cell phone and mailed me the pieces with a note saying I should destroy mine, too, so I couldn't be tracked. At first, he slept on friend's couches, we think. But eventually, he'd scare them, and they'd call us, and he'd leave. In April, we didn't hear a single word.

"I was coming back from Paloma's house, and it was dark," Hannah says. "This car pulls up alongside me. I didn't recognize it, so I kept walking. And it kept following me, and the driver rolled down the window. I'm thinking, great, can't wait for this jerk to start catcalling me or asking if I want a ride, but then he said my name."

"It was Danny?"

"I didn't recognize him, at first. I'd never seen him with a beard. And I said, where the fuck have you been, essentially, and he said, get in the car, essentially."

"Did you?"

"I thought—I don't know what I thought. I hoped he'd just been soul-searching, or something, gone on some road trip to clear his head. So, yeah, I got in the car."

Hannah pulls her hair back, twisting it into a ponytail with so much force it must hurt. I'm almost afraid to ask, but if I don't, she might not go on.

"And when you got in the car?" I prompt her.

"We drove around. We circled. Left turn after left turn."

That's to make sure no one's following you. If you still see them after four left turns, you're being tailed. I wonder if Hannah knows that.

"He was talking the whole time, about our parents, how I was in danger. And some stuff about UC Berkeley and an underground cult, I think, I'm not sure. He talked fast." She pulls her ponytail even tighter. "He always talked fast. Like if he didn't get it out, he'd explode. That was the weirdest part. Other than *what* he was saying—and the beard—it was still Danny. He was all there. There was just something . . . *else* there, too."

"What do you mean?" I ask.

"His delusion, I guess. That horrible, unshakeable, *real* thing. This was—" She swallows. "This *is* real to him. As real as this bench or that tree or . . ."

*Or your dreams, Hannah?* I think.

Hannah clears her throat. "So he was saying all this stuff, and I was telling him he was wrong, that he'd lost it. I'm not even being nice at this point. It's been so many months of my mom calling his RA, calling his friends, calling the police. My dad hasn't smiled since February, I haven't slept through the night in at least that long, and I'm so angry at him even though I know it isn't his fault."

"It wasn't your fault, either."

"I yelled at him. I called him crazy. Delusional. And other things. That part was my fault."

I wince, because that does hurt a person. "You were under so much stress."

"It broke his heart. I could tell. He said he was going out of town, somewhere Mom and Dad couldn't track him or send their 'people' after him. He said I had to come, that I'd never be safe here. He couldn't leave me alone here."

"You said no."

"Over and over until I was hoarse. Danny knew he was scaring me, and I could tell that broke his heart even more. We were still driving around, circle after circle, until finally he said"—she gulps—"that it was time to go. That we had to go. That I'd understand someday."

She's breathing fast now, and when I put my hand on her arm, I can feel her heartbeat pounding under the skin. Like mine, when I'm panicking. But she's not panicking. She's re-living.

"I did understand. I understood that I was not going back home tonight, not if he could help it. I understood that he was desperate. I understood that I had to make a choice, right now, or I might not be able to make one for a while. So I reach over—" She uncurls her arm into the empty air next to her. "And then I open the car door—" Her hand swings wide. "And then—"

"Then?"

"I jumped."

There's no air in my lungs. "You jumped?"

She nods.

"Out of a moving car?"

She nods again.

"Were you okay?" I ask, like an absolute child. Of course she was, or she'd still be in the hospital. Of course she wasn't, because she jumped out of a moving car.

"The falling was okay," she starts. "It didn't feel like anything. The falling felt safe. And I thought maybe I'd fall forever but then I hit the ground and at first you don't feel it, you know?"

I don't know. I don't know anything.

"You're just staring at the road. When you stand up, your legs are weak, because you landed on them, and your hands are wet, because you landed on them, too. Your palms are all blood and dirt and asphalt and so are your knees but you don't know that yet, you can't see them. And for a second, you can't even remember how you got there, in the road. But then you hear the car door shut and footsteps and you don't really remember even then but you run anyway."

"You ran after that?" I interrupt. "All scraped up?"

She shrugs. "Adrenaline is a hell of a drug."

"Hannah, I'm so sorry, I'm so—I don't know what to say."

"My dad didn't know what to say, either, when I called and he picked me up from the gas station. It was like he wasn't sure if he should be raging or sobbing." She laughs, and it sounds forced. "I was sobbing, that's the one I chose. After the adrenaline wore off and my whole body just . . . burned."

I wonder if it's anything like what I feel when I panic. I try to imagine it, but I can't. I'm so lucky I can't.

"You're so lucky you're safe," I tell Hannah.

"Safe?"

"Who knows what he could have done."

Her eyes flash. "He'd never hurt me."

"He made you jump out of a car!"

"No one made me do anything," she says, clipping her words off. "I jumped because I had to."

"You could have called the cops," I say. "If you'd had a phone."

"I had a phone then," she says. "But I kind of wanted my brother alive."

"What?"

"Sometimes, when the cops try to deal with someone living in a different reality, they get scared. Sometimes, when a person isn't together enough to realize *they* should be scared of the cops, bad things happen. Sometimes, people get shot."

My parents always told me to find a police officer if I was lost, or hurt, or scared. That they'd help me. I can't imagine how scary it must be to live in fear of the people who are supposed to help you. I'm lucky, unfairly lucky, to be unable to imagine.

"When he drove off—that's the last time I saw him. Mostly."

Mostly? I'm about to ask what she means by that, when she runs a hand along the red bracelet on her wrist. The one she found in my mailbox. And then it all clicks. The trips to People's Park. The packages tightly wrapped and handed over to Chris and Frank Zappa, the quiet conversations with the *Street Spirit* sellers and the stuffed fish in her tree. The uneasy sensation I have, sometimes, when I'm with Hannah. The feeling that we're being watched.

And then, Hannah takes a breath and tells me what I already know.

"Prophet Dan doesn't really exist," she says. "We've been looking for my brother."

"Oh," I breathe out. "Hannah . . ."

"You can understand," she says, almost as an afterthought, "why I'd want to find him. Now. Before the world ended."

I try to imagine Em sick, lost, in danger. It nearly rips my ventricles apart, just the imagining. Yes. I can understand.

"Why didn't you tell me?" I ask. "You could have told me who were we really looking for."

She shakes her head. "You didn't know me, you didn't believe in my dreams, yet. If I'd told about Danny right then, you would have thought . . ." She swallows, hard. "You would have thought I was like him."

It's probably true. I hate that it's probably true. "No, I wouldn't—"

"Of course you would have." She twists the sleeve of her hoodie. "Sometimes even I think it."

"You never needed someone else to interpret the dreams," I

say. "Did you?"

"I might have figured out the place on my own, with the eucalyptus, but I wouldn't have figured out the date. Even though it was so obvious."

"Because it's the solstice?"

"Because it's his birthday."

I don't have to ask whose birthday she means.

"You . . ." I pause, because I know she's just told me something huge, but why did she wait so long? "You lied to me, though. About everything."

If Hannah could lie about this, she could lie about other things.

She looks down at her lap. "I know. I'm sorry. I understand if . . . you don't feel like you can trust me."

Can I? Do I? I must, a little bit, because something in the back of my brain is already explaining this away, twisting it into something easier to swallow. Hannah lied, but because she had to. Hannah lied, but it's not like I haven't done that. Tal said I'm completely—what was it? Snowed. Like Hannah's words are relentless flurries, and they've buried me. Like she's a flesh-and-blood blizzard.

If Hannah could lie about this, she could lie about everything.

That's true. It's logical. It makes sense from the outside looking in, from a distance.

"But I swear, I didn't lie about seeing you in the dreams. I do need you." Hannah looks up and meets my eyes. She smiles. "I didn't know why, but I knew I needed you."

I'm not looking in, I'm not at a distance, I'm an inch away from Hannah, wrapped inside the center of her story. And if I shouldn't still trust her, after what she's said . . . well, fine. But I do. If I shouldn't still believe her, fine, but I do.

"I need you to help me find him," Hannah says. "Before . . ."

This isn't just a doomsday. It's a deadline. Hannah and I can survive an apocalypse, and I'm making sure my family can, too, but a person living in parks doesn't stand a chance.

"We'll find him," I promise. "We'll make sure he's safe before anything happens. He's still in Berkeley, isn't he?"

"He hasn't tried anything. Like with the car. But I think he stuck around to make sure I'm—" She looks at me. "I know how this sounds. But Danny was trying to save me. The wrong way, for the wrong reasons, but he was trying to save me."

"Maybe that's why he hasn't tried to, again. After you jumped out of the car."

"What do you mean?" she says.

"He saw that you could save yourself."

We sit in silence as the daylight fades. When the horizon is like the inside of a grapefruit, not quite orange and not quite red, Hannah stands. She offers me her hand and pulls me up, even though we both know I didn't need help. We go down the hill together.

## SEVENTEEN

I'VE PUT MY foot down. We're making flyers. I might not have all the details, and Hannah might not be on board, but we have a date and a location and a duty to the rest of the world. One day during lunch, I drag Hannah to the top floor of the Central Library, next to the vinyl section. No one's ever there except men with gray ponytails listening to the Doors and reliving their draft-dodging days.

At the table farthest in the back, Hannah sitting uncomfortably across from me, I make a mock-up flyer on orange paper. Orange like a nuclear warning symbol. Orange like a mushroom cloud. Orange like the apocalypse. At the top, it reads ARE YOU PREPARED? in the largest lettering I could fit. Below is Hannah's prophecy, only lightly edited. And at the bottom, and most important, is the date. December 21. Just over one month from now.

"I still don't think this is a good idea," she says. "And even if it was, every lamppost in this city is covered with flyers for weird stuff. No one's even going to notice yours."

"Ours."

"You're designing it. It's yours."

"You are just about the worst prophet in the world," I tell her.

"Uh, no, I'm not. What about the guy who had all his followers commit suicide?"

"Which one?"

"Thanks for making my point for me."

I set the marker down. "You know things other people don't. Things that will change their lives forever."

"So maybe let them enjoy the little bit of time they have." Hannah leans back in her chair. "It's not like they can do anything about it."

I believe in fate—how could I not, at this point?—but I don't believe in fatalism. I won't ever stop researching, or preparing, or making sure I'm in the best possible position to survive. It feels like giving up. I'm a lot of things I don't like, but I'm not a quitter. I don't give up without a fight, so Hannah's going to have to fight with me, whether she likes it or not.

"But don't you think they have a right to at least know?" I ask her. "To be prepared?"

I underline the question at the top of the page: ARE YOU PREPARED? It's mostly rhetorical. Of course they aren't prepared. Most people never will be. But everyone deserves a chance.

"You owe them that," I say.

Her mouth twists. "I don't owe anyone anything."

I fold my arms. "You owe me."

"Okay, that's not—" she starts to say, holding up a hand, but I cut her off.

"No, you do," I say. "I've lied for you. A lot. My parents don't trust me because of you. I've done a million things I wasn't supposed to do. I've gotten in so much trouble, all to help you."

"I didn't make you do any of those things," she says.

"That's not what I said! I did them willingly, I did them because I believe you," I say. "But I still did them *for* you, Hannah. Don't you think you owe me *something?*"

Silence. I stare at Hannah. She stares at the table.

"Yes," she says quietly. "I owe you a lot."

There's another long silence, like she wants to say something more. But she doesn't, so eventually, I clear my throat. "Okay. So, we're making flyers."

"Okay," she says, eyes still focused on the tabletop.

"Great." I push my first draft directly under her nose, so she can't help but see it. "See, we've got your prophecy, we've got the date, we've got the spot on the hill—"

"You can't tell them where," she says, reaching over me to grab the pen and crossing it out.

"What?" I sit back as she crosses it a second time, darker. "We have to."

"No."

"Hannah."

"It's just us," she says firmly, starting to write something else. "I've seen it, remember? You and me and no one else."

"You don't know that," I protest. "What if that's the only place that's safe, what if people need to be on higher ground, what if—"

"What if, what if," she repeats. "Sometimes I think you live on the planet What If, not Earth."

"Good one," I deadpan. "You should do stand-up."

She re-caps the pen and looks at me. Her face softens. "I'm sorry. But . . . bad shit happens, okay? Whether you plan for it or not. If you spend your life thinking about all the terrible things that could happen, you're going to miss every moment that's actually good. Trust me."

When she leans back, I see what she's written on the flyer.

LOCATION: *the place where the light comes in*

I wonder if that's why she gave away her things. Her clothes, her books, except for the ones her brother left behind. I wonder if they were some sort of sacrificial offering, for not appreciating the good moments. Less ascetic conviction, more crushing guilt. But it's not her fault. It's not her brother's, either, it's no one's fault. Doesn't she know that?

"Hey," I say, pulling the flyer back toward me. Trying to be casual. "Why did you—give up so much?"

She wrinkles her nose. "What?"

"Your stuff. Like your phone, or most of your clothing, or—"

"Did Tal tell you that?" she interrupts.

"No. Look, you have a total of maybe four outfits and I know your parents are professors, so it's clearly a choice," I reason. She stares at me. I cave instantly. "Paloma told me."

"God," she huffs. "Great."

"I only want to know why. Was that part of your dreams too, or—"

"It just didn't seem fair," she says, then clamps her mouth shut.

I sit back. "Fair?"

She swallows. "My brother doesn't have a phone. He doesn't have lots of clothes. Wherever he is, he's not comfortable. Why should I get to be?"

"But he chose that," I point out.

"It's not a choice if you don't think you've got any other options."

Is that really all this is for, fairness? She gave away her possessions so things would be fair between her and someone who lives on the street? I don't know what's in Hannah's head, and I won't tell her she doesn't know her own mind, but I think it's more than that. I think she's doing this to feel close to him. Wherever he is, whatever he's doing, she wants to feel what he feels. It's the only way she *can* feel close to him.

"So are you going to give these to people?" Hannah asks, taking the flyer from my hands and examining it.

"No, I'm going to make confetti out of them."

She gives me a look and hands it back over. "I mean are you just going to scatter them around town, or will you give them to people you *know*? People you care about. So they can be ready."

"I'll make sure my family's okay," I say. "You already know. Obviously. So who else?"

"Like maybe Tal?" she suggests lightly. Heat spreads across my face. Hannah's staring at me, searching me like I'm something under a microscope. "Or . . . Lia?"

The heat's on my neck and my shoulders now. I look down at the flyer. She sighs.

"I'm not trying to pressure you," Hannah says. "I don't want it to seem that way. But I think—"

"Yeah, I get it, you think you've got me figured out," I interrupt, shoving the flyer aside.

"I think sometimes people like us find each other," Hannah says, picking her words carefully, "because we need each other."

Is that true? Hannah and I aren't the same—not *exactly* the same, though maybe she assumes we are. Hannah likes girls. Only girls. That's not all the way true for me, I know that, but it is all the way wrong?

I shake my head. "Based on basically *nothing*, you think you know exactly how I feel."

Hannah moves to the chair closest to me. "I don't know what you're feeling," she admits. "But whatever it is, whatever you *are* feeling . . . it's okay. It's better than okay. You need to know that, and I'm not sure anyone's told you before." She leans forward, all but forcing me to look her in the eye. "Whatever you're feeling, Ellis, it's *you*. And you are good. So it's good, too."

She's wrong about one thing: I have been told that before. Not in this context, not the way she means it, but I've spent every day of my life being told I was created in the image of something perfect. That there are no errors in creation. I thought I believed that, but maybe I didn't, or haven't for years. Maybe I haven't been treating myself like I believe that. I can accept that I was fearfully, wonderfully made, or I can believe that I was a mistake.

Something warm is spiraling its way through my veins. Not hot like a brand, or a fire, but something softer. Like the sun coming in through a window.

I'm not a mistake. No part of me is a mistake. I can believe that.

The word *apocalypse* means a revelation, but that doesn't mean every revelation is an apocalypse. Or maybe it can be a little apocalypse, a *good* apocalypse. The word *apocalypse* means to uncover what's been hidden. Maybe this time, I'll draw back the curtain and like what I see.

I think I see it. I almost feel like I can speak it, too. I'm not all the way there, but I'm closer.

"I'll make sure," I tell Hannah, and it comes out a whisper. Soft and unsure, but spoken. "The people I care about . . . I'll make sure they know."

# EIGHTEEN

**I PLASTER OUR** flyers all around town—well, as far I can get on the bus and still make it home early enough that my lies about extra chemistry labs or math tutoring seem plausible. So that means they're mostly around campus, but I figure that's where the more open-minded people are hanging out anyway. The flyer goes up on every prepper forum I know, too, though I'm smart enough not to read the reply comments. For people who truly believe the End of the World as We Know It is imminent, they are oddly resistant to having an actual date for TEOTWAWKI. I also make a basic, free, and admittedly badly designed website with all the information Hannah's given me, plus some survival tips of my own.

It's not a lot. It's barely even a little. But it's something. It gives people a fighting chance.

I don't put any flyers up at church, though I'd like to. We're big on self-sufficiency, though, so I hope the ward will get through things okay. Most of the men were Boy Scouts. Most of the women can sew. Some of us are even descended from the original pioneers—"pioneer stock." I always thought it was kind of snotty, the way some people would drop that into conversation, as if having a great-great-grandma who buried three children on the way to Utah, or some breaded ancestor who carried children over the frozen Sweetwater River, made you a hero by proxy. But now I sit in a pew with my arms folded as my parents and sister talk to the friends they love, and pray that hardiness is an inherited trait.

There's a thump and the swish of loose fabric as someone slides in next to me. When I open my eyes, it isn't Em, like I expected. It's Lia.

She grabs my arm. "Ugh, Ellis. I've got to tell *someone*."

The hair on my arms feels static under her fingers. "What?"

"Bethany's great-grandma is visiting." She inclines her head at a blond, spindly, elderly woman talking to an even blonder sister missionary. "So I went up to introduce myself, and she asked where I was from."

I can already see where this is going. "And you said Berkeley."

"Well, I was born in Long Beach, so I said that. But then she said, 'No, I mean, what *are* you?' And I told her, 'I'm Samoan,'" Lia continues. "And *she* said, 'But you're so light! I'd never have guessed you were African.'"

I burst out laughing. "What!"

Lia shushes me, but she's giggling too. "Somalia, Ellis. She

246

didn't know the difference between Samoa and *Somalia*."

"Wow. Yikes."

"She's old, I get it, and from, like, very rural Wyoming, but holy shit." Lia rolls her eyes.

I'm almost shocked by the swearing. That's so not like her. Not that it isn't justified, but Lia's so perfect. Then again— maybe that's just the armor she wears to get through the day, to get through people not understanding who she is and where she comes from. Our ward is more diverse than most I've seen, but no one's immune to mistakes. No one's perfect, not even Lia. I built her up that way, without even meaning to. I met her when I was a toddler, but that doesn't mean I *know* her.

"Hey, Lia," I blurt out, my mouth moving faster than my brain. "Does your family have food storage?"

"Oh, yeah, some." She wrinkles her nose. "A lot of it is pisupo though." Then, off my confused look: "Corned beef."

Like I told Tal, there's danger to surviving solely off canned meat. "What about water?"

"I don't know."

"You should have water. Lots of water; tap is fine. You can fill up soda bottles, just make sure they're in a dark place."

I wouldn't normally advise that—used plastic can go bad— but it's only a month away. Better to have non-ideal water than no water at all.

"What about matches?" I ask. "Flashlights, batteries, extra blankets?"

"I'm really not sure."

"You should," I say. "It's important. If you don't, I know Sister Keller has a ton of extra supplies. You should ask her."

"How would that look, when she *just* taught a lesson on self-sufficiency?" Lia asks with a laugh.

"Ask anyway."

"Okay. But, Ellis . . ." She shakes her head. "I don't understand why you're telling me this."

I want to tell her. I want to tell her all the facts, the whole truth, Hannah's truth. But I don't want her to be scared. I want her to be happy, in the last days she might have. I used to think facts were the most important thing. Writing them down, memorizing them, giving them to others. But maybe sometimes, facts just aren't helpful. Maybe being prepared isn't the most important thing. Maybe Lia's happiness—as short or long as that lasts—matters more.

"I heard it's going to be a really rough winter," I say. "There might be power outages."

"Where'd you hear that?"

I pause just a second too long. "*Farmer's Almanac.*"

"Huh." She smiles. "You just know something about everything, don't you?"

In another person's mouth, that might sound snarky. But in Lia's voice, I can hear real admiration.

"That's nice of you," I say.

"No, I'm serious, you must be amazing at Trivial Pursuit."

"My family actually refuses to play that with me."

"Because you're too good?"

"Because I'm too competitive."

She laughs. "We should play it at Mutual, sometime. You and I could be a team. I'll take Science and Sports, and you'll do the rest."

My heart flutters under my ribs. "Deal."

"I should go find my family," she says, and starts to go.

"Wait," I call after her, and she turns back. "I—"

*When I talk to you, it feels like being a member of some special club.*

"I like you," I say, and her smile doesn't fade. "That's the other reason I told you about the . . . winter. I like you, Lia."

*When I look at you, it's like feeling the sun on my skin.*

"I like you a lot," I finish.

She doesn't hesitate, her smile doesn't falter. "Oh, I like you too, Ellis." She waves. "See you in class."

And then she walks away.

I take a couple of long, gulping breaths. She didn't pause, she didn't look serious or shocked or even surprised. She didn't know what I was saying to her. It's okay. That's okay. If everything I feel is okay, like Hannah said, then everything Lia feels—or doesn't—is okay, too. It doesn't mean what I felt was wrong. Or doesn't matter. Or isn't real.

*I'd want to know,* Hannah said to me one Sunday. *I'd want to know who I was. Before the world changed.*

And I do. I already did, and no amount of shutting down my

brain or locking it inside the cage I've made my body was going to make me forget it. I knew. But knowing is one thing. Saying it out loud is another. It's a different kind of knowing, the kind you can't come back from.

She didn't understand me, and that's okay. What would I even have done, if she'd said she liked me too, and really *meant* it? I'm not sure if I'd have been ready. I think I might need more time, to get ready for something like that. I'd need to tell other people first, My sister, my friends—my parents, eventually. I'd need to sit with it in my own head, say it to myself, not just another person. I'd to live it, not just live *with* it.

I need more days, I realize, with a kind of electric shock. I need more days in this life, the one I'm living now. But the giant cosmic clock is ticking. Time is one thing I just don't have.


Another sunny November day, another lie to my parents about math tutoring, another afternoon under Hannah's tree playing Five-Word Books. I'm getting better.

"Sea mammal obsession causes death," Theo offers.

"*Moby Dick*," answers Tal.

"Dude with schnoz ghostwrites flirting," Sam says.

"*Cyrano de Bergerac*," I say.

Suddenly, Theo is distracted by something over my shoulder. "Oh hell yes, Martin's here!"

"Really?" Sam says, turning around.

"Who's Martin?" I ask.

"I know it's not the first time I've asked," Tal says, "but are you *sure* you go to this school?"

"Martin the Ice Cream Guy!" Sam says, and Theo points over my shoulder. I twist around. A paunchy middle-aged man is pushing a metal cart over to a cluster of kids who all have their money out and ready. "He comes a couple times a week and charges less than 7-Eleven *or* E-Z Stop."

"Can you spot me, like, fifty cents for a SpongeJeff Yellowpants Popsicle?" Theo asks Sam, digging change out of his pocket.

"SpongeJeff?" I ask.

"They're not officially licensed, so they've got weird names," Theo says. "But FYI, Speedy the Tree Shrew tastes like Children's Benadryl." Sam tosses Theo a couple of coins and they both get to their feet.

Sam spreads his arms wide. "Martin, my man!" he shouts across the park as he and Theo leave. "Tell me you've still got Patricio the Plumber left!"

As soon as they're out of earshot, I turn to Tal and say what I've been wanting to tell him all afternoon.

"Hannah told me," I say. "You don't have to keep that secret for her anymore. She told me who we've really been looking for." He looks surprised, but doesn't speak. I guess I have to say the exact words. "Her brother."

"I'm sorry," he says. "I wanted to tell you from the second

251

you said 'Prophet Dan' at the library. But it wasn't mine to tell."

Right here, right now, I want to tell him about the end of the world. Is that mine to tell? Or is that Hannah's, too? Sometimes it feels like she's the sun, and we're all just orbiting around her.

"I can't make your choices for you," Tal says, eyes on the dirt. "I can't stop you from helping her look. But I can tell you, it's not doing her any favors."

"He's her brother."

"And he's got bigger problems than she can handle. This isn't on her to fix. The longer and harder she tries, the worse it is." He shakes his head. "It took me and Sam and Theo a long time to figure that out. Our help wasn't help at all."

The sun's going to explode, one day. In five billion years, no matter what happens in December, the sun will burn itself out. There isn't a thing anyone can do to stop it.

"She . . ." I hesitate, then try again. "She didn't trust me enough. To tell me the truth from the start."

"It took her months to tell *us*," Tal says. "It's not a trust thing, it's a Hannah thing. From what she's said, it's practically a Marks family tradition to shut your friends out while you're dying inside."

*They don't like being in the house.* That's what Hannah said, about her parents. They're dealing with Danny's disappearance just as badly as Hannah is. She's obsessing over it. They're pretending it isn't happening.

"It's more than that," I say. "She thought I'd judge her."

"Honestly?" Tal wrinkles his nose, looking a little guilty. "I might have thought that, too."

"Wow. Thank you."

"I would have been wrong! Clearly, she was wrong. You're a lot less uptight than you first appear."

"Again. Thank you."

"Oh God, that's not what I meant." Tal holds out his hands. "I'm sorry, okay? Really. I am sorry on both our behalves for wrongly judging your judgy-ness . . ." He stops, noticing the grin creeping across my face. He rests his chin in his palm. "Oh, are you having a good time, watching me grovel?"

Maybe a little. I smile. "Sometimes a girl just loves hearing a good apology, what do you want from me?"

Tal goes still. He stares at the grass for a moment. "What do *you* want?"

"It's a figure of speech."

"I know. But—" He leans forward. "What do you want? More than anything else?"

"What everyone wants. To survive."

He shakes his head. "No, Ellis. What do you *want*?"

"Survival is a want."

"Survival is an instinct," Tal counters. "Animals survive, bugs survive, bacteria survive. What are you surviving for? What's going to make it matter that you're still alive?"

What's the point of wanting things, when so many are sinful, or impossible, or both? What's the point of wanting things you can't have?

"What do *you* want?" I ask.

"I want—" He leans back on his hands. "I want to meet my dad's family, in Brazil. I want to get to know them. I want to make sure my half siblings know me, like really know me, even though I don't live with them and who knows what their dad says when I'm not around. I want my mom to stop worrying about me."

*Me too*, I think. Tal takes a breath.

"I want to go to college in a place with actual seasons. I don't know what I want to study there, and I want people to stop asking that like I should know already. And maybe this is petty," he acknowledges, "but I want to be fucking *happy*. I want to be the kind of happy that's two giant middle fingers at every person who told me I'd never be, unless my life was exactly like theirs. That's what I want."

What do I want? Do I want to move closer to him? Or do I want to run away? Could I want opposite things at the same time?

"Is that . . ." I dig my fingers into the dirt, as if that will keep me planted. "Is that all you want?"

"Is that not enough?" he asks with a laugh.

"Yes," I say. "But . . . is that all you want?"

Tal swallows audibly. "No."

He pushes himself off his hands and leans forward. There's

254

an inch of space between us, and less air. Or maybe just I'm holding my breath.

"Survive for something," Tal says, low and urgent. "*Want* something, Ellis. Want something."

We stare at each other for a moment that feels like eons. Tal reaches out for me, hesitant, like you'd do with a skittish cat. I scramble to my feet, all awkward limbs and confusion and a thrum of something warm and terrifying fluttering under my ribs.

"I'm sorry, I—" The feeling beats quicker, loud in its silence, and drowns out whatever lie my brain could think up. "I have to go."

As I walk away, I grasp for a word, a name for the feeling in my chest. I come up empty.

I wonder if there are some things even the dictionary can't define.

# NINETEEN

**THAT NEXT MONDAY,** Hannah finds me in the courtyard before first period.

"I've got something to show you," she says. I wait for her to pull something from her pocket, or out of her backpack, but she stands there, unmoving.

"Where is it?" I glance around, but there's nothing behind her, either.

"The City."

Berkeley is a city, Oakland is a city, even Piedmont is technically a city. But there is only one City. "San Francisco?"

"Yep."

"What is it?"

"It's not a thing," she says. "More like an experience."

I would follow Hannah into the depths of hell—I probably *will* end up following her there—but sometimes her vagueness is truly irritating. "I can't go after school. It's family home evening."

"Okay," she says. "Let's go now."

"But . . ." I look back toward the C-building, where first-period chemistry is waiting for me. "We have school."

She rolls her eyes. "Yeah, I know. We'll skip."

My parents have never explicitly told me I wasn't allowed to skip school, but I think it was implied.

"We'll be back by sixth period," Hannah promises.

"And when my parents get the absence email?"

"It'll say you missed one *or more* periods. You'll tell them you had a sub in history. They must have messed up the attendance sheet."

"Does that work?"

"It'll work once, for sure."

"I don't know."

"Have you ever skipped before?" she asks. I shake my head. "Don't you think you should have the experience once in your life?"

Skipping class: part of a complete and balanced high school experience. Like house parties with red cups. Or making improbable friends in Saturday detention. I'm not likely to be invited to any parties before the end of the world, and my school doesn't even have regular detention, so skipping class it is.

"Okay," I say, and Hannah's face blooms into a smile. "Lead the way."

"Uh, you don't know where the front gate is?"

My eyes go wide. "We can't go out the front!" I say, but

she's already walking toward the gate. I scramble to catch up. "Someone will stop us!"

She throws a glance back at me, then skids to a halt. "They will if you look like that."

I look down at my outfit. It's jeans and a coat. Not all that suspicious.

"The way you're standing," Hannah says with a shake of her head. "You look guilty. You look like you're asking to get caught."

I shrug at her helplessly.

"Walk like you've got somewhere to be," Hannah says. "Head high, eyes ahead, stand up straight."

I cringe at that last one. *Stand up straight.* Hannah's not looking down at me disapprovingly or prodding my spine as she says it, but I hear my mom anyway. I always thought she insisted on perfect posture because she wanted us to look graceful and happy, so everyone else would see us that way. I'd never considered it could be useful to me and me alone. I'd never considered that in her own strange way, she might have been trying to show me something. Gift me something.

I touch my fingertips to my hair, to my shoulders, to my waist, then let them fall to my sides. My spine straightens. Not like a cord being yanked, but like a sail being unfurled. I draw my chin up and look Hannah in the eye.

She smiles. "Perfect."

We walk across the courtyard, past the administration

building, and out the open front gate.

No one stops us.

Our BART train is crowded, so Hannah and I hang on to the straps. This is another thing I like about being tall—I don't have to stand on my toes to reach them, like Hannah does. When the train pulls into Embarcadero, the first stop in San Francisco, I look to Hannah for guidance. She shakes her head and snags two newly empty seats.

"How far are we going?" I ask.

Hannah looks out the window, into the darkness of the tunnel. "I was thinking Colma."

"That's what you wanted to show me? The giant cemetery city where the dead outnumber the living?"

"Where the dead outnumber the living," Hannah repeats. "You can be so dramatic."

"We're not really going that far, are we?"

"I was kidding about Colma, but we are going far. First Golden Gate Park. Then the Outer Richmond."

That's practically in the Pacific Ocean. "What for?"

"It's a surprise."

I fold my arms. "If I'm going all that way, you have to do something for me."

"Name it."

"Missionary work."

She looks pained. "Come on."

"We'll be in Golden Gate Park anyway. It's a perfect opportunity." Hannah wrinkles her nose, but I'm not backing down. I hold out my hand. "That's the deal. Take it or leave it."

She rolls her eyes, but shakes my hand.

Golden Gate Park should be the perfect environment for some light doomsday preaching. This is San Francisco, and we passed two other street preachers on our way here. At least we're not telling anyone they're hell-bound, like the man in the cowboy hat by the BART station was. At least we're not telling people their brains have already been infected by alien invaders, like the guy at the entrance to the park was, showing off the tinfoil on the inside of his winter coat. Ours is a friendlier doomsday. Peace, love, and armageddon. What could be better?

But the tech bros lounging on a fleece blanket and eating burritos just laugh. "Like the zombie apocalypse?" says the one wearing a Patagonia fleece. "I could do that. I'm hella good at *Overwatch*."

"Dude, the government would just bomb them," says his friend in the same Patagonia fleece, just a different color.

"They'd already be dead, man. They don't care if they get radiation, you'd just end up with something that could eat your brains *and* give you leukemia."

"I'll tell you what's a sign of the apocalypse," says an elderly man playing chess with an even more elderly friend. "That new tower they just built downtown. A thousand feet tall. Ugly as sin."

"They said it's the tallest piece of public art in the world," the other man says.

"Public art? Carl, it looks like a damn dildo."

"Well, so does the Washington Monument, Bob."

While I'm contemplating just how many phallic-shaped buildings there are, Hannah, who hasn't said a word so far, suddenly huffs and stomps away. I race after her, leaving the two old men in a heated, dildo-centric argument.

"What is your problem?" I say when I catch up to Hannah. She's been distracted since the moment we got here, eyes darting around, not even bothering to engage with our street contacts.

She keeps walking, hands jammed deep in her coat pockets. "I said I didn't want to do this."

"You didn't, technically."

"As if you couldn't *tell*."

I'm not the prophet, here. I'm not a mind reader, either. "Hannah, wait."

"What was the point?" she mutters, walking faster. "What was the point of that?"

"People have a right to know," I say. "We have a duty to tell them, to warn them—"

She spins around. "Why?"

I step back. "What do you mean *why*?"

261

"The world will end," she says, steely and sharp. "Whether people know about it or not, whether we tell them or not, it's going to happen and there's not a thing they can do to stop it."

"They could be prepared."

"Prepared," she says scornfully. "God, you love that word. It's like your fucking teddy bear."

Heat creeps onto my face and the back of my neck. "Don't."

"You can't protect yourself against everything. Sometimes terrible shit just happens and there's nothing you can do."

"Great advice," I snap back. "Why don't you take it?"

She throws up her hands. "What?"

"You gave away everything you owned." She takes a step back. "You gave up your phone, and haircuts, and a normal life. You made yourself a sixteen-year-old hermit, and why? Because you've made some cosmic bargain with the universe? Because you think it'll bring him back?" I close the gap between us. "Hannah. It won't."

She turns away from me. I'm instantly hit with a wave of guilt. I didn't need to say those things. It didn't help, even if it was true.

"I'm sorry," I say, and touch her shoulder.

"What do you want?" she mutters, shrugging me off.

"Same thing as everybody," I say, trying for a weak joke. "Basic survival."

Hannah shakes her head. "Survive for *what*?"

I pause, thinking of Tal. He told me to survive for something.

Hannah's using the same words, but she's not asking what I'll survive for. She's asking, why bother?

"Hannah," I whisper, but then don't know what else to say.

"So what if the world ends?" she says, quieter, calmer. "Not like it's a great world, anyway. It's mean, and cold, and so unfair that sometimes I can't believe it's lasted this long."

Her shoulders are quivering. So is her mouth. I know, without asking, that she's thinking of her brother. Alone, and in pain, and likely in danger. She's thinking of herself, alone and in pain, too, and powerless to help him. She's right. It is unfair. That word didn't always mean "inequitable." In the Old English, *unfægr*; it meant something ugly. Deformed. Hideous. And the world is unfair like that too. It can be so hard to see any beauty in it.

"I know," I tell her. "I know. But it's the only world we've got."

She nods, wiping the back of her hand across her nose. "I'm sorry."

"It's okay."

"That was so shitty, I'm sorry."

"I shouldn't have made you do that," I say. "You didn't want to. I'm sorry, too."

Hannah scans the park. "We can go home, if you want," she says, every word brittle. "He isn't here."

Oh. That's why we're in this park. I don't know how it took me so long to notice.

"Did someone see him?" I ask. "Did someone call you?"

"He's been here before, and it's the one place I hadn't looked in a while, so I thought—" She focuses her gaze on the wet grass. "No. No one's seen him in weeks."

"Not even Chris?"

She shakes her head. "It's never been this long before."

Hannah doesn't have to say it out loud for me to understand. Her brother has really and truly vanished. That word comes from a Latin root, *evanescere*. It means "to pass away," that polite way to say death. That polite way to speak something unspeakable.

"I'm so sorry, Hannah. I'm so sorry."

She keeps her eyes trained on the grass. We have to get out of this park. She'll only see him everywhere. I grasp her forearm lightly and take a step forward, a step west.

"Where are we going?" she asks, but doesn't dig in her heels.

"You tell me," I say. "Where are we going, Hannah?"


I've never been in the Outer Richmond, walking or driving. Hannah knows where she's going, so I follow in her stride, just a step behind. My dad always told me not to be a follower. Thinking back on it, though, there are plenty of people he'd like me to follow. Him, for one. Jesus, for another. It's such an odd thing parents do, make pronouncements that beg for exceptions.

But I listened, didn't I? I never followed anyone. I holed up in the library stacks. I made myself a nest inside my own brain. Then Hannah went and shook the tree branches, sending that nest toppling down. My parents are mad at her for doing it, and madder at me for letting her. But everything leaves its nest, eventually. Sometimes it takes a push.

We walk through block after block of houses with red stucco roofs, big sunroom windows drawing light and warmth inside. I wonder what we look like to someone sitting in the window seat. Do we look like truant kids, sneaking around the city? Do we look like the failed evangelists we are? Or do we just look like two girls, unremarkable and unnoticeable? I've always wondered what it would be like, to see myself from the outside.

We walk out of the residential streets and across an almost endless green lawn, past the Legion of Honor, into groves of cypress, bushy and tall. Then, suddenly, I hear it. I surge past Hannah, and now she has to rush to catch up with me. The ocean. I didn't know we were going to the ocean. The forest breaks, and there is the sky again, a haze of gray fog with cool blue underneath. There is the sea, dark waves and white foam, stretching so far it could be the whole world. *Sea* is a word with no known origin. *Sea* is a word that simply *is*.

Ahead of us is a part of the coastline I've never seen before. So much of the San Francisco waterfront is built up with piers, wax museums, and theme restaurants marketed to tourists in fleece jackets who expected California to be much warmer. This place, with its jagged, burnt sienna cliffs and silence, feels different. Pristine. Untouched. Wild.

"What is this place?" I whisper to Hannah.

"Lands End."

I wonder if there's an apostrophe in its name. Is this land's end, the stopping point of a singular place? Or is it the end of all lands?

"This way," Hannah says, and starts toward the shore. We're so close to the water that the salt sticks in my taste buds, briny and inviting. Hannah leads me to a big, deserted cliff. It's not one of the taller ones, and not as sheer of a drop, which I appreciate. Still, I'm careful to stay far back from the edge.

"This is my first memory," Hannah says, and I can barely hear her over the wind and the waves.

"What?" My hair whips around my face. I pull it back.

"This is the first thing I remember," she says, louder. "I think I was four. We came here, my whole family, after spending the morning at the aquarium. We stood at one of these lookouts. And I wanted to go down to the water, so I could see the fish. I wanted to get closer. Danny held my hand, and said I didn't have to see them, because I already knew they were there. But I still wanted to. I still wanted to get closer."

For a moment, we stand in silence, watching the waves crash against the smaller rocks below. They seem to hit harder each time, more force behind each saltwater swell. It must be high tide. When I look over at Hannah, her gaze is not out on the horizon, but down on the rocks.

"Come on," she says, lowering herself off the side of the cliff and onto a ledge.

Oh no. "Wait, stop, what are you doing?"

"Getting closer." She takes another step down, fingers gripping the plateau I'm standing on.

No, no, no. "Fine, there's a trail to the beach, use that!"

She ignores me and takes another step down.

"Hannah!" I shout. This is not safe. There were signs at the trailhead asking us to specifically *not do this thing*.

She looks up at me, eyes determined and bright. "I'm going," she says. She doesn't have to say "with or without you." I hear it anyway.

"Oh my God," I mutter, lowering my foot carefully down. It's not blasphemy. It is a genuine plea for Him to not let me die on this cliff. My foot wobbles, and I yelp, clinging to the edge of the rock with all the strength in my hands.

> *Turn back, you're going to fall. You're going to fall and you're going to die.*

I take another cautious step. I'm so close to the air, so close to falling. I wonder if this is how Hannah felt that night she jumped from the car. "Stop, I can't do this!"

She's several steps ahead of me, but she stops and twists her head back. "Yes," she says. "Yes, you can. Your body knows what to do, you just have to let it."

> *Give up, turn back, you're going to get stuck on this rock and the Coast Guard will have to lift you*

*out via helicopter but only if you don't die first,*
*which you will.*

I take a shaky breath in and hold it. One step. Another step. My feet find the footholds, my fingers curl around grips I can't see. Another step. Another inch.

*You can't do this.*

"You're doing great," Hannah calls back, though she couldn't possibly know that. "Almost there."

*You can't do this.*

Two more steps, and there is nothing I hear but the roar of breaking waves. There is nothing I see but the rocks in front of me, the next place to put a foot, a hand, a shaky knee.

*You can't do this.*

I can't. But I do. One foot in front of the other, tiny step by tiny step, I climb down the cliff.

Up ahead, Hannah has reached a plateau. She steps off it onto a freestanding rock just a few inches farther into the water, then holds out her hand for me. I take it, and she helps me over. I sink to the flat, damp rock surface, heart pounding and mouth dry.

"What the *hell*, Hannah?" I yell above the waves. "We could have fallen! We could have *died*!"

"But look at that." She nods her head back the way we came. Keeping all my limbs firmly on the rock, I twist back. The cliff above us looks almost impossibly tall and steep. "Look what you did."

Something incredibly irresponsible, and potentially fatal, involving at least three of my greatest fears. It was a terrible idea. It was beyond dangerous. But looking back, I can't help feeling a swell of pride.

Hannah sits down on the rock, closer to the edge than I am. "Over here." I crawl on my hands and knees to join her. Out in the distance, a wave ripples in, curling taller, reaching toward us. It's so close, and I wonder for a moment if I've traded death by falling for death by drowning. The wave crests and explodes several feet below us, and the spray mists us with salt water. It stings my eyes. It freezes my nose. It prickles my skin, and something deeper, too. I wipe my face dry, but then there is another wave, another wall of mist. I breathe deep, tasting the salt, feeling something inside me split open, a seam loosening, stitches unthreading.

The water swells and breaks, again and again, covering me in water and brine again and again, and I let it. I let myself feel my finger pads gripping the rock, my hair whipping in the wind, my legs pressing down on stone. I've spent so much of my life terrified of my body, all the ways it could fail or betray me. But Hannah told me to trust my body, and I did. I climbed down a cliff, and I didn't die. I stumbled, but I didn't break. I trusted that I could save myself, I trusted myself, and I make a silent vow that it won't be the last time. I've spent so much of my life thinking the things I wanted must be wrong, because I was the one wanting them.

*A life that is different than my mother's.*

*Lia Lemalu's hair in the sunlight.*

*Tal's hand on my arm, warm and gentle.*

Until the world ends, until the earth collapses in ice and storm, and throughout all eternity, I will trust myself. I will trust in the things I feel, because I am the one feeling them. I say these things in the name of Ellis Leah Kimball, I say these things in my own name, because I will not get another.

Amen.

# TWENTY

**"IS THERE ANYTHING** you'd like to talk about today?"

Most of the time, I shrug. Sometimes, I say no. On the rarest of occasions, I mention something minor, something we both know doesn't really matter. Today, I say:

"Yes."

Martha struggles to hide her surprise. "Great! What would you like to talk about?"

Something I've lived with for years and years. Something that's wormed its way into every waking hour. Something I want to be rid of for good.

"There's this voice," I tell her. "There's this awful voice in my head all the time and I can't get it out."

I think about telling her what happened in San Francisco. How the voice inside my head told me I'd never make it, I'd die, I'd fail. How I ignored it. How I climbed down anyway. But she might think me rappelling off cliffsides was a cry for help, or evidence that I'm a danger to myself. She might tell my parents. I can't let anyone take that day away from me. I need it. When the end of the world arrives, I will need that day.

"What does the voice tell you?" Martha asks.

"'You shouldn't have said that, you shouldn't have done that, your friends hate you, you don't *have* any friends. . . .'" I trail off at the look on her face. "Just that kind of stuff."

Martha stirs in her chair. "Can you describe the voice for me?"

"Describe it?"

"Yes."

"It's . . . mean."

"Okay," she says. "What else? What would it look like, if you had to give it a shape?"

"I don't know," I say. "I guess it's like this demon. Not a joke one, a scary one. Like a demon from one of those terrifying Renaissance paintings about Judgment Day and hell and they're all clearly drawn by the same dude and all you can think is, holy crap, what happened in that guy's life to make him paint this stuff?" I take a breath. "Do you know who I'm talking about?"

"Hieronymus Bosch?"

"Um, it's like *Where's Waldo*, except in this version Waldo is naked and you find him inside the mouth of a monster with a bird head and no torso."

She nods sagely. "Hieronymus Bosch."

"That's what it's like. Some horrible nightmare in a painting, except I can't close the book or leave the museum," I say.

"It's like a demon that climbs onto my back every morning and curls up on my chest every night. It's like a monster that remembers every stupid thing I've done and says all the things my mom secretly thinks."

*Why did you say that? You shouldn't have said that, she'll think your mom is awful and she's not. She'll think you're an ungrateful monster, and you are.*

"I didn't mean that," I say, scrambling. "About my mom. My mom isn't a monster, she's just . . ."

*Critical and overbearing and disappointed in you, they're all disappointed in you, confused by you, sick of dealing with you. Why shouldn't they be?*

"I'm sorry," I say, talking too quickly, talking so there isn't silence. "I know I'm being ridiculous, I'm self-aware, at least I'm self-aware, but—"

"Have you ever talked about this before?" Martha asks.

I think back. "When I was thirteen, I told my bishop. I didn't really mean to, it just sort of happened. I told him that I had these constant thoughts about how awful I was, how no one liked me and it was my own fault. I guess I wanted—" I falter, remembering. "Never mind."

Martha extends a hand. "Go ahead."

"It's stupid."

"Whatever you wanted," Martha says, "it was not stupid."

"He told me the voice I heard was the Adversary. He told me

Satan was trying to keep me from living the Gospel and staying active in church. He said to ignore it, and I tried, but all I really wanted was . . ." My voice box crumples. "I wanted him to tell me the things I was hearing weren't true. He never said any of those things weren't true."

"Ellis," Martha says quietly. She waits until I look up from the carpet. She locks her eyes on me like a laser. "It's not true. None of it is true. The things you're telling yourself are not true."

"Things *I'm* telling myself?" I balk. "I can't stop that voice, it just keeps talking, I don't know where it comes from."

"I think maybe you do."

I twist around and look out the window, at the tree, at the peeling bark on the tree, at the lines and the grooves in the bark. Anywhere but Martha. She waits for me, but I don't turn back around. I make my eyes go glassy, my heart go numb, my body go anywhere but here. When Martha finally speaks, she sounds miles away.

"It's not Satan," Martha says, and my eyes refocus. "There's no demon, or monster, or fallen angel."

My body pushes back, drags itself from outside the office, outside the universe, and plants itself back on the couch.

"The voice in your head is coming from you. Just you."

My heart stirs under its cold covering. It beats. Wrenches. Bursts.

I dissolve into a river of tears. A tidal wave, a tsunami, the kind that could wash away San Francisco or the entire world. Apocalypse by salt water. Martha reaches over and places something next to me, but I'm crying too hard to see what it is. I'm crying too hard to apologize for crying. When the tidal wave finally dies down to hiccups, I wipe my eyes with the back of my hand.

"What do you think these tears are about?" she asks.

My eyes burn. My face burns. "I'm sorry. I don't usually cry."

"It's okay to cry."

I know that. It's not like I was raised to be stoic and unfeeling. If anything, I was the oddball who shed zero tears during our yearly family viewing of *It's a Wonderful Life*, the girl who never cried when she shared her testimony at church or sobbed around the campfire on the last night of girls' camp.

"I just don't, usually."

"Why do you think it happened now?" Martha asks.

I well up again. "You said it's me. The voice is me."

"I said it's coming from you," Martha says. "Not that it *is* you."

"There's no difference."

"There is," she insists. "That voice is you speaking. But *you* are more than that voice. And you are much, much more than the things it tells you."

"I don't like feeling this way," I protest. "It's awful. I hate it. And you think I'm doing it to myself?"

"I think you're experiencing very painful intrusive thoughts. I

275

think you're engaging in a lot of self-critique. Yes, self-critique," she says, off my look. "But ultimately, this is a good thing."

"A good thing?" I cry. "It's a good thing that I'm ruining my own life?"

"It's a good thing because it means you aren't powerless. You are powerful. It means," she says, and leans in, "that you can tell that voice to shut the *fuck* up."

My mouth drops open. "Martha!"

"You don't have to use any words that make you uncomfortable," Martha assures me. "But for me, there are some things my nicest words just can't express."

I might slip into the lighter forms of swearing, but it's always with a twist of the intestines, a healthy sense of shame. I've never really considered that you could find strength in words like that. Defiance. Righteousness. Power.

All words have power. Not just the polite ones.

"I want you to close your eyes," Martha says. I do. "And let that inner critic loose." I open them again, panicked, and she holds up her hands. "Just for a moment."

I close my eyes again. It doesn't take long.

> *Martha feels sorry for you. Martha is paid to be nice to you and she can't wait for this session to be over. Martha feels sorry for you and she shouldn't, because everything that happens to you is your own fault. She said it herself.*

"What's that inner critic saying?" Martha asks.

"That if I'm sad, if bad things happen to me, it's because I brought it on myself." I leave out the parts about her.

"Is that true, Ellis?"

*Yes.*

"I . . ."

"Are you able to control the actions of others? Is that something you can reasonably blame yourself for? Are you in control of the entire world?"

> *You want to be. You are powerless and weak and every single thing you do has catastrophic consequences for the entire world.*

That doesn't make sense. I can't be both powerless and all-powerful. It doesn't make sense.

"Are you responsible for every bad thing that happens in your life?"

*Yes.*

"No."

I hear Martha breathe. Not a gasp. Not a sharp intake of oxygen, like she's surprised. A sudden exhale of carbon dioxide and satisfaction. "Good," she says. "You're right. That's exactly right."

It's such a small compliment. But it warms me from the inside out.

"Let's do one more," Martha says. "I want you to picture your family. Your father, your mother, and your sister."

"Am I with them?"

"Not just yet. Picture them all together, looking back at you. Hold that image."

I draw them up individually in my mind.

My dad, in his white coat.

*The look he gave you when you told him the world was ending.*

My mom, standing straight and tall.

*"We handle you with kid gloves."*

My sister, all charm and poise and goodness.

*"Why do you always have to make things worse?"*

"Are you picturing them?" Martha asks, and I nod. "If they could be here, in this session with you, if they could hear what you've told me, what would they say to you?"

*You ruined so many dinners. You ruined so many car trips. You ruined so many moments, little and large, you forced us to accommodate your fears, your needs.*

*We love you, but only because we are good people. We love you, but not because you are lovable.*

*You are an anchor around our necks, you are dead weight in our arms, you are, you are, you are—*

"What would they say to you, Ellis?"

"A burden!" I burst out, keeping my eyes shut as if that will keep the word shut away, too. "They'd say I'm a burden."

We sit in silence for a moment. "Is that true? Are you a burden to your family?"

> *Yes. But when the end of the world comes, you won't be. You'll know things they won't. You won't be a burden. You'll be their hero.*

"I don't know."

"You love your sister. You spend time with her, you're kind to her, you treat her with respect. Are you a burden to her? Is that a fair thing to call yourself?"

> *Yes. But when the end of the world comes, you'll protect her. You can be the sister she deserved to have all along.*

But everything Martha said was true. I do love Em, I do watch her dance, and braid her hair. Maybe—maybe the world doesn't have to end for me to be the sister she deserves.

"I guess not," I say. "No."

"Are you a burden to your parents? Is that a fair thing to call yourself?"

> *Yes. Yes.*

"Yes!"

Martha goes still. "Why? Why are you telling yourself that?"

I don't even have to wait to hear the inner voice. It boils up from the pit of my stomach and is out of my mouth before I can choose my words.

"I'm a burden to them because I'm anxious, and weird, and obsessive, and strange. I'm a burden because they have to drive more slowly on mountain roads, because my mom can't brag about me to her friends, because they have to spend their time talking about me and worrying about me, because they have to pay money for me to see you, because I'm sixteen and can't drive. Because I'm sixteen and can't handle anything. I'm a burden because I'm me."

We sit in silence. I blink back tears, because I am absolutely, positively not going to cry twice in the space of twenty minutes.

"Do you know," Martha asks, "the etymology of the word 'burden'?"

It's not Latin or Greek, so I'd guess proto-Germanic. Maybe something about farming. I shake my head.

"It's a great relief," Martha says with a sly smile, "to know just one word you don't. I hope you won't hold that against me."

"We all have our pride," I say, and she laughs.

"I'm not sure what language it comes from. I don't know what year you can trace it back to. But the word 'burden'—" Martha takes a breath. "The word for a *burden* is the same as the word for a *child*."

*Burden* and *child* are synonyms. Or they were, for someone, somewhere. Words can be revelations, and this is another one.

"A good parent would want to carry you. And if they couldn't, sometimes, it's because they're human. Humans are clumsy. Fragile things can break. It doesn't mean we mean to break them. Sometimes, we don't even know we've done it."

Something warm and hot is building behind my eyes. I look up at the ceiling. Martha keeps going.

"They were meant to carry you. Not just when it's convenient. Not just when you were small. For your entire life. You were brought into the world to be loved, and guided, and carried. That's the deal they made, the day you were born."

Without closing my eyes this time, I picture my family, again. All together, again.

My dad, in his white coat, saying that maybe he needed me more.

My mom, standing straight and tall, telling me my hair looked nice.

My sister, all charm and poise and goodness, teaching me how to spot the wall.

Martha gets up from her chair and sits next to me on the couch. She doesn't try to hug me. She doesn't even touch me. She wants me to know she's here, walking beside me.

"Are you a burden? I guess it depends on how you interpret the word. But if you're a burden, then every child is a burden. And Ellis. Please believe me. You are a worthy burden to carry."

Everyone just wants to be believed.

I want to believe Martha.

And as I collapse into tears yet again, I think I just might.

## TWENTY-ONE

**I'VE NEVER BEEN** alone under Hannah's tree before. I've spent a lot of time alone in my life, but in places that were suited for it. My room. The library. And maybe it's just the power of association, but Hannah's tree is an odd place to be alone.

I lie on the grass and tilt my face up at the sun. The closer we get to the end of the world, the more I seem to seek out warmth. Like a cat, following sunbeams. Or a person with an in-depth knowledge of what a mini Ice Age entails. One day far in the future, the sun will explode. One day, maybe even just a few weeks from now, there might not be sunlight. So I'll soak it up now. I breathe in deep, and sigh it out.

"Are you okay?" says a voice above me. When I open my eyes, there's Tal, looking down at me, his head titled. I sit up a little on my elbows.

"Yeah. Where is everyone?"

"Sam and Theo were hungry—they're going to Thai Temple.

Hannah had someone to meet. Didn't say who or where."

I bet I know who, and where. "And you?"

He shrugs. "I don't mind being alone."

"Oh." I start to push myself off the ground. "I can—"

But he's already sitting next me on the grass, a hand on my leg to stop me from getting up. "You should stay." Then, he quickly adds, "If you want to. Only if you want to."

"Okay," I say, and my palms are sweating. Am I nervous? I can't tell. My heartbeat's too fast and my stomach's twisted into a soft pretzel, but it doesn't feel like it usually does, like I've been backed into a corner or dangled outside an airplane window. For once, I'm not looking for an escape route. If I'm nervous, it's only because *he* seems so nervous.

"Cool," he says, and we both realize at the same time that his hand is still on my leg. I take a sharp breath in through my nose. He pulls his hand away like he's touched a mousetrap. I wish he'd put it back.

"What were you doing, when I came over?" he says.

I could lie in this situation. I probably should. I don't. "Thinking about the apocalypse."

He laughs. "You looked happy, though."

"I was thinking about the things I'd miss," I say. "Sunlight. Ice cream. Hanging out with you guys under Hannah's tree."

He goes quiet. "You'd really miss us?"

"Of course I'd miss you," I say, then look away.

After a moment of silence, Tal clears his throat. "Here's what

I don't understand. How are you so sure it'll—?"

"Well, the world's already a disaster, sea levels are rising every day, it's *in* the Bible—"

"You interrupted me."

"You interrupted *me*!"

"You did it first!" He puts his head in his hand. "God, okay. I was going to say, how are you so sure it'll be a literal apocalypse?"

I roll my eyes. "Who believes in a metaphorical apocalypse?"

"Lots of people. Lots of religions. I went to this other church—"

"You went other places?" I ask, surprised. I'd assumed if you leave the church, it's because you're done with religion entirely.

"Sure. My dad goes to this Methodist church now. It's cool. The pastor's a nice lady. It's not for me, but . . ." He shrugs. "Anyway, she said they don't believe in a literal apocalypse. That the story is more like a metaphor for how tough and shitty the world can be."

"The Book of Revelation is pretty clear," I say. "There's going to be a period of tribulation. With floods, and war, and disease—"

"But we've had those things," Tal says. "A thousand times over. What if this is the worst it gets? What if this world, the one right now, is that tribulation?"

A lady pastor. Scripture that's all metaphor. A universe that's already weathered the worst, and survived. It's so different than my world, but it doesn't seem like a bad world.

"Does your dad like it?" I ask. "The new church?"

"For now. He's always trying to find somewhere that fits and it never quite works. He was raised Catholic, but everyone in Brazil is. And then he came here for college, and just happened to meet two missionaries, and—" He shrugs. "They gave him what he needed. A community. Somewhere to belong. It was good for him. But then he needed new things. I used to think, if he'd had access to everything I do, no way he would have converted. But now I think he still would have, because he needed it."

"What do you mean, access to everything?" I ask.

"The internet." Then, off my look, "I'm serious. You don't have to think the info's accurate, that's up to you, but we *do* have a lot more information than our ancestors did. And infinitely more access to it. I mean, the temple ceremonies are on You-Tube, what else is left?"

My mouth drops open. Those ceremonies are sacred. There are some things even my parents can't tell me about their temple wedding, but it's on the internet? "You didn't *watch* one, did you?"

For a single second, he looks guilty. "I did."

"Tal!"

"I'm not saying *you* should." He shakes his head. "It doesn't mean the same thing to me as it does to you. My point is, we have more choices than anyone else in history. Whichever ones we make, we had more options. That can't be a bad thing."

I get why he thinks so, but even the idea makes my heart palpitate. If every choice in the world is open to you, how would you ever know which one is best? How could you ever really choose? It's simpler when things are laid out for you. Choices are good, of course, but choices are scary, too. Maybe *good* and *scary* aren't antonyms.

"If your dad hadn't converted," I point out, "he probably wouldn't have married your mom. You wouldn't even exist."

Tal picks at a blade of grass. "That might've been for the best."

"Don't say that."

"I'm not saying they don't love me," Tal says. "They do. But my dad would have a lot easier time dating without me around. And my mom . . ." He sighs. "She's got her new family. They all look perfect together. And then there's me, lurking in the corner, some reminder of the less-perfect family she used to have. I'm there, but it would be a nicer picture if I weren't. I'm like a . . ." He searches for a word.

And I know how it feels to search for something, anything, to make sense out of a painful thing. "Vestigial organ."

He raises his eyebrow. "A what?"

"Something in the body that used to serve a function but doesn't anymore. Like wisdom teeth. Or an appendix."

It's a weird, potentially offensive analogy, but Tal grins.

"I'm the appendix of my family. That's perfect. I'm keeping that."

Is there anything that makes your heart jump more, than someone wanting to keep your words?

"You're welcome," I say. "Nice to be useful to someone, for once."

He fixes me with a look. "Oh, what total bullshit."

My face gets hot. "Excuse me?"

"You're great," he says. "Don't you get that you're great?"

Now it's my turn to call BS. "I'm not."

"Girl, would you learn to take a compliment?"

"Well, I'm not that smart—"

"You're plenty smart."

"And I'm not that pretty—"

"I think you're pretty," he says quietly.

My breath catches. We stare at each other for a moment. I wait for him to say something else, to do something else. He doesn't. Maybe he's waiting for me, too.

"I'm not . . . sweet." I pull at the fibers in my coat sleeve. "You can't argue with me on that. I'm not even sweet enough to be a 'sweet spirit.'"

Tal sighs and looks off in the distance. There's a power in that, in not having to explain things. Tal is from my world, so he knows that "sweet spirit" is what church ladies call girls who are not quite attractive enough, not quite charming enough, not quite *enough*.

Tal focuses back on me. He moves a little closer. "Do you remember our freshman science class?"

"We weren't in the same class," I say.

He raises an eyebrow. "Yeah, we were. I sat right behind you." He flicks a piece of grass off my shoe. "Next to Hannah."

Something lurches in the pit of my stomach. *"Hannah?"*

Both his eyebrows are raised now. "Uh, yeah, that's how she and I met."

I don't remember that. I don't remember seeing her before that day in the waiting room. Hannah said we'd never met before. Maybe she doesn't remember either.

"You're sure we were in the same class?" I ask.

He nods. "Yeah, I swear. Freshman science. Third period with Mr. Spooner. You wore your hair in a French braid every single day."

Yikes. Accurate.

"It was probably around this time of the year," Tal continues. "Like, way too early for Mr. Spooner to have been so checked out, but he was. He had us doing some experiment. And Jessica Ritter—that was the year she was in the car accident, remember? She had that giant gash on her cheek, which it wasn't so bad with the bandage on it, but when it had to come off . . ."

I do remember that. It was noticeable, and not pretty, and her friends started avoiding her. This group of boys would bark at her when she walked in the room. Like she was a dog. They used to like her. But the second she wasn't something shiny in a store window, she was worthless to them.

"That day, during lab," Tal says, "Jessica asked Max Klein-felter for some iodine, and he said he would if she'd blow him. She told him he was a jerk, and then he said, 'You're going to have to get good at giving head, with a face like that.' And she dropped the iodine, and ran out of the room. No one followed her. No one did anything. But you . . ."

Me?

"You ripped a piece of paper out your notebook."

Oh. That's right.

"You ripped out a page and you wrote on it, saying you thought she was beautiful, a thousand times more beautiful than any of her friends, inside and out, and that you hoped a flaming piano would fall on Max Kleinfelter. You folded it up, and stuck it in her textbook, and just sat back down."

It comes back in a flood—the half-ripped paper, scribbling with the pen that bled blue ink all over my fingers, the fury I felt for stupid Max Kleinfelter and his stupid smug face, the anger I felt for Mr. Spooner not even noticing, the shame I felt for myself, because all I did was write a note. It's so odd to hear someone tell a story you didn't know they were part of. So odd to hear about yourself through someone else's eyes.

"Was your note *sweet*?" Tal says. "No, not really, you cursed someone with death by piano."

"He wouldn't necessarily have died," I point out.

"So it wasn't sweet. So what? It was compassionate, it was

righteous. It was *good*. Good is different than sweet. Good is so much better."

*Sweet* and *good* are not synonyms. It's a revelation. A small one. An important one. *Small* and *important* are not antonyms.

"I sort of figured . . ." Tal hesitates. "That's why Hannah found you, when she needed help. Because she knew you were the kind of person who would."

Hannah found me because she *saw* me. Not in some science lab, but in a dream, in the snow. Didn't she? I shake my head.

"I can't believe you remember that. I can't believe you saw that," I say.

"You're a lot less invisible than you think."

It's baffling, really, to think anyone would see me. Not as their daughter, or sister, or silent classmate in the corner. But see me, just as I am. See me, better than I see myself.

"Tal."

"Yes?"

"I—"

> Survive for something. Want something. Want something, Ellis.

"Do you know the etymology of the word 'pupil'?" I blurt out.

He blinks at me. "No."

"Can I tell you?"

"Okay," he says.

"I swear it's relevant."

"Okay," he says.

"'Pupil' comes from Latin, *pupilla*. It means a little girl, a little doll. It's the same in Greek, with the word *kore*. They gave the same word to a little doll and the center of the eye, because when you look into another person's pupil, you see a version of yourself, in miniature. But you have to be close, to do that, to see a person in a pupil. You have to get so close."

> *I want to be close. I want, I want—*

I grab Tal's hand and pull myself closer. My knee is touching his, touching bare skin through the rip in his pants, my heart is catapulting itself into my ribs, and there she is, in the center of his pupil, brown and green and unblinking. There I am. What a strange thing, to see yourself reflected in another person's eyes. What an amazing thing, to see yourself like they see you.

> *I want to keep seeing myself, I want to keep holding his hand, I want, I want—*

"Ellis."

"Yeah?"

"Do you know the etymology of the word 'kiss'?"

I do. Or I used to. "I don't remember."

His mouth quirks. "Can I kiss you anyway?"

> *Want something, Ellis. Want something. Let yourself want something.*

I breathe in. Release.

> *I want to kiss him.*

"Yes," I say, once, then again. "Yes."

291

He was the one who asked, so maybe I should have let him lean in, but I don't. I kiss him, terrified and overjoyed all once. When he kisses me back, the terror part melts away. I'm not supposed to be doing this, it's not like I don't know I'm not supposed to be doing this, it's just that I don't care. I feel like I've taken off a dress that's too tight. I feel like I've finally let myself breathe deep.

Tal breaks away. Oh no. Did he not want to? Or did he want to, but I was so bad at it he changed his mind?

"Are you . . ." He hesitates. "I only want you to do this if *you* want to do this. Not because you feel like you have to prove anything."

I don't understand what I'd have to prove. That I like him?

"I like you," I tell him. "I like you a lot, and I have for a while. I like you, and I liked kissing you, and I would like to kiss you again if that's mutually beneficial."

He barely suppresses a laugh. "Mutually beneficial?"

"Shut up, I know I'm bad at this!" I cover my face with my hands, but he pulls them away.

"You're not bad at this," he says. "It's just new."

I kiss him again, this time without hesitation. No hesitation, no terror, no fear. Not forever. Just for this one singular moment.

Words matter. Words are important, their definitions and histories are important, they mean something. Words tell every story that has ever been told, by fires in caves and castles and by prairie campfires. Under blue skies, under blankets of stars, in mountains and valleys and forests and deserts. Thousands of years, thousands of words, thousands of people who have loved each other, needed each other, grasped for each other in the dark of the world. But as I search for words, as I search for the etymology of *kiss* and *joy* and *fear* and *rapture*, nothing stays, nothing holds.

Some things are beyond words.

## TWENTY-TWO

**IT'S NOT THAT** I lie to Hannah about Tal. But I don't exactly tell her. I've barely even seen her, after our day in San Francisco. It's like she's avoiding me, and now that it's December, this is about the worst time for her to decide she needs her space. In theory, at least.

December 21 inches closer and closer, but it's weird. It doesn't feel like I thought it would, the end of days. The closer it gets, the more abstract it seems. And the more abstract it seems, the less space it takes up in my brain. Or maybe it's just being crowded out.

On December 4, someone pulls the fire alarm during sixth period, and school basically lets out early. I should use that as an opportunity to post more flyers, maybe around campus. But instead I hang out with Tal, Sam, and Theo under the tree, watching annoyed firefighters check the school.

On December 10, both my parents are out of the house. I

should be finding a way to stockpile more winter survival stuff. But instead, I spend the entire afternoon watching Em practice her routine for the winter recital.

On December 16, Tal asks if I want to skip fourth period and have a long lunch at his dad's house, which is a couple of blocks from school. I say yes, without hesitation.

I like Tal's house. It's only the second time I've been, but it's small enough that I already feel like I know my way around. It's cleaner than I expected a home with two dudes to be. The fridge is stocked, the counters are tidy, and the floor is clean enough that even my mom would approve. I've never seen my dad clean in his life, and he can cook eggs and not much else. "Oh, that's just men," I've heard my mom say. My dad's mom, too. But obviously, it's not true. I wonder what the men in my family could do if the women didn't treat them simultaneously like kings and children.

Tal's house is open plan, which I love, because it means I can sit on the very comfortable couch and still see him as he digs through the fridge.

"What about a frittata?" he asks. "Or . . . we've got leftover vatapá. It's a shrimp curry thing."

"The second one."

"Are you sure?" Tal throws me a look over his shoulder. "My dad makes it kind of spicy."

"I can handle it."

"Okay," Tal says, "but if frog's-eye salad at the ward potluck is more your style, that's cool. You don't have to prove anything here."

That reminds me of something I've wanted to ask Tal for over a week now.

"What did you mean, that first day we kissed?" I ask. "When you said I didn't have to prove anything?"

"Oh," he says. "Don't worry about it."

"I'm physiologically incapable of that. What would I want to prove?"

Tal closes the fridge door. He takes a seat next to me on the couch. "That you like guys," he says.

My stomach clenches. "What makes you say that?"

"Hannah said she thought . . ." He looks away for a moment, then back at me. "She thought I might not be your . . . type. You know?"

My stomach clenches tighter. I hold my breath. Tal notices.

"She only said that because I asked her if she thought you liked me," he says quickly. "She didn't say *why* she thought—"

"Hannah isn't—" I interrupt him, and he stops. He waits for me to continue. And I wait for some sort of new courage to burst out, to feel like the kind of a person who could say these things out loud. The kind of person who knows who she is. I wait to feel different, to feel ready, to feel *prepared*. But nothing happens. I still feel like the person I've always been—nervous, awkward, unsure. It's only that now, I have new things to say.

"Hannah isn't wrong," I tell him. "She's not all the way right but she's not wrong. I do like girls. I also like girls. Some girls. It's not—" I smile, suddenly, remembering one of my very first conversations with Tal. "It's not an either/or situation, for me."

I exhale. It was easier than I thought it would be. And of course it was. This is Tal. He comes from the same world I do, he feels the same things, he's said these same words to people who accepted him and people who didn't. I might not be saying these words, if he hadn't come into my life. I might never have realized I could.

"Okay." Tal nods. "Okay. So you're bi, then. That's awesome."

But maybe Tal and I aren't exactly the same. If only because he's had more time to wear these kinds of words, make sure they fit right.

"I think so," I say. "It seems right, it seems like it fits, but— I'm not positive. I don't know for sure. Can I wait on that, until I know for sure?"

"Wait on what?"

"Picking a label."

"That's chill with me. But I've got to tell you," he says with an apologetic shrug, "bi girls who hate labels is sort of a cliché."

"I don't hate labels. I just know there's lots of different ones, tons of them, probably ones I haven't even heard of yet, and . . ." I search for the right words. "I only just got here, you know? Let me take a look around."

He nods. "Take as long as you like."

"Well." I take his hand in mine, and draw him closer. "I like the view so far."

We abandon lunch. And TV. And my cardigan. He doesn't push me or pressure me. We don't do anything I'd have to confess to my bishop, but it's enough. Oh my gosh, it's enough. I'm starting to understand why some people get married in such a hurry.

Together on the couch, my head against his chest, he traces a pattern on my bare arm with a warm finger.

"Your skin's so soft," he says. "How do you get it so soft?"

A sixteen-year beauty routine of rarely going outside and never doing anything dangerous. "Well, not playing around with a lighter all the time helps." His hand shifts, and I place my palm on top of it. "No, don't stop. A couple more minutes and you'll pass the Universal Edibility Test."

"The what, now?"

"Prepper thing. It's how you tell if something's poisonous." I twist around and sit up on my heels. "First you smell it. . . ." I put a hand on his shoulder and sniff at his hair. He smells like coconut shampoo and cut grass. He smells like summer.

"Then, you hold it against your skin for fifteen minutes or so, to see if there's any reaction." I run my hand over his shoulder, down his arm. You're supposed to be watching for rashes or burns, but maybe goose bumps count, too.

"Then?" He puts his arm around my waist and closes the

space between us. "What's next?" he asks, like he already knows.

"Then," I say, "you can taste it. See what happens."

I kiss him, gentle and slow. Time might freeze. The world might stop in its motion. I wouldn't know. "Yep." I sit back. "I think you passed the test."

Tal shakes his head, the edges of his mouth quirking up. "So what you're saying is now you feel comfortable cannibalizing me?"

*Trying to Be Cute, Accidentally Implying Cannibalism: The Ellis Kimball Story.*

"I'm saying I think you're safe," I tell him, and he grins. I settle back down against his chest and close my eyes.

"The Universal Edibility Test," he says, after a minute of happy silence. "Who knew?"

"I did," I say, my eyes still closed.

"True. And that's what I like about you," he says. "All the best parts of those survivalist reality shows, none of the worst."

My eyes spring open. I sit up, pull back. "What do you mean?"

"You'd be the best person to get lost in the wilderness with. You'd know just what to do. I bet you're great at first aid, too."

"I don't know," I say truthfully. For all the planning and preparation, I have no clue what I'd be like in a crisis. Would I be calm? Would I get hysterical? There's no way of telling.

"You've got all the practical stuff down," Tal continues.

"But you're not building a bunker. You're not ready to pull a handcart to Missouri because some old dude told you the end was nigh. You're not an apocalyptic weirdo, like some people. You're not crazy."

I yank my arm out of his hand. "Don't say that."

Tal furrows his eyebrows. "That you're *not* crazy? Why?"

He wouldn't say that if he knew what I really think— thought? Still think? I did believe it, maybe I still do. I'm not what he thinks I am—what I was—no, am.

"That's a horrible thing to say," I tell Tal.

His mouth drops open. "But—I said you weren't—"

"You shouldn't say it at all."

He holds up his hands. "Okay, now I feel crazy."

I snatch up my cardigan, coat, and backpack. "You're not! You're not, I'm—" I shake my head so hard it hurts. "I'm going. I have to go."

Tal scrambles up from the couch. "Wait, wait."

"I just remembered, I have a math test."

"Ellis."

"I have to go."

Tal's shoulders are slumped, and he's still got one foot on the couch. He looks confused. *Confused* comes from Latin; *confused* once meant pouring together, mixing or joining. But it really meant throwing into disorder. Upsetting something delicate.

I've been teetering on this precipice for weeks, sitting on a cliff, right at the edge of belief and unbelief. The end of the world, just one step away, but the tug of hands on my shoulders, too, keeping me earthbound. Martha telling me I'm not a burden. The salt spray in my face at Lands End. Tal's lips on mine, hesitant and hopeful. I wanted those things. I loved those things. I wished those things wouldn't end, and neither would the world. I wished it wasn't true.

But it is true. If it isn't true, then everything I've done was for nothing. Every day I spent with Hannah, every lie I told my parents, every dollar I spent on supplies, every second of my life I spent thinking, planning, preparing. If it isn't true, I'm exactly what Tal said, and worse. It has to be true. *It has to be.*

"I have to go," I say again.

"I don't understand," he says, so simply and honestly it makes my heart split apart.

Of course he doesn't. No one does. And no one will, unless I tell them.

"I have to go," I whisper, just one more time, as he lets me walk out the front door.


Here are some things my high school has:

> The legally required American flag in each classroom, but half of them are upside down
>
> Substitute teachers who tell you their entire drug history, including that one time they technically died
>
> An annual tradition called the Senior Streak, in which twelfth graders clad only in body paint run through the central courtyard

Here are some things my high school does not have:

A dress code

A debate team

A halfway decent security system

No one stopped me as I walked onto campus ten minutes after the lunch bell. No one cared when I pulled a giant stack of orange flyers out of my locker. No one questioned me as I walked through the hallways of three different buildings taping the flyers to the walls. And now I'm in the administration building itself and *still*, no one appears to notice me. Did I turn invisible on my walk from Tal's house? Do I look so unthreatening everyone feels comfortable staring right through me? Does anyone take me seriously, or am I just a *joke*, am I just—

I shake my head and blink back the hurt. I'm not. They'll see that I'm not.

I tack a flyer to the bulletin board outside the admin offices, a bull's-eye in the center of the other flyers. Normal flyers, the kind that don't urge you to start stockpiling water and nonperishable food. Flyers for softball tryouts. Flyers for the spring musical—*Les Misérables*, which I would have liked to see, even if no high schooler can pull off Jean Valjean. Flyers for the state Quiz Bowl championship Theo would have gone to, if the world were not ending.

Which it is. It definitely is. Because if it wasn't, what would that make me?

I startle at the clip of shoes on the linoleum floor. I spin around and press myself against the bulletin board. It's Ms. Bayer, one of the assistant principals, and she doesn't even look my way as she shuts the door to her office and walks in the opposite direction down the hall, tapping on her phone. I didn't even know that was her office. I've only seen her in the courtyard during passing periods, clicking around in very high heels, yelling at everyone to get to class, and conversing with the water polo boys in a syrupy voice that is borderline creepy.

I stand still, feeling the blunt side of thumbtacks against my spine. I'm here, at the right place, at the right time. It's almost fate. The posters aren't enough, the posters were never enough. It's fate. I walk with purpose and quick steps around the stairs, down the hall, and straight into her unlocked office, shutting the door behind me. I fumble for the lock and turn it into place with a satisfying click.

I know exactly what I'm doing.

I run over to the phone on Ms. Bayer's desk. I scan the laminated instructions beside it. In another time, I would have hit each button slowly, uncertainly, checking and rechecking the steps, doubting and re-doubting myself.

I punch in the code without hesitation and scoop up the microphone. I flip the switch, and the on light turns green.

I have no idea what I'm doing.

"Attention," I say, too close to the mic, and it screeches. I pull it back a bit. "Attention, students, faculty, and administrators of Berkeley High School. Though mostly the students, because I'm guessing the adults are mad at me already. This is an announcement. It's not about clubs, or sports, or dances, it's about your lives. Your very lives are at stake, so listen up."

Now someone's at the door, shadowed and distorted through the frosted glass. The person tries the knob, and it rattles but doesn't turn. Someone's yelling at me to open up. Someone's yelling at me to stop, but I can yell at myself, too, and I'm yelling, *Keep going, Ellis, keep going!*

"As we speak, the world is coming to an end. Before the year is through, the world you've always known and loved—well, the world you've known, anyway—is going to end. Call it dooms-day, apocalypse, armageddon, the end is near. The end is near."

I said it twice. I didn't need to say it twice. For a second, I wonder exactly who I'm trying to convince, but my own voice drowns that thought out.

"A storm will come, snow and ice and cold, and bury San Francisco," I go on. "The sky will turn red. Stars will fall. Get ready now, get prepared now, don't wait. Stock up bottled water, nonperishable food, warm clothing, nonelectric heat sources. Kiss your crush. Tell your parents you love them. Don't go out with any regrets."

There are more people at the door now, at least three, and someone flailing their arms. There's shouting, too, but it's muffled. There are multiple people outside who are all furious with me, and I should be terrified. I *am* terrified. But I'm also grinning from ear to ear as I grip the mic and turn away from the door. Right now, I'm the one with the microphone. I'm the one with the audience. I have the voice that can't be silenced. And I'll enjoy it as long as it lasts.

"While I'm here," I say, leaning against the desk, "can I just say, this school is so freaking *weird*. I know high school is supposed to be a disaster just by definition, but have you ever thought about what you'll tell your college roommate? When she's like, 'Oh, I was homecoming queen,' and you'll have to be like, 'Oh, really? I spent homecoming watching children drink grain alcohol in a public park.' And she'll say that's very atypical, and then you'll one-up yourself by telling her about Senior Streak, and it'll be a weird conversation." I take a breath. "Or it would be, except none of us are going to college, because the world is ending in less than a week, which I think I mentioned."

Then I stop short, because I *want* to have that conversation, as awkward as it sounds. I want to have a thousand more awkward conversations, and good ones, and new ones—I want the universe to keep spinning. But it won't. It can't. Or I wouldn't be doing this.

"For as messed up as this school is, it's the best preparation for the impending apocalypse we could have asked for," I say. "No one here cares what you do, even when they definitely should, and that's going to be true in doomsday, too. No one here stops you from taking risks or making choices, no matter how young you are or how terrible those choices are. You should hold on to that. When the world ends.

"What else, what else." I twirl the mic cord, feeling oddly like a stand-up comic and also like I'm going to pass out. "Oh, well, not that I'm complaining, I guess, but what kind of school makes it this easy for me to get on the PA system, anyway? What is our campus security team for, exactly? The guard out front didn't stop me from breaking into this office because he was playing his Game Boy. That's concerning. Who still has a Game Boy? Also, someone should tell Ms. Bayer to stop flirting with the water polo boys. That's even more concerning."

There's a click behind me, metal against metal. I spin around just in time to see Ms. Bayer throw open the door, keys gripped in one fist. She strides over to me and holds out her other hand, palm up. That's fine. I said what I needed to. More than that, I said what I wanted to.

"Thank you, Berkeley High," I say into the mic. "It's been great. Fingers crossed we all survive armageddon, because I honestly think I'd miss you."

I lay the mic in her hand.

# TWENTY-THREE

**MS. BAYER CONFISCATES** my things and sticks me in an empty conference room. "Wait here," she orders. "We're calling your parents."

I'm not sure if that's intended to scare me, or comfort me. It does both.

When Ms. Bayer leaves, I don't hear the door lock. I briefly consider making a run for it, but there's a receptionist right outside. Even if I made it out the front door, what would be the point? As scary as this is, I got exactly what I wanted. The message went out. So why do I feel so sick?

This room is aggressive in its boringness. There's no artwork, no wall calendar to look at, and it's basement level, so the windows provide light and not much else. Occasionally, a person's legs come into view as they walk by. I settle on counting the squares in the linoleum under my feet. I've made it up to 328 when I hear someone say:

"Holy shit, Ellis Kimball. I never would've guessed you had it in you."

My head snaps up. Crouched by one of the street-level windows is Sam, and I have never been so glad to see anyone.

"Sam!"

I run over. I'm not quite tall enough. I drag a chair as quietly as possible and climb on it so that Sam and I are more or less eye to eye.

"What are you doing here?" I whisper.

"Cutting gym," he says. "I'd ask what doing you're doing here, but I'm pretty sure I know."

"Did you hear it? Did it work?"

"Oh, it worked," he says. "Radio broadcast? Doomsday? Mass hysteria? You're a prettier Orson Welles."

"Um, thank you?"

"This"—Sam holds up a flyer—"is hilarious."

Hilarious? I reel back and almost topple the chair.

"Not that it wasn't good," Sam continues, "but I think the Senior Prank is supposed to be done by seniors."

The Senior Prank also happens in the spring. "Sam—"

"Better than last year's, though. A bunch of paper cups filled with water in the quad? Uninspired."

"This wasn't—"

"I mean, was it as good as that time in the nineties they got a cow onto the C-building roof? Nah. But that's okay."

"So you're saying it wasn't as good as animal cruelty?"

"Or my brother's year, when they hired a mariachi band to

follow Principal Grant around all day. It was expensive and all, but that's a prank."

"Sam!" I hiss. "This wasn't. A. Prank."

He sits back on his heels. "Huh?"

"The end of world really is coming. And I thought people deserved to know."

"Are you messing with me?"

"Hannah's had visions."

Sam gapes at me. "Hannah had what?"

"Dreams," I clarify. "More than visions. Very specific dreams about the end of the world."

Sam stares up at the sky. He makes a noise somewhere between a sigh and a groan. "Ellis . . ."

"I'm—!" I say, and press on even though he throws up his hands. "She did!"

"She's been stressed out of her mind for, like, six months! She's basically disintegrating. This isn't a game, it's serious." He jabs at his chest. "And that's *me* saying that."

"I know it's serious. It's real, Sam."

He looks at me with a mix of sadness and disbelief.

"The end of the world is almost here," I say. And then, even though he won't get the Book of Revelation reference, "Surely, it comes quickly."

"God," he says through gritted teeth. "I really want to make a sex joke right now. But you've ruined it. You've ruined it with the apocalypse."

I laugh, even though this is possibly the least-funny situation

I could find myself in, barring the actual apocalypse itself. I should probably be crying. It would make more sense. Sam reads through the flyer.

"Freak snowstorm?" he says.

"Yeah."

"So, what, buy up all the blankets at the army supply store?"

Not a bad start. "And nonperishable food. Bottled water. Alternative heat sources."

"Sounds like camping."

"Forced camping."

"All camping is forced camping to me," he says.

We sit in silence for a moment. "Hey, Sam?" I ask, and he looks up. "When you see Tal, will you give him a message from me? I might not be able to talk to him again."

"They're going to send you to On-Campus Intervention, not ship you off to a Siberian gulag."

"Please."

He stuffs the pamphlet in his hoodie pocket. "Okay."

"When you see Tal, tell him none of this is his fault," I say. "Tell him I wish I didn't have to do this. Tell him sometimes I wish I didn't believe, but . . ." I smile, thinking of one of the first conversations I had with Tal. "But you can't force unbelief."

"Okay," Sam says. "Not his fault. Wish you didn't have to. Can't force unbelief."

"One more thing." I raise myself up on my toes, as if the

closer I am to Sam, the more it will stick in his brain. "Tell him that this can't be the tribulation period."

Sam cocks his head. "The what?"

"The tribulation. He'll know what it means. Tell him this can't be the tribulation because . . ." My eyes burn, and so does my heart. "Because the last three months were the happiest I've ever been."

Sam looks at me sadly. I'm not sad. I meant it.

"Can you remember one more?" I ask. "It's the last one. I promise."

Sam nods.

"Tell him I wish we had more time."

Sam reaches his hand through the crack in the window. I raise mine up. Only our fingertips can touch, but it's enough.

"I'll tell him," Sam says.

"Everything?"

"You've got a way with words." Sam snakes his hand out. He stands. "I don't think I'll forget them."

"Thanks, Sam."

"Anytime."

When he leaves, I twist my head as far as it will go, watching as he gets smaller in the distance. It feels like when my parents dropped me off at sleepaway camp for the first time. Like a tether's been cut, or a muscle's been severed, and I'm facing an entirely new existence. Alone.

I step off the chair. Rather than dragging it back to its old spot, I place it facing the door. Whatever's coming through, I'm facing it head-on.

After what feels like an eternity of staring at the door, the knob turns. Mom emerges in the doorway. I knew she'd be the one to come get me, and I kept trying to picture her reaction. Trying to prepare. Like research, but for emotions, which almost never works. I'd prepared for Mom being quietly furious, rage under a layer of carefully applied foundation. But she just looks . . . defeated. Battered and tried, her whole body waving a white flag. Being defeated implies an enemy, though, doesn't it?

It only takes one horrible second to realize that the enemy is me.

Mom jerks her head at the door. "Come on."

I stand. I reach for my backpack before remembering it's not with me. "I need to get my stuff."

Wordlessly, she hands over my backpack.

When I walk out the door, Mom puts her hand on my shoulder and guides me down the hallway, toward the glass front doors.

"We're going home?" I ask, because I thought there would be more. More talking, more discussion, more questions. No one's asked me a single question. Don't they have questions?

"Yes," she says. "We're going home."

"She doesn't want to talk to me? Ms. Bayer?"

"I explained the situation," Mom says.

"But you don't even know what the situation is!" I protest.

"I know plenty."

She's already made her mind up about everything. Not just Hannah, not just faith or the right way to fold dish towels, but everything. Including me. We walk the rest of the way to the car in silence. We start the drive home in silence, too. But then something pricks in my heart and deflates the quiet.

"So am I suspended, or what?"

I don't know why I ask. In a week, it won't matter.

"I handled it," Mom says. "Nothing's going on your record."

I don't know why I'm relieved. In a week, my record won't matter, either. I shouldn't care, why do I care?

"Then why can't I go back to class?" I ask Mom.

"We came to an alternate arrangement."

"What arrangement?"

"We'll talk about it later."

"I deserve to know what's happening to me."

Mom veers off the road so suddenly I brace myself on the dashboard. She parks. She turns off the car. And then she bursts into tears.

"I don't know what's happening to you, Ellis," she sobs. "I don't know why you're doing this, I don't understand a thing you've done."

I've never seen her cry like this. I've seen her cry quietly, artful and delicate tears at the right moments. I've never seen her collapse.

"Mom," I whisper. "Mom, please, stop."

"I want to," she says, her voice raw. "I want to understand so badly, but I don't. I don't. I don't know how to help you. I don't know what to do."

"Please," I say again, because she's scaring me. Is this what it's like, to watch someone break down? To see them sliced open by their own thoughts and know you can't do a thing to stop it? Is this what Mom has seen me do, over and over and over?

She's sobbing through each word now. "All I want is to help you and I can't. What kind of mother can't help her own baby? What kind of mother am I?"

Something hot and searing sticks in my chest. Because deep in the darkest part of me, I've wondered the same thing. All my life, I've wanted to grab on to her skirt and beg her, "Why don't you love me, *please* love me." I've wanted to grab her by the shoulders and demand, "Why don't you love me, you should *already* love me."

She does love me. She loves me so much it's ripping her in two. She just doesn't understand me. *Love* and *understand* are not synonyms.

I grab her arm. "Mama."

She looks up at me, red-eyed and blotchy-faced, that veneer of perfect washed away.

"I'm sorry," she says. "I'm so sorry." She wraps her arms around my neck, awkwardly. I hug her back, though I don't understand exactly what she's apologizing for. That can come later. You can love without understanding.

We hold each other, uneasily but tightly, for a long moment. Mom breaks away first. She digs in her purse for a napkin and gingerly wipes away the parallel lines of mascara running down her cheeks.

"Let's go home," she says.

# TWENTY-FOUR

**I WONDER HOW** much of my life I've spent on couches while someone tries to figure me out.

Days, for sure, between Martha and the therapist I had when I was eight and my teacher said I wasn't "emotionally connecting with other students." I still maintain the other students weren't connecting with *me*, though I now acknowledge it's hard to connect with the girl who can't stop talking about the destruction of Pompeii.

If you include my parents in that list, it's got to add up to weeks, at least.

I don't understand why we couldn't have talked about this in my room, where at least I could have curled up under blankets while my parents stared at me like a zoo animal. When my dad got home, my parents claimed the entire second floor so they could whisper about me for a half hour while my body attempted to melt into the couch.

I don't know exactly what they talked about, but they must have decided something, because now they're seated in two chairs in front of me.

"First of all," Dad says, looking at Mom out of the corner of his eye, "we know you've been having a tough time."

"Psychologically," Mom adds.

"With your junior year being stressful. We know that heightens your feelings of anxiety."

"This isn't about school," I protest.

"Then what is it about?" Mom asks.

"It's about the end of the world," I say.

"Oh, for goodness' sake," Dad says.

"I feel like my flyers were pretty clear."

"They were terrifying," Mom says, "if that's what you mean."

"The apocalypse is a scary concept, Mom, so sure."

"There is no apocalypse coming," Dad says. "I thought we'd gotten past this."

"I believe there is."

Dad puts his head in his hands. Mom purses her lips.

"I know you don't believe me," I say. "That's fine. It's your right not to believe me."

"That's very kind, thank you," Mom deadpans.

"But other people had a right to know, you know?" They both look at me blankly. "The kids at school had a right to decide for themselves, too. So I had to tell them."

317

"How do you think you'd react," Dad asks, "if you were in class, and all of a sudden, someone came on the loudspeaker and told you exactly how you were going to die?"

"I didn't say they'd die!"

"You said the world as they knew it would be over by the end of the year."

"That's not the same as dying."

Dad shakes his head. "If someone did that to you, you would be a wreck."

Is he right? Probably. But this was necessary.

"Well," I say, and it comes out a whine, "I didn't know how else to tell them."

Mom sighs. "And I suppose there's no convincing you that you shouldn't have told them at all?"

I stare at my shoes. "Were people—were people really scared?"

"Ms. Bayer said it was—" Mom looks at Dad. "Light pandemonium."

"That's a made-up word," I mutter. "'Pandemonium.'"

"No, it isn't," Mom says.

"Yes, it is," I shoot back. "John Milton made it up as his name for Satan's hell-palace in *Paradise Lost*."

"Ellis," Dad says.

"He didn't just make it up, he stuffed Greek and Latin words together to make it up. It's ridiculous."

"Yes, that's what's ridiculous, here," Mom says.

"Lisa," Dad says.

"Do you have any idea what we just went through?" Mom says. "Do you have any idea what I had to say to that woman to keep your record clean?"

"What did you tell her?"

Dad takes over. "Mom told her it was an isolated incident brought on by extreme stress and that with some time and distance, you would be able to overcome it."

They're so sure time is limitless. I'd like to be that sure. I'd like to believe I have all the days in the world to spend with Tal and to watch Em dance. Instead, I have this sense of doom, dark and shadowed, wrapping its arms around my chest.

"I convinced her," Mom says, "you should be given that. Time and distance." She pauses. "Physical distance."

"Physical . . . ?"

Mom and Dad look at one another.

"We're going to Utah for Christmas," Dad says.

"I know that." They made those plans a month ago. Never mind that their plane won't be able to take off after the storm. "On the twenty-third. After Em's recital."

"Yes," Mom says, "but you're going ahead of us."

I recoil. "When?"

They look at each other again.

"When?" I repeat.

"Tomorrow," Dad says.

The sun explodes. The earth's core collapses.

"Tomorrow?" I whisper.

"You'll stay with Aunt Tonya until we get there," Mom says. "We'll all be together on Christmas."

"You're sending me away," I say, half accusation, half question.

"We're removing you from the stressor," Mom says. "We're taking this doomsday plot out of the equation."

I won't be here on December 21. I won't be at the top of the hill with Hannah. I won't be there to make sure things go the way they're supposed to. Panic rises. Panic reigns.

"You can't do this," I say, fast and urgent. "You don't understand what could happen if I'm not here, I have to be here, she *told* me—"

"She's disturbed," Mom says.

"Overly imaginative," Dad says, spreading his hands. "And charismatic, I'm sure, honey, but that's why we're doing this."

"Because you want the world to end?"

"Because we want to make sure you're safe," Dad says. "For the rest of December, you'll be with family. Somewhere safe, and protected. And when January comes and the world doesn't end, you'll see we were right. And things will go back to normal."

"I have school," I protest. "You said they didn't kick me out."

"They didn't," Mom says. "Your teachers said you can email in anything that was due this week. You'll be back at school in time for midterms in January."

"They were really very accommodating," Dad says.

"And obviously, you are never seeing Hannah again," Mom says.

"It wouldn't be good for either of you," Dad agrees.

"We'll work out logistics in January," Mom says. "You're not taking your phone to Utah. We'll start with that."

"But she doesn't even have a cell phone!" I shout. "She gave it to Frank Zappa's owner!"

"What?" Dad says.

I close my eyes to stop the buzzing in my brain. "Please," I beg. "Please don't send me away. Bad things will happen if I'm not here. Really bad things. I know you don't believe the world is ending, I know you don't believe Hannah, but don't you believe *me*? I'm your daughter. Don't you believe *me*?"

"We believe that you believe," Dad says.

"But we also know you're hurting yourself," Mom says, grabbing on to my hand. "We also know you're wrong."

I wrench my hand out of hers and stomp through the living room, into the kitchen, and down the stairs to the basement, picking up my backpack on the way and slamming the door behind me. I curl up on the lumpy, discarded chair by the washing machine and dig through my backpack. My Altoids box of everyday carry is still there, though someone's clearly looked through it. My phone is not. From this spot, I can hear everything upstairs. The clack of my mom's heels, the clomp of my dad's size 12 feet. The running water as my mom starts to get dinner ready. And then I realize—they'll let me stay down here for hours. Until dinner, probably. They know I need my space.

And that means I have time. Not much. But some.

They can't hear anything in this concrete cave, not from where they are, but I still creep as quietly as I can to the basement's back door. The inside lock opens, and then I'm outside, alone, undetected. I close the door slowly, silently. I have no phone, which means this'll be a surprise. I have no real plan, either.

But I have time. I have time to find Hannah.

I'm lucky I remember where Hannah's house is. I'm less lucky that it's a mile away from mine. I'm even less lucky that it starts sprinkling as I cross the Cal campus. We could hide around here. Cal has lots of warm, dry places to hang out, and I bet the library's open late, for all those overachieving Public Ivy Leaguers. But then again, campus is so close to both our homes, and probably crawling with police officers and security guards. Maybe we'll go into the hills, disappear into Tilden Park. We only have to make it one more week. In the grand scheme of human existence, that's nothing at all.

I wipe my wet shoes on the plaid doormat. I peer up at the gray house and into the second-story bay windows, hoping to catch a glimpse of Hannah. I rap on the red door.

It creaks open just enough for me to see one wide blue eye and a tendril of long curly hair.

"Hi," I whisper.

"What are you doing here?" she whispers.

"I came to get you."

The door opens just wide enough for Hannah to slip outside. She leaves it open, just a crack. She wraps her arms around herself. She's only got a long-sleeved shirt on, no coat or hoodie. And no shoes. We're going to have to fix that.

"That was quite a performance today," she says. I guess she didn't skip fourth period.

"I had to do something."

"Oh God," she says, and sighs. "I know I haven't been around much lately, but what were you thinking, saying shit like that on the intercom? We need to lay low until the twenty-first, okay? Just be chill, just—"

"Who's inside right now?" I interrupt.

"My mom," Hannah says, throwing a look back toward the door.

"Then let's do this fast," I say. I count off on my fingers. "You need your warmest coat, and your warmest boots. Food if you can grab it, bottled water—"

"Ellis," she says, but I'm not done, and time is of the essence, so I ride over her.

"If you have anything wool, take it, doesn't matter what it is, stuff it in a backpack."

"Ellis!" she snaps, then clamps her mouth shut for a moment. "What are you talking about?"

"They're going to send me to Utah. Tomorrow. So we have to leave. Now."

She winces. "Your parents were that mad?"

"Apoplectic. Devastated. Let's go."

Hannah looks down at her shoes. "No."

No? What does she mean, *no*? "We have to," I tell her. "You need to get what you can, then we'll go back to school—I have some emergency supplies in my locker. We'll figure it out. We'll figure it all out, but you need to get your stuff and we need to go now."

"This has gone too far," she whispers. Her head shakes, and so does her voice. "I didn't mean for this happen, I swear, I just wanted to find Danny. But you took it too far."

Because I locked myself in some admin office? Because I did what she wouldn't, because I actually *warned* people?

"They'll be glad I did," I promise. "When the snow comes, when the end of the world comes. Everyone will be glad I told them."

She shakes her head again. "The end of the world is not coming."

The earth's core cracks beneath my feet. Iron and nickel explode up like the Yellowstone Caldera.

"What?" I croak.

Hannah steadies herself on the red door. She looks me in the eye. "The end of the world is not coming."

"But . . ." My brain is spinning; the words aren't coming.

"But you—your dreams—"

"Everyone has dreams, little kids have dreams, my *dog* has dreams."

"Your dog dreams about squirrels, not the apocalypse!" I shout. Hannah throws a panicked glance behind her.

"Be quiet," she says through gritted teeth.

Why should I be? She said it herself, no one's inside but her mom, and her parents already know—

No.

"Your parents don't know about the dreams," I say, and the look she gives me is as good as a nod. "They don't know, you never told them, you never told anyone but me."

"Wait," she says, but I can't.

"Why are you in therapy?" I demand. "It's not for your dreams, it's not because your parents think you're delusional, why do you go?"

"Because I had to jump out of a car," she snaps. "Because I can't let him go. Because I've been dealing with some *serious shit*, Ellis, you don't need a diagnosis to have *problems*."

"You lied to me," I croak.

"I never told you why I saw her, I never said—"

"You said you'd seen it. You'd said you'd seen the end of the world."

"I know!" she says, burying her face in her hands. "I know, but if I'd told you about everything all at once, you would have freaked out. You would have judged me."

"That's not true."

"I needed a way in, and then you brought up the end of the world, and I only . . ." She clamps her mouth shut. Like it's too hard to say more. She doesn't need to, I'm piecing it together myself.

"You wanted my help. You wanted me to help you find your brother and you figured out what I was most scared of in the entire universe and you told me it was happening!"

"I needed you," she says, as though *need* makes it better. "I needed you, and I needed you to trust me, so I said what I thought would work, but then it just sort of spiraled, and you made those posters, and started telling people, and—"

"And you let me do it! Even though you knew it wasn't—"

"I know, okay? I know." Hannah rubs at her eyes like they hurt. "I guess I didn't realize how seriously you'd take it."

*"The end of the world?"*

She shushes me again. "And when I did realize, I tried to . . . back off. I swear. I went looking for him on my own, I stayed out of the Park because I knew you'd be there, I thought if I kept my distance maybe it would be better. For you."

All those days I didn't see her, or hear from her. She spent all those days alone. Because she couldn't bring herself to tell me the truth. It makes my heart ache and my teeth clench all at once.

"Yeah, if you tried that hard, how did we end up here?" I demand.

She winces. "I don't know. I kept promising myself this was it, and then I kept breaking the promise. I kept finding you, I kept wanting to find you. I kept getting pulled back in."

I thought Hannah was the sun, and I was just an orbiting planet. Or a piece of metal drawn to a magnet. It's not true. We were both the magnets.

"You kept pulling me back in," she says, and it feels close to an accusation.

"This isn't my fault!" I throw back at her. Salt stings the corner on my eyes. "You lied to me. You used me. And for *what*?"

"I can explain that part," she says, but I'm already taking a step back, then another.

"I don't want you to explain." I spin around so fast it feels like my brain rattles.

"I didn't lie about everything," she pleads. "Not everything. Wait, please."

I turn back around. She's got one hand on the door, one hand reaching out to stop me.

"I still need you," she says.

Worlds crumble. Worlds end. Words fail.

I walk away, leaving her in the doorway.

Water sloshes out of my shoes and drips down from my drenched hair as I walk in my front door, realizing too late I should have come up through the basement stairs. Dad is still in the living room, poking at his phone. His mouth drops open when he sees me. "What on Earth—why are you soaking wet?"

"I'm going to pack," I say, and it sounds flat and muffled in my ears.

"Lisa!" he calls into the kitchen. I head him off by walking into the kitchen myself.

"Ellis," Mom gasps as I grab an entire package of Oreos from the pantry. "Did you go outside? We thought you were down in the . . ." She trails off as I grab a Coke out of fridge. "That is not an appropriate snack."

"Hannah's a liar." I pop open the soda can. "She lied to me."

"What?" Mom says.

I take a long gulp. "Hannah lied to me. I'm going to pack for Utah."

Then I leave her in the kitchen, eyes wide and saucepan boiling over, and go straight to my room.

## TWENTY-FIVE

**WHEN I WAS** little, I thought America looked just like the fifty states puzzle I had. When viewed from above, I imagined, you could see each state's name in bold black letters stretched across the ground, clean borders with clear-cut lines. From my window seat in the second-to-last row, I can't tell where Utah begins. I can't feel the split second I cross out from the wilderness into home. But when the Great Salt Lake comes into view on the horizon, a little blue pool hemmed in by desert and mountains, I sigh. This is a homecoming.

I was born in California and lived my entire life in the same zip code. Berkeley is the place that raised me on its chaos and oddball charm. Seventeen square miles of hills and canyons, elite universities and tent cities. Berkeley is my hometown, and it always will be. But Utah is my home, too. A different kind of home. An ancestral home. A place of belonging. A legacy.

When I land at Salt Lake City International, I ride the

escalator down with a just-returned sister missionary, exhausted but bright-eyed, in a long skirt and sensible, beaten-up shoes. Her family is just past the security checkpoint with balloons and "Welcome Home" signs, and they scream in unison when they see her. And just to their left is Aunt Tonya, staring at me with obvious disappointment.

Em was always the Golden Girl, from the moment she was born. What choice did I have but to be the Perpetual Disappointment? Every family needs one. So I've fallen on my sword. It's actually very noble of me.

The car ride to Aunt Tonya's house is silent. And so are the next few days, as I mope around her house in Spanish Fork. Or as everyone here pronounces it, "Spanish *Fark*." Spanish Fark in Utah County. Happy Valley. And yes, we're all so happy here. I'm so happy I could vomit rainbows. I'm so happy I could shove an ice pick in my eye.

It's too far from the city to get anywhere without a car, not that anyone would let me go. Aunt Tonya's kept me on the shortest of leashes, and I don't expect that to change when my cousin Sarah gets done with finals tomorrow and flies in from Hawaii. I don't even expect that to change when my parents and sister arrive the day after that, on the twenty-third.

But to my shock, today features a surprise field trip.

"I want you dressed in fifteen minutes," Aunt Tonya says, passing through the living room with a basket full of laundry.

"Why, where are we going?" I ask.

"The Renaissance."

*Of course, let me grab my corset and petticoat,* I almost say, but restrain myself. "The Renaissance?"

"Grammy Kit's nursing home," Aunt Tonya says. "Fifteen minutes."

The Renaissance is a two-story brown-brick building on the outskirts of Salt Lake City, and you could mistake it for a real house, except for the bank of wheelchairs on the covered entryway and the sign proclaiming it "an award-winning senior care facility."

Aunt Tonya parks near the front, and I grab my bag from the backseat.

"What's all that?" she says as we walk to the building, eyes on my backpack.

"Homework stuff." I choose not to mention my everyday carry pack at the bottom, or my wallet stuffed with quarters, in case the nursing home has a pay phone and I can sneak away and call Tal, or Em, or—

No. Not Hannah. Not even if she had a phone.

"Uh-uh," Aunt Tonya says. "You're here to spend time with Grammy Kit, not hole up in a corner. This isn't a vacation."

I wonder in what joyless universe homework is considered a vacation activity. "It's for school."

"And this is for service." I follow behind her through two sets of doors, heavy and opaque. A lock clicks behind us.

Aunt Tonya moves through the hallways purposefully, greeting green-uniformed workers by name. I try to stop my stomach from flipping at the piped-in fifties music, the locked, motion-sensored doors, the smell of bleach and urine and lavender air freshener. We stop at a door that reads KIT HOLLEY.

Inside the room is a tiny, hunched woman in an easy chair. If you didn't know, you might not guess that she spent her teenage years running cattle on her family farm, or that she spent her adult years wrangling children, nursing her husband until the bitter end of pancreatic cancer, and managing their small grocery shop, all at the same time.

You also might not know what a pair of lungs she packs inside that small body, but only until she opens her mouth.

"Ruby!" She hollers as Aunt Tonya shuts the door behind us. I look around for a healthcare worker, but there's no one in the room but us. Aunt Tonya has her mouth set in a thin line. Grammy Kit is staring straight at me.

It takes me a second to realize that Ruby is me. Or at least, Ruby is who she thinks I am.

"Ruby!" She repeats.

"It's Ellis, Grammy," I say, trying to swallow the lump in my throat. It's not like I couldn't have predicted this. She doesn't remember my mom, her own daughter, why should she remember me?

"Good lord in heaven," she says. "What are you wearing?"

I look down at my outfit. The jeans are pretty standard, so

it must be the shirt. "It's flannel."

"You look like a field hand."

"I'd be a pretty bad field hand."

"Nonsense," she says. "Wasn't me with that blue ribbon calf in fifty-nine."

It wasn't me, either, but why not? Whoever Ruby was, I'd rather be her than me.

"I'll let you in on a secret," I say, and Grammy Kit leans forward. "It was really a pig painted black and white."

She stares at me for a moment. Then she throws back her head and cackles. Aunt Tonya purses her lips.

"Mama," Aunt Tonya says as Grammy Kit picks at a back molar. "Ellis is going to keep you company today. I'll come back after dinner."

After dinner? It's barely noon. "When's dinner?" I ask Aunt Tonya.

"Four p.m. I can pick you up around five."

That's a long time to hang around here by myself, but I nod. Aunt Tonya shuts the door the behind her as she leaves.

Grammy Kit pokes me in the arm. "Thought she'd never leave."

"Tonya? She'll be back."

"She's gone. You can tell me."

"Tell you what?"

"About George, you goose. Did he kiss you?"

I shake my head. "Grammy Kit, I don't know any—"

"I won't tell. Swear." She holds out her hand, wrinkled and trembling. She extends her little finger. Huh. I curl my pinkie around hers, and she lifts up, then down, like a handshake. Ruby must be a friend. Or, must have been a friend, long ago, when they were young enough for pinkie swears, but old enough to kiss boys.

"Yes," I say, because what's the harm? I think of kissing Tal five days ago. Five eons ago. My eyes prick. "He kissed me."

Grammy Kit grins. "He'll have you in a white dress before supper," she declares. "And out of it before morning."

My mouth drops open. *Was that a sex joke?*

"George is all right," she says approvingly. "Doesn't tear around town in his car like Bobby." She sighs. "But oh, those eyes."

Bobby? Bobby like my grandpa Bob? I never met him, he died before I was born. I sit down on the bed, next to her easy chair.

"Tell me about him."

She blinks. "You know Bobby."

"Tell me anyway."

So she does. She never talked about him when I was younger, she'd always change the subject when Mom brought him up. Maybe it was just too painful, like tearing stitches. But he's alive in her mind, and he comes alive to me as she talks. Grandpa Bob speeding down rural roads in his truck, Grandpa Bob giving her his class ring, Grandpa Bob stealing a pig for a senior prank. She'd never have done this if she were well. But in her mind, he's alive. In her mind, there's no pain.

"It's four," she says, finally, though it's twelve thirty. "You want to watch *American Grandstand*?"

"Um. *Bandstand*?"

"Yes."

"Sure."

"I can never find that clicker," Grammy Kit grumbles. "I think they steal it."

"Who does?"

"The shopgirls."

She must mean the nursing home workers. She thinks this is her house, and also her store, and maybe some back porch where she and Ruby sipped lemonade and gossiped about boys. This is her reality, as real as the soft sleeve of my flannel shirt against her arm, as real as the bird squawking outside her window, as real as anything that has happened to her. Reality comes from the Late Latin *realis*, meaning "actual." But before that, in Medieval Latin, *realis* didn't mean "actual." It meant "belonging to the thing itself." I was never quite sure what that meant, but now I think I do. *Reality* is not a singular noun, even though the dictionary says it is. Reality is a plural, a million things at once, seen from the eyes of a million people at once. Reality belongs to the thing itself, and the thing itself is us. Our reality belongs to us, and we belong to it.

I'm brought out of my head by the sound of furious, frustrated

335

clicking. Apparently, they didn't steal the remote. "Can't get the darn thing to—" Grammy Kit hits the remote against the easy chair, which accomplishes nothing. "It's broken. I'll find the receipt."

I pry it out of her hand. "Let me give it a shot. What do you want to watch? I don't think *American Bandstand* is on."

"The news, then."

"Do you know which channel?"

She tilts her head. "Ruby, honey, there's only four."

I bring up the guide screen and click on the first news program, on channel 758. It's national news, and two anchors are discussing the latest possibility of a government shutdown.

"She ought to be wearing a hat," Grammy Kit says, looking disapprovingly at the blond female anchor. "Imagine, being interviewed for television and forgetting your hat."

We finish the segment on the government shutdown and then a piece about an unlikely friendship between a husky and a potbellied pig before the Ken Doll–esque male anchor turns it over to weather. Grammy Kit's not likely to find that interesting, so I raise the remote, but then stop, frozen, at the sight of the national weather map.

Sun in Florida. Rain on the Eastern Seaboard. And there, hovering above the San Francisco Bay, a giant snowflake.

"Well, as you can see, Frank," the weather lady's saying to the anchor, "we've got this cold front coming in from the north—"

She keeps talking, stuff about cold fronts and air pressure and winds from the west, but I can barely hear her over the pounding in my chest and my head and my ears.

"So there's a possibility San Francisco might see snow?" Frank the Anchor asks.

"A distinct possibility, yes. And the inland areas are almost certain to see at least a few flakes."

Berkeley is inland. My home is inland. *Hannah is inland*.

The anchor and weather lady are laughing, like this is a fun little surprise, but I'm whisper-screaming at the TV, "When? WHEN?"

"What, dear?" Grammy Kit says.

"When can folks expect to see that snow, Mariana?" Frank the Anchor asks.

"It might be as early as this evening, Frank," Mariana the Weather Lady says.

Oh my gosh. It's tonight.

Oh my gosh. She was right.

I turn off the TV because I can't think with it on, I can't think with Frank and Mariana joking about sledding down Lombard Street. I can't think because I don't know what to think.

Hannah lied. Hannah said she lied, she told me she lied. But there's going to be snow in Berkeley on December 21. A freak weather event on the right day and in the right place.

And I'm in Utah.

I stand up, boneless and bloodless and shaky. The end of the world as we know it is coming, and I'm not there. Hannah swore things would be all right, but only if I was there. I should be there, with her, watching the newscast and packing our go bags, making sure my family's set with supplies for at least seven days. I should be there, but I'm here, in a Salt Lake City nursing home with a woman who thinks I'm her childhood friend and has outdated opinions on women's hats.

I pace. But there's barely enough space in this room to pace, between the hospital bed, the easy chair, and the portable toilet. Three steps to the left, three steps to the right. I don't pace. I flounder.

"What are you looking for?" Grammy Kit asks.

I breathe out. "An answer."

"To what?"

"I don't know," I say. But no, I do. I know what I'm looking for, and she's the safest one to tell. She won't remember in an hour. I kneel down next to her easy chair.

"I'm looking for an answer," I tell her. "I'm looking for a sign that tells me where I should go. I'm looking for a clue that tells me what to do. I'm looking for something that tells me what I should believe. I'm looking for a . . ." I grasp for the word, near enough to snatch from the air. "I'm looking for a revelation."

Grammy Kit stares at me, long and searching. Maybe I'm only imagining it, but for a second, her eyes look sharper. "Well, doll," she says, "I don't think you're going to find that here."

The words hit me like salt waves, like cold water on your face in the morning, something brisk and urgent that says, *wake up, get up.* The sign I'm waiting for isn't coming. I have to choose, and I have to choose alone.

I've made so many choices in my life, but how many of them were really mine? I made choices because Hannah said the world was ending, and I believed her. I made choices because my parents and my church said they knew best, and I believed them. I made choices because a voice in my head said I should be afraid of the world and myself, and I believed it.

But here is something else I believe: I was put on Earth, given a body and brain—*this* body, *this* brain, imperfect and odd—to make choices. What's the point, if I never make a true one?

> *What do you want, Ellis? Want something, choose something, Ellis.*

I'm standing in this tiny room, narrow and cluttered and dark, but that isn't how it feels. It feels like the horizon line at Lands End. It feels like the sky above Utah Valley. It feels—I feel—limitless. Boundless. Or maybe just unbound.

> *I want to go home.*

I want to go home. I want to see the snow fall. Whether Hannah is there or not, whether the world ends or spins eternally, there's nowhere else I would choose to be.

"I'm going home," I say to Grammy Kit, because someone

needs to know, and I need to hear myself say it. She blinks, then nods.

Okay. Okay. I need to keep my head. Attack the problem logically. First, and hardest, Aunt Tonya. I grab the bedside phone, scramble to find the cell number in Kenny #14, and dial. She picks up on the first ring.

"Mama?" she says, sounding surprised.

"It's Ellis."

She sighs as if to say, *You couldn't even last a half hour?* "What is it?"

"I was calling to ask—" I should have taken a second and practiced this lie. "One of the nurses came by and told me they're doing a movie night: *42nd Street*. It's after dinner and she said I could stay for it. Can I?"

"You want to stay for it?" I try not to be offended by the surprise in her voice.

"It's basically my favorite movie," I say, and that's not even a lie. "Grammy Kit showed it to me the first time." That's not a lie, either. "Please?"

"What time should I get you?"

"I think around eight."

There's silence on the line. "All right. We'll save some dinner for you. The cafeteria there is hit-or-miss."

After I hang up with her, I poke my head out the door and flag down a nurse. "Excuse me," I say, trying to keep my voice even and not vomit all over her white orthopedic shoes. "Is there a good cab company nearby? My aunt isn't going to be able to pick me up after all."

"I'll call one for you," she says, then adds, softer, "The residents' phones can't do it. Too many escapes."

I thank her, and she promises to come get me when it's outside. Once she's down the hall, I shut the door. Breathe in, hold. Breathe out, hold. I kneel down by the easy chair again and grab Grammy Kit's hand.

"Grammy Kit," I say, and she frowns, as if I've called her Captain Crunch. Right. Ruby, I have to be Ruby. "Kit," I try again.

"Yes?"

"I have to go, okay? I have to go somewhere now."

She smiles slyly. "George waiting out back?"

Sure, that'll do. "Yes. George is waiting for me. But you can't tell anyone where I've gone."

"Oh, Ruby, you be careful."

"I will. I promise I will. But you can't tell anyone or I'll be in such big trouble you can't even imagine. Okay?"

"If your mama calls," she says, "I'll tell her you're spending the night over here."

"But I can't talk. If anyone wants to talk to me, I'm in the bathroom. Okay? You promise?"

She holds out her pinkie. I wrap it in mine. She leans in close. "Go get 'em, doll."

★ ★ ★

341

The internet is a beautiful thing. I know lots of people are con-vinced it's the downfall of humanity, responsible for everything from carpal tunnel to serial killers. And yeah, those 1940s sci-entists building computers the size of houses would probably never have guessed we'd eventually all keep one in our pocket and use it to watch videos of cats and/or browse apocalypse preparedness forums. Maybe they'd feel like we ruined their achievement. But I will say this for the internet: it makes it really easy to buy a plane ticket.

I bought mine at a library near the airport, too scared to go straight there and buy one at the counter. They'd take one look at my face and know something was up. They'd have American Express on the line post-haste to report me for credit fraud, even though the card is technically in my name. Even though my parents bought my flight *here* with the same card, to boost my frequent flyer miles. And sure, it's only supposed to be for emergencies, but if armageddon isn't an emergency, I don't know what qualifies.

I'm third in line to have my ID checked by the TSA, and my hands are clammy, my ticket clutched in a death grip.

> *They know who you are. They know what you're doing, they can see it on your stupid, guilty face.*

Oh, not now. I thought maybe it would go away. After that therapy session, after I shut it down once, I thought maybe it would stop. But it can't, can it? It's me. It's part of me. I can't rip it out or will it away.

> *They're going to catch you and detain you and*

> *send you back to Spanish Fork; it's going to hap-*
> *pen, you know it is.*

No. That's a lie. I know the sky is blue. I know my name is Ellis. I know I'm second in line. But I don't know what's going to happen, I don't know what I don't know, *it's lying to me.*

> *What if the school put you on some government*
> *watch list, what if you're on the no-fly list—*

What if, what if, *what if*? What if I just didn't listen? What if I heard it—because I don't think it'll ever really be silent—but what if I just didn't listen?

I'm first in line. The ID checker beckons me forward, and I go with a smile, ticket and passport in hand. He waves me through the checkpoint without a second look, and the gate agents even smile at me as I board the five fifteen direct to Oakland.

My middle seat doesn't offer much of a view outside, especially since my window seat neighbor has the screen shut. We're getting closer to home with every passing second, and I can almost feel the change in the recycled airplane air. The plane bumps and bounces over the Sierra Nevadas.

> *The plane's going to crash and you're doing to die.*

I hear it, every word. But I try to hear it like white noise, sounds that can fade into the background of my mind. Just because I hear it, doesn't mean I have to listen.

> *How pathetic would it be to die in a plane crash*
> *just hours before doomsday? You're going to crash*
> *and die.*

I might. But probably not. It's so unlikely. Everything's okay. I focus on those words until they're the ones I hear.

*Probably not, so unlikely, everything's okay. Probably not, so unlikely, everything's okay.*

"Folks, an update from the flight deck," the captain says over the intercom. "We're just about to begin our final descent into Oakland. Might be a bit of a bumpy landing—looks like they've got some snow."

There's murmurs throughout the plane.

"Snow in the Bay," says the businessman in the aisle seat next to me. "Can you believe it?"

"I always did," I reply. He frowns at me, then goes back to his book.

Abandoning propriety, I lean across the sleeping man in the window seat and push up the screen.

Outside, the sun is setting.

Outside, there are snowflakes, perfect and fragile and real, falling from the sky.

Here are some things I will miss when the world ends:

An ice-cold cone from Yogurt Park, so big it threatens
    to topple
Sitting in the Park with my back up against Hannah's
    tree, Tal beside me
Telegraph Avenue on a warm Saturday afternoon,
    smelling like incense and good food and home

344

I make this list in my head as I crisscross a snowy downtown Berkeley. It probably isn't the smartest thing to do, wander aimlessly out in the open as a criminal. Because yes, running away from home when you're a minor technically *is* a crime. I've looked into it. I didn't really run away from home, though. I only ran *back*. But I doubt the police would appreciate the distinction, so I keep my hood up as I wander on an endless quest for a pay phone.

I finally find one in the Berkeley YMCA. Just up the street from school. Right back where I started. The very first thing I did after the cab dropped me off—several blocks away, in case my parents were already tracking my credit card—was break into my high school. Or, really, just walk inside, thanks to the staff party apparently raging in the C-building teachers' lounge. I crept down the second-floor hallway as quiet as I could, to the very last locker bay and my unauthorized second locker. Three turns of the lock, and I had my emergency bag. Enough food for three days, if you ration carefully. A space blanket. A first-aid kit the size and weight of a hardcover book. A flashlight.

In the YMCA, I dump both backpacks against the wall and dig change out of my wallet for the pay phone. I've never used one before, so it takes a couple of tries and about three dollars, but finally, I hear ringing on the other line, and I will the universe to let him pick up.

"Hello?"

Just hearing his voice makes me want to crumble. "It's me."

A pause, an inhale, a recognition. "Ellis?"

"Yeah."

"Oh my God," Tal says. "Are you okay?"

"I'm fine."

"Good. Okay, good." He breathes out. "I'm so sorry, I'm so sorry about what I said at my house, I didn't know—"

"I know," I tell him softly. "It's okay, I know."

"I was wondering when you'd call. When they'd let you. They didn't send you to one of those troubled teen places, did they?"

"What? No."

"Utah's full of them."

"How did you know I was in Utah?"

"I asked my sister to ask your sister. She said you'd gone to Utah, but wouldn't say more than that."

"Oh."

"It must be boring as hell. And cold as shit. Is it snowing there?"

"I, um. I don't know."

There's a beat as it dawns on him.

"Where are you calling from?"

"A pay phone."

"Jesus Christ, Ellis, *a pay phone where*?"

His exasperation makes me want to laugh and sob at the same time. "Here. I'm home."

"Berkeley?" he says. "You're in *Berkeley*?"

346

I nod, then realize he can't see that. "Yeah."

Another beat.

"Did your parents bring you home?" he asks. I chew the inside of my cheek and say nothing. "Does anyone know that's where you are?"

"Just you."

There's a scuffling sound on the other end. "I'm coming to get you."

"No," I say, then again, louder, because I can tell he's moving around, maybe grabbing his keys. "No, I have to—you can't come get me."

"You don't have to go home," he promises. "You can stay with me and my dad, we'll figure it out, we'll—"

"It's snowing!" I yell into the phone. "Tal. It's snowing."

I hear him sit down with a thump. "I know," he says carefully. "I know what you think that means, Sam showed me that flyer you put up, but that doesn't mean anything."

"This is the first snow in years. The first *real* snow, more than an inch, since the nineteenth century. They said so on the newscast."

"You ran away because of a newscast?"

"I ran back," I counter. "I wanted to see it."

"There's nothing to see!" he protests. "This isn't the apocalypse, and Hannah never should have told you it was. She knows that, believe me, she feels so terrible for doing it. But this is a freak snowstorm, nothing else. What do you think you'll *see*?"

"She said I had to be with her," I tell Tal. "I know a lot of it was lies, but I don't think that was. She said I had to be with her or it would all go wrong. I know you don't believe me, I know you don't believe at all, but I have to be there."

He sighs, deep and heavy. "I'll go with you," he says. "Tell me where."

I almost do. I almost do, because I'm scared, and I miss him, and I trust him not to tell anyone else. But my breath catches in my windpipe, itchy and gnawing, so I cough instead.

"Ellis," he says. "Just tell me where."

"I can't," I say. I think this moment was meant for me and Hannah, alone. I'd assumed we couldn't get any converts because I made a terrible missionary and Hannah made a worse prophet, but maybe . . . maybe we weren't meant to convert anyone. Maybe even our failure was meant to be.

"You don't have any survival gear," Tal says, trying to reason his way out of an unreasonable situation, as always. "If it's really the end of the world as we know it, you'll die. Wherever you're going, you won't make it."

I don't tell him about my emergency bag. "I'll be okay."

"You're really going to do this?"

"Yes."

I wait for him to yell at me. I wait for him to plead with me. I wait for him to threaten to call the police, or my parents, or my bishop. He's quiet for a very long time, and I almost think the call's been dropped, when finally he says:

"I will be here." My heart bursts under my ribs. "I will be here when the world doesn't end. I will be here even if it does. Even if I'm frozen in a block of ice, when you want to find me, you'll know where to go." His voice cracks. "Right?"

"Yes," I say, more a sob than a word.

"You'll come find me?"

"I'll come find you," I say. "I promise."

And that's when the call really does drop.

One more thing I will miss when the world ends: the smell of books.

Very old books, like the ones that used to be in Grammy Kit's house, smell like tree trunks and smoke and vanilla extract. Brand-new ones smell crisp and clean, like ink and dryer sheets mixed together. If you research it, which I have, you'll learn the vanilla smell comes from the lignin in the wood paper, a complex polymer close to vanillin. The dryer sheet smell is probably the finisher they use in production. Those are the facts, and facts do matter. But when you're inhaling that scent for what might be the last time, facts barely matter at all.

Even in the library computer room, I can still smell the books. Faintly, from far away, but there. That smell, the one that's cocooned and calmed me since the first day I toddled into a library and scooped up as many books as I could carry, that smell is still there. I fill my lungs with it as I read through my email one last time.

TO: Dr. Andrew M. Kimball, Lisa Holley Kimball, Em&m
FROM: Ellis Kimball
SUBJECT: The Things That Shall Be Hereafter

I'm safe. That feels like the first thing I should say. I'm sorry. That feels like the most important thing I should say. I'm sorry for using the emergency credit card. I'm sorry for escaping Utah. I'm sorry for the 16.5 years of worry. I know, from the moment I was born two months early, I've worried you.

I had to. That feels like the truest thing I could say. We all have choices, we all have agency and choices and the freedom to make them. But sometimes, something bigger than us pushes our hand. I feel like I had to. And I believe in the things I feel.

Em: It's all going to be all right. I promise. I'll see you soon. Keep yourself spinning.

Dad: I don't think Mom found my secondary stash of supplies. It's in the basement, in the clothes storage, behind my baptism dress. And I want you to know—I've needed you just like you needed me.

Mom: It's okay that you don't know how to help me. It's okay that you don't understand me. Sometimes I don't understand myself, either. I'm starting to. We'll do it together.

I love you. I hope I spend the rest of this short life by your side, and eternity, too. I changed my mind—that's the most important thing I can say. I love you.

—Ellis

My mouse cursor hovers above the send button. I shut my eyes and listen to every familiar sound. The squeak of shoes on the beige floors. The rattle of a book cart down the hallway. The swish of turning pages. The thump of my heart beneath my ribs, beneath my skin, vulnerable and thin, but powerful all the same. Endlessly shedding and regenerating and growing. The deep layers of your skin—with your scars and freckles and birthmarks—stay with you for life. But that first layer, the one that brushes up against the world around you, that one replaces itself every twenty-seven days. Every twenty-seven days, you're inside a new skin. Every twenty-seven days, you get a new chance.

In this skin, I made choices, good ones and bad ones, and some I'm not sure about yet. In this skin, I kissed a boy and broke my parents' hearts and broke out of Utah. And if this is my last skin, well. I'm glad it was mine.

I hit send.

## TWENTY-SIX

**BY THE TIME** I reach the trailhead, the sun's already set. I should have gotten here earlier. I shouldn't have spent as much time writing my final message to my family. But I owed it to them. I owed them something. It's just that now, I have to climb this hill in the dark.

The snow is still falling, but it's not sticking. The flakes are cold as they hit my face, but melt nearly the second after. I can't see the ground all that well, but there's no crunch under my boots, just slippery dirt. It's wet snow, "bad snow," my grandpa Jack would say, because it's not good for skiing. It's heavy, but it's practically sleet.

My feet are damp, half from the snow, half from the effort of scrambling up the hill, and I wish I had wool socks. I wish I had my headlamp, the new one. With the sun down, I can barely see my own feet. At least I have a flashlight. I don't know how Hannah's going to get up this trail without one.

I stop, for a moment, my chest seizing in a vise. What if she doesn't come? What if I'm up there all alone, and she never comes? She has to have seen the weather. She wouldn't leave me. She'll be there. She has to be there.

Just thinking about being alone at the lookout floods fear through my muscles. There are mountain lions in these hills. Years ago, one wandered into downtown and the cops shot it. In true Berkeley fashion, a funeral was held for the cat.

*You could be eaten by a mountain lion.*

*You could be crushed by a storm-damaged tree.*

Just because I hear it doesn't mean it's right. Just because I hear it doesn't mean I have to listen.

*You could fall off the side of this trail and smash your head open, and that's where you'll die. No one would find you. You'd be all alone.*

There's only me and the snow, me and the wind, me alone with myself and all my fears.

*You'll never be rid of me. I'll always be here. You'll always hear me.*

I've only been given one body. I've only been given one brain, miswired and odd and mine. But my voice—not just what spills over my vocal cords and into the world, but the things I say to myself—that's something I get to choose. I'll always hear it, but that doesn't mean I'm doomed to hear what I've heard before. There are so many words in this world. I can learn new ones.

I'm at a standstill now, blinking into the darkness ahead and the darkness behind me. Should I turn around? I could find my way back. I could find my way back home and hug my parents one last time. I could hold Em's hand as the world spins off its axis. I could end life as I've known it in the warmth and comfort of the house I was born in, with the people who brought me into life. Who protected me. And who loved me, all of them, the best way they knew how. Or I could keep walking into the cold unknown.

I walk forward.

The higher I climb, the darker the sky gets, and the wetter the ground becomes. I should have paid more attention, when Hannah and I were here before, to the terrain. But I didn't think I'd be walking alone. I'm careful as I go, sliding my feet more than lifting them. My hands are ready to catch me if I fall, because I desperately don't want to. It's amazing how much you notice when there's nothing to see. I hear the wind whipping through the trees and shrubs. It's harder now than when I was downtown, and it bites at my exposed ears and sends dirt and snow flying up to sting my eyes. I smell the eucalyptus grove as I pass through it, then nothing but cold air. I feel each patch of wet grass, each jagged rock, each stone groove in the trail, and I stick to the grooves as much as I can. They don't slip as much under my shoes.

And I sense, rather than see, that I'm getting closer. The light is better, so the trees must be thinning. There's one more turn, one more little incline before the trail flattens. Before the bench. Before the place where the light comes in. As I make that last turn and struggle up that last incline, I sense, rather than see, that I'm not alone.

"Hannah?" I whisper into the blackness, more a prayer than a call. When I round the bend, I turn to my left, and the world is bright again. All of my city is stretched before me, sparkling with light, house lights and streetlights and car lights moving down Broadway. All of Berkeley is illuminated. All of Berkeley is still there. San Francisco is hazy in the distance, but I can just make out the tops of the towers. San Francisco is still there, too.

At the cliff's edge is a person in shadow, long hair escaping from a pulled-up blue hoodie, staring out across the icy bay.

"Hannah!" This time it is a call, a shout across the wind.

She startles and spins around, but I still only see the vaguest outline of her body. She takes a step forward, then I do, then we're both running, colliding with each other in the dark.

"You came," she whispers.

"Yeah," I say, my hand clutching the cotton fabric on her arms. She's not wearing enough; where's her coat, where are her gloves? "It's snowing."

"Yeah," she says back.

"I didn't know if you'd be here."

I feel her muscles quivering under my hands. "I knew you would."

I let her go, though I don't want to, and fumble in the

emergency backpack from school. I paw around until my fingers latch on to something thin, crinkly, and lifesaving. I pull it out and drape it around Hannah's shoulders.

"What—?" I feel her fingers grab the edges.

"Space blanket. Pull it tighter." It'll keep her warm for now, but not forever. "You didn't bring a coat."

She sighs, a huff of warm breath. "I had to make a break for it."

"Yeah, me too," I laugh.

"How did you get over here? The bus?"

"A taxi. Then a nonstop flight from Salt Lake to Oakland. Then another taxi."

*"What?"*

I explain, in very abridged form, my exile to and escape from Utah.

"I can't believe it," she says, her hair flopping onto my shoulder as she shakes her head. "I can't believe you did that."

"You knew I'd be here," I say. "You didn't think seven hundred miles was going to stop me, did you?"

She squeezes my arm, and that's answer enough. I look out at the city. "Oh," I say, and my breath hangs in the air like fog. "It looks like a Christmas tree. All lit up."

Hannah whips her head around, and I realize I mentioned Christmas. Just like she said I would.

"You told me you lied," I say. "You said you lied, but it's snowing."

"The dreams were real," she tells me. "That's what I was trying to tell you, before you left. I didn't lie about the dreams. Just what they meant."

"What did you think it meant?"

"Every time I woke up—" The wind howls and whips at our clothing. "Every time I woke up, I knew that I had to make it here. To this hill. When it snowed. If I came to the right spot, his favorite stop, if I was here . . ." I hear the tears, rather than see them on her face. "He'd come home."

"Danny?"

She nods. My heart aches. It was never the apocalypse. It was never the end of the world. Hannah told me what I wanted to hear, and I heard it. Hannah told herself what she wanted to hear, too. That her brother's safety was within her control. That if she gave up her possessions, or stopped cutting her hair, or gave up her days and nights looking for him, that she could protect him. This was just one more cosmic bargain she'd made with the universe. Nothing more.

"The other things—the city, the red sky, I don't know," she goes on. "They never felt real. I never really thought they would happen. But you were real. I saw you in my dream, and then I saw you in the real world, and I knew I'd see you here." She squeezes my hand. "You were the only real thing."

Hannah didn't make it snow. She can't control the weather, that was going to happen regardless. It was inevitable. But us being here wasn't. I squeeze back, as a sudden thought strikes me.

"What if this only happened *because* you saw it?"

"What?"

"You saw us here, in your dreams, together. You thought it was fated to happen, that nothing could change it. But that meant you went looking for me, and found me, and I believed you. You created a way for it to happen, and that's the only reason it *did*, because you already believed it would." I grip her hand harder. "What if we *made* it happen?"

Just then, the wind picks up, sending freezing dust and snow into the air. Hannah coughs, and I shield my face.

"Jesus!" she yells, then coughs again. We huddle against each other, clinging to one another. The gales are hard enough, heavy enough, that it feels like we could be catapulted over the edge of the lookout point. I force my eyes open to see how close we are to the cliff drop. I look out toward the water, and my heart stops.

"Hannah!" I yell, dirt and snow in my mouth. She keeps her face turned away, so I shake her shoulder. "Look!"

Her head turns, and she must see what I see, because she gasps. The wind is churning the snow as it falls, and picking up what hasn't melted. The world in front of us is white and gray, all sleet and sand. For a moment—just one singular moment, from one singular perspective—San Francisco disappears into the storm.

Hannah and I are still clutching each other, half blinded, when the wind falters. Across the bay, a tower spire pokes through the clouds and the snow. As the gusts diminish, slowly, bit by agonizing bit, the city comes back into view. Still clouded, still difficult to see. But there.

Beside me, Hannah is still gasping. She's gulping for breath, over and over, like she can't get air in her lungs.

"It's still there," I say, relieved and terrified all at once. "It's still there."

Hannah says nothing. I can't see the expression on her face, but I know she just saw a dream transform into reality, then disappear into the ether just like San Francisco was supposed to.

"It's still there," she agrees, barely audible.

We're together. We're at the place where the light comes in, on the day one becomes two and two becomes one, and we saw San Francisco vanish. We're here. The world is still here.

I grasp for the answer, struggle for an explanation, but there is only cold, black air and a world that continues to spin, unchanged. Hannah's dreams were real, but the apocalypse wasn't. Her cosmic bargain wasn't, either. But the dreams were real; the dreams became reality and I don't understand why. I point my flashlight all around us, searching desperately for another clue, another fact, something to help this make sense because it doesn't *make sense*.

I shine my flashlight to our right, close to the sloped edge of the overlook. My vision snags, and my heart plummets into my wet shoes. My flashlight has landed on a large, prickly bush, just a short slide down the hill.

And a foot.

I stumble back, half screaming, half choking. My hand fumbles in the dark and finds Hannah's. I latch myself on to her freezing-cold hand and squeeze so hard she yelps.

"What?" she says. "What's wrong."

"There's—" My heart is threatening to launch itself out of its rib cage, my mouth is dry, adrenaline shooting through my veins. "There's a person."

"What?" she says again.

"In the bush, in the bush, there's—"

I shake my flashlight at the spot to direct her eyes. Now Hannah squeezes back. "Oh God."

The light stays on the foot. It doesn't move. Hannah slides her own foot toward it, tentatively.

"Hey," she calls out. "Are you okay?"

My eyes go wide. I pull her closer. "What are you doing?"

"He's not moving," she whispers. "If he wanted to kill us he would have."

"You don't know that. You *do not know that*."

"He could be hurt." She takes a step forward. Then another. I don't let go of her hand, and she doesn't let go of mine, so she's dragging me with her on each step. I keep the flashlight ahead, though my hands are shaking, and we both nearly slip on a large patch of ice right at the edge. I keep the flashlight on the foot, but as we peek down the slope and into the bush, the glow expands. There's a foot, then the tattered edge of jeans.

Then a dirty hand with dirtier fingernails across a thigh. A red-and-black coat, a sweater under, a dark beard. Finally, a face, a whole person. Young. Male. Unmoving.

Hannah screams. I'm confused, because he still hasn't moved. There's no reason to scream. She drops my hand and slides down into the dark. I drop the flashlight, startled, and scramble to retrieve it. When I find it and focus it back, Hannah is on her knees, her entire body shaking like the trees in the wind. I lower myself down the wet, snowy slope, still sensing a trap, but not about to abandon her. One hand is on my flashlight, the other on a branch. The slope isn't that steep, but it's slick beneath my feet, and I don't want to fall. She's stopped screaming, but she's now crying hysterically, and I still don't understand why until she chokes out a word. One word.

"Danny."

Oh God.

Oh my God.

I sink down next to her. Hannah's got her hands on his shoulders, and she's shaking him like a rag doll.

"Stop." I reach out to her, but she bats my hand away. "Stop, Hannah, stop, he could have a—" I don't even know what he could have, but I know you're not supposed to shake an unconscious person. "Is he breathing?"

Hannah bursts into fresh, panicked sobs at that. My fingers feel numb and swollen, but I manage to snake my hand around hers. Danny's got one hand clutched to his chest, a crumpled piece of paper in his fist. I start to shove his arm away so I can check his breathing better, but as I do, my flashlight illuminates the paper.

It's orange. Day-Glo orange.

"Our flyer," I whisper to Hannah, but I don't think she hears me. "He found our—" He's here because he saw a flyer. He's here because he alone, other than us, knew what Hannah's prophecy meant. The place we were going, the place where the light comes in. He's here because he wanted to protect Hannah.

I shake my head. It doesn't matter why. It will later, but not now, because right now, he's the one in need of protection. My fingers grasp for his coat buttons and undo them. I lean forward, then recoil at the smell. He clearly hasn't bathed in a while, and even his sweater feels slick with sweat. *Pull it together!* I scream at myself, because Hannah won't, and someone needs to. *Who cares what he smells like? Your ancestors crossed the prairie in handcarts. They forded flooded rivers. They battled locusts. Put your shoulder to the wheel, Ellis.*

I hold my breath and lean in, my hand searching for a heartbeat. I find it, the thumping matching mine, which isn't good, because mine's too fast. I feel the rise and fall of lungs, too. He's breathing. His body is pumping blood. He's still here.

"He's breathing," I croak out to Hannah. "Okay?" I feel light-headed for a moment and brace myself with a hand on the grass. It comes back wet. Not like snow. Thicker, stickier—

I direct the flashlight at my own hand. It's red.

"Oh," I breathe out. "Oh no."

"What?" Hannah cries.

"He's bleeding. We have to find where he's—"

He must have slipped, at the edge. Fallen. Hit something.

"Oh God, oh God, oh God," Hannah's repeating over and over, clutching at Danny's clothes.

I shake her shoulder. I need her help. "Hannah."

She only sobs.

"Hannah!" I shake her shoulder once more, but she's beyond hearing. She has to snap out of it. I don't know what to do. She has to tell me what to do. I waste precious seconds staring at her helplessly before realizing: Hannah can't tell me what to do. If anything's going to happen, it'll be because I did it myself.

We need 911. We need 911, and we need an ambulance with medicine and doctors and wheels. Doctors on wheels. Doctors on ATVs. *Jesus, Ellis, get it together.* We need to call 911, but my phone is a mile away in my dad's desk drawer, and Hannah's is with Chris and Frank Zappa. Danny's was smashed to pieces months ago.

Problem: We need a phone and we don't have a phone.

Solution: Find a phone.

Problem: No one else is on this trail.

Solution: Get off this trail.

I look up, over the edge, at the dirt path leading back the way I came. I almost start running then, but stop myself, because I have to be logical. Even when the world is falling apart, you

363

have to be logical. It took me forever to get up that path, it's twisty and steep. It's always harder to go down something steep. Didn't I learn that at Lands End? Climbing back up was so much easier. More dangerous, maybe, but faster.

I close my eyes, trying to take myself back to the day I was here with Hannah. I shove myself into the memory. Sunshine. The bay, sparkling and blue. So quiet, except for the cars—

The cars. The road. The house at the top of the path. A house means people.

I want to run down. I want to run down, because that's the way I came from, that's something I know. But I know what I have to do. I have to run *up*.

I kneel down next to Hannah, who is sobbing so hard I wonder how she can breathe. "It's going to be okay," I say. "I'm going to get help." I fumble around in my backpack. I grab her arm, uncurl her fingers, and jam a flashlight into her hand. "Figure out where he's bleeding. Put pressure on the wound. Hard, do it *hard*."

She sobs, but I feel her nod.

"I'm going to get help. Stay here. Don't move, don't move yourself, don't move him." She cries louder. "Do you hear me? *Stay here*."

I feel her nod again.

I don't want to leave her. I can't believe I'm leaving her. But I drag myself over the edge and sprint into the darkness, up the hill, knowing I'm going faster than is safe and not caring at all. My chest is already on fire by the time the ground starts to climb under my feet, a sign that I'm starting the steep ascent. The flashlight's no real help. A single pillar of light against pitch-darkness. It's nothing. I shine it all the same. The toe of my shoe catches a rock and I crash to the earth, dust in my mouth and a searing sting in my knee.

The girl who used to live inside my skin would have curled into a ball. The girl who used to be me would have refused to go on. I get up. One foot on the ground, then the other. One step forward, then another.

It's so slow. I'm so slow. The steps are steeper and harder, each one, and the snow is clouding my vision and my flashlight beam. What if I don't make it? What if I freeze to death here, fall to my death here, what if Danny is dying, what if Hannah has gone into shock, *what if what if what if.* What-ifs don't make the path flatter, maybes don't make my legs stronger. What-ifs don't solve a single thing. I'm done with them.

I fall, slipping on wet scrub grass. I get up. I climb faster, gasp for air harder, fall again, get up again. My hair is plastered to my forehead, every muscle I have is on fire, my skin is bruised and scraped raw, but my feet feel the ground rise up to meet them. Level ground is coming. I know the road is ahead even though I can't see it. So I run on screaming tendons, I run faster than I've ever run in my life. I'm running so fast, so blind that I don't see the trail gate until it's in my gut, knocking the wind out of me.

A gate.

The gate.

I'm so close.

I clamber over it, though I'm sure there's a way around. My foot slips on one of the bars. I catch myself from falling, but twist my wrist around too far. It burns. It's fine.

My feet hit concrete. It's solid, so solid, more stable than anything I've ever felt. In the flashlight glow, I can see the other gate, the one surrounding the house, the one I'm really looking for, up ahead. This one's too tall to climb over. How am I going to get through? The snow's falling heavier, and I can barely hear the party inside the house. If I can't hear them, what chance do they have of hearing me?

On my bruised legs, I race up to the door and pound on it with the wrist that isn't twisted. "Help!" I scream, and draw back my fist to pound again, but the door eases open, just an inch. I push, gently, testing, and it swings open. I'm through it before I can even question why it isn't locked, stomping over cobblestone and grass, snow in my face, snow in my eyes, and then snow in my mouth as I pound on a smaller door, a front door, and demand to be let in.

Someone opens the smaller door. I don't know who. I don't look at their face before I stumble through the threshold and shoulder my way into the warmth and light ahead. I wonder if this is what death feels like. I wonder if I am dead.

When I brush snow and salt from my eyes, I'm standing in a

beautifully decorated living room. There's a Christmas tree by the floor-to-ceiling windows, which look out onto the white world outside. Two dozen people in dresses and sport coats are staring at me, drinks in their hands and shock on their faces.

"Call 911!" I shout into the room, and it's so big the words ring back in my ears. "Someone, please, call 911!"

No one moves. Do they speak English? Do *I* speak English? Maybe I really am dead. I turn my wrist. It hurts. I'm still alive. I'm still alive, but Danny might not be, so why aren't they calling?

"Call 911 *now*!" Still, no one moves. "I don't have a phone and someone on the trail is hurt and if you don't call, someone is going to die tonight."

Everyone pulls out their phones at once. It takes me a second to realize that what I said sounded very close to a death threat.

"It's ringing." A young woman in a sparkly red dress presses her phone to her ear. "H-hello?" she says to the dispatcher. "There's this girl, she burst into our party and said someone's hurt, I don't—"

She's doing it all wrong, she's too vague, too slow. I snatch the phone out of her hand and twist around so she can't grab it back. "The emergency is an unconscious nineteen-year-old male bleeding from an unknown source on the Stonewall-Panoramic Trail in Claremont Canyon at the first lookout point. The first good one. With the view. With the bench."

"The victim is unconscious?" the dispatcher asks.

Didn't I just say so? "We couldn't wake him up."

"Is the victim breathing?"

"He was when I left."

"Miss, where are you calling from?"

"A house, the house at the top of the hill, but the victim is at the first lookout point and needs medical attention."

"What is your name?"

What does that matter? She's wasting time. "His name is Daniel Marks and he's with his sister who's completely freaking out."

"No, Miss, what is *your* name?"

"Ellis Kimball, it's Ellis Kimball, but their names are Daniel and Hannah Marks and you need to call their parents. Their parents' names are—"

My mouth is suddenly a desert. My throat is suddenly filled with cement. What are their names? I can't remember their names and I can't breathe and I can't stay standing.

When I stumble, I grab on to the closest thing to me, something prickly and dry that jingles as I try to steady myself against it. It's not strong enough. I'm not strong enough.

My knees buckle first, then the rest of my limbs follow. My vision pinpoints to a small spot on the green rug. It looks so comfortable, and yes, I will stay right here, this is fine, this is good, so I don't understand why someone far away is gasping, and someone else is grabbing me hard underneath my armpit and trying to haul me up. The carpet is perfect, it cushions my head like my favorite pillow. It cushions my fall like a parachute landing pad. I let go of the something prickly and dry, and it rattles and shakes.

The last thing I hear is something shatter against the floor by my head. The last thing I see is a big, golden, broken star.

Then everything is nothing.

## TWENTY-SEVEN

**IMAGINE THAT THE** universe is a film that has already been completed, and you've been given the reel. Each frame is one moment in time. A character inside that movie could only see them in order, moving from one numbered frame to the next, but you hold the entire story in your hands.

Imagine that the universe is a colony of ants living in a vast, treeless desert. As far as they know, the world is one flat plane—they live in two dimensions. But imagine that one day, a single blade of grass begins to grow. One ant climbs up it and discovers the reality of height. A brand-new world.

Imagine that the universe is one big cement block, floating in space. Inside that block is all of the past, the present, and every moment of the future . . . and us. We are inside that block, too, experiencing time the only way we can. Second to second, always in the present, stuck in an unending forward motion. But imagine you could step outside the block. You would see the universe as it really exists, time as it *doesn't* exist, every single moment occurring at once.

That's how this feels. Like I'm outside time. Beyond it. Somewhere deep and dark, staring back at the universe with new eyes.

I blink into bright lights.

"Hey," a shadow above me says. "Can you hear me? Are you awake?"

"Yeah," I say, though I don't know if it's true for both questions. "Yeah."

"Oh, thank God," a different shadow says.

"You fainted," says the first shadow, slowly taking form as a person with two arms and two eyes behind two glass lenses. My mouth is full of cotton. My legs are full of sand.

"911?" I ask through the cotton. Was that real? Did I make the call? Or was that just a dream?

"They're on their way."

Hannah. Danny. "My friend—my friend is on the hill, and her brother—"

"It's okay," says the girl in the red dress, holding her phone protectively to her chest, like I might snatch it again. "They'll find them. It's okay."

"The world," I say. "The world is still here."

"Huh?"

"The world didn't end. Did it end?"

"No," says the guy with glasses.

371

"I think she's delirious," says the girl in the sparkly red dress.

My eyes feel heavy again. No, I'm staying awake. I have to stay awake.

"It's a plowing metaphor," I say. "Did you know that?"

"Okay, she's definitely delirious."

"Exactly," I say. "Delirious. *Delirium* is the noun, *delirium* is Latin, *delirium* combines the prefix *de*, meaning 'away,' with the word *lira*, meaning 'furrow.' 'Delirious' means off the furrow, off the path." I sweep my arms out. "It's a metaphor. The whole world is a metaphor."

"What the fuck," says the blond guy.

"Mike!" says the girl. "Not helpful."

"You're the one who said her activation phrase, Lucy."

"Her what?"

"Activation phrase. Like sleeper agents have. The secret ones, from Russia."

"Are you drunk?"

"I am clearly not drunk *enough*."

An EMT, young and slim, arrives, and the guy with glasses points her over to me.

"My name's June," the EMT says, sitting down next to me on the couch. "What's your name?"

"Ellis."

"I heard you fainted, Ellis."

"I guess."

"How are you feeling right now?"

"Okay. A little . . . fuzzy."

"What have you eaten today?"

It takes me several long seconds to remember. "A piece of toast. And milk."

"When was that?"

Breakfast time at Aunt Tonya's, though it might as well have been a decade ago. "Nine a.m.," I say, and don't bother to account for the time difference.

"That's the last thing?" she says, and I nod. "You probably have low blood sugar." She pulls a little carton of orange juice from her bag, the kind my mom used to pack in my lunch for school field trips. June inserts the straw for me, and I slurp it down, only realizing when it's gone how thirsty I was. She promises we'll get me a snack in a moment.

"Is this yours?" she asks, retrieving my coat from the couch arm.

They must have taken it off me when I fainted. I nod.

"You should put it back on," she says.

"I'm not cold."

"You will be, when the shock goes away."

I don't think I'm in shock. That should feel like numbness, shouldn't it? I feel like I've grabbed hold of an electric fence. But I shrug the coat back on and zip it up.

"Is Danny okay?" I ask. "Please tell me, I won't freak out. I didn't freak out before; Hannah did, but I didn't."

"They got him off the hill," June says. "They'll take good

care of him." She pauses. "Is that her name? The girl with the long hair. Hannah?"

Wait. How does she know Hannah's hair? I swing both feet onto the floor. "Where is she? Is she here?"

Before June or anyone else can stop me, I'm out the front door, through the garden, and following red lights to a paved back road I didn't know existed. Hannah is sitting in the back of an ambulance, her legs dangling over the edge, cocooned in a blanket. Another EMT is speaking to her. The snow has stopped, and the road is illuminated by the lights on top of the ambulance. They're so bright and steady, it almost doesn't look like a night sky anymore. The sky almost looks—red.

A red sky before midnight.

"Hannah!" She looks out from her caterpillar cocoon, and her face crumples. I rush over, but stop a step short, not sure if I can touch her. Not sure if I'll hurt her. Not sure what to say. "Hannah."

Her eyes are watery and puffy, and her cheeks have deep tear tracks down them, but she looks otherwise unharmed. "You're okay," she says, on a sigh of relief.

"Of course I'm okay."

"You ran up a mountain in sneakers."

"A hill," I say. "I'm fine."

"Did you see him go by?" she whispers, teary again. "Did you see them put him in an ambulance, or—"

I shake my head. "Why didn't they take you with him?"

"They said I couldn't ride along," she hiccups. "I was hyperventilating. They couldn't take care of him and me."

"He's going to be okay." I don't know that, but it's what Hannah needs to hear. It's what Hannah needs to believe.

"I'm sorry," she sobs. "I'm so sorry."

"For what?" I ask, bewildered.

"I'm so sorry I lied to you, I'm so sorry I told you the world would end."

Doesn't she see it? Doesn't she realize how right she was?

"I need to get her heart rate down," the EMT says, stepping in front of me.

"Wait, I—"

He boxes me out of the way. I'm about to object with harsher words when there's a hand on my shoulder. I turn around to see a police officer beside me, June trailing behind him.

"Are you Ellis Kimball?" the police officer asks.

"Yes." It comes out a whisper. I clear my throat. "I'm Ellis Kimball."

"I'm Officer Harris. May I ask you a few questions?"

He's phrasing it like a request, but I get the distinct impression it's not. Still, I nod, and he guides me a few feet away, toward the house. Away from Hannah.

"Are you aware your parents reported you a runaway?"

So few people seem to appreciate the distinction between running *away* and running *back*.

"No," I say.

"No, you aren't a runaway?"

"No, I wasn't aware they reported me as one."

He sighs. "We've alerted them that you've been found. They're very happy you're safe, in case you care."

Wow. Expert guilt trip, Officer Friendly. "I do."

"You've used up a lot of resources tonight, do you know that? You and your friend."

Wow again. Find an injured person and they act like you've started a wildfire. "We didn't mean to."

"Really?" he says. "Because what I think is you and your friend were joining up with that street kid—I'm not going to say for what—when he . . . what, OD'd?"

My temper flares at how many hurtful, cruel assumptions a person can make in twenty seconds. Danny slipped and fell; that's the only explanation I can think of. The ground was slick, we found him down the slope, there was blood, why would this jerk go straight to drugs? I know why.

"That's not what happened," I say, struggling to keep my voice even. "That's not what happened at *all*."

He spreads his hands. "Enlighten me."

Here are some things I tell Officer Harris:

> I went up the hill to see the snow falling.
>
> Hannah and I discovered Danny, her brother, hurt and unconscious.
>
> Hannah stayed behind to watch Danny while I ran up to the house to call 911.

Here are some things I don't tell Officer Harris:

> I went up the hill because I thought the world was ending.

> Hannah's brother, Danny, has been homeless and living with a mental illness.

> Hannah stayed behind because she was hysterical, and I basically stole someone's phone to make the call.

> Details.

Officer Harris takes a few notes, but doesn't seem overly concerned. "We'll have you make a full report later," he says. "Are you ready to go home?"

I don't know. I'm ready to hug Em. I'm ready to have Dad call me Elk. I'm even ready to have Mom untuck the hair behind my ears. But I've hurt them, all of them, so deeply, and I know it. I hope they'll accept why I made the choices I did, even if they can't ever really understand them. Maybe, like the end of world, family is more complicated than we give it credit for.

"Do you know how he is?" I ask Officer Harris.

"The street kid?"

Hannah's brother, who'd die to protect her. His parents' oldest child. The kind of person who'd bring muffins to lonely old ladies and leave secret gifts for the sister he couldn't talk to.

I bite the inside of my cheek so hard it tastes like metal. "His name is Danny."

"He's stable."

Relief floods me. Or, no, that's not right. Relief does not drown me. Etymologically, relief means something raised, something rising, and that's right. Relief lifts me.

"When can Hannah go see him?" I ask.

Officer Harris looks past me. "Looks like she's going now."

I whirl around. They're packing Hannah into the ambulance, closing her up inside. I dash away from Officer Harris and back over to her.

"I want to ride along," I tell the EMT.

"Not a chance," Officer Harris declares before the EMT can even blink, heading our way. I climb into the ambulance next to Hannah anyway.

"You were right," I whisper.

She blinks at me. "What?"

Officer Harris is behind me now, and I grab Hannah's hand.

"You were right," I tell her again, louder. "Everything you said was going to happen did happen, Hannah, you were right."

She frowns, and I hope she's thinking of the city disappearing in the snow, the red sky at night. And there are things she doesn't know about yet, things she didn't even see, like the star falling from the sky.

"It didn't end," she says. "The world didn't end."

"Come on, kid," Officer Harris says to me, but I'm betting he won't physically drag me away from a sick girl in an ambulance, so I stay.

"Maybe there are more worlds than we thought," I say.

Hannah only frowns harder.

"I'm giving you ten seconds," Officer Harris says, like my mom used to when I was a kid. Unlike her, I hope he's bluffing.

I squeeze her hand tightly. "You found Danny. Danny is stable. Danny is safe." She inhales sharply, unsure whether to believe it, wanting to believe it.

The world might be a self-fulfilling prophecy, or it might just be a giant metaphor.

Maybe it's a Gettier problem, where nothing is quite like it appears, but that doesn't mean you can't find something true.

Or maybe the world is a small, solid block in a vast universe, part of a larger story than we can hold in our hands. Something bigger and greater than anything we can see with imperfect, human eyes. But that doesn't mean the world we can see isn't a miracle.

I lean in. "It's a brand-new world, Hannah."

Officer Harris has his hand on my shoulder, and I think he's tugging, but I barely feel it through all the layers of clothing, all the layers of fear and dread I'm just now ready to shed. With one last squeeze, I let go of Hannah.

I climb out of the ambulance and allow Officer Harris to think he's pulling me away. Everyone has their own reality. Far be it from me to disturb his. From a distance, we both watch in silence as the EMTs close the ambulance. In the sliver of the light in the closing doorway, Hannah looks back at me. I raise my hand. She smiles.

The door shuts. The engine starts. The ambulance turns the corner.

She's gone.

I look up at Officer Harris and straighten my neck, then my shoulders, then my spine, just like my mother taught me.

"I'm ready."

# TWENTY-EIGHT

**THERE ARE SO** many ways a world can end.

A nuclear war.

An underground volcano in Wyoming.

A city that vanishes for only a second, a brother who's missing until he isn't, two girls standing together on a hillside because the universe wanted them there.

It could end in fire. It could end in flood. It could end with me dying of embarrassment up at the pulpit, before I can even finish my testimony.

As I start to get up from the pew, Mom touches my arm. I stop. After a moment of hesitation, she reaches toward my ponytail and tucks a loose strand of hair behind my ear. "So they can see your face," she whispers. "I want them to see you." I smile back at her.

I walk to the front of the same church where I was blessed as a baby, and just before I reach the stairs to the podium, I hesitate. In front of my whole ward and Lisa Holley Kimball herself, I touch my fingertips to my head, to my shoulders, to my waist. I let my hands fall. I go on.

At the podium, I adjust the mic. Before, I might have just hunched over. But this is my testimony, and I shouldn't crouch just because the last person was shorter.

"I don't know the church is true," I say. I hear someone take a sharp breath in through their nose. I understand. This is an atypical script. "I don't know that Joseph Smith was a true prophet. I don't know that I'll be with my family for all eternity. I don't know that. Not a single person on Earth knows that, and not a single person on Earth knows those things aren't true, either. I can't tell you I know those things, not honestly, and I'm trying to be more honest. So instead of the things I know, I'd like to tell you the things I believe."

There are some things I *do* know, though I won't say them out loud, here. Some things are mine to keep.

"I believe in grace," I say. "I'm grateful for every little of bit of grace I receive. I believe in trying to give it back. I believe that miracles can happen."

I don't know if I'll ever be the perfect daughter my mom saw in her dream. I don't know if I'll embarrass Em again, or make my dad sick with worry again. I don't know if I'll ever fit into my family like a puzzle piece.

But I do know they love me. I know that they've never been happier to see me, or more furious with me, than when Officer

Harris brought me home. I know they've never been more baffled by anything than the story I told them about the end of one little world. And I'm lucky, because I know they believe in miracles, and you don't have to understand a miracle to accept its existence.

"I believe in goodness, which isn't the same thing as niceness. I believe in choosing what's right, and sticking up for it, even when it's hard. Especially when it's hard."

I don't know if Tal and I will be together forever, eternal companions in this life or the next. I don't know how many days, or months, or years we'll sit under oak trees and debate the afterlife, or challenge each other to Five-Word Books, or kiss in his bedroom, close enough to see ourselves in each other's eyes.

But I do know he showed up to today, to support me, because I asked. I spot him in a pew near the back, his little sister on one side, and on the other—

I nearly whisper her name into the mic. *Hannah.*

I haven't seen her since that first day after, in the hospital. And I didn't expect to, not until her brother is a little better, and her family is a little more healed. Her world is re-forming after the Big Bang, primordial ooze settling and growing into something strange and new and scary and hopeful. I'm not the center of her universe right now, not even close. I didn't ask her to come. But here she is.

"I believe in . . ." I have to search for the word, because I didn't practice this. I didn't plan it. But that doesn't mean it shouldn't be said. "Loyalty. I believe in loyalty, and being a good friend, and choosing friends wisely. That doesn't mean choosing friends who are the same as you, though it could."

Sam. Theo. Hannah, who made sure I met them. Hannah, who knew I needed them just as much as I needed her.

"It means choosing friends who love you for who you are, who see who you could be even when you can't. It means loving yourself just as much as they love you."

But then I stop again, because I wonder: If Hannah sees me better than I do, what does she see? Who does she see standing on this platform? Does she see the girl who saw who *she* was, under all that grief and pain? Does she see the girl who came back for her, crossed mountains for her, faced every fear and more for her?

Hannah wasn't my savior. I wasn't hers. I don't think there's a word for what we are to each other, and I don't need one.

"It means loving yourself just as much as you love them," I say, and for a moment, there is no one in this room but me and Hannah. It's hard to see through blurry eyes, but I think she's smiling at me. I think she understands.

I look up at the ceiling and try to get myself under control. I've got more to say. Just a little bit more, and there's nowhere I'd want to say it but here, beneath the same rafters I've spent every week of life. Under my own roof.

"I believe in the Gospel, and I believe in being the kind of person the Savior wants us to be. I believe that this place is my home. I believe I'm the person I am because this has been my home."

I don't know if I'll stay in the church, the community, the culture that created me. I don't know if I'll live the kind of life my parents and ancestors did, or if I'll forge my own path in the dark. I don't know if I'll stay or go, though I want to stay. I want to stay just as much as I want to live happily inside my own soul. I'll stay as long as I can do both. I do know that if I'm ever forced to choose, I will choose myself.

"Belief is different from knowing. There are so many things in the world we don't know, and I used to be scared of that. I used to think I needed to know. But I don't, and I can't, and I never will. And that's okay." I take a breath. "I think belief might even be better, because belief is choice. It's something you give to yourself."

I look out into the audience. To my parents, my sister, Tal. And Hannah.

"I say these things in the name of Jesus Christ . . . and in my own name, too. Amen."

I step back from the mic, and hold myself still as silence buzzes in my ears.

In this pause, time seems to stall. My brain is ready and waiting to cycle through everything that could go wrong. Bishop Keller could faint. The Relief Society ladies could gossip about me for all eternity. Lia Lemalu could never speak to me again.

But then again—Bishop Keller could applaud me. The Relief Society ladies could tell my mom they liked my testimony. Lia Lemalu could smile at me and tell me I said just what she was thinking. I don't know which scenario, one among thousands, will play out. I am in one singular moment, lived from one singular perspective, and I don't know what's ahead.

I give myself over to the not knowing, because it feels right, and I believe in the things I feel. I trust in the things I feel. I trust myself.

There are so many ways a world can begin. And here is one.

# ACKNOWLEDGMENTS

## OR, A BRIEF LIST OF PEOPLE I'D WANT ON MY SIDE IN THE EVENT OF APOCALYPSE

Ben Rosenthal, my brilliant, insightful editor, who saw the heart of this book from the very first draft. I can't wait to tell more stories with you.

Sarah LaPolla, my amazing agent, who is always there to answer my questions, talk through a problem, and support me every step of the way.

The entire team at Katherine Tegen Books, especially Mabel Hsu, David Curtis, Liz Byer, Bethany Reis, Tanu Srivastava, Aubrey Churchward, and of course, Katherine Tegen. Thank you for making this book a reality.

My writers' group: Emily Helck, Brian Kennedy, Siena Koncsol, and Michelle Rinke. Thank you for every single piece of feedback and every single moment of friendship.

My early readers: Cindy Baldwin, Caroline Davis, Sam Galison, Naomi Krupitsky, and Michelle V. I'm eternally grateful for all your comments, expertise, and encouragement.

The Electric 18s, the Class of 2k18, and all the other wonderful, talented authors I'm lucky enough to call my friends.

The entire population of Berkeley, California. Thank you for making me the person I am today. I wouldn't have wanted to grow up anywhere else.

My family and friends, who have always supported my writing and generally tolerated my fear of heights, needles, flying, fire, small spaces, the sound chalk makes, asking salespeople for help, the basic concept of eternity, and mice.

Leah, who has made me a better and braver person since the day she was born.

Rob, who read this book before anyone else and sees me better than I see myself.

And most of all, my parents, who have been by my side through every little apocalypse.

TURN THE PAGE FOR A SNEAK PEEK AT KATIE HENRY'S

*This Will Be Funny Someday*

# CHAPTER 1

HIGH SCHOOL MIGHT be a total joke, but that doesn't mean everything is.

Some stuff just isn't funny. Like plane crashes. Or the Black Death. Or William Shakespeare's *Hamlet*—not that Jack Brawer, varsity lacrosse captain and officially the world's worst scene partner, isn't doing his best to turn it into a comedy routine.

"'My lord,'" I say, staring down at my script so I don't have to look at Jack. "'I have remembrances of yours, that I have longed long to re-deliver; I pray you, now receive them.'"

I reach into my cardigan pocket for the—oh, *shit*. The prop letters are still on my desk. I mime handing something toward him, still not looking up, just willing him to *do the damn scene, Hamlet.*

"Wait, whaaaaaat?" Jack says, high-pitched and mock-surprised. I close my eyes. "I didn't give you shit, Ophelia. Have you been getting into the meth again?"

Laughter, then Ms. Waldman's voice: "Jack, that's not the line."

"You're always telling us about the intent, that's the *intent* of the line."

"William Shakespeare did not intend to say anything about meth."

"It's a modern twist."

"'My honor'd lord, you know right well you did,'" I say, louder than both of them, because it's bad enough being up here in front of everyone, it's bad enough Jack is messing up the scene on purpose. "'And, with them, words of so sweet breath composed—'"

Jack snatches the script out of my hands.

I think: *How can a person be this big of a dick?*

I think: *Alas, poor Jack. I knew him well, Horatio, until I had him assassinated for pulling this shit.*

I say: Nothing.

But I do grab it back.

"So are you honest?" Jack asks, vaguely close to his real line this time. "And by 'honest,' Hamlet means, 'Are you a total whore?'"

More laughter, mostly from the corner of the room where Jack's friends sit, their arms sprawled over the backs of their chairs, their pelvises spread so wide it looks like they're about ready to give birth.

I don't understand why Ms. Waldman makes us do these

scenes. The class is called Shakespeare Seminar, not Shakespeare Performance. If I'd known I'd have to talk this much, I would have just taken American Lit with all the other juniors, instead of petitioned my way into a senior class.

More importantly, I don't understand why Jack couldn't have warned me he was going to do this, the half dozen times we practiced the scene in the hallway. At least then I'd have been prepared, at least I'd be in on the joke—

And then I do understand. I *am* the joke.

"Jack, if you can't respect Isabel as your scene partner, you're going to fail this assignment," Ms. Waldman warns. That's an empty threat. Jack doesn't care about failing this assignment. He's already been accepted to Cornell, early decision, a legacy kid. Come September, he'll be hundreds of miles from here, probably being hazed by his equally terrible frat brothers. The thought comforts me.

I make the executive decision to skip ahead in the scene. "'Could beauty, my lord, have better commerce than with honesty?'"

Jack makes the executive decision to go straight for the kill. "Get thee to a nunnery! And by 'nunnery,' I mean brothel or something, even though they aren't the same thing at all. Except I guess in porn."

"Okay, you're done." Ms. Waldman waves her hand.

"Remember that for the final, everybody, Shakespeare was into nun porn."

Ms. Waldman gets up from her seat in the back, heels scraping against the floor. Jack nudges me. "What about you? You into that?"

I think: *Well, I'm not into ruining someone's day for fun.*

I think: *I'm not into so obviously peaking in high school. How about you?*

I say: Nothing.

But I feel my face burn.

"Oh, she's blushing!" Jack says. "Confirmed, Shakespeare *and* Isabel—"

"That's *enough*." Ms. Waldman gets in between us just as the bell rings. She and Jack immediately start talking over each other. Jack with words like "just a joke" and "lighten up" and her with words like "unacceptable," "ridiculous," and "textually unsupported."

Ducking out of both their conversation and their space, I hurry to my desk in the second-to-last row. Jack and Ms. Waldman have moved onto arguing over whether the behavior referral she's giving him is "fair." I think "fair" would be letting me follow him around his next lacrosse game screaming out-of-context Shakespeare quotes, but no one's asking me.

Jack leaves in a cloud of Axe body spray and unjustified ego, but before I can escape out the door, too, Ms. Waldman's voice jerks me back.

"Isabel, hold on a second, okay?"

I stop, reluctantly. She returns the referral pad back to her desk drawer and motions me over. I go, even more reluctantly. She's the kind of teacher who starts the school year by making a big deal about how she's "always around" if anyone "ever needs to talk." The kind of person who thinks you should automatically trust her because she's young, and wears blouses with cats on them, and rolls her eyes at the school song.

"I'm really sorry that happened," she says.

I shrug. Smile.

"I just want you to know, it's not going to affect your grade. I can tell you'd practiced."

Then she waits, expectantly.

"Oh. Um. Thank you," I tell her.

She waits some more, but I'm out of ideas. She tilts her head. "Are you worried about your grade, at all?"

I shrug again. Smile again.

"You haven't participated in the class discussion at all this week," she says, and it's almost apologetic. As if it's her fault, not mine. "Or last week."

I haven't read the Geneva Code, but if the concept of participation points isn't listed as a war crime, then it's bullshit.

"It's only January," she continues. "There's lots of time to turn it around. Your first essay was fantastic."

"Thank you," I say.

"You know, some people just have a harder time talking in public. I totally get that." Ms. Waldman leans a bit closer.

5

"But . . . sometimes people are quiet because something's going on. You know?"

Something grips my stomach and twists. "Not really."

"I'm not saying there is," she adds quickly. "But if there were, my door is always—"

"Open," I say, edging my way toward that exact door. "I know."

She sighs. "Just make an effort, please. Say something once a week. Okay?"

*I'd rather feed my fingers to a Venus flytrap*, I think.

"Okay," I say.

Jack is waiting for me outside. Though I do my best to avoid his eyes and make a break for Alex's physics classroom, Jack plants himself right in my path.

"Hey, about that . . ." He jerks his head back to the classroom. "We're cool, right?"

What does he expect me to say? If we weren't, if I said we weren't, it wouldn't mean he wasn't funny. It would mean *I* was a joyless bitch. Either way, he wins, and I lose.

"I didn't know you were going to do that," I say, as if stating the obvious will cause him to spontaneously grow empathy.

Jack runs his hand through his hair. "Yeah, I meant to give you a heads-up, but then I was late, so."

A rock-solid defense. First Cornell, then Yale Law, then representing oil companies that suffocate baby ducks. It's written in the stars.

6

"The guys on the team dared me," he says. "So, you know, I had to do it."

I think: *A dare?*

I think: *What are you,* five?

I say: Nothing.

He punches me in the arm, softly, but harder than he thinks. Then he grins, toothy and secure. "I knew you'd be chill."

And that's when I do the worst thing. Or maybe the third worst thing, after murder and arson. I smile back.

It can't look like a real smile, I think as Jack turns to go, apparently satisfied. It doesn't *feel* like a real smile. It feels forced and vaguely sinister, like the antique porcelain doll in my grandmother's parlor. And though I suspect that doll is the veteran of several Satanic rituals, at least she has an excuse. At least she didn't paint that smile on herself.

I slump against the lockers, close my eyes, and resist the urge to brain myself on the cool metal behind me.

"Isabel." Five fingers are curling into my shoulder. "Hey."

When I open my eyes, there's Alex, standing in front of me, looking concerned. He also looks like he just stepped off a photoshoot for a Ralph Lauren ad, but he always does. I didn't start dating him because his hair is shiny and artfully disheveled and you can see his upper arm muscles under his uniform button-down shirt. I started dating him because he shared new things with me, like all the black-and-white movies he loves, and he remembered the things I loved, too.

It isn't anything like the three-day not-dating I did at sleep-away camp in middle school, where a boy would say he liked you, maybe grab your hand with his clammy fish palm, but then mostly ignore you. Alex asked me to be his girlfriend before the first date was even over. "From now on, it's just you and me." And I thought that was just a line, but whenever we're alone together, that's how it feels. Like there's nothing else in the universe but the two of us.

I'm not going to pretend like the whole Kennedy-cousin look isn't a bonus, though.

"Are you okay?" he asks. "What happened?"

"Nothing." I push myself off the lockers and smile at him, closemouthed. "I'm fine."

He nods and interlocks his hand in mine. I'm not a huge fan of public displays of affection, not to mention they aren't allowed at school. But even though we've been dating for four months, Alex still always wants to hold my hand in the hallway. Which is sweet. And kind of performative. But still sweet.

"You weren't waiting for me outside physics," Alex says as we walk toward the cafeteria. He's almost pouting, like if I'm his mom, late to pick him up from preschool. Though I doubt she's ever picked him up from anything. His parents are a little weird—he has a seventy-year-old dad with the equivalent net worth of a small developing nation, and a fortysomething mom with the personality of a wolverine that only flies first class.

In the end, Alex was raised by a series of nannies, a no-limits credit card, and an internet router with zero parental controls. So I understand why he's clingy, sometimes, and I try to be nice about it. Even when he isn't.

"Sorry," I say, squeezing his hand. "Ms. Waldman needed to talk to me."

"God, she's such a bitch," he mutters under his breath, and I prickle, because that's not fair. He wouldn't call her that if he knew she was just trying to help me. But before I can tell him, he's reaching over to smooth down a loose strand of my braid. "I like your hair this way. You should do that way all the time."

Only if I didn't value my sleep. The chipper vlogger with effortless pastel beach waves might have 130K subscribers, but she's kidding herself to call this look "quick and easy."

"Not all the time," I laugh. "It takes forever."

He frowns. "But I like it."

Alex's phone vibrates in his pocket, and he lets go of my hand to fish it out.

"Something really weird happened in Shakespeare Seminar today," I say, then pause for him to ask what. He doesn't look up from his phone. "Remember how I was telling you I had to do a scene? From *Hamlet*. In front of the class." I wait again.

"Uh-huh," he says, texting someone.

"And my scene partner was Jack Brawer—"

"Oh, cool," Alex says.

"Yeah, he's . . . so cool," I say, and my performance as Girl Who Thinks Jack Brawer Is Cool is even worse than my performance as Ophelia. "We'd practiced the scene a bunch, but then when we got up to do it—"

Alex sticks his phone under my nose. "Check out what Kyle sent me."

It's a GIF of a small child being chased by a pack of aggressive-looking geese. One eventually tackles him. "Wow. That is . . . disturbing."

"What?" He sticks his phone in his pocket. "It's funny."

"So anyway, when I got up to do the scene with Jack—"

Alex points at me. "See, *he's* funny."

"Yeah, actually, he—"

Alex cups his hands. "Kyle!"

Just outside the cafeteria doors, Kyle and his girlfriend, Chloe, turn around. Alex picks up the pace, and I jog to keep up with him. It's fine. I'll tell him about Shakespeare Seminar later.

As always, we sit at the table closest to the lemonade dispenser, in the same seats, with the same group of Alex's friends. They're all on junior-varsity lacrosse, and I've never been able to figure out whether they're all friends because of lacrosse, or they all play lacrosse because they're friends. I think I was supposed to befriend their girlfriends—Margot and Chloe and whoever is on Luke's rotating schedule as he strives to have sex with the entire junior class—but it never quite worked out.

Margot catches my eye across the table. "I—your—"

Four words, or maybe five. Definitely about me. But I can

never understand people in places this loud.

"Sorry," I say, leaning closer. "What?"

She repeats it. I mean, I assume she repeats it. I can *hear* she's speaking, but I have no idea what she's saying.

"I, um." I smile, tight, hoping she'll get it. "Sorry."

Her forehead wrinkles, but she tries again, and I try to focus on watching her lips. I can't ask a third time.

There's a tap on my shoulder, and when I turn, Alex is holding out his phone, which is open to the notes section.

*She likes your necklace.*

"Oh!" I swing back around to Margot. "Thanks, it's new. My mom gave it to me for Christmas."

"It's pretty," she says. I'm 70 percent sure that's what she says, but Chloe nudges her to ask something, and I'm saved.

"Thank you," I whisper to Alex.

"Sure," he says.

Alex isn't the most sensitive person—there are about 618 adjectives I'd pick before that—but he's always been great about my hearing. It's not really my hearing, since my ears are fine. It's the way sound travels from my ears to my brain. I know when people are talking, I can *hear* them speaking, but sometimes—especially if the room is loud, or they mumble, or have a different accent than me—my brain can't process *what* they're saying.

It's annoying for me and probably everyone else, too. Alex never acted like it was.

I start to dig back into my salad, but I have the prickly, unsettling feeling like someone's watching me. I twist around in my seat, looking across the cafeteria, to the corner by the bulletin board. Sure enough, Naomi Weiss is staring back at me. It's so weird—knowing a person so well for almost ten years, and then not at all for the last four months.

Naomi and I became friends in second grade, more out of convenience than real compatibility, at first. She was quiet; I was quiet. She didn't have anyone to partner up with in PE; neither did I. But the longer you stick with someone, the more they become a part of how you see the world, even if you both spend most of your time in easy, uncomplicated silence. We spent hours at her dad's house, Naomi with her herds of pastel ponies, me with legions of plastic dinosaurs. Weekends and winter breaks and hot summer days at my apartment, Naomi on her computer, fixing bugs in her code, me on my bed, thumbing through my dog-eared, broken-spine copy of *Encyclopedia of Plants and Flowers*.

It worked. Until it didn't.

Without even realizing it, I'm standing up from the lunch bench, starting to disentangle from Alex's foot, wrapped around mine.

"Where are you going?" Alex asks, craning his head to follow where I'm looking.

"I—" The truth is, I don't really know. "I was going to get a cookie."

Alex keeps his eyes toward Naomi's table, but puts a hand on my shoulder and gently presses down. "I'll get it. You don't have to get up."

I don't have to sit, either. But I do.

As Alex saunters over to the food line, Margot and Chloe watch him go. They share a look with each other, then turn in unison to me. "He is so *sweet*," Chloe says. Or mouths.

She's right, of course. They can all see it, and if I told them otherwise, they wouldn't believe it. Not that I would, because it *is* true, of course it is. He is sweet.

When I look to Naomi's table again, she's turned back around.

For the rest of lunch, I nibble at the chocolate chip cookie Alex bought me and listen to conversations I can't quite hear. I've got it down to a science, nodding when everyone else does, laughing at the right moments. Maybe it's not a science; maybe it's really an art. Like woodworking. Or taxidermy.

When the rest of them get up to bus their trays, Alex puts his hand around my waist, pulling me close. "Come over to my house for dinner tonight."

There's an itch in my chest, like I can't quite breathe deep enough. "I can't tonight."

"What?" His hand drops to his side. "Why not?"

"It's Charlotte and Peter's last night before they go back to college."

"You'll see them again in, like, March."

I shift to my other foot. "My mom said to come home."

"You don't have to do whatever she says."

I think: *Yeah*.

I think: *Just whatever you say*.

I say: Nothing.

"God," Alex huffs. "Fine, I had this whole nice night planned, but whatever. Not like I care."

"I didn't know that. If you'd told me, I could have—"

"It was a surprise, Isabel," he snaps. "Do you know what a 'surprise' is?"

I shrink back. "I'm sorry."

"You don't have to be— That's not what I—" He crosses his arms. "All I wanted was to spend time with you, do something nice for you. And now you think I'm so mean."

His shoulders are still stiff and his arms are crossed, but the only thing on his face is hurt.

"No," I say as a hot wash of shame floods me, because I didn't mean to do that, make him look like that. "I just—"

"I'm sorry," he says, "I'm sorry, I don't want you to—"

"I don't, and everyone's mean sometimes. It's—" I fumble around for something to end this conversation, something to make this less awkward and easier to forget. I laugh a little. "It's like we learned in statistics class, right? Mean is the average, so . . . maybe the average person is mean."

He stares at me blankly.

"You know," I explain, "because the mean and the average

14

are . . ." His expression doesn't change. I clear my throat. "It's a joke. A math joke."

He shakes his head and grabs the rest of the chocolate chip cookie off my lunch tray. "I wish you wouldn't do that."

"Do what?" I ask.

"Try to be funny." Alex breaks the cookie and hands me half. "You aren't good at it."

# Comedy, chaos, and an Inquisition

A DIVINE COMEDY

Heretics
ANONYMOUS.

KATIE HENRY

"Hilarious, irreverent, charming, and an absolute delight!
This book is everything I hoped for and more."

—Robyn Schneider, bestselling author of *The Beginning of Everything*

KATHERINE TEGEN BOOKS
An Imprint of HarperCollins Publishers

www.epicreads.com

# JOIN THE

# Epic Reads

## COMMUNITY

**THE ULTIMATE YA DESTINATION**

◀ **DISCOVER** ▶

your next favorite read

◀ **MEET** ▶

new authors to love

◀ **WIN** ▶

free books

◀ **SHARE** ▶

infographics, playlists, quizzes, and more

◀ **WATCH** ▶

the latest videos